Blood of the Pelican

The sequel to
The Ormolu Clock

To Janet

With Kind Regards

Jessie Ritchie

About the Author

The author wishes the reader to note she is a novice in the literary world and has great respect for professional writers. Her first book *The House with No Roof* was written entirely from the stories her forebears told her of the East Neuk in Fife others entirely fiction. In the creation of the sequel, *The Ormolu Clock*, Jessie Ritchie travelled far and wide and did the necessary research for authenticity. The guide in the Russian palace, the librarians in Sri Lanka and Spain were very helpful. The third work in the trilogy, *Blood of the Pelican*, had to be written from memory as Covid put paid to any chance of doing research in Kenya and the current situation prevented further research in Russia, but she wishes to thank all those who helped her in the past.

Blood of the Pelican

The final work in the trilogy to
The House with No Roof
and
The Ormolu Clock

by
Jessie Ritchie

DIADEM BOOKS

Published by Diadem Books

Cover artwork by Alex Bird

ISBN: 9798377766575

This book is dedicated to all who work for peace in the world.

ACKNOWLEDGEMENTS

Nate and Nana, my very young writing soul-mates. Young Emma my mod tech genius. The Pelican League. The U3A, creative writing. Ben in memory of Anne. The staff at Primavera. The support from friends and neighbours, Lorna, Lesley, Angela and Anne. A plethora of family pets, Siamese cats, German Shepherd dog and rough collies over the past 50 years. My lovely immediate and extended family, whose unwavering support and encouragement have resulted in the achievements of a nearly 80-year-old woman. My forebears, without whose stories and memories shared with the author during her youth, Jessie Ritchie's Scottish Romantic fiction trilogy would never have been written.
Thank you.
Jessie Ritchie

To everything there is a season
and a time for every purpose, under heaven.
A time to be born, and a time to die; a time to plant,
and a time to pluck up that which is planted;
A time to kill and a time to heal;
a time to break down and a time to build up;
A time to weep, and a time to laugh;
a time to mourn, and a time to dance;
A time to love, and a time to hate,
and a time of war and a time of peace.

The Leightham Family Tree (Scotland)

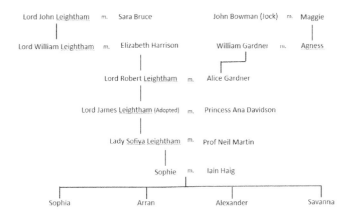

Lord John Leightham m. Sara Bruce   John Bowman (Jock) m. Maggie

Lord William Leightham m. Elizabeth Harrison   William Gardner m. Agness

Lord Robert Leightham m. Alice Gardner

Lord James Leightham (Adopted) m. Princess Ana Davidson

Lady Sofiya Leightham m. Prof Neil Martin

Sophie m. Iain Haig

Sophia   Arran   Alexander   Savanna

The Skavronsky Family Tree (Russia)

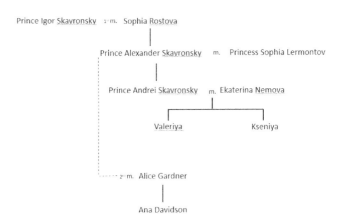

Prince Igor Skavronsky 1-m. Sophia Rostova

Prince Alexander Skavronsky m. Princess Sophia Lermontov

Prince Andrei Skavronsky m. Ekaterina Nemova

Valeriya   Kseniya

2-m. Alice Gardner

Ana Davidson

The Harrison Family Tree (America)

1859 Peter Harrison (unmarried)

Son (Adopted)   Daughter (Adopted)

Andrew Harrison m.   Margaret McAllister

Bruce Harrison   m.   Roberta Anderson

Rachael Harrison   m.   Lord Robert Leightham

Betsie   m.   John Geiger

Johnny Geiger

BOOK THREE

Blood of the Pelican

Introduction

WITH A HEAVY HEART, Lady Sofiya Leightham leant against her bedroom window and looked out over the estate gardens towards the River Forth. The clocks had moved forward, heralding the arrival of spring and longer days, but the nights were still cold. The central heating had been changed from all day, to mornings and evenings. It was April, 'Primavera', new beginnings, but Sofiya was in a sombre mood, not helped by the unexpected arrival of a brown envelope with a handwritten address and an American stamp delivered by the postman earlier in the day.

The millennium had come and gone at an alarming speed; a once-in-a-lifetime occasion never to be forgotten. She remembered the firework displays echoing from as far away as Edinburgh, exploding and lighting up the night sky, the low intermittent howling of boat-horns on the river, from harbours and dockyards, that could be heard from miles around. Bonfires blazing on the surrounding hills, maybe even seen from outer space? People gathered inside the marquee and congregated outside around a roaring bonfire on the estate grounds, enjoying a barbeque, free bar and Scottish country dancing to a ceilidh band that Sofiya had arranged for them. The unique, haunting sound of bagpipes filled the local Scottish people's hearts with pride.

There had been excitement and anticipation among the crowds waiting to hear the sound of church bells heralding in the 21st century. 'Happy New Year!' rang out, as the bells chimed in unison from town to town and village to village. Many a dram of Scotch whisky was downed in celebration that night and to keep out the cold.

'To everything there is a season under heaven'. Sofiya reflected on the verse from the Book of Ecclesiastes. Time, time, time… the words folk groups sang in the sixties about the seasons which were reflected in the gardens of Leightham House. Colourful, floral tributes to nature, month by month, were planned and planted by knowledgeable gardeners over the centuries: snowdrops and crocuses in January that pushed their way up through the estate lawns disappearing at the end of February, as did a sea of bright yellow daffodils at the end of March. Dense, tall, evergreen rhododendrons lining the main drive and the estate's walkways were now heavy with thick buds, ready to burst into bloom from April onwards. A large evergreen bay tree, with aromatic leaves for use in the kitchen, would burst with a new growth of small, pale-coloured leaves at the end of each branch.

A large, Chinese, golden magnolia tree displayed a canopy of cup-shaped yellow, pointed, waxy flowers that bloomed before its leaves, a tree so rare no one could put a name or age to it, but the local council ordered a Protection Order once it had been identified by the head gardener of the Royal Botanic Gardens. Soon bright coloured camellias would bloom from evergreen bushes and climbing, vibrant pink and purple clematis would cover the side walls of the house all summer long.

Among the many varieties of trees at Leightham House, a prized 'handkerchief' tree, the size of an old oak, had bloomed there for over a hundred years. Small, reddish purple flower heads, looking like acorns surrounded by a striking display of white florescent bracts that resembled pinched handkerchiefs were ready for blossoming in late spring. Some called it the 'ghost tree'. The Davidia involucrata's leaves hung in long rows beneath its branches, fluttering in the breeze giving a

2

ghostly appearance when the moon shone at night. A mid-18th century rarity discovered in the Sichuan province of China by a French missionary, Armand David, and brought back to Britain by a 19th century botanist, Ernest Wilson. He was shipwrecked on his return from China but he still managed to save his precious seeds and cuttings.

By June the roses in the rose gardens would burst into colourful perfumed bloom; in the greenhouses and the walled-garden, vegetables planted by the house gardeners, and newly pruned fruit trees would explode with an abundance of produce for the kitchen and local markets. Knee-high, stone Victorian planters, on either side of the front entrance doorsteps, would brim with red geraniums, pink fuchsias and blue lobelia. Ready to greet visitors were the hanging baskets in the back courtyard hanging on Victorian, wrought-iron wall brackets, displaying a plethora of variegated, double-headed pelargoniums, begonias, petunias and green ivy, hanging as if suspended in mid-air. The grounds, greenhouses and gardens were carefully maintained by the estate's head gardener, Ronald MacKay, a local man credited, and rightly so, with green fingers.

Jimmy Ramsey, the estate manager, and his wife Bunty, housekeeper to her ladyship, lived in one of the renovated cottages on the estate. Jimmy went down the mines when he left school at a young age expecting to be a coalminer all his life, but decided, after Margaret Thatcher, the UK's Prime Minister, ended the miners' strike, that mining was no longer for him. He had watched his dad suffer from chronic lung disease from inhaling coal dust all his working life. Jimmy was grateful to get free housing and paid work in Leightham House and he repaid his employer by casting an eagle eye on every aspect of the house and estate management.

At times Jimmy and Ronnie's friendship reminded Sofiya of the woman she thought was her great-aunt

Jane's stories about auld Tam's and Jock Bowman's nights in their local pub, The Pirates. But Ronnie did not have a horse named Nellie nor a 'kirt' to bring the two of them home after a night's drinking in the Leightham Arms. They didn't play cribbage either. Instead, they shouted themselves hoarse watching the 'footie' on the pub's TV. And because of the 'drink driving' ban, they had to walk home hanging on to each other for support and singing Tina Turner's hit 'Simply the Best', interspersed by the odd chorus of 'Scotland the Brave' and 'Flower of Scotland 'at the top of their voices after a Rangers and Celtic match depending on who won. After a night's drinking, Jimmy usually went home with Ronald and spent the night on the couch in Ronald's living room to avoid the wrath of Bunty's tongue for coming home drunk.

But Sofiya took cold comfort from what should have been heart-warming thoughts of the renewal of life on the Leightham Estate that she had been instrumental in resurrecting from half a century of neglect. It was April and the arrival of a letter had brought back in vivid detail all that had happened to her.

However hard she tried to forget the worst time in her life, the memories resurfaced every year. Yes, there had been deaths but they had been loved relatives and close friends who in the fullness of time had died along with a few untimely ones. The deaths of family members and friends were to be mourned; then, in the fullness of time, their lives celebrated with happy memories when the pain of bereavement subsided. April had nothing to do with death; it was to do with a life.

Sofiya fingered the necklace she wore round her neck, a simple gold chain with a large solitaire diamond in a claw setting suspended from it. With every movement the diamond glittered, undiminished from the day it had been re-set from her American engagement ring. She was also wearing a pair of real pearl earrings, a wedding gift forwarded to her from her American friend, Mary, who was to have been her bridesmaid in Texas at her wedding to Johnny Geiger. A thick gold wedding band that had been her husband Neil Martin's grandmother's, Rena McKay, was the only other piece of jewellery she wore and she had never taken it off from the day her husband put it on her finger. She had loved him, but she was never in love with him. He knew this when he married her but he never questioned her love. Along with her watch these were the only pieces of jewellery she ever wore.

Shaking her head, Sofiya began to wonder where the time had gone since the millennium and the other New Years that had passed in the previous century, since the devastating news of her parentage had been revealed. That day seemed so long ago now, but time had <u>not</u> stood still.

PART ONE

Chapter 1

S OFIYA THOUGHT BACK to the journeys she had taken over the years after the death of the woman she thought was her great-aunt Jane. Having discovered the woman was in fact Alice Jane Gardner, her real grandmother, who may have faked her death and could still be alive at that time. She also had to find the truth about her birth parents and her forebears.

How did Janet arrive in Scotland and end up on auld Tam's doorstep? Were her birth parents still alive? Did they move to James Paxton's (whom she found out was really Lord James Leightham, Lord Robert Leightham's son) her birth father's coffee estate in Kenya as her grandmother had intimated? Did they leave Ceylon before or after the country's independence? And the most burning questions ... why had they sent her back to Scotland and where was her original, her real, birth certificate? She had several ancient documents that had fallen out of the ormolu clock's base at the reading of the will, but several were still missing. Did her birthparents know their mother Sofiya's grandmother had not kept her but instead had had her adopted with a false birth certificate?

Once she recovered emotionally and physically, she felt it was time to start her enquiries for the information she needed to answer her questions. A search for information regarding her great-grandparents, Wullie and Agnes Gardner and her great-great-grandparents, Maggie and Jock Bowman proved to be the easiest. Initially it seemed it would be difficult after her fruitless search for headstones in the Pittendreal cemetery. Perhaps, with the exception of Jock Bowman, they had all been buried in

Peterhead; maybe she should try the graveyards there? But a phone call to and an appointment with Anne, a helpful young clerk in the local County Building Bereavement Services, eventually gave Sofiya all the information she needed.

"Dae ye hiv ony information at aw'… birth, marriage, and death certificates?" Anne had asked when Sofiya phoned. "Yes, I'll bring them with me," she assured Anne.

Sofiya thought back on the day she had taken grandmother's ormolu clock to young Alex Bird, auld Alec Bird's grandson, the jeweller's on Leightham High Street. She had never been absolutely convinced the entire contents in the base of the clock at the reading of the will had been revealed and young Alex Bird had agreed with her that there could be another inner, secret chamber.

"They masterpieces wur designed by clock-makin' geniuses. An a see why ye think that there micht be mair tae reveal. The openin' in the base is obvious…a simple clip catch." Then after a few minutes Alex announced, "Think a've sussed it! Wait there till I git ma tools." On his return, Sofiya saw he had the finest, tiny-headed flat screwdriver she had ever seen. "Cannae be too careful wi' fine workmanship like this, ye ken, and it's meant tae be concealed, the inner secret opening, a mean. Whaur did ye say the clock cam frae?"

Sofiya told him, probably Russia.

The young man opened his eyes wide in astonishment. "Hiv ye ony idea whit this is worth?" Alex gasped, as he carefully examined the clock's tortoiseshell dial, its delicate hands that ticked away the minutes and hours, and the tiny key to wind it up, so delicate in comparison to the rest of its large, broad, high, gold base. Turning the clock round and opening the door at the back he examined the inside, its striking mechanism and seven-jewelled movement with his jeweller's magnifying glass lens supported between his eyebrow and cheekbone. Alex decided there were no keys hidden behind the clock's cogs and wheels. So, turning the clock back round he carefully laid the clock on its back and began to examine the base.

"This micht be Louis XIV and if it wur brocht frae Russia it's hid some journey tae get there and then tae Scotland. Look efter it."

With professional expertise Alex flipped open the now empty base, then tried to open the circular metal discs in the base of each foot by inserting the flat screwdriver under each of the four feet to no avail, but he spotted the last one had a tiny hinge. With the flat screwdriver he flipped it open and it gave way to reveal a tiny keyhole. Gently turning the screwdriver in the keyhole, with a loud click suddenly the entire base separated from the plinth, burst open and an old faded photograph and several folded documents fell onto the shop's counter with something concealed among them.

"Ah' weel, I wisnae expecting that! Oh, ma guidness me, there's a brooch! Noo, a've seen that afore. Na, no the brooch, but drawings o' it. Ma dey, auld Alec Bird... ma mither thocht Alec too auld fashioned, so I got 'Alex', he kept a record o' aw his designs. He was richt particular aboot his work. That's a wee lassie's brooch. Whit a beauty! A silver caramel sweetie wrapper twisted at baith ends, richt? But a dinna ken wha Alice wus." He frowned at the gold inscription in the middle. "But maybe ye ken wha the bairn wus? This is fine silver... look at the hallmark, the thistle, that's Edinburgh's. Ma dey must have sent it to be assayed there. Noo, wull a' pit the clock aw back the gither fur ye?" he asked Sofiya, after she lifted the brooch and collected the documents but she offered no explanation as to who Alice was, only nodded her response.

This was the original child's brooch her great-great-grandfather Jock Bowman had given his granddaughter Alice Jane Gardner, not the Fabergé one Prince Alexander had copied from Alice's drawing for his granddaughters and Alice in Russia.

"A'll tak some measurements and mak a new key fur the foot in the base and only ye an' me wull ken hoo tae get intae it, if in the future ye want tae hide somethin' yersel." Young Alex Bird winked.

The enclosed documents included notification of the Banns that by tradition were posted on the church notice board three weeks before a marriage and called out during the Sunday morning services. All were printed on good quality blue paper, the words surrounded by a garland of flowers and the names all written in the fine small Italic scroll of a bygone age. But Sofiya already had the death certificates of her great-grandmother's family, given to her at the reading of the will.

But at last, here were almost all of the certificates Sofiya had been looking for: Her father, James, falsified birth certificate with Frederick Paxton as his father, but no mother on it and registering his place of birth as London. James's original Scottish one with mother Alice Gardner, and father unknown. Her mother Ana's Scottish birth certificate registering her place of birth as Edinburgh, the one with her father's name Alexander Davidson, and her mother Alice Gardner Davidson, nothing to identify her Russian connections. Her parents' marriage certificate and her own original birth certificate, but there were no death certificates for her parents. And still no sign of the vital document she needed, the marriage certificate for Lord Robert Leightham and Alice Gardner. The photograph was of a woman in a Queen Alexandra's nursing uniform. Sofiya knew at once who it was... her mother, Ana. Sofiya swallowed hard to stop from bursting into tears in front of the young man.

Armed with the death certificates of her forebears Sofiya made her way to Anne's office. After a few minutes Anne returned from a back room with a heavy, leather-bound tome and thumping it down on her desk, she proudly announced, "Pittendreal church records fae the end of the 17ᵗʰ century. Tak yer time. If they're in Pittendreal cemetery the information and the exact location of the graves wull be in there."

The beautifully handwritten church records confirmed not only the dates of their deaths but the burial sites of their graves. Sofiya quickly realised all her forebears were buried there, including the two little girls named Jane who had died before their third birthdays. Her great-grandparents had not remained in Peterhead as grandmother had told her they had! That was confusing because her great-grandmother Agnes Gardner's death certificate said her death from TB had occurred in Peterhead, but how did she come to be buried in Pittendreal cemetery?

"Oh, my God!" Sofiya burst out to the astonishment of the clerk; she had suddenly remembered being shown the photograph of grandmother's dead mother and being told she had died in Canada. It had all been lies: her grandmother's fictitious family had never emigrated to Canada after WW1 and her grandmother's fictitious father had never attended the auction of Russian antiques in New York. The photograph could not have come from Canada. Sofiya shook her head. How could she have been so unobservant and not seen the photographer's name *J.S. Ireland, Photographer, Leightham,* on the corner of the photograph? Sofiya's only excuse was the shock at seeing a photograph of a dead woman was why she had missed it.

They were all one and the same family Wullie, Agnes and their daughter, Alice Jane Gardner. The Gardners had left for Peterhead after their daughter Alice had disappeared while staying with the Phimister sisters. Agnes Gardner must have been photographed in Leightham when they brought the body back from Peterhead before they buried her! This was confirmed by the dates and burial site in the church records. Her grandmother's wealth came directly from Russia, not from the New York auction rooms, and had been sent to Scotland by her husband, Prince Alexander Skavronsky, before the revolution.

Anne arranged for two council workmen who looked after the cemetery grounds to meet Sofiya at the cemetery and between them they would find the gravesites, using the information from the church records.

"Richt, Dougie, start ower there aside the west dyke and a'll awa tae the Kirk wa', and start there."

"Wan, twa, three, fower," the lads counted as they paced out the distance, heel to toe, heel to toe, using their workmen's boots as measures.

"That's twenty-eight paces frae the Kirk wa' and seventeen paces frae the west wa'."

Dougie and big Sandy Anderson looked towards Sofiya as they met. "They're in here, Mrs!" Sandy indicated the location of the two gravesites, pointing down at two patches of bare grass side by side. Perplexed he shook his head, "Nae tomb stains thou, sorry."

Sofiya burst out laughing at the antics of the two men locating the graves and calling her 'Mrs'. Dougie and Sandy obviously relieved, joined in the laughter and having done their job, shook her hand and wishing her well took their leave... mission accomplished. There was no doubt in Sofiya's mind her great-great-grandfather, Jock Bowman, had planned the whole thing from above to make her laugh, just as she had laughed at her grandmother's story of the mourners at Jock's funeral who instead of following the horse-drawn hearse, by mistake followed auld Tam's kirt loaded with horse manure up the Comentry Road, when in fact he had been buried in Pittendreal church cemetery all along.

Standing alone after the council workmen left, Sofiya walked over to the magnificent but now badly discoloured headstone of an angel with the epitaph *'For a Dead Princess'* engraved on its plinth. She vowed to have Janet's headstone thoroughly cleaned and she would contact Thomson the engravers in Leightham and order two granite headstones, to be placed side by side on her forebears' graves. She would arrange with the local florist for flowers to be placed on all three graves every month.

After that day Sofiya realized she would need to shake herself, get out of the miasma of grief and self-pity. She was descended from better bloodstock than that. She had to get back to real life and begin the journeys she knew she had to take for her peace of mind. There was nothing to stop her and she had the means to do it, thanks to her grandmother, Lady Alice Jane Leightham or Princess Alice Davidson Skavronskya!

Chapter 2

A SUDDEN SPRINGTIME SQUALL was blowing from behind the Mary Isle. Only a few line-fishing boats were out; changed days from the time of Sofiya's great-great-grandfather, Jock Bowman, when the river was thick with fishing boats and trawlers were out on the Forth and the North Sea in all weathers. Old photographs of rows of tightly packed fishing boats in Pittendreal harbour showed you could walk from one pier to the other, boat by boat, without getting your feet wet.

A large cruise ship was making its way out to sea from Rosyth Dockyard which was no longer a naval port but was now privately owned and catered for merchant ships and cruise liners. The dockyard also refitted Royal Navy submarines and stored decommissioned trident missile submarines that once slithered up and down the waters unobserved, like giant black whales deep beneath the waves making their way out to sea for secret destinations. *What would her father, an Admiralty Pilot at the Royal Navy base till he retired, think?* He was so well respected as a pilot, that an American admiral sent a signal to the Admiralty in Rosyth, requesting that only Captain Fairgrieve should pilot American warships in and out of Rosyth harbour.

These were the good memories of her childhood and of her dad telling her amusing stories about his work. *Were they true? Who knows?* She remembered him telling her that when his tugboat *Marauder* was towing the huge nets needed by the Royal Navy destroyers for target practice, he sent an urgent signal to one of the captains, "We aim to please…you aim, too, please!" Sofiya never found out if it was true or not, but it did sound a bit like Royal Navy humour!

Her dad also had strong views regarding the ill-treatment of women and children. It was his opinion that any man who abused a woman or a child was an unmitigated coward and should be severely punished. While growing up she and her dad frequently discussed which university she should apply to and which car she should buy, but on the subject of those who abused women and children... there were no ifs or buts.

In the fifties, the days before health and safety laws, her dad took her to work with him during her summer holidays. When she went sailing with him on his tugboat she would watch him jump off the quay into what seemed like Para Handy's Clyde puffer, the *Vital Spark* as it was so small in comparison to the ship he would be piloting. As the *Marauder* bobbed up and down with the swell, just managing to stay alongside the *Ark Royal,* she watched her dad climb the side of the enormous aircraft carrier by a rope ladder that had been thrown down the starboard side for him to board. It was so dangerous... her heart was in her mouth watching him swaying from side to side on the ladder until he disappeared through a wide hatchway halfway up the side of the carrier. Although he never let on, he was probably glad to walk through the hangar deck, to eventually reach the ship's conning tower, to pilot her in.

She remembered standing with him in the tug's wheelhouse at close quarters to the *Royal Yacht Britannia,* as the Queen with Prince Philip walked along her port side, unseen as yet by the cheering crowd on its starboard side, where those on the quayside were waiting for the royal couple to appear on the bridge to wave to them. Sofiya remembered these occasions, watching her dad nonchalantly stirring three teaspoons of sugar into his cup of seaman's extra strong, boiled tea, thick with condensed milk that the tea-boy had brought him. Tea, so thick, a teaspoon could stand up in it. At times Sofiya thought her dad had the second sight with one eye on his tea and the other on the royal yacht. The *Marauder* was 'standing by' alongside the *Royal Yacht*, but dare not touch it as it cast off and left Rosyth on its way up north with the Queen on her annual Scottish holiday. Once the yacht was underway and her dad had finished his tea, the tug could 'stand down'. *Britannia* had her own pilots and her dad often joked they would have arrested him if he tried to climb aboard and pilot her. *More RN humour?*

His loyal crew nicknamed him 'hurricane Jim'. It would be a calm, sunny day when they left the dockyard. The *Marauder* would sail past the breakwater, then under the road and rail bridges and by the time they reached Inchkeith, a few nautical miles out into the Forth, a storm would blow up out of nowhere! While the crew sheltered in their bunks being seasick, her dad would be in the wheelhouse, one hand on the helm and one behind his back, totally unfazed.

Frequently it was even worse sailing in the North Sea during the winter months with gale-force winds and colossal waves breaking over the bow. On these occasions most of the crew would be below deck, but not her dad. One day her dad heard his nickname for the first time when a new tea-boy trying to keep his balance in a sudden squall was on deck directly below the wheelhouse window. He asked auld Buchan, the bosun, "Whit happened?" Auld Buchan replied, "Dae ye naw ken? Yer sailing wi 'Hurricane Jim'!" Secretly pleased, her dad had laughed when he told Sofiya the story. Hurricane Jim had a droll sense of humour.

Life had changed out of all recognition; Jim would be hard pressed to recognise this world if he was somehow able to return to it. Sofiya's dad had taken a great interest in all the outer space exploration since the 70s. She wondered how he would feel about the latest space quests to discover what other stars and planets existed…what was 'beyond the beyond'?

Although he never commented by word or deed, she could sense his relief when her wedding to Johnny Geiger was called off. She instinctively knew of his concern regarding her intention to marry Johnny. Not entirely because it took her away from him, her family and home but, although similar, it was still a different culture to the one she had been brought up with. And she remembered his abhorrence of the racism in America.

Sofiya's dad therefore was happy to 'give her away' at her wedding to Neil Martin, a Scotsman. She wore her birth-mother Ana's silk dress that she had found in the attic of Mount View. Sofiya recalled how proud he had been in the role of 'the father of the bride'. With his chest puffed out he escorted her up the aisle of Leightham Parish Church and proudly made his way back down the aisle to the 'Radetzky March' with Neil's mother, Susan, on his arm. Wholeheartedly throwing himself into the celebration at the reception with family and friends at Cards House in Edinburgh and downing more than a few drams of whisky to toast the happy couple, he managed to stay sober long enough to throw confetti as she and Neil drove off on honeymoon.

Her dad had realized she could not face holding the reception at Mount View, however much she loved the house. It would bring back too many memories of the devastation from that storm, that unforgettable August day, which should have been one of the happiest days of her life, but had been ruined, and was now imprinted in her brain forever. She would never forget that occasion or another unhappy memory that followed not long after. Her dad knew everything about her, every last secret and he neither judged nor condemned her, silently supporting her one hundred per cent in every decision she made.

How she missed him! She had been his 'pet'. He died in his sixties a cruel painful death from smoke-related lung cancer. She had begged him over the years to give up smoking but he was so addicted to his cigarettes with their heavy tar content, that he just couldn't stop smoking. That addiction probably had begun in his early youth and the war years hadn't helped. But her fondest memories and his legacy to her was that he could make her laugh and comfort her when she felt low in spirits, even after all these years.

She remembered the day after he was admitted to hospital for tests the first time, and her mother's frantic phone call to her in a state of panic, demanding to know if her dad was with her. There were two policemen at the door telling her mum that her dad was missing from the ward. One of the young policemen using the walkie-talkie radio on his chest was advising whoever he was talking to, to take care when approaching this man as he might be dangerous. *Dangerous?! Her dad...?!*

Her dad arrived home about an hour later totally unfazed, wondering what all the fuss was about, having walked over the fields in his slippers and pyjamas. His explanation was simple. He had gone to the nurses' station and asked if they were finished with him. The nurse said, "Yes", meaning, for that day. But he took it to mean that they were finished with him altogether and left without waiting for Sofiya's mother to bring his outdoor clothes and to take him home. 'Hurricane Jim' to a T! More tests followed, but this time in a hospital in Edinburgh. Sofiya's mum quipped on the way home: "Well, I hope he doesn't try to walk over the Forth Road Bridge in his pyjamas!"

Within days of his death and before his funeral, he was at it again, determined to make Sofiya smile through her tears. In some kind of pagan cleansing ritual her mum and Sofiya scrubbed and cleaned every carpet, every moveable and machine-washable object in the house, including clothing. Sofiya guessed it was to take their minds off his death. Mr Wright, the funeral director, phoned to remind them to take the death certificate to register Jim's death as soon as possible so he could arrange the date, flowers and so on for the crematorium.

On their way out to do just that, they realized the death certificate was missing! Sofiya had put the death certificate in the pocket of one of her blouses and her mum had put the blouse in the washing machine that morning! That necessitated a further trip to her dad's GP surgery, to get his GP to sign another death certificate. It goes without saying they both burst into a fit of laughter. Sofiya thought the newly qualified young doctor was going to split his sides open. He had never had to issue a repeat death certificate before; maybe a lost prescription but not a death certificate!

A further phone call from Mr Wright informed them that the bottom half of Jim's pyjamas hadn't arrived at the funeral parlour with his body and asked that they please bring them. That sent Sofiya's mum into a frenzy of activity searching for the missing bottom of the pyjamas Jim had been wearing the morning he died. Her main concern about the garment being lost, which she repeated loudly over and over again, was that the pyjamas were new, and she had only just bought them from M&S! "So what, mum?" said Sofiya who had tried to calm her down. "Are you going to wear them?!" Sofiya heard the phone ringing again...God, what next? It was Mr Wright asking if they would bring the bottom half of her dad's false teeth to the funeral parlour as they hadn't arrived either!

Time doesn't stand still and there was nothing more to do except collect his ashes from the crematorium after the cremation and take the solid wooden casket they had been sealed in, to rest overnight in Rosyth Dockyard church. The captain of the dockyard had very kindly allowed them to take the casket out on her dad's tug the *Marauder* with his old crew the next day, to cast the casket into the Forth as his final resting place. After a short service conducted by the dockyard chaplain on board the tug it was time to say goodbye. Sofiya removed the casket from her dad's WW2 merchant navy flag she had wrapped round it in remembrance. Jim had rescued the flag from the sinking merchant ship before getting into a lifeboat the day his ship was torpedoed by a U-boat in the North Sea.

Handing the flag to her mother, feeling very sad, Sofiya leant over the side of the tug to drop the wooden casket overboard, but her dad wasn't finished yet! Out of nowhere a wave appeared, the tug lurched sideways and Sofiya dropped the heavy box which crashed into the wave and an almighty fountain of water rose up, drenching her from head to foot! Vaguely in the background she thought she heard her mother say, "I don't think he wants to be put in there."… *bit late now, Ina,* she thought.

With seawater dripping down Sofiya's face and to the utter astonishment of the crew and the dockyard chaplain, she turned, looked out towards the two bridges spanning the Forth, stood to attention and gave the Royal Navy salute…hand flat, palm facing downwards 'smartly' on the way up to the side of her face, slow on the way down just as Jim taught her as a girl and she shouted above the noise of the waves, "Aye, aye captain 'hurricane' Jim, signal received loud and clear, but you didn't have to half-drown me in the process, dad. You win, I give in. I will stop mourning your death and start celebrating your life. All is 'shipshape and Bristol fashion'. You can rest in peace now."

Chapter 3

T HE CRUISE LINER sailed past the Mary Isle on its way to the Baltics or perhaps the Mediterranean. Sofiya smiled at the memory of her grandmother's story of Sofiya's mother, Ana, being seasick in the Bay of Biscay, on her way to Ceylon in WW2. At that time, she had no idea Ana was her mother. Seasickness wouldn't affect the passengers nowadays, as on large cruise ships the addition of stabilisers extending out from the hull on both sides, preventing excessive rolling of the ship from side to side in rough seas and strong winds. The passengers these days would be able to eat and drink to their hearts' content whatever the weather.

Tall, slim, seemingly ageless, her auburn hair as vibrant as ever and apart from a few laughter lines on her pale face, Sofiya had changed little over the years. She wore a pair of straight-leg 'Marks' jeans, and remembered that in her youth the original brand name had been 'St Michael's'. Her simple cashmere polo-neck sweater had been bought from the same 'M & S' on Leightham High Street. Marks and Spencer now supplied affordable luxury for all, with several of their own brand names of clothing to choose from. With a pair of soft comfortable loafers on her feet, she had been ready to take the dog out for her daily walk. A light-weight, puff quilted jacket completed her outfit, changed days from the old duffle coat she wore as a student.

Thankfully there were very few occasions these days she needed to get dressed up for; comfort was the name of the game rather than fashion. *When was the last time I wore a designer outfit?* And somewhere in one of the old trunks in storage gathering moths, was the blue Balenciaga dress she had worn to impress her grandmother, the dress her American friend, Mary Smith, had given to her before she left America. *And where is my Jackie Kennedy pillbox hat and my stiletto shoes?* Her dad had said the stiletto heels were only fit for planting leeks! She wondered what they would be worth on eBay along with several other designer outfits she had bought over the years from Chanel and Yves Saint Laurent. *Perhaps the items could raise money for charity?* They were of no use to her now, even if they did still fit.

Sofiya slumped down on one of the two Parker Knoll chairs she and her grandmother had sat on at Mount View. Cathie had had them brought from the house, but not the painting that had hung on the wall behind her grandmother. It was a painting she had stared at as if hypnotised during her early visits to her grandmother as a young woman fascinated by the story of 'the house with no roof'. Her grandmother had suggested from the start of their meetings, they were the picture frame of her story and what she would tell her was the painting itself, the people, the landscapes and the colours. Sofiya had often imagined the central figure was her grandmother's friend, Alice, 'Alice in Wonderland'. But after the woman's death it was Sofiya who had gone through the 'looking glass' and had emerged from the imaginary 'rabbit hole' transformed as Lady Sofiya Leightham ... not Alice.

Her grandmother had moved the painting to the dining-room wall above the sideboard some time before their last meeting, stating that Sofiya was paying more attention to the painting than her story. But it was as if her grandmother had had a premonition as to what would happen the day her will was read. The painting had crashed off the dining-room wall, spraying Johnny Geiger with shards of glass after he had jumped up from his chair as he and the others sat listening to the reading of the will.

He had abandoned her at the very moment she was at her most vulnerable and needed his support more than anything in the world. Sofiya hated that painting and the memories it brought back and she had it reframed and donated it to charity.

But she loved the two Parker Knoll chairs on either side of the coffee table in the large bay window in her bedroom. Recognizing the handwriting she threw the envelope with contempt onto the table.

It landed between the latest printouts Wilma Paterson had worked on. Wilma an I.T. specialist, she had met at a party a few years before. Sofiya had warmed to the woman and before she realized it, they had become good friends. She had no idea why she felt such confidence in someone she hardly knew or why she was sharing all her long-hidden secrets with. Sofiya had confessed to having a mass of jotters and typewritten notes, memories from her youth of her visits to her grandmother and Sofiya's daughter Sophie had challenged her to transfer these notes to a computer so that she and the grandchildren would know the family's history. Sofiya also admitted to Wilma she was having trouble transferring the work. To make matters worse she had sent 50,000 words into cyberspace never to be seen again and she had almost given up on the idea.

Laughing, Sofiya told Wilma she was mod-tech illiterate and the machine hated her! Wilma smiled and reassured Sofiya, "Don't worry, Lady Leightham. I was a computer programmer in the days when a computer was so large it and its peripherals occupied a room the size of the ground floor of a house and the information was put in by punched cards and transferred to decks of magnetic tapes. So I will help you get to grips with modern technology! To business… I suggest you treat yourself to a laptop and here's my advice to avoid any future catastrophes: 'breakfast, dinner and supper'."

Sofiya frowned. *What on earth?! Why was she talking about… food?*

"Remember to first 'save' the work you have just done on the laptop; that's 'breakfast'. Second, regularly download the work to a memory stick; that's 'lunch'. Last, print a hard copy… 'supper'. Breakfast, lunch and supper. That way you can't lose work that would be hard to replace." Sofiya laughed out loud and shook her head because with her past experience, it made right good sense.

"Give me all your hard copy to date and I'll go through it, do the corrections and bring it back for you to make the changes. But remember I'm *no* ghost writer. It will be all your own work, although we might have the odd disagreement regarding repetition of sentences and suggestions may be made of how one sentence will say exactly what you are trying to say, instead of three!"

"Remember Wilma, doctors' notes are clinical statements of fact. I am a novice writer! You will have your work cut out. What about payment?" Sofiya asked.

"Nothing…!" Wilma insisted. "It sounds so interesting. I want to read your story from start to finish and I want to be the first to know the ending. So, get on with it!"

To say thank you, Sofiya arranged for Wilma and her dog to have holidays at her estate in Aberdeenshire. Old Lord John Leightham, Robbie's grandfather had somehow managed to save the estate and the sale of some of the land had paid the death duties on both properties when he died.

* * *

The unopened envelope spun round on the highly polished surface, and landed face up. It was an envelope with a foreign stamp, but was not an airmail letter; the overland posting must have taken weeks to get here. It seemed to challenge her, but still Sofiya refused to open it to read its contents. The letter also brought back memories of the kindness, support and care of dear people at that time: Cathie, Irene and her mother-in-law to be, Susan, one of the most decent, practical, down-to-earth human beings she had ever met. She could not have survived but for their help and unconditional silence at the time of her greatest need. Unspoken they simply closed ranks around her.

Looking out of the window, she tried to draw a line under the past, to stop thinking about her own personal history, to think of happier times. But the month of April always brought that memory back with a vengeance and this letter made it worse. To ease her painful memories, she distracted herself by looking back on the wonderful journeys to other countries she had taken, to countries that might hold clues that would help her come to terms with her life and prove one way or another who she really was.

Chapter 4

S OME POSITIVE developments had happened in Sofiya's lifetime: Glasnost and Perestroika; the fall of the Berlin Wall in 1991; the re-joining of East and West Berlin and the collapse of the USSR. In the mid-1980s during Glasnost and Perestroika, which were a series of political and economic reforms in Russia, it might have been a good time for Sofiya to visit in her search for information, had she waited. By then Russians might have been more open to help her regarding her royal ancestors. Also, in the mid-1980s DNA fingerprinting was invented by a British geneticist and this would have been invaluable to Sofiya. That, however, lay in the future.

In the early 1970s she had argued with herself that to go to Russia then was the best plan; she couldn't risk waiting. If she waited perhaps the elderly, retired Russians who held the information relevant to her search, might have died. She made the decision to go and it had turned out to be the right one, leading to one particularly emotional and rewarding experience for her.

In St Petersburg Sofiya had hired a young, unsmiling guide, Marina Vishneva who spoke perfect English and took Sofiya's request for information very seriously. When she realized why Sofiya was asking so many questions, Marina relaxed, began to smile and enjoyed spending several hours with her, over and above the time she was being paid for. She took a great deal of interest in Sofiya because of the possibility she might have Russian blood in her veins and Marina had an interest in early Russian history and the number of Scottish people who featured in it, such as Charles Cameron architect, Doctor John

Rogerson personal physician and Captain John Paul Jones rear admiral in the Imperial Russian Navy, who were all employed by Catherine the Great.

The guide pulled out all the stops to see if Sofiya recognized any part of the Skavronsky Palace or its contents that her grandmother had described. Marina took her not only through the grand rooms of the palace, where Sofiya saw on the entrance hall wall, a large oblong, empty space with previous markings, which suggested might have been where the painting of the girl on the horse had hung. Marina also took her to the kitchens and the laundry, the extensive grounds including the orangery, the Dutch cottage with its Delft blue and white tiles lining the walls, Dutch furnishings and artefacts, and the family's Russian Orthodox Church, where Father Mikhail had married her grandparents, Prince Alexander and Alice Gardner.

Marina explained how a canal had been dug from the Neva River to create a boating lake in the palace grounds, so the palace guests could entertain themselves rowing on it. There was sufficient accommodation to house 2,000 guests in this palace outside St Petersburg and the owners were said to be wealthier than the Tzar. Sofiya was surprised when the young guide told her the Russian nobility in previous centuries had their 'serfs' trained to become artisans. Imported *objes d'art* were prohibitively expensive so the nobility would buy limited examples and have the artisans copy them. The artisans became so professional and skilled they could earn their own money by reproducing the *objes d'art*. It also surprised Sofiya to hear the term 'serf' as Emperor Alexander II had abolished serfdom in 1861.

Walking round the palace it became abundantly clear to Sofiya why there had been a revolution: the vast wealth of the nobility and upper classes was in such stark contrast to the abject poverty of the poor. Marina suggested various libraries and museums that might have old registers, if Sofiya knew names, dates of births, deaths, any information at all of the people she was looking for, but warned her, that for safety's sake in the days post-Revolution, many had changed their family name so as not to be associated with the nobility. And many documents had been burnt by the Bolsheviks during the October Revolution.

"Did you say that one of your predecessors might have danced with the Mariinsky, the Kirov ballet company?" Marina asked Sofiya. Sofiya nodded. "Well," continued Marina, "the company might still have records of all its past ballet dancers. It was established for more than 150 years before the Revolution but the ballet company went into decline and was closed for some months until it reopened as The Soviet State School of Ballet in 1918. After the Revolution it was able to maintain its repertoire with a pre-Revolutionary teacher and director."

Sofiya remembered the letter grandmother gave her to read in which Princess Shusha first said she had signed with her initials K D, as she had not dared to risk signing it Kseniya Davidson, or Skavronskya, but she hadn't. To further confuse whoever read it and to protect her anonymity, signed it K.A. (Alexander her grandfather's first name). When Sofiya asked if the Skavronsky family had other palaces or estates in other parts of the country Marina shook her head, but thought it could have been possible because many of the nobility and their family members had several estates in St Petersburg they never visited, as well as having property in Moscow. Marina suggested that Sofiya try the monasteries as they were also a good source of pre-Revolution information and as Sofiya knew the name of the priest that married her grandparents, they might have a record of him.

Sofiya did not inform Marina that her grandmother was still married to Lord Robert Leightham at the time of her wedding to the prince but in her defence, she didn't know her husband had survived the sinking of the *Titanic.* Sofiya was glad she had no claim to the Skavronsky Estate. It was beautiful, but it belonged to the Russian people and was being well cared for by the Russian government.

Before they parted, Sofiya asked Marina, "Why did no one smile back at me? Why did Russian people not respond? Why do they always look away?" Marina explained, "They think you are either simple- minded or trying to trick them, so they keep themselves to themselves."

When Sofiya was walking round the grounds of the palace, she felt the hairs on her arms rise. Her grandmother had arrived there to work more than half a century before and Sofiya recognized much from grandmother's description of the grounds and the palace. In one of those moments when her imagination must have been playing tricks on her, Sofiya thought she saw the two little princesses Lera and Shusha, with their grandfather Prince Alexander dressed in his 1812 Hussar uniform, playing in the gardens with their Scottish Collie dog, Hamish, which was barking, demanding they throw the ball for him. She felt the same sensation then as when she first became aware of Tchaikovsky's music, or the day she thought she saw a man on the beach in Pittendreal playing with his German Shepherd dog.

It had made her shiver; she could not explain why. She was not afraid but knew these visions were meant only for her; no one else could see or experience them. All these images confirmed her innermost feelings and even her dreams. She remembered the day she stood in the ruins of Leightham House and a piece of masonry fell at her side, the same piece of stone Cathie took out of her tote bag and threw at Johnny Geiger striking him across the cheek when he walked away from her.

Sofiya also journeyed to East Africa, visiting the tea and coffee estates in Kenya, Kericho and Thika in the vain hope of finding some trace of her birth parents, who might have been alive at that time. It was an irrational hope as there had never been any letters from her parents for years in the documents grandmother left behind. There were only the letters before and during WW2. Her parents' marriage certificate and her own original birth certificate, which had been revealed from the inner secret compartment of her grandmother's ormolu clock, when Alex Bird opened it. The trail went dead after that.

In Nairobi smiling library and museum staff had pulled out every stop to help 'memsahib' search for the information she was looking for during the time of the Freedom Fighters, then known as the Mau-Mau; especially a young librarian, Miss Moonira Rampuri, who was not the least bit fazed by her request for information on what was still a sensitive subject in the early years of Kenya's independence when Jomo Kenyatta was its first president. Moonira kindly invited Sofiya to come home with her. She told Sofiya some of her relatives were living and working in Scotland and her family would appreciate hearing about the country first hand. At times she felt overwhelmed by the hospitality of the museum and library staff in all the countries she visited, who took such an interest in her search for information.

Chapter 5

W HEREVER SOFIYA TRAVELLED, she was always glad to return home to Scotland. Scotland was in her heart and in her blood. It astonished her at times that Scotland, a small country of around five million people, was so well known worldwide. Burns suppers take place at the end of January from St Petersburg to Tokyo and beyond, to celebrate the birth of Scotland's national bard, Rabbie Burns. Travelling by train and aeroplane, Sofiya was amused, at times surprised, at some of the questions she was asked by fellow passengers. Whisky was always at the top of the list. Sofiya had never tasted whisky, but she told enquirers her dad had sworn by whisky as a cure for all ills and had such respect for the golden liquid he called it 'Himself' the boss or in darker tones 'The Craitur' the beast, or rather the devil! And visitors should try drinking Scotch whisky from a traditional Scottish drinking cup, the Quaich and remember any country can make whisky, but only Scotland can make Scotch.

Once, much to her astonishment, a fellow passenger on board a flight asked her if she had ever seen Nessie. "No," Sofiya answered. "Loch Ness is an exceptionally deep, long stretch of water, bordered on either side by magnificent high mountains and Nessie only appears to a chosen few!" And, as if embarrassed, in lowered tones... a question asked mainly by women, "Is it true that Scotsmen wear nothing under their kilts?" Without embarrassment Sofiya would reply, "Yes, if they are *true* Scotsmen." There were times when Sofiya was tempted to add, that's why Scotsmen are so fertile, as production of the male seed takes place at a lower temperature than body heat.

Foreigners from many countries visit Scotland during the annual Edinburgh Festival in August and Sofiya was often told that they would never forget hearing the skirl of the massed pipes and drums at the Military Tattoo when Scottish regiments marched up and down the esplanade of Edinburgh Castle in full Highland dress to the sound of the bagpipes, and drummers twirled their white pompom drumsticks up in the air as they play.

Visitors were impressed by the unforgettable sight as the bands marched in their tall, black, ostrich feather bonnets fluttering in the wind, braid-trimmed jackets, long white horse hair and black tasselled sporrans and kilts swinging from side to side, tartan plaids pinned at one shoulder hanging to below the knee, knee-length tartan socks with the *Sgian Dubh* 'black knife' tucked inside, white spats meeting black brogue shoes. The drum major in full Highland dress with his Malacca cane mace, held close to his chest, stretches it out to signal a change of direction to the marching regiment. And to think that wearing of tartan was banned by the Hanoverian King George I of England in the aftermath of the first attempt by the Jacobites to restore the Stuarts to the British throne in 1715!

It filled Sofiya with pride to think of visitors enjoying the Highland dancing, watching the handsome men with their kilt pleats swinging high in the air, (almost proving Sofiya's point that no underwear is worn with kilts) as they performed the 'sword dance' with its intricate steps over crossed swords on the ground in front of them, never touching the swords with their feet. In earlier times it was only the men who performed Highland dances to show off their strength and stamina. Men and women in groups of six or eight on the esplanade, men in their kilts and women in white dresses, their tartan plaid shawls pinned at the shoulder with Cairngorm brooches, display Scottish country dances which are often a part of Scottish weddings.

Scottish distinctive tartan designs are woven in pure wool with criss-cross horizontal and vertical bands in multiple colours; the colours and striped checked patterns identify individual Scottish clans. As well as the traditional tartans, hunting tartans, modern tartans are still being created. The relatively new Royal Stuart tartan was created in the 1800s for the Hanoverian British royal family.

And no one ever failed to tell Sofiya of the emotion and the tears that came to their eyes whatever country they came from when the lights went out at the end of the Military Tattoo and a spotlight shone on a lone piper, high up on the castle ramparts playing a last solo bagpipe piece, perhaps the laments 'The Flooers o the Forest' or 'Sleep Dearie Sleep'. The roar of applause that erupted at the end of every Tattoo could be heard well beyond the historic castle walls.

The undeniable unique sound of the bagpipes would accompany the clansmen into battle and raise the fighting spirits of the men. During the Second World War captured German snipers were asked why they didn't shoot Lord Lovat's personal piper, Bill Millin, who, unarmed apart from his Sgian Dubh, walked up and down the beach playing the bagpipes as the soldiers came ashore from the landing crafts on D-Day. The snipers' response was they didn't want to shoot 'Dummkopf', a dumb head! When Bill Millin quoted the regulations regarding restricting the playing of bagpipes in action to Lord Lovat, Lord Lovat is said to have replied "Ah, but that's the English war office regulations. You and I are both Scottish and that doesn't apply to us." Perhaps the snipers also recognized the bravery of the man, a fellow soldier.

Sofiya was often asked if she liked the sound of the bagpipes. Well yes...she admitted she liked to hear the young lads playing for the visitors in the big cities to earn a bit of money, but privately thought of the times when her husband, Neil, decided to practice his bagpipes. Ordered to play outside the house, he would march up and down the courtyard, while Sofiya and her daughter, Sophie, would cover their ears with pillows to drown out the screeching sound of the amateur piper. Who did Neil Martin think he was ... the 'Laird o' Cockpen'?... a good job they lived in the countryside or he would be arrested for disturbing the peace!

Sofiya informed visitors that the bagpipe music, the 'Flooers o' the Forest are a' wede awa' was a lament played by a solo piper only at funerals. It was composed to commemorate the defeat of James IV, grandfather of Mary, Queen of Scots, at the battle of Flodden Field in 1513. It is an emotional expression of grief for life lost, and pride for those killed in battle ever since. Visitors know about William Wallace from city-tour guides and the movie, *Brave Heart* and most know that lakes are called lochs in Scotland. There is, however, one lake in Scotland, Lake of Menteith and it was Sir John Menteith who betrayed Sir William Wallace to the English in 1305. The statues of William Wallace and Robert the Bruce are on either side of the entrance to Edinburgh Castle.

If visitors had time they could visit Bannockburn near Stirling with its imposing statue of Robert the Bruce on his horse which celebrates the Scottish victory over King Edward II of England, who tried to conquer Scotland but failed. It was one of the many battles to retain Scotland's independence. Would a time come when Scotland would become an independent country once again?

Sofiya reminded visitors to set their watches but not be startled when the One O' clock Gun is fired from the castle every day except Sundays. With a 20-inch barrel

'Mons Meg' one of the largest cannons ever built, gifted to King James II of Scotland in 1457, was now a field gun and had been given a recent MOT. Sofiya also spoke about John Knox, a follower of John Calvin, the protestant reformer. John Knox introduced the Presbyterian form of Calvinism to Scotland, and he railed against the 'monstrous regiment of women'. He was apparently referring to 'Bloody' Mary, the Catholic Queen of England and Marie de Guise, mother of Mary, Queen of Scots. There was also the story of Jenny Geddes who in 1637 threw her stool at the Dean of St Giles' Cathedral for preaching from the new English-style prayer book. Sofiya liked to tease visitors by saying Scotland had its own Robin Hood in the form of Rob Roy MacGregor.

Sofiya encouraged other fellow travellers to visit 'The Kingdom of Fife' widely held to have been one of the major ancient, Pictish kingdoms, known as Fib and whilst there to visit St Andrews, the traditional home of golf and the first university in Scotland and the third oldest university in the English-speaking world. The proud symbol of Scotland known throughout the world is its blue Saltire flag, with the white diagonal cross. St Andrew believed himself unworthy to be crucified on a cross shaped like that of Christ's and was martyred on a diagonal cross. St Andrew was also the patron saint of Russia and St Petersburg...*now why did I say that*? Sofiya wondered, but she now knew why.

If they visited Dunfermline Abbey visitors would see a cast of 'The Bruce's' skull, also where his body is buried, but not his heart which he instructed should be removed after death and taken to the Holy Land. Instead, his heart was carried in a casket into battle in Moorish Spain and is now interred in Melrose Abbey. Thanks to the movie, *The Da Vinci Code* there is speculation whether the Holy Grail rests in Rosslyn Chapel, a chapel which may have a connection with the Knights Templar.

No one could ever imagine such a small country could be so full of culture and history as is Scotland. Sofiya remembered a conversation with her grandmother back in the 60s who said we needed more women in power and Sofiya assured her grandmother to give it time. And now Scotland has a woman poised to become its First Minister. To what heights could she scale on the world stage? Scotland, a small beautiful, country with couthie people, loved by those who know her, Sofiya never failed to wonder at the contributions to the world in this and past centuries by Scots folks. Perhaps her grandmother got it right – the Scottish people did get their brains from eating so much fish!

Chapter 6

IT **SEEMED** so long ago now, that fateful day when they had gathered to hear the reading of the will of the woman Sofiya thought was her great-aunt. Sofiya's world had been turned upside down when Miss Helen McDougall, her grandmother's long-time friend, made a life-changing announcement. She revealed that Sofiya's great-aunt's name was Alice Jane Gardner and she was her grandmother! Once Sofiya recovered from the shock of that incredible disclosure and Johnny Geiger's appalling accusations, she decided that even if she discovered her birth parents were alive, Ina and Jim would always be her mum and dad. She had her own granny and dey with whom she had spent many happy hours of her childhood; that could never be changed.

Aunt Nan, Aunt Jessie and her beloved cousin, Margo, they were her family. Sofiya wiped a tear from her eye when she thought of Margo's untimely death from cancer in the same week as Princess Diana died. How grateful she was to have Margo's daughter, Paula, phone her. "We women must stick together and support each other whatever happens," Paula said. Paula's resolve was important for now and the future when Sofiya would no longer be around.

Even although inclement weather had been forecast, it would not be as bad as years ago, thought Sofiya. Sofiya remembered winter days of thick pea soup fog and smog from coal fires and industry, bumper-to-bumper traffic that meant road closures; several feet of snow and ice for weeks at a time, dangerous for transport, ambulances and fire engines; people falling, breaking limbs on the ice;

doctors and district nurses struggling to make house calls to their sick housebound patients – all were distant memories. Environmental change as well as climate change had arrived.

But nothing stays the same forever; life goes on regardless she thought, only to be interrupted for the second time that day by Bunty Ramsey her housekeeper. Was there never any peace? No, thank goodness there never was any peace on the Leightham Estate, never a dull moment. The grounds served as the hub of community activities throughout the year. A fall of snow brought the grounds to life in the winter: the screams and laughter from excited children and their parents sledging down the hilly slopes behind the house; hot chocolate and hot dogs served by Bunty Ramsey and Vivienne MacKay; followed by a traditional Burn's Supper at the end of January.

Once a month from the end of March, on a Saturday, there was a farmers' market where fresh fruit and vegetables, and other produce from the farms were sold from stalls set up in the lower grounds. There were also book and clothing stalls. Sunday-school picnics, end-of-term school picnics and races for the pupils were other events which were held on the estate towards the end of June. Sofiya remembered these events from her own schooldays and had decided to reintroduce them. On the lower lawns cricket was played every Saturday throughout the summer as well as tennis matches on the estate's courts.

There were music festivals from late spring, weather permitting, and these started with an Easter performance of Handel's 'Messiah', performed by local amateur musicians and choirs, and continued with professional orchestral concerts throughout the summer until autumn. At well-attended concerts, the audience sat on rugs on the estate lawns with picnic baskets enjoying glasses of wine served by Bunty and Vivienne. Ronald MacKay patrolled the gardens during these performances to keep an eye on his precious trees, plants and shrubs... just in case they might get damaged, and Jimmy Ramsey kept an eye on the cars being directed to the parking area by two young lads from the village and made sure no one went near the house. As far as he was concerned Leightham House belonged as much to him as it did to Lady Leightham! But he turned a blind eye to youngsters enjoying a snog in the woods.

Local children avoided guising at Leightham estate during Halloween; the long dimly lit eerie walk to the house put them off. But not at Guy Fawkes, bonfire night, when there were sparklers, fireworks and a bonfire to enjoy. It was a house, a home, brought to life by her daughter, her son-in-law and her grandchildren and all their friends, her niece and family, family pets and good people from the local community working to keep the place alive; alive with birthday parties, anniversary celebrations and especially at Christmas when indoor and outdoor fir trees glittered with tree lights and a delicious Christmas dinner was cooked by Bunty. There were gifts under the Christmas tree for everyone, family and estate workers, from Santa Claus, better known as Jimmy Ramsey or was Santa Ronald MacKay? The house's activates were brought full circle with fireworks and hot mulled wine for the locals to welcome in the New Year, Hogmanay, a Scottish traditional Scottish celebration that was now enjoyed throughout the world.

At times Sofiya wondered if she could have settled in America. Maybe she'd had a lucky escape. Any length of time spent away from her beloved country brought on feelings of homesickness... she just had to get back home. She had loved Johnny Geiger, but would that love have been enough to leave her homeland and family for good? She had had a good marriage with Neil Martin. At times she felt she was following in the footsteps of her grandmother, who had lived with her unrequited love for Robbie Leightham. But as far as Sofiya could make out from the stories her grandmother told her, her marriage to her prince had been a happy one. However, having to abandon her child before leaving Scotland for Russia had brought sympathetic tears to Sofiya's eyes.

Had all the ghosts, the secrets from the past finally been laid to rest? Yes, all but one. A shadow of gloom, a shadow of unexplained sadness hung over the house every April and Sofiya refused to answer enquires as to why she seemed to be so low in spirits then, till all who knew her stopped asking, leaving her in peace, to her own deep thoughts. Even to her own beloved daughter, she refused to give an explanation but maybe with the unexpected arrival of that letter today, maybe it was time?

Chapter 7

S IGHING, SOFIYA turned away from the window and took a deep breath. It was almost time to go downstairs and get ready to take her 8-year-old granddaughter, Savanna Alice Haig to the local swimming pool. By the age of three Savanna refused to wear armbands at the family home's pool in Spain and by the time she was seven, Junior Scottish Swimming Champion Richard Laird, who coached her recommended she join the local swimming team. How proud Sofiya's dad, once a local swimming champion himself, would have been of his great-granddaughter. Sofiya was not surprised to learn that Richard's great-great-aunt, Emily Laird, was the librarian in Pittendreal library and it was she who played the organ at Janet McDougall's funeral.

What would she have done without her daughter? Her daughter, Sophie, when she was growing up as an only child, declared that she would have many children and with her laid-back husband Iain Haig, had four, two boys and two girls, the joy of Sofiya's life. Arran and Alexander were into football, which mercifully didn't involve her.

Today was no different than any other but it was hard not to look back even with the everyday distractions and interruptions demanding her attention. Earlier in the day there had been the usual ruckus at the back door with the dog barking her lungs out as the postman arrived with the mail. Later in the afternoon when Sofiya normally liked to relax, put her feet up and enjoy a cup of coffee while looking out of her bedroom window, she had been interrupted by a knock at the door and Bunty Ramsey burst into the room.

"A'm awfy sorry Miss Sofiya, A nearly flung this oot wi awe that trash mail that arrives in the post they days!" Bunty handed a letter to Sofiya. "It's fur you. There's no many folk write letters thae days and this wan was tucked in the back o' aw thae daft adverts that arrive wi the mail. Hoo mony folks buy insurance frae an advert on a bit o' paper, or a year's delivery o magazines? A' like tae buy the *People's Friend* masel frae the supermarket when I'm oot daen' the shoppin'. And awe they adverts fur food! Indian, Chinese and pizzas tae be delivered tae the hoose!"

"Many people order food to be delivered these days, Bunty. In my mother's time, as you well know women handed in their notice when they were about to get married, but with the arrival of family planning they can now continue with their careers for as long as they want, up to retirement. What's the point of women learning a skill, attending a training course, going to college or university, just to stay at home, unless of course they wanted to? And single-parent families! I admire them, take my hat off to them. It's not easy, in this day and age with the expense of child-minding, unless there are grandparents to help, and rent, mortgage and utilities to be paid, food, holidays and the like. To have any standard of living in the western world, women have to work. Why shouldn't they enjoy having some food delivered or go for a take-away during the week or at the weekend to save them cooking? Good for them."

Bunty nodded her head in agreement as she busied herself tidying Sofiya's bedroom. "A agree wi ye, but the problem fur us is aboot gettin' somethin' tae eat fur oor dinner the nicht!" She picked up carelessly tossed shoes and slippers, put them at the bottom of the wardrobe and closed the door after hanging up clothes that had been dropped on the floor. Not for the first time Bunty thought Sofiya was the untidiest woman on the planet!

...food? What's she on about now? "Well, you rescued my letter but I don't think it's the postman's fault it got mixed up with the trash mail. And you are right… It is unusual to get a personal handwritten letter these days but…" Sofiya was thinking that it was a pity Bunty hadn't thrown the letter out with the rubbish.

"A'm no blaming him. He's new, Miss, the postie that is," Bunty began. "A've run efter him afore tae warn him, but never caught up wi him till the day."

"Bunty, why have you started to chase the poor man to warn him about what?" Sofiya pursed her lips and dipped her head into her chest to smother a laugh at the thought of her buxom housekeeper running after the postman. She needed a reason to smile and laugh especially now having recognized the handwriting on the letter.

"It's that dug. Well, it's no really her fault. A swear she hears the mail van comin' chuggin' like 'Postman Pat wae his black and white cat'. Up gan the ears, she gits up frae the kitchen flair and runs tae the back o' the door, drinks in the smell o' the man through her nose and waits heid doon fur the letters tae drap. That auld postie, Eck Harrower, he's just retired and he's the wan tae blame. He tormented her as a pup. That auld Victorian letterbox, it's that big and wide and so Eck used tae push the mail in and oot teasing her until she caught it in her teeth and hauled it in! Eck thought it was a fine joke. The strange thing is, she jist gets the bundle o' mail atween her teeth, gies it a guid shake and draps it on the flair. A' used tae think she read the mail and decided nanc o it was fur her… so she spits it oot."

Bunty, stopping for a breath, shook her head. She lifted the teacup from the bedside cabinet, replaced it on the saucer which was still on the tray on the coffee table, while trying to lift biscuit crumbs from the floor. She stood up thinking she would get the hoover out once her ladyship went to the swimming.

Sofiya thought it was a pity the dog didn't tear or better still eat today's mail. She realized someone might lose a finger or their fingernails if they got their hand too far in the letterbox so would ask Jimmy to install a wire basket behind the letterbox.

"Here, let me gie ye a laugh... miss."

Sofiya shook her head...miss? She hadn't been a miss for years now and no amount of arguing with Bunty on how to address her had made any difference and it would be nice to have something to laugh about.

"A went tae the door tae warn the young postie. A saw he was aboot tae drive awa again, so a went chasin' efter him and managed to stop him the day! A telt him aboot the dug and ye'll never guess what he said tae me! 'Oh, a thocht it wus you pullin' the letters in.' 'Eh?! A telt him,' dae ye think a've nothin' better tae dae than stond inside the back door and snatch the mail frae you?'...Cheek!" Bunty shook her head, "Ye couldn'a mak it up. Mind ye, that dug earns her keep. Laila works fur her livin'."

"...earns her keep. What do you mean, Bunty?"

Chapter 8

SOFIYA REMEMBERED the day the dog arrived. Jimmy and Ronald came into the kitchen with the puppy in Ronald's arms. Sofiya, Bunty and Vivienne were sitting at the kitchen table going over the Tea Room accounts before they were sent to the accountant, and Bunty was the first to see the men arrive.

"Git that filthy beast oot o' here!" Bunty demanded.

"Haud on noo Bunty. That's no oor decision to mak, it's her ladyship's." Jimmy responded.

"Where or who did you get it from, Ronald?" Sofiya asked, remembering her grandmother's story when she was a little girl, bringing a cat home and Sofiya's great-grandmother, Agnes Gardner's words about the animal being a filthy beast.

"A fund her in the park bein' teased by some bairns. They wer'na really hurtin' her, so I guid thaim a lecture on being kind to animals or a wud tell their faithers. Then a noticed the pup wus a German Shepherd and jist look at thay muckle big paws! Goodness only kens whit size she'll be when she's finished grown and dinna worry aboot thay stupit lookin' lugs hingin' ower her een; they'll cam upricht in time. A've phoned aw the local vets' surgeries, put notices on the lampposts, phoned the Bobby, but naebody seems tae ken onythin' aboot a missing dug."

"Weel, it's nae biden' here." Bunty was adamant.

"What dae ye want me tae dae, Bunty, haund her back tae the bairns, or the rescue service and hope she gits a guid hame?" Ronald argued, "Whit dae you think, yer ladyship?"

"Sorry, Bunty, you know me, I'm a soft touch where animals are concerned. It must have been the animal deprivation I suffered in my childhood. My mother wouldn't have an animal in the house but when I grew up she couldn't stop me bringing Samson, my first Siamese cat home. Mum thought he would go with me when I moved… out." Sofiya stopped herself in time from saying, '… moved to America'. "My dad loved animals and German Shepherds in particular. My only concern is Samosa. You know how possessive Siamese cats are and I believe German Shepherds are known to dislike cats! But, yes we will give the dog a trial." Sofiya nodded.

Bunty wondered why anyone would call a cat after an Indian fried pastry. Why not pakora or poppadum? It was a good job they didn't live in the town, she thought, because if they did their Indian neighbours would be bringing them food, thinking they were hungry when they shouted for the cat to get her in at night! It was strange to think that no one including Sofiya would have known what samosas were in the sixties. Indian snack food and chilli dips were delicious and who could refuse them?

"A tell yae whit, yer ladyship. She looks aboot six weeks auld and thay dugs are highly intelligent and trainable. We'll keep her on a lead while Samosa's aboot and train the dug tae tolerate the cat," Jimmy suggested but knowing the cat, he realised it probably would need to be the other way round. "Noo, what are ye thinking aboot a name, yer ladyship?"

"Mm. Let me think. Laila… yes that's it, from Majnun and Laila. I believe it's thought to be a version of *Romeo and Juliet* of the East. I like it and the cat is named after a delicious Indian food – their names will match each other." Sofiya reached out to pet the puppy, which promptly nipped her hand!

Bunty shook her head, "Jist look at that smug expression on her face. She's taen us aw fur gowks."

As it turned out a dog lead was unnecessary. When the cat spied the pup, her royal Siamese highness jumped down from the kitchen worktop, hissing like a banshee, came in sideways head down, tail furred up like a fox's and as the pup gave her a playful bow, Samosa with one swipe of her paw established who was going to be boss. As the pup went off to lick her nose the cat jumped back up on the worktop and started to groom herself. From then on, they were the best of friends. Samosa insisted on sharing Laila's basket in the kitchen and when the pup grew to full size, Laila had to roll onto her back to let the cat sleep on her stomach!

"You were saying about ordering a take away and why did you say the dog earns her keep Bunty?"

"Weel, yon dug thinks she owns this hoose, you and the bairns in particular, as weel as the folk she's kent since she was a pup, but strangers are in fur a big surprise," Bunty nodded knowingly. "Laila welcomes awbodie intae the hoose but it's a different story when they try tae lave it. Aye, the tail wags nineteen tae the dozen at the plumber or the electrician, nuzzlin' her nose intae their hauns fur a biscuit, but the minute they try tae leave it's a different story." Bunty shook her head, laughing.

"It wud be the same wi a robber. She wud be grinning frae ear tae ear, as if tae say, 'Help yersel tae whatever ye fancy.' But her hail body would change when a burglar tried tae lave. The heid gans doon, the tail stops waggin' and the lips begin' tae curl. The minute the burglar stonds still, the tail wud start waggin' again and she'd be grinning in triumph. Ha! Naebody's allowed tae go till we tell her 'Leave!' Only then she'd let thaim oot the door. Gawd help the burglar if we're nae here. She'd keep him cornered and eat him alive if he tried tae move! Ye dinna need a burglar alarm. Aye, she earns her keep richt enough and eats the best o' food we buy her as weel! Which reminds me food…Whit aboot the nichts dinner?"

"I thought you were grilling steak?"

"Ye'll be lucky. Whit dae ye prefer…Chinese, Indian or Pizza?"

"Now what, Bunty?"

"A left fower sirloin steaks on a tray at the back o' the worktop to defrost this mornin', then a went oot tae dae a bit o shoppin'. When a got back a wus surprised no tae find Laila in the utility room whaur a leave her when a gan oot. Instead she wus lying flat oot on the kitchen flair, her ears flat aside her heid and a glaikit look on her face and only the last three inches o' her tail wus waggin'! I hidna closed the kitchen door richt afore a left!"

Bunty gritted her teeth.

"A questioned her, Miss Sofiya. Laila…!?" At the time Bunty couldn't believe she was having a conversation with a dog. "She pushed hersel further doon intae the flair pretendin' whitever it wus a wus askin' aboot, hid nothin' tae dae wi her, although guilt wus written aw oor her face. A looked ower at the worktop. The tray had fower semi-circular pieces of fat on it…nae meat! Suddenly it clicked. She'd chacked her teeth roond each steak, eaten the beef and left the fat behind!! Like a said afore… What tak-a-wa dae ye want, Indian, Chinese or pizza…?"

Sofiya couldn't hold it in any longer and burst out laughing. "Bunty, how could anyone be angry at such an intelligent dog…maybe she was watching her weight? Pizza will do fine and get it delivered. I like pepperoni so does Savanna. Get an extra one and she can take it home with her after the swimming."

"It's nae laughin' matter, Miss Sofiya. Oh, my gawd jist look at the time! A'm awa doon the stair ma bairn will be here in nae time." Bunty leant forward and picked up the tea tray.

"Wait, Bunty! I just want to say how grateful I am to you and Jimmy. What would I have done without him to give Sophie away at her wedding to Iain? Jimmy playing football with Arran and Alexander and teaching the boys to play the bagpipes. And you baking, knitting and sewing with the girls, are making such unforgettable memories for the future for them, as well as keeping our culture alive. Thank you."

"Ach, haud yer wheesht! Dinna mention it. It's Jimmy and me that's grateful. Ah, a think Savannah's here already. Jist listen tae yon racket! Wow, wow, wow...Wow, wow...Wow! Yea wid think thon dug wus askin' questions and answering them hersel... stupit beast."

Sofiya heard Bunty continue to talk to herself, as she went downstairs.

"Bliddy dug, and screeching cat, clawing the furniture tae ribbons. Ye wud think we hid a Bengal tiger in the hoose. It's worse when Miss Paterson brings that dug o her's wi her, thay twa dugs bowfin' at each ither, knockin' awethin' ower. And that puir lawdie frae Aikman's the grocer's tryin' tae chow his wi through a haunfae o' GoCat left on the kitchen worktap fur Samosa, he thocht it wus Bombay Mix! The place is turnin' intae a Zoo. It's a guid job they bairns disnae hae ony animal o their ain or they wud bring them as weel." Sofiya's son-in-law was allergic to animals and sneezed from the minute he arrived in Leightham House. "It's gettin' mair like bedlam everyday..." complained Bunty then she sneezed.

"I heard that Bunty!"

It was time to read the letter. Sofiya could not think of another reason to delay. Sitting back down in her favourite spot she lifted the envelope from the coffee table and ripped it open before she changed her mind. It was from Johnny Geiger. Holding the letter she began to read.

Chapter 9

"G RANDMA! It's me," Savanna shouted at the top of her voice. The eight-year-old ran down the back stairs from the courtyard amidst the ruckus of the dog barking, announcing her arrival. She burst into the kitchen ready to throw herself at her grandmother and give her a hug around the waist as usual. "Guess what mum's bought me?" Instead of her grandmother being there, Savanna ran right into the arms of Bunty Ramsey. "Oh! Sorry, Mrs Ramsey, sorry… Where's grandma?" Savanna frowned looking round the kitchen as she petted Laila, scratching the dog's ears.

"Dinna fash yersel, Miss Savanna. Yer granny'll be doon in a minute. She's still pitten her lipstick on. Laila, wheesht!"

"Where's Samosa, Mrs Ramsey?"

"Aye, the Leightham Hoose predator… oot scaring the wild life hauf tae daith. Ye should hiv been here yesterday, Savanna. She brung a wee moose in, puir little thing, terrified oot its wits and madam Samosa nae in the least bit interested in killin' or eatin' it, tossed it up in the air, then let it go till it tried tae hide under the fridge. Ye could hiv helped me rescue the wee soul and pit it back outside."

"That would have been fun."

"Nae much fun getting' scarted tae bits by thay claws…pest o an animal!" And not for the first time as she looked at Savanna, Bunty thought …that bairn looks like the girl in the painting hanging in the hall…*Ach yer imagination's gan daft.*

Savanna laughed, but she knew that Mrs Ramsey was remembering being one of Samosa's victims having been scratched by the cat in the past. "I'll ask mum if we can take Samosa home with us."

"Whit! Dae ye want yer faither tae sneeze himsel tae daith?!"

Sophie ran into the kitchen to catch up with her daughter. "Where's mum, Bunty? She's usually down here waiting to take Savanna to her swimming club."

Sophie was puzzled. Her mother made a point of being in the kitchen early to wait for her granddaughter to arrive because she knew they would come in the back entrance, as Bunty always kept chocolate biscuits in the kitchen for Savanna to take to the swimming with her.

"A ken it's a wee bit odd, but she's still up the stairs. But… it *is* April?" Bunty raised her eyebrows and lowered her voice so the child wouldn't hear what she was saying, shrugging her shoulders as if to say 'what do you expect?' But Savanna was paying no attention to the two women. "It's aboot time ye fund out whit that's awe aboot, Miss Sophie, it's depressing tae live wi every spring fur aw thay years. Enough's enough." Bunty hesitated wondering if she had said too much or should say anything else, then decided to tell Sophie. Leaning forward she whispered, "A great big letter arrived the day fur her ladyship. Maybe she's reading it, that's why she's late. Dae ye want me tae gan and git her…tell her yer here?"

"A letter … in an envelope… a handwritten letter?" Bunty nodded. "That's odd. I didn't think anyone wrote letters now. I can't remember the last time I received a letter. It's only ever birthday and Christmas cards… Everybody communicates by email these days. No, Bunty, I'll go up in a minute… Savanna, hand out of the biscuit jar!" Sophie warned her daughter. "And stop feeding Laila with them. Chocolate is not good for dogs."

"I didn't, mum! I was just holding one behind me and she went round to the back and took it out of my hand." Savanna answered.

"Mm, some excuse."

"Ach, lave the bairn alaine. She's nae duin ony herm. Noo, whit were ye saying, ma pet? Whit's yer mither bocht ye?"

"A new swimsuit, Mrs Ramsey...look!" Savanna shouted full of excitement. She put her half eaten biscuit in her mouth and dug into her club swimbag she brought on club days, along with her swimming kickboard bag. "It's a Speedo and a new rubber cap with the club team crest on it. I hope this one stretches better than the old one. I've got such thick hair, Mrs Ramsey, that even when it's in pleats, I always have to get one of the older girls to help me get it on, it's so tight," she announced with the biscuit still in her mouth.

"Take the biscuit out of your mouth, Sav, when you are speaking!" Sophie ordered.

"Wait till I show Richard my new swimming costume." Savanna's voice suddenly started to rise, "Mum, mum!! Where are my goggles?" Savanna frantically searched inside her swimbag, tossing the towel and her 'onesie' onto the floor, "Oh, here they are at the bottom. Phew, that's a relief!"

Crisis over, Bunty smiled. "Let the bairn enjoy her biscuit. Richt, let me see yer new costume then. Wow that's a beauty, and ye'll swim like a fish in that." Bunty admired the swimsuit then turned to Sophie, "Yer no normally this early, Miss Sophie. Whit's up the day?" Bunty asked as she bent down to pick the swimming gear off the floor and put it back into the swimbag.

"Savanna! Help Mrs Ramsey clear up; there was no need to empty the bag all over the floor! You spoil her, Bunty." Sophie smiled at the housekeeper, a friend; the Leightham Estate wouldn't be the same without her. She continued, "To answer your question...teacher training or something, Bunty. The parents were phoned and asked to come and collect the children early. Personally I think

54

there was a problem with the ceiling in one of the classrooms and they wanted the children out of the building. I felt sorry for Holly and Arwa's mums. They both work, so when something like this happens it causes childcare problems for working mothers. If Savanna hadn't been going swimming, I would have offered to take her two school friends home with me and they could have played together till their mothers had finished work."

Not for the first time Sophie realized she was privileged to have the choice of whether to work or not. "There's good news for working mothers though, Bunty. The Scottish Government has legislated for fifteen hours of free nursery-school care for three to five-year-olds, and that might increase sometime in the future and of course, college and university tuition fees are government-funded in Scotland. How many young people lost out in the past because their parents did not have the money to support their children to further education? My parents never had to think the cost of my education. I was one privileged kid… enough about that. How about you, Bunty? Do you have your free bus pass for senior citizens? "

Sophie was thinking that her grandmother, Susan Martin, had always voted for the Conservative Party. They would have acknowledged Scotland had benefited from having its own parliament in Edinburgh once again. Devolved powers for Scotland had been established in 1999 and since then the Scottish government had alleviated the effects of the bedroom tax, had written off poll tax debts and abolished prescription charges from cradle to grave. She also knew her mother's adoptive parents had been staunch Labour supporters, but granddad Jim would have thoroughly approved of the successful socialist political party in power in Scotland's government. However he would have been horrified at the arrival of Polaris missile nuclear submarines at Faslane in the Gare Loch. He would have asked why the nuclear weapons had been sited in Scotland despite very strong nationwide protest.

Sophie remembered a conversation her mother had had with her grandmother regarding the need for more women in positions of power and her mother's answer had been the same as her grandmother's… give it time.

"A do and it's awfy grand, Miss Sophie. Vivienne… Mrs MacKay that is, we baith use oor free bus passes tae gan tae Edinburgh fur the day and hae a look aboot the shops and hiv oor tea in Miss Margaret's tearoom in Princes Street afore comin' hame. The bus picks us up and draps us aff at the bottom o' the drive… easier than the train and nae hingin' aboot a cauld railway station."

"Iain's last two patients have cancelled their appointments. He says they must be saving their toothache till Sunday when he's on call! So with the school getting out early Iain's picked up Arran and Alexander and has taken the boys for extra football practice. Mum only needs to drop Savanna at the swimming baths, and Iain on his way back will wait till Sav's finished and take her and the boys home."

Sophie had a sudden thought. "Since I am here earlier than usual, mum and I can have a cup of tea together. I rarely get time to sit with mum these days; someone should have told me four children were a lot of work before I had them," Sophie laughed.

Bunty was thinking it was a good job Sophie and Iain had worked out where the children were coming from, or goodness knows how many they would have ended up with! But she couldn't fault them as parents. "A tell ye whit, Miss Sophie. A've hid an idea. A'll tak the bairn swimming the day and wait till her dad arrives. A've got the car oot the back. Jimmy's no needin' it. He and Ronald are awa tae Edinburgh, and they'll no be back till late."

"Oh please, please, mum… let Mrs Ramsey?" Savanna pleaded with her mother. "But don't forget to tell grandma I love her when she comes down."

"You are on! I'll text Iain on the mobile let him know. Off you go the two of you. Bunty, not too many sweets, please, and I won't forget to tell grandma, Sav."

Bunty smiling nodded in agreement with the child's mother, but said to herself, *That'll be richt! Nae sweeties? Hoo often do a git the chance tae spile the bairn?* "But first, Miss Savanna, dae ma a favour. Gan awa ben tae the utility room. Laila'll follow ye. Her biscuits are in the cupboard under the sink… only ain or twa noo! Then leave her in there, shut the cupboard and the utility doors tight ahint ye and it's a deal."

"High five, Mrs Ramsey!" Savanna giggled jumped up and soundly slapped hands with Bunty mid-air, and ran off with the dog in hot pursuit.

"I'll nip up the stair and tell mum the good news… might cheer her up. Be an angel and put the kettle on for me, Bunty, before you leave. On the other hand, Bunty, mm… no…" Sophie thought for a moment. Iain could come for her on his way back from picking up Savanna rather than going straight home; she didn't have to drive. It was Saturday tomorrow so she could come back and collect her car then. "Wait a minute, Bunty. Mum and I can have a sun-downer …it's almost Happy Hour! Is there wine in the fridge? I know she likes Cava. You know when I was growing up I never saw my mother with a glass of wine in her hand…changed days."

"Aye, a've bin here lang enough tae mind thay days and naebody wud dare light a cigarette in front o' her or in the hoose then and noo. Seems tae me she started tae like a gless o' wine no long efter yer faither died, although she's *gey* disciplined, never mair than twa glesses at a time. Wine in the fridge? Jimmy keeps enough wine and spirits in the wine cellar tae stock a pub! There's aye twa bottles o her favourite Spanish Cava in the door o' the fridge and ye'll get champagne glesses in that cupboard ower there. Funny... her ladyship disnae like Champagne. Says it gies her a sair heid efter wan gless, but she kin manage twa glesses o Cava...nae problem. Oh! A hiv tae order pizza fur her ladyship. She thocht Savanna wud like ane as weel. Whit aboot yersels? Wull a order fur aw o ye?" Bunty asked as Savanna arrived back in the kitchen.

"No thank you, Bunty. It's Friday and we always get fish and chips from Marcello's on the way home."

"A dinna blame ye. Yon fish suppers are the best in Scotland. Noo, we're awa, Miss Sophie. Cum on, ma pet, or we'll be late. Whar's yer bags."

Taking hold of the swimbag and kickboard bag in one hand and Savanna's in the other, Bunty marched to the backdoor. Savanna skipped up the backstairs with her friend and Bunty retrieved the child's booster seat from the boot of the car. Savanna jumped in clicking the seatbelt into place. Sophie shaking her head wondered what the two of them were talking about, as she observed Savanna engaging Bunty in what looked like a deep philosophical discussion.

Chapter 10

I *BETTER get on and pour mum's drink and get upstairs before she comes down. Now where did Bunty say the glasses were kept?* Sophie loved the view from her mother's bedroom. Whenever she sat on one of the big chairs in the bay window, it brought back happy memories of her childhood, kneeling at the coffee table with her homework and her father helping her. It also had served as a place of solace after her father's untimely death and where she had been comforted by granny Susan and her mother.

Thinking about her past made Sophie ponder her future. She wasn't sure if she wanted to inherit the rest of her mother's fortune or the estate. Was she up to the job with its 24-hour-a-day commitment? With four children to contend with, were they not her first priority? And not for the first time she thought the property might be better off in the hands of the National Trust for Scotland. Sophie knew her mother had set up ample financial trust funds for her grandchildren and had divested a great deal of her wealth to Sophie years ago, on the advice of her accountant and lawyers to comply with the seven-year rule on inheritance tax. But then Sophie remembered she had her eldest daughter Sophia to consider. Sophia was descended from Scottish nobility, Russian royalty and hardworking Scots fisher-folks. Perhaps her daughter would feel differently and would want to inherit Leightham House, the estate and the title in the fullness of time.

Sophie, stop daydreaming! Where did Bunty say the wine glasses were kept...? The first cupboard was the wrong one but there was a packet of Doritos in it. Finding the glasses and taking the Cava out of the fridge, she proceeded to fiddle with the metal clasp till it finally popped open, spilling some of the fizz over the table.

With a glass in each hand and bag of Doritos between her teeth she bumped the kitchen door open and made her way up the kitchen stairs to the entrance hall of Leightham House.

For a few moments Sophie stood in the middle of the wide hallway and stared at the life-sized painting of a girl riding a magnificent, black stallion, and was struck as always by it wondering who the girl might be. From another century a beautiful young girl just out of childhood, riding side saddle, wearing an elaborate, tight fitting, pale blue, lace trimmed blouse and a long, soft, white, silk skirt draped over the horse's back to its hocks. On her head over her thick ringlets, was a very large hat decorated with feathers, and a flowing silk scarf. The painting was hung on the back wall in the hall. Sophie knew her mother had brought the painting from Mount View, but her mother had always given vague, evasive answers to any of her questions regarding the painting except to say it was her favourite.

Continuing up the stairs, Sophie's thoughts turned back to her mother's melancholy in the month of April. Sofiya could have taken her vast inheritance and disappeared to a life of the rich and famous. Instead, her mother became the local philanthropist, taking over from the Phimister sisters who had built the local school and provided childcare for the under-fives and also emulating the mysterious benefactor who donated a great deal of money to Pittendreal, with bursaries to help local children attend university among other things. The community had guessed, and rightly so, that their benefactor was Alasdair Forman and the money came from the Russian gold roubles he had discovered in the box his ill-fated fiancée Janet, had owned.

Sophie's parents had had their first wedding reception in Cards House in Edinburgh. Sophie knew her mother had had no real attachment to Cards House in Edinburgh, and knew the beautiful mansion held sad memories for her grandmother. Sofiya had converted the house to holiday flats for local, low paid or single parent families to enjoy a week's free summer holiday every year, with their only expenditure being the bus fare to Edinburgh and food. Visits to the zoo, the swimming baths and tickets for the cinema were funded by Sophie's mother. Sofiya had set up a trust fund with a local solicitor, so social workers and health visitors only needed to apply on behalf of their clients and families for a holiday.

After the deaths of Cathie, Irene and her special-needs granddaughter, Sofiya embarked on another generous charity enterprise and had Mount View adapted for young people with disabilities, so they could live and work as independently as possible with every modern aid to facilitate independence, with staff on call night and day if there was a problem. Sophie remembered with affection Cathie and Irene patiently teaching her and Irene's granddaughter how to bake scones. She remembered also pushing the girl round the gardens in her wheelchair to find Easter eggs. Harriet may have struggled to speak but Sophie would never forget her infectious laugh. Sofiya had taught Sophie from early childhood that all children were special, but children with special needs and disabled people should be supported, respected, loved and cared for.

Sophie recalled one miserable wet Saturday afternoon, when she was a schoolgirl; she and her friend, Gillian, who had come for a sleepover, went up to the loft for something to do. There they had found a large, sealed, strong cardboard box stored away at the back with a

'Neiman Marcus' American label on it. Forcing the box open the girls were astonished to find under the tissue wrapping, the most beautiful, seed-pearl encrusted, lace, and silk grosgrain, wedding dress, obviously unworn, with a separate detachable train and the longest silk illusion veil they had ever seen. Beneath the dress, in more tissue paper, was a long slightly yellowed, Victorian era christening robe of fine embroidered Indian cotton. Sophie knew at once what they were and although she had never seen either of them before, and swore Gillian to secrecy, hoping her mother would never find out they had opened it. Quickly replacing the garments in their tissue paper and before ramming the lid back on, Sophie caught sight of a large, flat, brown envelope, lying at the bottom of the box.

She remembered the christening robe was mentioned several times at the start of the story her mother had written for her grandmother and how Maggie Bowman had shortened it for her granddaughter, Alice Jane, to be christened in because it was too long. Thinking about it now, Sophie wondered if there was some significant reason for it to be kept hidden away in the attic? When was the last time it was used? It hadn't been used for Sophie's own christening. Photographs of that day showed her dressed in a different christening robe. Nor had it been used for the Humanist naming-day for Sophie's own children. Sophie remembered seeing a photograph of Irene's granddaughter in a christening robe that looked identical to the Victorian one she and Gillian had found in the loft. What was the significance of that?

Sophie continued to reflect on the possible reason for her mother's distress. She had read all her mother had written on behalf of grandmother and she knew her grandparents' history on her mother's side and the fact her mother's fiancé, an American airline pilot, had deserted her at the reading of her grandmother's will. Good riddance, Sophie thought at the time when she read that chapter. But Johnny Geiger's rejection of Sofiya had happened one August many years ago.

Every September before the winter set in Paula, her mum's cousin Margo's daughter, and Paula's daughter, Lorna, came to stay for a holiday and they always did what Sofiya called the graveyard trail. They took flowers and placed them on the graves of their loved ones, family and friends. They celebrated the lives of those who had gone before them and who would have wanted her mother to smile and remember happy memories. But none of them had died in the month of April.

Had something happened between her mum and dad maybe before Sophie had been born? Was it because of her mother's inability to tell her father she loved him? The untimely, tragic death of her father had stunned them both, but they had supported each other through their grief. She remembered her mother punishing herself telling Sophie once she had grown up, of the guilt she felt; she had not loved him as she should have. But her dad died on a cold December day, so that could not be the reason either.

Sophie remembered her granny Susan's wisdom in telling her that life was short at its longest. How very true… but she also said to live every minute, draw a line under the past and look forward to the next day because you never know what it might bring or what was round the next corner; it could be worse or a whole lot better. Now it was time to demand her mother tell her the truth and it was up to Sophie to tell her to draw a line under the past. Whatever it was they could get through it together by supporting each other.

Chapter 11

S OFIYA slumped back in her chair as the pages of the
letter dropped around her feet. She just couldn't come
to grips with what she had read. *Think, think!* she ordered
herself. Well, if Geiger was going to take any further
action he'd better get on with it. But it didn't give her
much time to decide what to do next and Sofiya didn't
trust him, not for one minute. For a moment she felt as
though she were being sucked back down Alice in
Wonderland's rabbit hole, the same one she had emerged
from many years ago.

Then Sofiya began to feel indignant. How dare he!
Why was he trying to exonerate himself now? To say
sorry for what he did to her so long ago…the bastard. She
couldn't care less about him, but she cared about her
family and herself. Why hadn't he contacted her before?
To use DNA and genetic testing to prove their biological
parentage and to keep such important information a secret
for all these years …She could have given him that
information from her side of their family years ago. He
obviously didn't want to know the truth back then.

Sofiya shook her head as her anger subsided and she
began to question the science behind his claims
concerning their forebears. From the mid-1980s her
husband, Professor Neil Martin and his two professorial
friends, Abe and Imdad, had worked together on blood-
related human DNA fingerprinting and inherent blood
diseases such as porphyria and haemophilia. The accuracy
of their scientific work was widely acknowledged but they
accepted the need for further research. She wondered how
accurate the test results were that Johnny Geiger had

purchased. Knowing him she thought he could have bribed someone to give him the results he had sent her. Did he have fingerprints, blood-stained clothing or hair from the hairbrushes of his deceased family or her's? No, she bet he didn't.

If what he had written was the truth he must have had the bodies of his mother and grandparents exhumed, dug up to collect the samples of teeth, bones, nails or hair. The bodies would have been too decomposed to get much else. Maybe they had been embalmed. Would that have made a difference? *Sofiya, wake up! Remember Tutankhamun's embalmed remains. His DNA extracted thousands of years after his death.* A host of questions raced through Sofiya's mind but the most pressing problem was what to do now. On top of that she knew she could not put her daughter off any longer. She would have to tell Sophie the truth.

Devastated, Sofiya clutched both sides of her face with her hands and rocked slowly back and forward in her chair. *Oh my God...Savanna! I have to take her swimming! I can't take her in this state. What am I going to say? What excuse can I give...?*

*   *   *

Sophie carried the two full glasses of Cava carefully in both hands trying not to spill them but felt the need to hurry as the packet of Doritos between her teeth made her drool. Negotiating the bedroom door handle with her elbow, she went in and put the wine glasses down on the bedside cabinet and turned her attention to opening the packet of Doritos. "Good news, mum. Bunty is taking Savanna swimming. You and I are going to enjoy drinking your favourite wine and we will talk about something I have been meaning to ask you." Lifting the wine glasses and the Doritos, Sophie went over to the window and put them down on the coffee table.

Sophie was startled to see sheets of foolscap paper scattered on the floor. Worse still, here was her mother, motionless and white-faced in her grandmother's old chair. Horrified, Sophie's mind instantly darted to that chapter her mother had written about her grandmother which described finding the old lady in the very same chair in Mount View. Sophie felt as though she had witnessed the scene before… déjà vu. But the coffee table had a pile of hardcopy on it, not a photograph of a dead woman.

"Mum! What's wrong? Will I phone for the doctor?"

"No, no I am alright. Don't worry. I will be fine in a minute. I got some unexpected news." Sofiya indicated the letter on the floor, "I just need time to digest the contents and think about what I am going to do."

"No!" Sophie decided to assert herself irrespective of her mother's state. If she missed the chance now, when would she get another? "No, mum, its time you answered my questions and <u>we</u> will decide what to do. I am not a child. Do I have to live the rest of my life wondering what happened to you? No! I am not asking you, I am demanding you tell me what causes you such sadness every April. Enough of this, year after year. I swear I will never tell anyone, whatever it is that you tell me."

Sophie realized this wasn't going to be easy. "Mum, we are a family. Look how much we all love each other and you taught us to be like that. You are the matriarch. You and dad taught me to have respect for human life, honesty and decency and anything we were told in confidence was never divulged to anyone. Here, take a sip. We can sit for a moment and you can gather your thoughts. But I insist you tell me now!" Sophie began to think she hadn't made much of an impression on her mother, so decided on another tack.

"Stop beating yourself up, mum. What happened in your young life to cause you such misery? Did you make a mistake at work…misdiagnose a patient; did a patient die in your care? There can't be a doctor alive who hasn't had that happen to them and these are such negative thoughts. On the other hand, look what you did for our community with your inheritance. You became a modern-day philanthropist. Draw a line under the past and think positive thoughts, not negative ones."

"You told me of childhood visits to the woman you thought was your great-aunt, and also about your cousin Margo and the women in our family and how you became obsessed with a 'house with no roof' when you passed the house on the car journeys to Pittendreal. When you grew up you felt you had a connection to the house and you wanted to know more. It was grandma Ina, who suggested you ask the woman the whole family thought was a distant relative. Your grandmother made a deal with you to write her memoirs but never admitting whether it was fact or fiction. *You* had to decide which parts were true if you wanted to be told her story. What a predicament! You comment several times in your notes how you felt a bond with her. The woman was your grandmother, not a great-aunt; she never came clean as to who she or you really were." Sophie shook her head perplexed.

"There has been the odd occasion, especially in the month of April when I have wondered if you are repeating the life of that old woman. You seem so alone at that time. Sorry, mum, but it seems to me she was an embittered, lonely old lady who died alone *by choice*. It was sad she gave up her baby son and was estranged from her daughter because of Ana's innocent love for the wrong man, but she didn't have to live alone. She chose to have you, her granddaughter, adopted.

"You could have been together as a family. Please don't feel bad about that. It was not your fault if that's what troubles you."

Sofiya gasped at her daughter's analysis and Sophie got the impression she had hit a nerve.

"Yes, she had you adopted, but she didn't exactly abandon you altogether; she moved from Cards House in Edinburgh to Mount View to be near you. But that's all in the past now." There was still no response from her mother. Sophie shrugged her shoulders. "Well, here's the deal. I have read all your previous work up to the time of your great-aunt, your grandmother's death, but I don't know much about your own life before you married dad. So here is another challenge since you seem unable to tell me face-to-face...write it down!"

This challenge roused Sofiya.

"No! No! I found it hard to call her my grandmother at first because never in my life did I know her as that and she never chose to tell me herself and I had my own beloved grandmother at that time." She held her hand up to prevent her daughter protesting. "And, I *have* already written down my own life story for you." Sofiya pointed to the pile of hard copy on the coffee table. "That is as close to the truth as I could get with the information I was given and the research I did at home and abroad trying to find out about my parents, my birth-right and our forebears." Sofiya looked at the papers on the coffee table for a moment before continuing.

"My grandmother told me that parts of her memoirs were fiction, weaving me into a story about the characters in a painting that hung on her wall as if I were one of them. I guess I fell for it, was beguiled because of my obsession with Leightham House. You said you felt I was repeating her life and I have had to use my imagination to tell you my story, just as my grandmother told me hers. But she made me promise never to reveal what I had written about her until after her death so you must swear never to reveal what I have written about me." Sofiya stopped for a moment to allow her daughter time to digest what she had said. "Some of my story is very personal and it would be embarrassing for both of us to discuss it. But it records what I discovered and what I went through and some of that is not very pleasant. In the meantime life must go on as normal."

"Has Wilma copy-edited this?"

"Yes."

"What does she think?"

"Wilma is my friend. She never gives an opinion, never tries to alter my work. She simply makes sense of what I am trying to say and once you have read the chapters about my life and you read the letter that might have serious repercussions for the future, I will decide what has to be done."

"No, mum, I will decide what has to be done and *we* will go forward together. Trust me."

Sofiya felt as though a weight had been lifted from her shoulders. She reached out for her glass and drank from it.

Finishing her drink Sophie put her wineglass back on the coffee table as she knelt on the floor at her mother's feet and began to gather up the pages of the letter. Like a bolt of lightning her mother's hand shot out and grabbed her tightly by the wrist so she had to drop the pages. "Ouch! What?! What did I do?" Sophie yelped.

"Before I give you the letter to read, you must read all that has happened first." Sofiya released her grasp and picking up the pile of hardcopy put it into her daughter's hand. She looked down at Sophie who was still on her knees. "You said you felt I might be repeating the life of my grandmother. You are right. I did something once not unlike her and for that I am deeply ashamed. You challenged me to write about my life. Well, here it is."

Sophie looked at the pile of hardcopy in her hand and slowly the truth began to dawn on her.

Sophie stared at her mother, realising it was more important than ever she read the documents her mother had just handed her...the letter could wait.

"Go home, Sophie." Her mother's voice interrupted Sophie's train of thought. "Take care of your family. Once you have read all I have given you to read today, we will meet and I will give you the last chapters and the letter to read and answer your questions. Remember, I am made of stronger stuff now. I am no longer a vulnerable young woman." Sofiya reached behind the cushion on her chair and brought out the package Sophie had seen in the attic.

"My grandmother told me when we came to the end of her story that it was all fiction. The information she gave to me years ago in this package is anything but fiction. I never felt the need to open it before today. She must have had a premonition that at some time in the future I might need it. Now I have the means to deal with Johnny Geiger."

Sophie left her mother's bedroom having agreed to her conditions not to ask questions or to discuss what was written on the hardcopy printout until she had finished reading it. She decided that just as her mother had gone to Mount View to discuss her grandmother's story she would insist they meet periodically to discuss her mother's memoirs. She and her mother would be repeating the same arrangement her mother had had with her great-aunt Jane, her grandmother. Sophie shivered at the thought... history repeating itself? Sophie felt as though her mother's grandmother, more than half a century later, was reaching out to women in her family. What secrets would her mother's work reveal?

Walking downstairs to wait for Iain to collect her, Sophie realized it was now more imperative than ever that she read her mother's memoirs, to read about her mother's younger life and how she became Lady Sofiya Leightham, owner of the Leightham Estate and 'The House with no Roof'.

Chapter 12

ALL SOPHIE WANTED to do was to collapse on the floor as she arrived back from her usual Sunday morning run. Gasping and panting, she bent double, her head touching her knees before standing straight up with her arms above her head, thinking her ballet lessons hadn't been such a bad idea after all as she twisted from side to side until her breathing slowly returned to normal. It had been a late start for her daily run, as she and Iain had been out to dinner with Sophie's old school friend Gillian and her husband Simon the night before and they had partied late into the night. All Sophie wanted to do now was to get out of her sweaty running gear and into the shower.

Lord! Was there never any peace in the world? They're all up. The noise from the kitchen and the smell of bacon frying confirmed that Iain was cooking the breakfast. The thought of a tasty bacon roll was tempting enough to put off going for a shower, so taking a few gulps of water from her water bottle, Sophie made her way to the kitchen, calling out as she walked along the corridor: "Iain! I'm back. Mm, that smells good." Sophie had to raise her voice to be heard above the usual Sunday morning ruckus that had broken out between Alexander and Savanna.

"You're in my seat, Alexander! And dad made that roll for *me*!" Savanna lunged forward in an effort to snatch the roll from her brother. Savanna and Alexander were almost the same age and were continually involved in one disagreement or another. At present they were in a pushing contest to see who could unseat the other from the same chair, although there were vacant chairs on either side of them.

"That's enough, you two!" Iain shouted, "Alexander! Sav always sits in that chair... move! Why are you annoying her?"

Alexander gave his dad his usual nonchalant, indifferent look and shrugging his shoulders slid along to the chair next to him with his Apple iPad in one hand and the bacon roll still in his other hand well out of Savanna's reach. Nothing ever bothered Alexander, and if it did, you would never know it.

"Here's your roll, Savanna. Now eat it and no more noise, my head's thumping."

"Had one too many last night, Mr Haig?" Sophie grinned at her husband as she entered the kitchen.

Iain gave his wife a sheepish look. "I'd give you a hug, darling, but you don't smell so good, Mrs Haig. Your breakfast isn't ready yet. I've got the other two to feed so go on and get your shower first and bang on Sophia's bedroom door as you pass it. Tell her to get up, her breakfast is ready. Boy, can teenagers sleep."

"I'd give you a hug in return, handsome, but you don't smell so great either." Sophie grinned.

"I know... I know I need a shower but the kids were up and demanding to be fed. You would think they hadn't had a bite to eat for years. You go first, I'll come up after you have finished."

"Promise?" Sophie grinned.

Sophie walked back down the hall pulling at her clothes that were sticking to her body and banged on Sophia's door. At the same time she tossed a coin in her head as to whether a shower or a soak in the bath was more appealing...*Sunday... too much to be done, better take a quick shower first,* she decided. *The school uniforms are to be sorted out for the morning, the school shoes to be cleaned, the lunch boxes washed and make sure all the school books are in the school bags. A woman's work is never done as my wise old granny used to say.*

After lunch Iain left with the boys for football practice and a telephone call from Sophie's friend, Eleanor, was like manna from heaven. Sophie would not have to take the girls to the dress rehearsal now for their up-and-coming end-of-term annual dance-school show. Eleanor had offered to come with her daughter Jennifer to collect Sophia and Savanna, take them with her and then drop the girls off on the way back, which meant Sophie had the afternoon to herself for the first time in weeks.

Every weekend Sophie was determined to sit down and read the manuscript her mother had given her in April, but something had always turned up to distract her like the annual celebration of her mother's birthday on the 17th of May, which Sophie always organized.

This year, Sophie had arranged for a large open-fronted tent to be erected in the cove on Leightham beach with a soft drinks and ice cream kiosk for the children and a bar for the adults. Sharon Anderson and her partner Ruth had sold their business several years ago, that had been financed and then bequeathed to the two women by Sofiya's grandmother. The Shazanna café, an innovative self-service restaurant and grill, had been a great success and Sharon had remained friends with Sophie's mother.

Sophie at times thought that Sharon was trying to make up for Sofiya's wrecked wedding reception and the aftermath by insisting on organizing the food for her mother's birthday celebrations every year. Sharon organized a barbecue pit and rotisserie for a roast of beef. Bunty was sworn to secrecy as usual and was invaluable in organizing the fiddly bits: heating trolleys, tables, chairs, wine glasses for the adults. And woe betide anyone who dropped litter on the beach because they would have Jimmy Ramsey to answer to.

The Scottish weather decided to behave itself for once and everyone had enjoyed themselves eating, drinking, the children building sand castles, wading and swimming in the freezing cold water of the Firth of Forth. As the sun was beginning to set over the River Forth, Sharon, as always produced the birthday cake and everyone, family, friends, estate workers crowded round the bonfire that had been set earlier in the day by Ronald and Jimmy, to warm themselves and to sing 'Happy Birthday'.

When Sophie had arrived home after demanding that her mother tell her the reasons for her state of mind every April, she had with her the manuscript her mother had given her to read. Sophie had locked the papers in the desk drawer in the study but it was out of sight … out of mind. Sophie's conscience bothered her at times when she remembered about it and now today was the perfect time to sit down and read her mother's memoirs. Sophie poured a glass of wine. *Well… it was Sunday afternoon.* She grabbed a pencil and one of the kid's jotters and having no other immediate commitments she relaxed and gave her undivided attention to what her mother had written. Sophie took the opening chapters from the pile in the desk drawer and made her way to the lounge.

She sank into the armchair and had a sudden fleeting thought: *Am I replicating my mother's experiences with her grandmother?* But instead of being face to face with the woman as her mother had been, Sophie was alone and unable to ask her questions as she read her mother's work. At least she wouldn't have to suffer the ridiculous fantasies that her mother had had about being in a picture hanging on the wall, or being Alice in Wonderland or coming out of a rabbit hole. They both now knew full well who the fictitious character, Alice, was. Sophie decided to write down her thoughts and the questions she would ask her mother when they met up.

Taking a sip of the wine Sophie began to read *The Continuation of the House with No Roof.*

PART TWO

Chapter 1

Continuation

WITH CATHIE'S ARM around her waist Sofiya was escorted to her car in the car park of Mount View after the reading of the Will. The full magnitude of being her great-aunt's sole heiress, the enormity of this life-changing event slowly began to sink in. Cathie sensed Sofiya's state of mind was changing and she started to worry about her.

"Dae ye want me to cam wi' ye, ma lass? A dinna like the look o' ye... yer awfy pale. Ye'v hid a shock, ye ken. A'll sit aside ye and a'll get the bus back?" Cathie offered.

"You're a darling, Cathie and I love you, but I need you to be here to organize clearing up this mess." Sofiya thought of making a sick joke. *Send me the bill... I can afford it now.* "Next time I come to Mount View, I want no trace of what should have been one of the happiest days of my life. I would trade every penny my great-aunt left me for a few short hours or one day on my honeymoon with the man I love and I thought loved me."

"Naw, ye dinna mean that. Yer meant fur better things, ma lass, than trying tae please a man that haes nae respect fur ye. There's a lot o' need in the world and in oor wee toon. Yer great-aunt or raither yer granny, left ye plenty bawbees tae dae a lot o' good wi' it. Noo awa hame. Yer mum and dad, they'll be worrit aboot ye. Tak yer time drivin' on they roads... they're dangerous and phone me when ye get hame, let me ken ye'v arrived safe and soond." Sofiya started the car engine and drove out of Mount View's driveway.

Sofiya had very little recollection of how she got home that afternoon except one. The unforgettable, vivid memory of the astonished expressions on the faces of the workmen about to bulldoze Leightham House to a pile of rubble, when she arrived at the worksite threatening to call the police and her lawyer, if they didn't pack up, leave and get off *her* land. "I am the owner of this estate. I am Lady Sofiya Leightham and Leightham House is mine," she had railed at the hapless demolition crew.

"It's Saturday! Dae ye think we're here by choice?!" one of the workmen shouted above the chorus of abuse from the others. The workmen took off their hard hats and made their way towards the bulldozer. The driver in the crane's cabin lowered and folded in its tower, swinging it over and above the cabin, got out then made his way to the main road. A voice from among the demolition crew shouted at Sofiya: "It wus nae skin aff his ef...en nose tae leave." A second voice shouted: "Thank you, missus. The Leightham Arms is aboot tae open. We're awa fur a pint!"

A further selection of choice words assaulted Sofiya's ears. "Yer aff yer bluidy heid, wumman, taen' on this pile o' rubble. Best o' luck tae ye!" But one comment stuck in Sofiya's memory.

"Ma dey wrocht hard on this estate monie years ago. Maybe they auld ruins should be preserved fur posterity, gien a new lease o' life. Her ladyship is tryin tae protect oor culture, oor past history, no destroy it!" Then the young man approached Sofiya and said, "If ye decide tae rebuild gie me a shout. A'd gie ma richt airm tae work on the hoose or the groonds, Lady Leightham. And ma dey auld Wullie Gibson worked on the estate afore the roof wus taen aff, he telt me a story and left me a letter aboot the hoose, afore he deed, ye micht be interested in."

"Ach, awa wi' ye, Billy Gibson. Ye'v been readin' ower monie history books and it's gaun tae yer heid. Are ye comin' wi us or no?" The men turned and made their way along the main drive to the village, regardless of whether 'Billie' was going with them or not.

But the site manager was not going to give up that easily. With the clipboard under his armpit he drew a sheet of papers from his pocket and waved them in front of Sofiya. "Am no finished wi' ye yet. Ma boss is awa fur the weekend, but here's the demolition order frae the cooncil offices. A'll tak yer word fur it, but the crews awa and that means a've nae wey o' securing the site. I'll be back first thing Monday morning wi ma boss tae check yer story *and* see that barbed wire haes been replaced roond the hoose *and* there are chains and padlocks on baith the entrance gates, along wi public notices on them sayin' DANGER KEEP OOT!!

"Jest gie me a minute. A'm gaun tae write a note that a've warned ye o' the danger and that the cooncil will *no* be responsible if onybody is been injured ower the weekend. It's *you* that'll be blamed… *no* me!"

Shaken a little after her confrontation with the site manager, Sofiya got into her car and looking back at Leightham House she drove off. It might have been her imagination playing tricks on her, but a gaping hole in one wall resembled a smile. Perhaps the house sensed relief at its stay of execution, and unlike the last time she stood near the house the building hadn't dropped a chunk of granite at her side.

Arriving back home the house was quiet and almost in darkness, but her dad was waiting for her in the hall as she opened the front door. Calm, patient as always, he offered Sofiya none of the usual platitudes. Taking her tote bag, he told her to go and have a seat in the living room, the kettle was boiled and he would make a cup of tea. There was no sign of her mother who was probably in bed having taken a fistful of Valium. For the first time in her life she felt like telling her father to forget the tea and pour her a double whisky! As he left the room he called back to

Sofiya, that he would be taking six-months leave of absence from his work to accompany her to every meeting and would be there to give whatever support she needed.

"Dad, where's Samson?" Sofiya asked as Jim returned with the tea.

"Where do you think the local predator is? The moment I opened the front door when your mother and I got back he shot out between my legs. He's out hunting for mice. He brought six home last week, remember? ... mistake! That's him at the back door howling to get in. I swear he can hear your voice from miles away. I'll go let him in. You! Drink your tea."

* * *

Six months later, Sofiya lay in bed in the bedroom that had been hers since childhood, staring at the ceiling. *Had it all really happened? Was there never to be any respite?* Every day she had had to shake herself, force herself to get out of bed and face another round of pressing problems and endless meetings and discussions with her lawyers, bankers and Leightham Town Council. She had lost count of the number of times she had to sign documents and forms. Were they legal and what surname should she use...her adoptive parents' or her newly acquired title?

There was one problem after another because of her false birth certificate. Sceptical councillors who were doing their damnedest to prove she wasn't who she said she was, argued with her lawyers until at last they agreed she was the legal owner of Leightham House and estate. It went through her mind the councillors had finally agreed in order to save the council the cost of demolishing the building. As for the financial side of things... she could never have done without the services of Mr Townsend, a chartered accountant she had employed to deal with the financial details of her grandmother's investments and bank accounts. It seemed like months since she had time to focus on herself and another growing problem she had been ignoring.

Sofiya's dad was her saviour. If it hadn't been for his patience, understanding, love and support, she would never have survived. "What will happen, dad, if sometime in the future I find someone I want to marry?" she asked him. "I don't want to stay a spinster all my life... and what about the children I might have?"

Sofiya remembered the grin that spread over her dad's face as he replied, "I think we will face that sometime in the future when the situation arises, which I have no doubt it will. Meanwhile...a day at a time. What's more important is your health and peace of mind. Tomorrow, we are going to start making appointments and you are going as a private patient to a consultant haematologist. I believe the best centre for genetic research is the Hammersmith in London. They have been researching blood diseases since 1934. It's more than likely you have no genetic defects, or they would have shown up by now. Doctor or no doctor, you need to be reassured, so no argument... we are going. As for your state of mind... no one can decide what to do about that and you should know better than anyone that you have to make that decision for yourself."

Captain Fairgrieve had become captain of Sofiya's ship before it sank altogether.

Chapter 2

FROM THE DAY of the gut-wrenching news that her birth mother and father were her grandmother Alice Jane Gardner's son and daughter and half-brother and sister, her family had closed ranks around her. Ina and Jim confirmed their absolute support and stated emphatically she was their daughter whatever happened. Granny and her cousin Margo in particular, kept trying to shield her from the reality of the situation. But if her aunt Jessie had asked one more time, "How are you, ma lass?" Sofiya would have screamed, "How do you think I am?" Aunt Nan kept telling her to pull herself together. Sofiya cringed at the thought of the reply she had given her aunt. "You tell *me* how to pull myself together! How would you feel with the news I have been given? I don't know who I am." After Christmas and the New Year, which had been disasters, their visits became few and far between.

At times she felt as if her mother was suffocating her, being over-protective assuring Sofiya all would be well, tiptoeing around her as if she was walking on a tightrope, buying her useless gifts and cooking endless meals that Sofiya couldn't eat, she felt so sick. "I'm not ill!" she had shouted at Ina, wishing she had swallowed her words at the sight of her mother's crestfallen face, but that seemed like months ago.

Sofiya became aware of an eerie silence and wondered where everyone was and where was her cat? The animal had hardly left her side and had been her constant companion, sleeping with his head on the pillow beside her for the last six months. Samson had sensed her every mood, purring loudly, pawing gently at her face when she tossed and turned in bed unable to sleep, before curling up at her shoulder. Her mother never complained about Sam now. It still seemed like yesterday the day her world came crashing down around her. And where was dad? For months he had come up to her room every morning, quietly tapping on the bedroom door and entering with the statutory cup of tea in his hand. The silence abruptly ended with the kitchen door opening and slamming against the kitchen wall. Sofiya then heard her parents arguing, their voices increasing in volume.

"No, Jim!! No, you can't do this. She's still not well. I won't let you! I'm coming upstairs with you," her mother shouted.

"Stay where you are, Ina! Get your coat on. We are going out once I've dealt with her." Sofiya sat bolt upright in bed as a sharp rap on the door announced her dad entering her room. Sofiya noticed a strange look on his face, one she had never seen before and there was no cup of tea in his hand.

"Get up!!" he shouted at Sofiya, "Get up and make your own cup of tea!" as he went to the window and threw open the curtains. "You have *one* hour to get dressed, pack your case and get out of this house!" Jim was red in the face. She had never seen her dad in such a temper.

"Dad?!"

"Jim, please!" her mother's voice echoed up the stair.

"Be quiet, Ina! Are you going to move or will I put you out in your nightdress?" he threatened.

"Put me out?! Where's Samson?" Sofiya threw back the bedclothes.

"Oh, is that all you're interested in... a blasted cat? He's at the front door packed in his carry-basket and ready to go with you, along with the rest of your stuff. Now for the last time, pack the last of your things and don't forget to take your passport with you."

"Why, dad? What's changed, what did I do?" Sofiya asked close to tears.

"That's just it, what have you done? *Nothing!!* I'm sick of it. I'm sick and tired looking at your pathetic face. We are all fed-up pussyfooting around you 'your Ladyship'. Your mother and the rest of the family have had enough walking on eggshells. They are at their wits' end with what to do with you... you spoilt brat. Christmas without a single thought for anyone but yourself. And what about New Year? That's a joke! What's new about it? Nothing... just more of the same self-pitying you!"

"Please, dad!"

"Shut up... and don't call me dad, not until you come back vaguely resembling the strong, confident daughter I once knew."

Sofiya was flabbergasted. She had never heard her dad use abusive language before.

"Get out and deal with whatever the hell is bothering you! You're not short of a bob or two. Get to India. There they have ashrams or meditation places of some kind. Away and chant a mantra... whatever they call it. I hear the Beatles have gone to India to visit a 'guru' named Maharishi. If he helps them, maybe he will help you. Get back to America, get an appointment with... what do they call them?... 'shrinks' *if* you have more faith in them there than the psychiatrists here. Take a month, take two...You're not ill. Your blood tests are normal. It's your blasted brain that's sick. You're accepting defeat without even trying to tackle whatever it is that's bothering you."

"Where will I go, what will I do with Samson?" Sofiya asked, hoping her father would change his mind.

"I phoned Cathie earlier. She's expecting both of you."

Sofiya could not believe her ears. Cathie was in on it too.

"You think you are so clever, don't you? Well prove it. Your car keys are in the ignition waiting for you and that damn Neiman Marcus box that's been staring us in the face for the last six months is on the back seat. Bloody well deal with it or I'll take it to the back garden and set fire to it... I am sick of the sight of that box. Get up. I want you out of here before your mother and I get back. I am not a religious man, but to quote the Bible, 'Physician, heal thyself'. Well, you're a physician…get on with it and heal yourself." Her father left the room and moments later Sofiya heard the front door slamming.

And then there was silence except for a distant pathetic meowing and the sound of Samson clawing at the sides of his wicker pet-carrier trying to get out, in protest at being trapped against his will. Sofiya realized that was how she felt, trapped by circumstances against her will. The verbal slap in the face her father had just given her was exactly what she needed to break out of the cage she had built round herself. It was time to deal with the situation, return to the land of the living, to no longer dwell in the land of the past.

* * *

Sophie's jaw dropped when she read what her mother had written. "Oh my God, I don't believe it!" she gasped out loud. Although she had been very young when her granddad had died, she vividly remembered him as a kind, gentle, loving man, the man from her childhood who hid Easter eggs in the garden for her to find and took her on excursions on the ferry boats… he had thrown her mother out and using such language and in such a manner! Totally out of character. And granny shouting, frantic, almost hysterical trying to stop him… For the first time Sophie thought it was no wonder her granny needed Valium to calm her down. But there had to have been a good reason for her grandfather's behaviour."

Opening the jotter Sophie wrote in capital letters:

QUESTION 1. Why did granddad throw my mum out and in such an awful way when she was so vulnerable and in such a dreadful state of mind?

Although Sophie realized she was unlikely to get an explanation any time soon, this question would definitely be top of her list to ask her mother. Getting up from the chair Sophie went to the fridge to top up her wine glass and settling back down continued to read the next chapter.

Chapter 3

SOFIYA opened the front door with her keys and let herself in.

"You're back, what a relief! I've been worried sick. I'll never forgive your father for what he did." Ina reached out and held her daughter tight. Sofiya tried to free herself from her mother's suffocating grasp by gently pushing her away.

"Mum…mum! Dad was absolutely right to do what he did. It was the incentive I needed to go and sort myself out and stop wallowing in self-pity." Tears began to fill Sofiya's eyes.

Jim had hung back from the two most important women in his life, before moving towards Sofiya to untangle his daughter from her mother's bearlike grip.

"Welcome home, Sofiya. Well, you're not quite like your old self yet, but pretty darn close and a thousand times better than the last time I saw you. Welcome home, ma pet."

Sofiya put her arms round his neck before bursting into tears as he held her in his arms.

"There, there, you have a good cry. Considering what you have been through, who could blame you? Ina, away and put the kettle on, make us all a cup of tea. Dry your eyes, it's over now… new beginnings, eh?"

Reaching for a handkerchief in her pocket Sofiya dried her eyes and blowing her nose looked at her dad. "Dad, you have no idea how many times I have longed to hear those words 'make a cup of tea'. Oh, it's so good to be home, but in some ways it will never be over."

"You didn't need to leave!" a voice from the kitchen rang out.

"Ina!!" Jim shook his head. "Auch, you don't know what you're talking about," he called back with a knowing look on his face.

"I have something to tell you both, about a decision I have come to."

"Hold on, here's your mother with the tea. Sit down, drink some first and then tell us both what you have been up to and how you reached whatever decisions you've decided to make."

"Mum...dad, I did go back to America. I had to, or I would have spent the rest of my life wondering what my future would have been like in the States, irrespective of whether I married Johnny Geiger or not." Sofiya paused for a moment thinking of her last encounter with him and how badly he had treated her. "That chapter of my life is over, closed for good and never to be discussed or reopened. Mum?" She looked straight at her mother.

Both her parents nodded in agreement.

"This time I returned to America a fully qualified doctor, an M.D. and I was offered a job. With my professional qualifications and experience there would be no obstacle to my getting my Green Card and applying for citizenship. I had kept in touch with my two American colleagues whom I met during my student years. They were about to open the first overnight artificial kidney haemodialysis unit in Texas. When I explained what had happened and that I didn't want to return to Texas, they immediately contacted their colleagues who, in 1964, had opened an overnight dialysis centre in Seattle, Washington State, not to be confused with Washington DC the capital. I took a flight to Seattle from New York and I was treated like an honoured guest. Under the present circumstances it was very tempting to accept their offer of a job but I declined it."

Jim sat quietly drinking his tea waiting to hear what Sofiya would say next.

"I turned the job offer down. Listen to me. I am *not* going to America to work and I have come to the decision I am not going backwards in life; I am going forwards and I am leaving a career in medicine altogether."

Ina almost choked on her tea, "No!"

"That's right, mum. I feel I can do more for our community with the financial resources my grandmother left me, than writing prescriptions for antibiotics and sick lines. Our NHS is the envy of the world, but at times it is completely abused by the patients. If they lived in America they would know all about it; expensive private insurance does not cover every illness and can run out before the patient has recovered. And you have to pay the pharmacist for every medicine the doctor prescribes."

Ina's jaw dropped at the thought of how much her Valium prescriptions would cost.

"If you have a medical condition of interest to the NIH doctors and are willing to be admitted to specialist wards for research, sign the permission form and be part of a research study, then everything is free and they do have excellent research programs. Where I worked in my student year, the ambulance services were owned by the funeral parlours and I was told they collect the dead bodies at the site of road traffic accidents first before they take the injured to hospital, as they make more money from the funerals. I don't see things changing, until perhaps a President some day in the future has compassion for America's citizens who can't afford health care.

"I flew back to New York. What an amazing city and there is so much to see. But it was while I was sitting in Central Park that I came to the conclusion that America was not for me though wonderful for holidays, sightseeing and entertainment. A lump came to my throat when I had to admit I was homesick. I felt without my family there to support me, I would be dependent on acquaintances, friends and my ability to earn a lot of money. I remembered as a student in Texas I applied for a credit card from Neiman Marcus. I wanted to buy some designer clothes I couldn't afford otherwise and was turned down because I had no debt! I had to be in debt before I could get credit!" Sofiya stopped before continuing.

"An American friend once told me that after three weeks' unemployment in America you would be bankrupt and there is no safety net. And I think what finally made my mind up, was that in that 'great democracy', I don't know how long I would be able to live with the level of racial prejudice that exists there. The African Americans fought a hard, peaceful battle in the face of vicious opposition for the right to vote recently, but I think it will take many decades if ever to resolve these issues. Africans were taken to America in chains as slaves against their will, unlike the Europeans and other Nationalities who on the whole chose to emigrate. But the original inhabitants, Native Americans, Cherokee, Navaho, Sioux et cetera, misnamed as 'Indians', they too encounter prejudice. No, it is not for me."

Sofiya looked towards her dad momentarily, looking for confirmation she had convinced her mother. Very discreetly Jim nodded assent. Putting her cup down on the coffee table, steeling herself for the next bit of news Sofiya had to tell her parents, she continued.

"I am not going to come back to live with you both. Not only do we need a break from each other... let's face it, it's about time I stood on my own two feet. Most of my friends have already left home and have bought their own flats or houses. I don't need to do either, thanks to the fortune my grandmother left me."

"But where are you going to live... in that derelict ruin?! Or are you going to rent a caravan? Oh! By the way, where is the fur coated predator? Is he in your car?

I've had the chairs recovered recently ready for him to start clawing at them again… aye, that'll be right! Not!"

Sofiya laughed much to the delight of her father.

"No, mum, your chairs are safe. Samson is not coming back. He's still with Cathie and Irene. Samson and Cathie have fallen in love with each other and he's now sharpening his claws on an old chair Cathie put in the kitchen for him. I've missed him. So that's my news. I am going to stay with Cathie and Irene in Mount View until I decide what I am going to do in future."

Sofiya expected a chorus from her parents begging her to stay, but instead her mother, unable to contain herself any longer, burst out: "You'll never guess what's happened. Irene is not that long back from London. You've been in America so you won't have heard the news."

"For heaven's sake, Ina, she's only just back in the door. Give the lassie a break, let her get over her jet-lag before you begin filling her head with the local gossip."

"Well since she's determined to move to Mount View… and it's not gossip, she should be aware she won't get much sleep with a bairn howling half the night."

"What are you talking about, mum? Irene is back from London?"

"Well, Irene's daughter Anne… you remember, you were at school together… she trained as a nurse in Edinburgh. It appears she did her fourth year in the eye pavilion as a staff nurse. Anne has a special interest and experience in ophthalmology, whatever that means. Anyway… she got a job in Moorefield eye hospital in London a couple of years ago and now she's got a job offer from a teaching hospital in Australia, all expenses paid to teach… something about eyes." Ina frowned

"Get on with it Ina. We don't have to listen to the full story."

91

"Give me a minute, Jimmy! I think Anne was waiting for the work permit to arrive... Well anyway, while Irene's daughter was waiting for this to happen, she had an affair with a mature student who was studying in London and he left to go back home when his visa ran out, not realizing she was having his bairn. As far as I can make out from Cathie, the wee soul has some medical problems and Anne had to decide whether to emigrate or stay here, because she couldn't take the infant with her. Anne had no one to look after the wee lassie, either in London or in Australia. She had to decide whether to give up her job in London or the offer from Australia. Either way the lassie was torn because of the bairn's problems... don't ask me what's wrong with the infant..." Ina paused for a moment to let that information sink in.

"Well Irene was having none of that, her daughter having to give up work altogether and Cathie agreed with her. Irene went down to London and brought the wee soul back to live with her and Cathie."

Ina dropped her voice as if not to be overheard.

"I've heard the wee one hasn't been christened yet. Maybe they will ask you to be godmother."

"Enough, Ina! You're making half of this up," Jim snapped at his wife, shaking his head and raising his eyes up to the heavens. "Sofiya, you go, stay with Cathie, Irene, the bairn and Samson. You are still a doctor with some paediatric experience. I am sure they will welcome your advice when it is needed."

"Thank-you, dad, I will. You have no idea how lovely it is to be home among the people I love the most in the world. Dad, I have been thinking about rebuilding Leightham House. I have more than enough money to do it and I get the feeling my grandmother would approve. I am sure she would have rebuilt it herself but couldn't because no one knew Leightham House belonged to her. Rebuilding it would have given it away that she was Lady

Leightham. Anyway, that's beside the point. If and when you are both ready you might consider moving in with me. I'll make sure there's a whole suite of rooms just for you two, so you can squabble in peace. The rooms will be fully equipped for you when you are in your wheelchairs!"

"Good grief! I keep forgetting how wealthy you are, Sofiya. One thing is for sure, it hasn't gone to your head and that's a kind offer to have us live with you but we are not in our dotage yet. Your mother has got her choir practice and we have our bowling. We couldn't leave our friends and I couldn't leave my work. Leightham is too far for me to drive to the dockyard in the winter months. But, Sofiya, I want to be involved with the rebuilding. In fact I know a brilliant builder, Allan Dickson and he will have contacts with architects, plumbers and electricians et cetera. When you are ready to start I'll give him a shout and put you in touch with him. You might find him a bit odd but you won't be disappointed. Now away to Cathie's. Does she know you are coming?"

"Yes, dad, she knows. Oh, by the way dad, I want to do some travelling in the near future, so I will leave you in charge of the rebuilding of Leightham House."

"Away and get over your jetlag. I believe it takes a few days to get back to not wanting to eat your dinner in the middle of the night. And leave the rebuild in my hands I'll look forward to that." Jim was delighted thinking of the excuse and the peace and quiet and the legitimate reason to get away from Ina's nagging voice.

Sofiya picked up her tote bag and made her way to the front door with her parents following behind her. "I'll see you at the weekend. I might even go bowling with you." The three of them laughed and held each other close. Yes, it was good to return and get back to some form of normality and hopefully new beginnings.

* * *

Sophie realized her mum had to go back to America to face her demons and lay to rest the ghosts that might have haunted her for the rest of her life. She had to come to terms with the past and what might have been her future in America but Sophie felt something was missing. Sophie wrote in the jotter:

Question 2. Did my mother meet with Johnny Geiger while she was in America? And if she did, what was the outcome from that meeting; she didn't even mention him in the last chapter? There has to be more to it mum, but obviously you are not ready to tell me yet.

Sophie sat back in the chair and reflected on what she had just read and was full of admiration for her mother, for her resilience in the face of such adversity.

Sophie hearing the sound of a car in the drive, quickly wrote in the jotter:

Question 3. Why had her grandmother not told her mother the truth about her parents before she died. And what happened to her grandmother's body?

Question 4. Did mum become the baby's godmother??

The peace of the day was well and truly shattered. "Oh Lord, the gang's back!" Sophie uttered as the front door burst open and a chorus of young voices assaulted her ears. She had been concentrating so much on the manuscript and reading it over line by line a couple of times to make sure she had understood every word and had been so deeply engrossed she had not noticed the time.

"Dad collected all of us and we got McDonald's for supper... chicken nuggets and chips for us and a hamburger for you with *NO CHEESE*!!" All four voices joined in.

Before replacing the manuscript in the desk drawer and locking it, Sophie quickly glanced at the first pages of the next chapters and realized her mother had out of context, jumped to the rebuilding of Leightham House? *Now that will be interesting to read.* Then she caught sight of the opening lines of another chapter. Her mother stated she had used her imagination to write the chapter about Alasdair Forman. Obviously her mother had been upset about the dreadful accident that led to the death of Janet and not realising she was possibly one of her mother's forebears when her grandmother told her that story. Perhaps her mother felt using her imagination to write a happier even fictitious ending for the poor man, was a way of saying how sorry she felt for him, because she couldn't find a trace of the man after WW1.

Sophie locked the drawer, made her way to the kitchen and joined her family, laughing with them about the fact that she didn't like cheese on her hamburger. It was Sunday night, the night before school on Monday and Sophie wondered when she would get the chance to continue reading and what she had just read and the glimpse at further chapters left her well and truly hooked.

PART THREE

Chapter 1

Rebuilding Leightham House

"S OFIYA, PLEASE keep in mind when you read the following chapters that are based on events from my own life between the1960s and the 1980s and some are very personal, but I wanted to tell you everything, including events that happened long before I was born. I looked back on the day I read Lord John Leightham's letter, dated 1912 to Miss Tarvet and I was struck by how many people's lives had been dramatically changed by a single moment, or in modern technology… a pixel on the screen of their lives.

"*If* – my great-grandmother, Elizabeth Leightham, had not gambled away the family fortune…

"*If* – my grandfather had not left on that fateful journey to America to try to save Leightham House, my father James would not have been adopted.

"*If* – my grandmother had not fled to Russia in fear, my mother Ana would not have been born.

"*If* – my mother, Ana, had not met and married my father, her half-brother, James, during Ceylon WW2…

"*If, if, if,* the list goes on and on.

"I had to get answers. First of all, I decided to find out what happened to Alasdair Forman. Did he travel to Spain? Was he involved in WW1? And who was Janet? I knew from visits to my grandmother that Janet probably Russian, but how had she found her way to Scotland in the 1890s and at such a young age? I was determined to find out and believe me that journey to do research regarding Russian Royalty during the Cold War years, before Perestroika, Glasnost and the Berlin Wall coming down was scary. I had moments when I thought I was being followed by the KGB... but money talks in any currency! And I had the unexpected joy of meeting a Russian relative and finding out the answer to the mystery of what had happened to probably my great-aunts, princesses Lera and Shusha.

"I had read the letters from my mother to my grandmother from the then Ceylon and realized there was no point in travelling there, Sophie. I have included information regarding my parents' marriage in Ceylon, gleaning the details from their marriage licence and copies of church records in the then Naval Dockyard in Columbo which were sent back to my grandmother. The transition to independence in 1949 was peaceful for what is now Sri Lanka, so why did they leave? I also remembered my grandmother telling me in one of her stories that James Paxton, my father, had tea and coffee estates in Kenya. Therefore, it was obvious I had to go to Kenya to find out if my parents had moved there and if possible, why they had sent me back to Scotland at such a young age. Maybe they were still alive when I went there in the early 1970s.

"The transition to independence in Sri Lanka was peaceful, but it was anything but peaceful in Kenya. The British forces had nothing to be proud of considering what they did to the Kenyan people. And, there was also what the Kenyan tribes did to each other. I did find the answers during my visit thanks to a wonderful Asian family who invited me to their home and gave me all the support I needed, but you can read about that visit later. Strangely enough, that visit gave me some measure of closure *and* the answer to another puzzling question.

"I have also included memories of my marriage to your dad and how we felt about each other. My opening chapters begin with the rebuilding of Leightham House. I have written the following chapters in the form of a novel, just as my 'great-aunt Jane' demanded I write hers. I only hope that someday in the future, my descendants will read my history and the history of our forebears. I have added explanations at the beginning and end of each episode, to keep you up to date, Sophie. I begin with the restoration of Leightham House."

*　*　*

Sofiya had no idea until the reading of her grandmother's will that she would inherit Cards House in Edinburgh, Mount View in Pittendreal, and a vast fortune in Russian gold roubles, artefacts and paintings from Russia, Europe and beyond. There was also the mind-blowing revelation that great-aunt Jane was Alice Jane Gardner, her grandmother. Sofiya had been told that Alice Gardner had married a Russian prince and that's where all her inherited wealth had come from. But the biggest shock of all was that she had inherited Leightham House, the estate and the title of Lady Leightham.

Looking back on her childhood, Sofiya had been intrigued, almost hypnotised by the derelict mansion on the hill and no one in her family could give her an explanation as to why the roof had been removed in 1912. Prompted by her mother she had asked 'great-aunt Jane', as she might be the only person who knew the answer. Sofiya had met with the old lady by herself many times over the past two years and the crotchety old woman told her the history of Leightham House and its inhabitants. She had been unable to embrace the old lady before she died and tell her she loved her and that there was no need to forgive her, the last words her grandmother had mouthed to her as she left Mount View. Nor was there a grave to place flowers on. Had the woman simply disappeared? It was all very mysterious!

But today almost a year later, the present situation in Mount View was getting Sofiya down. Cathie and Irene's over-protective care of her and Irene's granddaughter, Harriet, was beginning to get on her nerves and the local townsfolk had started to ask why she was still living with them. It was time, time to move on and decide what to do next, as she had given up practicing medicine. The answer was staring her in the face, or rather staring at her on the hill every time she drove past it. She would rebuild Leightham House and she, the new Lady Sofiya Leightham, would live there. Money was no object and she also needed somewhere to put all her fine objects, furnishings and paintings that were in storage.

Sofiya got out of her car at the back entrance of Leightham House and with a great deal of difficulty managed to unlock the padlock, remove the heavy chain and drag open the old, metal gate with more than half a century of rust on it. She wondered if the builder her father had recommended would have the knowledge to research and locate the necessary building materials to reconstruct such an ancient building in the present day.

"Good grief," Sofiya muttered, "I should have worn boots and hired a Land Rover. Just look at the state of the road...more like a farm track! I hadn't realized how much it had deteriorated from the last time I drove along it."

Leaving the gate open for the builder, Sofiya got back in her car and managed to negotiate her way along mud-filled ruts, potholes and ditches and with the windscreen wipers working overtime clearing mud off the windscreen and branches of the overgrown bushes hitting the car, she finally made it.

"I'll wait for the builder outside the courtyard. Sofiya, you are talking to yourself, old girl! Well as granny used to say, 'You couldn't talk to a wiser friend'. Mm, I'm not sure how wise this is though."

Sofiya walked from the once magnificent, high-arched, back entrance to the quadrangle of the derelict house. One of the original, heavy wooden, metal-studded gates was still there hanging off its hinges, the other missing. She was reminded of the first time she visited the ruin, standing among the weeds in the courtyard, when suddenly a deafening sound made her jump out of her skin!

"That sounds like the builder now. What did dad say his name was? ... Alan Dixon, master builder. What a racket! What on earth is the man driving?!!" Sofiya wanted to cover her ears as an old truck of unknown make or year, broke through the overgrowth and parked next to her mud-splattered BMW.

A man in his late fifties, five-foot six in his stocking soles, scrambled out of the ancient truck his rear end first! As he reached back into the passenger seat to retrieve something, the unbelted trousers were dragged down almost exposing the cleft in his buttocks! Turning to face Sofiya, he introduced himself as he hitched his trousers up with his elbows.

"Alan Dixon, at your service, Mrs, but a'bodie cries me Dixie." Considering the man's hands were full of papers, it was not a surprise to Sofiya that he did not offer her his hand but instead tipped his forehead with it, which temporarily worried her in case his trousers fell down altogether!

Somewhere in the back of her mind Sofiya remembered her father saying that Mr Dixon always wore a deerstalker hat and was quite a character. That was an understatement!

"Mr Dixon, I am Lady Leightham. I am not married and do you realize one of the sections of your deerstalker is hanging over your ear?! What happened to it?"

"Aye, a ken, it's that bliddy dug o' mine, Boots, he chaws awthin. He took ma deerstalker aff the hall stand and chowed the button aff last week and a hidna hid the time tae look fur it and sew it back on. Tae be honest, am nae sure if he swalled the button. He chaws awthin' includin' a brand-new pair o'ma boots."

Dixie wasn't looking at Sofiya while he gave this oration; he was looking up at the sky as if asking for divine intervention.

"Your dog is named Boots, Mr Dixon…Dixie?"

"Well, it's like this, Mrs Leightham. He's a pure bred Italian spinone and he cam wi pedigree papers. His pedigree name is *Iron Duke*. Well, we awe ken frae history, who he wis… the Duke o' Wellington. Then a' got anither spinone, tae keep him company, yea ken…try tae stop him eatin' awthing' including a new pair o' ma wellington boots. Her pedigree name… Lady Wilhelmina. She becam Welly and him Boots! They're big lumps o' guid nature but need a lot o' exercise tae keep them frae getting' intae trouble."

Struggling to keep a straight face, Sofiya told Dixie, "I like dogs, Mr Dixie. Where are they?" Sofiya almost jumped out of her skin, as Dixie let out an ear-splitting roar.

"Dinna you dare!! Get back in that truck!"

Sofiya looked down and nearly burst out laughing. Two large, woolly, curly-haired dogs that looked like two-sweet faced old men, had silently jumped out of the back of the truck and Boots was about to lift his leg against hers, when Dixie shouted! Boots, as if shrugging his shoulders nonchalantly at his master, meandered casually over to Sofiya's BMW and lifted his leg against the front tyre instead. Ignoring his master's orders Boots sat down on his rump and proceeded to scratch his stomach with his back paw as if it was infested with fleas. Finally, licking his private parts and yawning, he collapsed on the ground, grunted and proceeded to fall asleep. Welly, on the other hand, was twisting, rolling on her back before disappearing into the undergrowth.

Chapter 2

"**M**R DIXON…Dixie…!"

But before she could utter another word, Dixie announced, "Here Mrs, tac a look at they architect's plans fur a braw new modern hoose wi every amenity. Awe we hiv tae dae is bulldoze the auld hoose and tac awa the rubble then build you a brand new modern hoose aroond the auld quadrangle. We'll pit a fountain in the middle, install under-floor heating and awe the bedrooms wi 'en-suite' bathrooms, a shower room next tae the master bedroom, the hail flair wi non-slip marble, kind o' Spanish like and windaes fur the lounge and master bedroom the hail length o' the wall tae tac in the view…" Dixie waxed lyrical, indicating they should move to her car bonnet so he could spread the plans out.

Sofiya put her hand up. "Mr…Dixie, I've heard enough. I have changed my mind." Sofiya was thinking her father had made a bad mistake. She would have to dismiss the man and find someone else. This was not what she wanted at all.

Dixie butted in to her thoughts.

"A' kent it, I kent it frae the very start. A telt yer faither, Jimmy, we better get the young architect that a ken, tae draw up ither plans, jist in case. He his a special interest in auld historical hooses. Here he comes noo, Mrs."

Sofiya went forward to meet the young man as he ducked his head coming out of his old mini minor, a relic from his student days, and offered him her hand. Out of the corner of her eye, she saw Dixie chasing the dogs back into the truck and heard him shouting for her to hear,

"A'll need tae tell the fermer, tae git rid o' they coos oot o' they fields!! Welly's been rowen in a coo pat. She's stinking!"

A tall, handsome, intelligent-looking young man, with a number of scrolls under his armpit, walked towards Sofiya and shook her hand. "Your Ladyship, I am Nathaniel Irvine and I am delighted to be working for you." Her father had been right; Dixie and Nathaniel were the right men for the job.

Maybe a wee bit envious of the attention the architect was receiving, Dixie butted in to temporarily halt further discussion with the young man.

"Noo, this is oor team o' builders. Billy Gibson, he's a jiner, but he's a liking for gardening, a'd hing on tae him efter the reconstruction's finished if a wis you. Oh! A jist minded his dey, Wullie Gibson, worked on the estate till the roof was taen aff in 1912.

"Jim Wilson, a qualified electrician, he'll bide on the job till he leaves tae jine the police force. He wants tae be a detective. His family cam back frae Africa years ago. A think his dad wis a train driver oot there. Aye, and a' the essential painters, decorators, plumbers and plasterers. Oh, a nearly forgot, Harry Fairgrieve, interior designer. He his a special interest in restorin the interiors of 18th century mansions."

Am I about to get a complete family history of all these workers? Sofiya turned her attention to the young architect and held up her hand to stop Dixie talking. She wanted to hear what the young man had to say.

"Lady Leightham, I believe you want Leightham House restored to its former glory? I have done research in the Mitchel library, your ladyship, and I am of the opinion, Leightham House was designed by the same architect who designed Shawfield Mansion in Glasgow. It was built by and for Daniel Campbell and probably with some input by one of the Adam brothers' circa 1750's palladium style.

Without a doubt Robert Adam installed the fireplaces in Leightham House. We can replace them for you. My friend who is a surveyor and I could see from the open roof to the basement, as very few of the floors have survived. I know companies that reproduce Rennie Macintosh windows, wrought-iron gates, fences and the like.

"Your ladyship, it is the interior that needs the most reconstruction. Here are the original floor plans of Shawfield Mansion, which we need, because I failed to find any photographs pre-1912 for inside Leightham House. Shawfield Mansion no longer exists, but I am convinced if we continue with the original lay-out of the three Shawfield floors, hall and staircase, you will not be disappointed. Leightham House can be rebuilt because the remaining granite walls are sound...no evidence of crumbling. Someone 'capped' the original outer walls, maybe in the hope the house would be restored some day. The foundations are solid... no evidence of subsidence according to the surveyor. If you are happy with that, we will construct the main house first, so you can move in and we can complete the out-buildings at the back of the quadrangle after that. Both the walled gardens will be up and running in no time once their walls have been repaired and minor repairs to the watchtower can also be done later. Oh, by the way, everyone calls me Nate."

Sofiya was stunned. These two men were professionals in their individual fields of design and construction and she had no doubt they would know where to access the necessary materials, whether original, reproduction or new.

"Mr Dixon...Dixie...Nate, I am about to leave on an extended visit to Spain. I am not sure how long I will be away, but if you have any problems or queries get in touch with my dad. He will deal with everything. We have made arrangements with the bank to deal with the financial side.

Give my dad the estimates, costs and the bills and he will arrange payment and you will give him the receipts.

"And Nate," Sofiya turned to the young man, "this will give you time to draw up plans for the old stables to be converted to a café and, isn't it about time someone thought about easy-access, a ramp or something, for people who have mobility needs?" Sofiya thought of the struggle Cathie and Irene were having at times lifting Harriet's pram upstairs, never mind when she was older and would need a wheelchair. "There's no rush, but the old garages are to be turned into self-contained flats and put stores and garages on either side of the quadrangle gate." Nate grinned and tipping his forehead with a finger, he proceeded to roll up the scrolls he had spread over the bonnet of his mini minor.

As Sofiya left she heard Dixie shouting after her: "Aye, nae problem, hen! A'll meet wi Jimmy in the Leightham Arms fur a pint and we can discuss onythin' that needs tae be sorted oot. But what aboot a nursery Mrs Leightham?"

Cheek! Sofiya did not respond to Dixie obviously teasing her, but made a mental note to get her own back at a later date. She began to laugh; she had enjoyed the last hour of hilarious entertainment with 'Dixie' and his dogs, learning the history of ancient buildings with Nate and the banter about a nursery.

Driving off Sofiya felt as if the weight of the last six months had been lifted from her shoulders with the prospect of a happier future living in the house of her dreams. She was suddenly propelled forwards as her forehead nearly hit the top of the steering wheel.

"Lord! I should have demanded Dixie do something about this road first! I'll ask dad to tell him to do it before I get back."

Driving along the back entrance to the house it was hard not to look back. Sofiya suddenly shivered, the hair standing up on her arms. She couldn't get it out of her mind, the picture of her heavily pregnant grandmother, Alice Gardner, fleeing along this very road, perhaps with the deafening sounds of Leightham House being demolished ringing in her ears? She was no longer laughing. Sofiya knew how her grandmother must have felt when the rug was pulled from under her feet, thinking back to how as Johnny Geiger had pulled the rug from under hers.

Stop it!! Be grateful you live in modern times and you are not repeating the life of your grandmother. But it was hard not to remember women like the Phimister sisters who put their lives on hold to save her grandmother from the disgrace and humiliation of giving birth to what her parents and the community saw as an illegitimate child. And Janet, a registered midwife, who took Alice Gardner in, a very ill young woman and did not report the situation to the maternity services against her better judgement, risking her livelihood and possibly a jail sentence if Alice had died in her care. She would never forget as long as she lived, the understanding and support Cathie, Irene, Susan Martin and her father had given her in her hour of need after Johnny Geiger left her.

Enough, Sofiya. Leave the past where it belongs… in the past. Time to plan your future. Spain first I think, to find a trace of Alasdair Forman after he left Scotland. Then home to inspect how the renovations are progressing and regardless of the danger, I must visit Russia. I must try to find how Janet, a very young girl, fled from Russia and was found on the doorstep of auld Tam's cottage and met and nearly married Alasdair. Who was she? And if she'd not saved Alice Gardner's life none of this would be happening. I owe her a deep debt of gratitude.

When I return from my journey to find my birth parents, if they are still alive, I want them to know our family home has been rebuilt and I want them to return, someday. I know I was born in Ceylon, now Sri Lanka, so why did my parents leave for Kenya and why did they send me back to Scotland? Kenya would be a good place to start. That's more than enough to be getting on with, old girl. Sofiya brought her mind back to the present day.

"When did Cathie say the Rugby season would be starting? I might get in touch with Neil Martin to see if he would still like to go to a match at Murrayfield when I get back from Spain. You are talking to yourself again, Sofiya!"

* * *

"Sophie, here it is, chapter and verse and the evidence from the research I did in Spain, beginning with what happened to Alasdair Forman after he left the psychiatric hospital in Edinburgh1913."

PART FOUR

Chapter 1

Spain and WW1

S OFIYA planned to drive overland to Spain by way of France and insisted on travelling alone. She wanted to lie on a sun-soaked beach by herself and come to terms with the shock and emotional blows life had seen to assault her with in the last year. Spain had become the number one destination for British holidaymakers looking for inexpensive holidays and guaranteed sunshine… sea… and sangria! Ibiza was a popular choice but Sofiya had no desire to visit a tourist destination, or take a three-hour flight to a crowded hotel. She had driven on the right side of the road in America, so driving on the Continent held no fears for her. She would hire a car and take her time driving to the various destinations relevant to her search for answers to her questions.

Taking a flight to London, then the ferry from Dover to Calais, she hired a car and visited the Somme. Sofiya failed to find evidence of the death of Alasdair Forman on the war memorials of WW1 at the Somme, as she had failed to find evidence of his death in the documents in the Military Archives at home. It became clear he might not have died in WW1. The War Memorial in Pittendreal had both Tom McDougall and Brian McKay on them, but Alasdair Forman's name was not there. It was as though Alasdair Forman had simply disappeared.

Sofiya took her time driving through the villages of France booking into small village hotels on her way south. Arriving just south of Monte Carlo, and remembering her grandmother's stories regarding her great-aunt Elizabeth

Leightham and her grandfather Robert, her enquiries soon paid off. In one of the Cathedrals of the Côte d'Azur a pleasant young priest took an interest in her request for information and agreed to meet her the next day at the Café de la Place. He assured Sofiya the archives, stored for hundreds of years, would contain a record of all burials, the names of every person and the burial site of a particular person buried in the graveyard. If she could give him an approximate date of the death, it would make it easier.

A bowl of delicious French onion soup, French bread, tarte au citron and a quiet night's sleep in the village hotel did her the world of good. The priest met Sofiya as arranged at the café, with a big grin on his face. The look on the priest's face reminded her of the triumphant look on the face of Anne in the local County Buildings, when Anne produced the church records from the 17th century, having found the dates of Sofiya's Scottish forebears' deaths and burial sites in Scotland.

"I think I have found what you are looking for, madame," he announced, hardly able to contain his excitement. "Look, here in this book of burials 1850 to1920! After that the cemetery was closed." The young priest shrugged his shoulders up to his ears, put out his hands, made a face, pursing his lips and raising his eyebrows, with a wide smile announced, *"Oui! Oui! Elle est ici!"*

Sofiya's schoolgirl French was rusty but she understood every word and was pleased when the young priest accompanied her to the cathedral's cemetery, to make sure she found the correct grave site. There was no doubt it was the grave of her great-grandmother Lady Elizabeth Leightham, undisturbed for years. The cause of death had been given as a heart attack, but Sofiya did not enlighten the priest that Elizabeth Leightham's death was by suicide. The date in the cathedral register – April 1912

– confirmed it was Elizabeth, a disturbed, troubled, relatively young woman living at a time when there was little help for drug addiction and mental illness.

Sofiya remembered the story being told by her grandmother, Alice Jane Gardner; her grandfather Robert Leightham arriving in Monte Carlo to deal with his mother's death before he boarded the ill-fated *Titanic*. Sofiya had bought flowers at the local street market to take with her and after the priest offered a prayer to the deceased at the gravesite, she laid them on Elizabeth's grave. Would she ever return? No, she felt that part of her family history, should…'rest in peace'.

Sofiya drove on along the coast of Spain. She knew from old postcards and letters that Alasdair had been in Spain before WW1. Now it was time to find out what happened to him.

Chapter 2

AFTER WHAT SEEMED like months of ferry and train journeys and thumbing lifts from French and Spanish vehicles Alasdair felt he had arrived, had gone as far as he wanted to go. With every step, after leaving Scotland with his troubled soul and depressed state of mind, he finally seemed to be at peace with himself. In time he might even forgive himself, but he would never forget. The farther away he travelled, the more accepting he was that Janet's death was a tragic accident. Strange though it might seem, on the journey, he could hear Janet's voice inside his head pleading with him to forgive himself, as she had forgiven him.

It was an accident, Alasdair. No one is to blame. Go forward and live your life. We will be together some day through all eternity, that is a certainty... I promise you. From the bottom of my heart, I forgive you; it's time to forgive yourself. Mercifully the farther he went, the voice began to fade and he could hardly remember how Janet's voice sounded.

Sweating in the glorious sunshine, walking along the Spanish coast line Alasdair found himself on a sandy beach with sparkling waves gently moving to and fro as they washed the shore. Dumping his knapsack on the sand, Alasdair looked around to make sure the beach was deserted. It was mid-afternoon and he knew the local Spanish people living in the village close to the beach would be enjoying their traditional afternoon siesta. Sitting down he kicked off his hiking boots, took off his socks, trousers, gaiters and thick khaki shirt. Barefoot, he stood in his long-johns and semmit. He looked out over the deep blue Mediterranean towards the coast of North Africa. Closing his eyes momentarily and taking in several deep breaths, he felt his mood change from morbid self-condemnation to one of hope.

Running over the hot sand Alasdair threw himself into the next wave and dived under the water, only the sound of the waves above him. He luxuriated in being beneath the water and not having to think. Drifting for a short time, he felt he was being washed clean. He surfaced for air then swam out as far as he could. Realizing he could swim no further he halted, treaded water, gasping, breathless from the exercise and looked towards Gibraltar which was not that far away. Alasdair decided he would definitely visit the Rock of Gibraltar, one of the Pillars of Hercules at the entrance to the Mediterranean and take a trip up the Rock to look at the incredible views and maybe see the Barbary macaques, the only uncaged troop of monkeys in Europe. The sun was beginning to sink towards the West. A cool breeze fanned the waves, his head and shoulders. It was time to swim back and find somewhere to eat and sleep for the night.

Recovering from his exertions, he swam at a leisurely pace back to the beach. It was when he stood up he realized his long-johns and semmit weren't exactly the best swimsuit as the garments were now twisted under his armpits and hanging low down on his hips. His hair might have gone grey overnight from shock, but he was still a handsome young man. His body, now strong and muscular, had benefited from his long walks as he hiked his way across the Continent, carrying the heavy knapsack on his back. He was a far cry from the pale-faced, thin man who looked like he had aged overnight when he left the psychiatric hospital in Edinburgh.

Standing up and dripping wet, Alasdair walked out of the foaming waves swirling round his knees toward the sand, shaking the water out of his eyes and hair. He was startled by the sound of a woman's laughter that was growing louder by the minute. He had forgotten to check if anyone had arrived on the beach. But what was she laughing at...him?

When his vision cleared, in front of him stood a young woman next to the pile of clothes he had dropped on the sand. He had to blink twice wondering if he was seeing things. He was struck by her sparkling dark brown eyes that were so full of life. Her long, black hair was swirling around her shoulders in the breeze and she was wearing an outfit that vaguely resembled a gypsy's, including a high comb on the back of her head and lace veil. Was his mind playing tricks on him? For a few heart-lifting seconds, he thought it was Janet. *Don't be ridiculous, Alasdair. Get dressed. Maybe this young woman knows the local area and could help you find accommodation and food.* He walked over to his clothes and bent down to pick up his shirt. The woman was still giggling and covered her mouth with her suntanned hands.

"Oh my God!!" he exclaimed when he saw the waves had burst open the lower buttons of his long-johns and his private parts, thankfully limp from the cold water, were hanging outside the opening for all the world to see!

Quickly Alasdair turned back towards the sea and began to shove his male organs inside his long-Johns. Thinking he was unlikely ever to see her again he paused... *What am I doing...so what?! It's too late now, old boy. You're going to have to pick up your clothes anyway or get dressed in your soaking wet underwear!* He decided to brazen it out. Calmly turning round to face the young woman he removed his soaking wet underwear and he was now stark naked! Lifting his trousers, he shoved his wet, sand-covered feet into them as best he could, which was no mean feat as he tried to keep the sand out of his trousers. Suitably attired in his thick tweed trousers that were itching his damp skin and with his shirt stuck to him, he looked straight at the young woman, who now seemed to have recovered from her fit of the giggles and to Alasdair's surprise she did not look the least bit embarrassed.

"My name is Míriam. How did you get here?" The young woman spoke perfect English.

Alasdair decided the best way to deal with the situation was to pretend none of the last few minutes had happened. Having overcome his embarrassment, he lifted his knapsack and slung it over his shoulders; he took hold of the laces of his hiking boots, tied them together in a knot and casually draped them round the back of his neck to avoid the sand filling his boots. Taking his time, he looked directly at her as he answered, "That's a good question, Míriam. How did I get here?"

Chapter 3

"**W**HEN THEY DISCHARGE him from that dreadful place he will come home and live with me. That would be the best thing for him. Eh won't heve him going back to that awful place and em all alone since Angus died," Audrey lamented with her exaggerated Morningside accent.

"Yes, a great loss, Audrey. But widowhood suits you and that dreadful place saved Alasdair's life. I'm sure we have been through this before when Alasdair first decided to leave and to work in the field of medicine he wanted to work in and not become some posh consultant or professor. You ignored my advice then. You are a control freak, Audrey. You railed against him taking the job which, I have to remind you, was recommended by his godfather, Harry Henderson. He broke free from your control. So, hell mend you, Audrey. He will never return home now! One more 'woe is me' look on your face and you are on your own. I have had enough of your self-pity. So unless you cheer up I will leave you here right in the middle of Princes Street."

"Oh, Marjory, I have lost my precious son, my baby, forever…" sobbed Audrey. "Will he ever get out of that awful hospital and return home to me? They only let me in once to visit Alasdair when he was admitted all those months ago and from then they refused to let me in. How could those doctors be so cruel…do that to a mother? Eh can't believe it," Audrey stuttered, while dabbing at her dry, tearless eyes with an equally dry handkerchief to produce the heartbroken effect of a distraught mother for all to see.

She never seems to forget to bring a handkerchief with her these days, Marjory thought. "Give it a rest, Audrey.

People are looking at us and it was your son who banned you, not the doctors. It's nearly six months since Alasdair's unfortunate, tragic accident," Marjory hissed at her. "You lost your son, but Alasdair lost the love of his life, the young woman he wanted to spend the rest of his life with and he feels he was responsible for her death. But was he totally responsible? Why did he feel the need to leave with Janet so early in the morning, as if he had something to hide? We will continue this conversation later, but for the moment, if you don't stop your pathetic wailing… I am going home!"

Audrey sniffed. "But you don't understand. You have never had…"

"Children? No, as you so kindly remind me on a regular basis. Now are we going to Miss Margaret's Tearoom for afternoon tea or not? Make up your mind before I change mine. Yes? Then maybe you could put a bit of a smile on your face and put that blasted stage-prop handkerchief back in your handbag. For God's sake, that's not helping you or your son. You're fooling no one, Audrey, and maybe just maybe, Monsieur Gregory will come out of hiding and serve us. That might just make it seem life has returned to some form of normality."

Climbing the stairs to the tearoom, Audrey stuffed the offending handkerchief into her handbag.

Ever since the news of the dreadful accident Mrs Forman's son had been involved in, Monsieur Gregory had almost taken to the hills when he saw the ladies arriving for afternoon tea. He had genuinely felt sorry for one of his best customers. But after the first few weeks of lending a sympathetic ear, he realized Mrs Forman was thriving on it and enjoyed the attention of the other customers by telling anyone who would listen, the story over and over again. Even Mrs Bateman tried to check her friend by snapping at her to stop it, but it didn't have any effect. Gregory thought Mrs Forman was something of a drama queen and would have triumphed as an actress on the London stage.

Chapter 4

HARRY HENDERSON, who had witnessed tragedy in war and in his profession, would never forget the scene in front of him till the day he died. He had driven like a lunatic along the coast road after young Brian McKay phoned him with the news of the tragic accident. Peeping the car horn with the flat of his hand several times, Harry managed to clear sufficient space from the villagers gathered on the pavement to park his car behind the police mortuary van and Wright's hearse. Elbowing his way through the crowd, he reached the drive of Alasdair's house and saw the model T Ford parked as far down the drive as it would go. The sight of Alasdair, rocking back and forwards with the lifeless body of a young woman in his arms was heart-breaking.

There seemed to be blood everywhere: Alasdair's face was covered with dried blood and the front of his shirt was soaked with it. Alasdair kept putting the dead woman's hand on his face and shouting, "No! No!" every time it fell back on the ground. The memory would haunt Harry for the rest of his life.

"Thank goodness you have arrived, Harry." Brian spoke softly, crouching on the ground beside his mother. Looking up at Harry very alarmed and worried he shook his head. *"He won't let her go."* He mouthed the words slowly so Harry could lip-read and understand what he was trying to say.

Harry would not normally choose to kneel down on his rheumatic old knees, but today he did not notice the discomfort as he knelt down beside Alasdair, the young man who was more like the son he never had than his protégé, who was holding the lifeless body of a young woman close to his chest. Horrified, Harry recognized the young woman was Janet, the local district nurse. Tom McDougall seemed to have just performed some sort of marriage ceremony, as the stalwart matrons of the village arrived. Harry could see a wedding ring on the third finger of Janet's left hand.

"Come on noo, ma bonnie lawdie... let her go," Rena coaxed Alasdair. Harry had tried and failed to persuade Alasdair to give him Janet's body.

Looking straight at the distraught man, Rena felt it was time to exert all her motherly concerns. "Gan awa wi doctur Henderson, Alasdair. You've hid an awfy fricht. Yer white as a sheet. It macs richt guid sense. Awa an get a cup o' tea an dinna worry, we'll tak richt guid care o' Junet an aw thin' else."

Before relinquishing Janet's body Alasdair looked up at Patrick Wright the undertaker and insisted that under no circumstances was the wedding ring to be removed from Janet's finger. "Oh my God, Janet... forgive me, forgive me," was Alasdair's last pitiful cry as he released Janet to the care of Rena.

Harry had to get Alasdair out of there as it seemed there was a row beginning to brew regarding *who* was going to deal with the body and make the funeral arrangements. There was also a heated discussion between Rena and Doddie Spence, who was insisting the body should be taken to Leightham police mortuary pending a sudden death enquiry! Rena instructed Doddie to look at Janet's left hand and told him there were no suspicious circumstances... just a terrible accident and any enquiries would almost certainly render doctor Forman suicidal.

Harry struggled to get Alasdair into the car and away as quickly as possible in case Alasdair overheard Rena's last remark and decided to act on her depressing thought.

Out of the corner of his eye, Harry saw Fimmy Phimister slipping her arm through Tom McDougall's. She encouraged him to leave the now more or less empty driveway. Tom was visibly shaken. He couldn't believe what had happened and he was grateful to Fimmy. *How cruel life could be. Two lives wrecked: one dead and one on the way to the psychiatric hospital without a doubt,* he thought.

"He was, is, my best friend, Miss Phimister. I have known him since we both moved to Pittendreal virtually at the same time. He is godfather to my daughter, Helen. I knew he was in love with Janet. He had been unwell and quite literally Janet had saved his life all these years ago. He confessed he was in love with Janet, but felt he could not subject her to the humiliation of being judged by the snobbery of his social peers in Edinburgh."

Fimmy nodded her head, encouraging Tom to keep talking.

"My wife and I arranged to adopt Janet and organized a birth certificate for her so she could apply to do a course in Edinburgh and gain her nursing qualification; it would be against the law for an unqualified practitioner to practise any form of nursing the sick. I think something had come between Alasdair and Janet although he never told me what.

"But why were they leaving for Gretna? Why didn't he tell me he wanted a private wedding? I could have arranged a wedding for him and Janet with the contacts I still have in Edinburgh! What was he afraid of or hiding? And here's a strange thing. A few months ago, after the roof was removed from Leightham House, Alice Gardner went missing! Do you know anything about her or her whereabouts?"

"I don't know, Mr McDougall." Fimmy's innocent expression would have fooled no one. "You have lost your friend for the moment, but the village has lost both its doctor and their district nurse in one go. I don't envy you the task, but it will mercifully occupy your mind for a bit; go home and write a eulogy befitting a wonderful, mysterious young woman. Now I have to go and collect some things to prepare Janet's body for the wake."

Chapter 5

I T WAS OBVIOUS by the time Harry arrived home Alasdair no longer wanted to live. During the whole journey Alasdair kept begging Harry to stop by his surgery and leave him there with the drug cupboard keys so the world would think there had been a break-in and he would disappear never to be heard of again. He didn't want to live without Janet. *God in heaven,* Harry thought, doing his best to calm the man. Settling Alasdair in one of the bedrooms, Harry went straight to the hall cupboard for his old medicine bag to get the medication he wanted. He would lock the bag in the garage when he had finished with it.

Harry decided the best thing to do was to knock Alasdair out with an injection of morphine. However, before succumbing to the drug, Alasdair managed to concentrate long enough between trying to focus on Harry and his head hitting off his chest, to plead with Harry who managed to understand the passionate, slurred speech from the distraught man.

"Harry, phone Brian... tell him to go to my bedroom. In the bottom of the wardrobe there is a box. It belonged to Janet. Among the clothing there are important documents. They must be taken to Edinburgh University language...for translation. I made a sort of will. It's in the box... two letters...in case anythin'...happen'...Take to Andy Coull, the bank manager at the Bank of Scotland with Janet's gypsy clothes... I'm not delirious. My lawyer in Edinburgh, the name is on...envel..." At that Alasdair's head hit his chest.

Harry phoned Brian and arranged to meet him on the High Road to Pittendreal at the now locked back-gate entrance to Leightham House. Harry knew he could leave

Alasdair, now semi-unconscious, for several hours without him waking up.

Brian felt guilty using Alasdair's car but there was no option; to go to the stable and hitch up Alasdair's old horse and buggy would take time. In any case the car would have to be moved as soon as possible to clear the drive at Alasdair's house to allow Janet's coffin to be carried to the hearse. As promised, Brian was waiting and handed over the box to Harry. Harry sought Brian's professional advice on what was the best course of action regarding treatment for Alasdair, considering the state of mind the man was in.

Without hesitation Brian promptly replied, "Oh, my God, Harry! He must *not* be left alone for one second longer than is necessary. I will follow you back to your house, and phone my old professor of psychiatry at the Royal from there and have Alasdair admitted this afternoon. Let's go. I don't have my medical bag with me and I doubt Alasdair will agree to swallow any oral barbiturates. In his state of mind he probably feels he should suffer. Dear God, what an undeserved punishment to have to live with the rest of your life. He will never forgive himself, one of the dearest, kindest men on the planet."

Harry wondered if he should tell Brian his thoughts on why Alasdair had made such a baffling decision to leave the village with Janet, but decided against apportioning blame to Alasdair's family. After all, at the end of the day, what did it matter now? Harry decided to try and cheer Brian up and make him smile a little.

"Ach! Dinna you worry, son. I still had my old bag with all my needles and drugs. You don't have to give him anything. I filled his backside with morphine before I left. I doubt he will wake up before he's in his hospital bed!"

Chapter 6

A LASDAIR was now on a reduced dose of the barbiturate medication he had been dependent on and the psychiatrists were pleased with his progress. But what about his future? Marjory breathed in deeply and was taking comfort from the thought that after a long hard, depressing winter, spring was finally on its way. Walking up the garden path to the front door in the early spring gloom, she noticed in the garden either side of the path, the snowdrops were withering back into their bulbs for next year and would soon be followed by the bright yellow daffodils. At times over the last few months she had wished life was just that simple. Deep in thought she wondered if this situation would ever come to an end. Marjory searched in her handbag for her door keys.

While Alasdair was still in the psychiatric ward, Marjory had visited her godson on a regular basis but he had spoken only to thank her for visiting and quietly asked her to return. Last time she visited she saw he had been moved to a single room. *At least he's made some progress,* Marjory thought. The general wards were depressing enough without having to stay in them indefinitely, with a nurse watching every move and the added humiliation of being accompanied to the toilet and bathing.

Still fumbling for her keys, Marjory suddenly became aware of a figure crouched on her doorstep. A man was sitting on the cold stone with his head on his knees.

"What do you want? I'll go to my neighbour and call the police!" Marjory shouted, as the man stood up. Marjory was shocked. He was almost unrecognizable outside the hospital with his white hair and skeletal frame.

"Jesus! Alasdair, you almost gave me a heart attack!! What on earth...? How did you get here? Did they discharge you?"

"No, aunt Marjory, I signed myself out. The doctors did try to stop me, initially, but then they decided that I wasn't a danger to the public. Huh, a danger to the public! And they agreed I might do better facing the future and coming to terms with what happened by myself. I made them promise not to tell my mother if she turns up at the hospital... I can't face her yet. And please don't tell her I am here."

"Come in, son. I will make you a cup of tea and sort out a bedroom for you. You are perfectly safe and it's not that difficult to keep your mother away."

A month later Marjory had to admit, Alasdair had made very little progress. He wasn't getting up till after lunch time and returned to bed before the news was broadcast on the radio in the evening. Besides, it was becoming more and more difficult to put Audrey off. This couldn't go on much longer. It was time to give it to him from the shoulder and she knew the very person to do it.

When Marjory returned having told Alasdair she was going out shopping, she found him in the family room staring out the window. Rising up he made to go back to bed. "Stop! Alasdair, you are no better now than you were six months ago, or when you signed yourself out of the psychiatric hospital last month."

"Lunatic asylum, you mean," Alasdair answered in a flat lifeless voice.

"Don't say that, but you can't sit here day after day staring at the walls and I don't know how much longer I can put your mother off. I am running out of excuses and she is becoming suspicious, Alasdair.

"Your mother has been genuinely worried about you and we both realize now the reason for deciding to marry in secret. It was partly because of our snobbery. Your mother and I learned a little bit about Janet at the meeting in Pittendreal, when the mysterious bequests were read out. Janet was a very decent human being. Kind and caring, she never apportioned blame to anyone and certainly would not want you to blame yourself for what happened."

"Aunt Marjory... don't speak her name,"

"It's about time somebody did!" a sharp voice from the sitting room called out. "It's about bloody time. People are tip-toeing around you, terrified to open their mouths or tell you like it is! But I am not. It was an accident! Now off you go, young man, and top yourself. Janet would want you to, to take her revenge and put all the good folk who care for you here and cared about you in Pittendreal out of their misery. Maybe they would arrange a funeral for you, despite never being thanked for organizing the burial of that young woman. You are so consumed with self-pity you haven't even bothered to go and see her grave for yourself and put flowers on it... you said you loved her?!"

Alasdair's jaw dropped open as he entered the sitting room to find it was his old professor of surgery, Sir David Scott who knew him so well from his time at university. Alasdair's shoulders dropped with relief and he unashamedly burst into tears. The man was right.

"Oh, aunt Marjory." Marjory nodded her grateful thanks to the professor as she took Alasdair in her arms and comforted him, whispering in his ear, "New beginnings, new beginnings, son."

Sir David spoke up. "Healing will not begin till you, however painful, acknowledge the past face on. I suggest, no I am telling you, go back to the scene of the tragedy and make your peace. You will never forget, but forgiving yourself will begin the closure, Alasdair."

"Wise words, Sir David, and I will take your advice and return to the village where I know I will be welcomed and perhaps with their support I will visit the cemetery."

Alasdair turned to Marjory. "Have you got a backpack up the loft? Pittendreal will be my first stop on my journey to recovery." Marjory smiled and nodded as she turned to the professor to express her gratitude.

* * *

Managing to put a pitiful smile on her face, Audrey nodded to Fred the waiter, who came forward to take the ladies' coats as they arrived. He was experienced enough to know how to put on an act, to say the right things because he knew the ladies' tips were always generous. Fred took their coats and asked them to wait at the door of the tearoom till he returned from the cloakroom to escort them to their favourite table, as Monsieur Gregory was busy in his office. Audrey on his return as always went ahead. Marjory held back and managed to whisper in Fred's ear, "For God's sake, Fred, dig Monsieur Gregory out of hiding. I don't blame him, but assure him Mrs Forman is improving. But have a glass of whisky ready as she might have a relapse when I give her my news!"

Audrey waited till he left before demanding to know why she might need an alcoholic drink, having overheard what Marjory said to Fred.

"Alasdair has been living with me, Audrey," Marjory confessed.

"What?!" Audrey blasted forth. "And you never told me... his mother!" she shouted. Throwing her napkin on the table, Audrey stood up and made to grab her bag as if to run to the door.

"No, sit down! You are making a fool of yourself."

Monsieur Gregory told her if she screamed like that again he would bar her from the tearoom for good! She was disturbing the other customers.

130

"We are going to your house right now, Marjory Bateman. I want my son, my boy," she hissed. *Here we go again.* Marjory shook her head.

"Alasdair is out of the hospital? How or why? Last time I tried to visit Alasdair the doctors said he wasn't ready to be discharged as he was still ill. Do you have psychiatrists doing house visits? No, that's it. I'm off. Monsieur Gregory, call me a taxi cab!"

"Audrey, wait. He's not with me now. He left the hospital a month ago and still was making little progress. About a week ago and with harsh, firm, truthful words from his old professor, Sir David Scott, we made the decision and quite rightly to encourage him to leave. He first of all went to Pittendreal, to face his demons and he has now left for Europe. I know where he is. He's quite safe, much improved and sorry, Audrey, I can't risk him having a relapse. He will return home when he is ready…"

But Marjory was thinking, *Not only were his mother and I inadvertently involved in the incident, but what if what Harry Henderson told me in confidence is true? I have lost my godson, but Audrey has lost her son and possibly a grandchild. Alasdair must have known this…* Marjory doubted they would ever see him again.

Chapter 7

ALASDAIR boarded the train at Waverley Station for Fife and left Edinburgh behind. He wondered if he would ever return home as the train crossed the Forth railway bridge, an incredible construction, a man-made, steel-plated wonder. As the train pulled into Pittendreal Station and he alighted, he remembered the first day he arrived; seemed like a long time ago now. Full of hope, enthusiasm and anticipation of a new future working among the fisherfolks, he also remembered the first time he met Janet at the delivery of Aggie Gardner's baby. Alasdair's handsome face was void of expression. He did not want to be reminded of the worst day in his life. Would he ever be free of the memory of holding Janet in his arms for the last time? But to reach his destination he would have to pass the scene of the tragedy.

Alasdair was well aware that until memory of Janet was laid to rest, he would never recover. Swallowing hard, fighting back tears, he walked towards his old house and surgery. But to his absolute amazement the building had been bulldozed, flattened, eradicated. In its place were the beginnings of what looked like a lawn and garden. The sight of several benches and a small play park for children with swings and a seesaw comforted Alasdair. After all Janet had delivered half of the young population in the village and it was a fitting memorial. Alasdair began to feel it was possible, as he had hoped it would be, to take a journey of remembrance and closure. He could begin to celebrate her life, live again and take some solace from the memory and in future be able to look back at their time together in Pittendreal.

Alasdair slipped unseen into the village and stayed at the manse with the McDougalls. The day before he left, very early in the morning in semi-darkness, accompanied by Tom he went to the cemetery. The visit would live in his memory forever, but he had to say goodbye to his beloved Janet and make his peace with her and himself. Alasdair placed a large wreath of red roses at the foot of the gleaming white marble plinth, on which a life-sized white marble statue of an angel had been newly erected in Janet's memory. The simple words *For a Dead Princess* were engraved on the plinth. Tom and Alasdair stood together in silence. Then Tom recited the Lord's Prayer. After the two men said Amen, Tom turned to face Alasdair and said, "Alasdair, I want to quote a passage from the Old Testament, a few lines from the Book of Ecclesiastes that I find very comforting at times like these."

To everything there is a season and a time to every purpose under heaven:
A time to be born, a time to die; a time to plant, and a time to pluck up that which is planted;
A time to kill, a time to heal; a time to break down and a time to build up;
A time to weep, and a time to laugh; a time to mourn and a time to dance;

Tom then continued to the most important line, in his opinion, for Alasdair:
A time to love, and a time to hate; a time of war and a time of peace.

Alasdair took comfort from these words and he felt the hellish burden he had been carrying lifting. There was no doubt Tom knew his job. "Thank you, Tom."

"Alasdair, you cannot know how I felt when I got the phone call from your aunt Marjory to say you had signed yourself out of the hospital and she had found you on her doorstep. I felt helpless, not unlike the way I felt preaching the sermon at Janet's funeral when I gave the shortest eulogy of my whole life. Alasdair, I was gutted, could hardly speak. Ministers of the church are expected to comfort others, not feel they need to be comforted themselves. But tomorrow will be different. I will preach a fine sermon and I know our little congregation will be overjoyed to hear about your visit and the beginning of your recovery. Instead of asking the congregation to pray for you, I will ask them to celebrate your return to life. Are you sure you won't stay?"

"Thank you, Tom, but no. I want to get on my way and I am not ready yet to meet all those wonderful patients of mine. I'm not ready to face them or their sympathy. Please give them my kindest regards. Young Brian has taken my place. Just as owners are as good as the last biscuit they give their dog, so we doctors are only good until the new doctor comes along!" Tom and Alasdair burst out laughing at the thought. "But in this village full of good fisherfolks that's not true and I must go before I start to miss them."

"Right, let's go. The sun is almost up and Isabel will have cooked the breakfast. I have tomorrow's sermon to write this afternoon, but how about a game of chess this evening? It will be like old times, Alasdair."

"Sounds good to me, Tom."

* * *

The next day Alasdair had packed and was ready to leave early after breakfast. Isabel brought the coffee in and spoke on the subject of Janet for the first time since he arrived.

"When you arrived, Alasdair, I was worried. I could hardly recognize you. You looked like you had been to hell and back but look at you now, a different man. These few days have made a big difference to your outlook on life. And I thought you would like to know that Tom, the village ladies and I have arranged to care for Janet's grave and the white marble headstone. It's so beautiful and befitting and we will make sure fresh flowers will be placed on it till you return to look after it yourself. Now drink your coffee before it gets cold."

"Thank you, Isabel. You cannot know how comforting that is to hear, and I am very grateful."

Isabel left the coffee pot for the two men to help themselves and talk. Suddenly the door burst open and unannounced a young man burst in and helped himself to a cup of coffee.

"So... you're back, old man. Have you forgiven yourself yet? I hope so. Forgiven yourself for leaving me stuck with your old chess partner! He keeps beating me. Thank you very much, Alasdair." Doctor Brian McKay grinned before rushing over to grab Alasdair by the hand and shook it vigorously.

"Brian, how good it is to be back among you, but I have to leave you all again. I have been given some good advice from Sir David Scott. It makes right good sense, I cannot ignore it. I don't want a relapse. I am convinced next time we meet it will be under different circumstances... I hope better ones."

"Yes, it will be different, Alasdair." Brian's jovial expression had changed. "There are rumours from the Continent of serious unrest: groups of terrorists and terrorist activities, social unrest in the population. I am not sure about better circumstances."

"You're right, Brian," Tom joined in. "Here's my advice, Alasdair, for what it is worth. Physician go heal thyself. Take a break away from these shores. Make peace with yourself in the knowledge you will never forget Janet and there's nothing to forgive. Stop being such a martyr when there is so much good you could still do in the world."

Brian nodded his head in agreement with Tom, but he had also noticed the changes in Alasdair's appearance and hoped he was up to the challenges ahead.

"War is coming, Alasdair. The Germanic and Austrian socialists are unstable and Britain's royal family origins are German. There may be social unrest here, but whether the Kaiser may or may not cause a war, remains to be seen."

"That's true, so I insist wherever you go write to me once a month if possible or we will worry ourselves sick," Tom added.

"Whenever it is possible to post a letter, you will receive one," Alasdair promised.

"And if war does come, Scotland will be dragged into it whether she likes it or not. We will join up together, Alasdair. The army will need doctors to tend to the wounded, and I bet this war will be pretty savage with bloody hand-to-hand fighting. Oh, and of course a minister to tend to their souls. Naturally we couldn't do without you with us, Tom," Brian added.

The three men burst into laughter. For Tom and Brian it was music in their ears to hear Alasdair laugh. "Thank you very much, Brian. I know you two couldn't do without a Scottish Rabbie Burns, a loving, parsimonious, sanctimonious minister with you to keep you out of trouble." Again, the three men laughed.

The door of the sitting room burst open for the second time that morning and in came Rena McKay, who walked straight over to Alasdair and threw her arms around the man as if she would never let him go.

"A' kent ye were here," she whispered in his ear as Alasdair managed to free himself from the arms around his neck before she strangled him.

"Noo, you listen tae me… yer like ma ain son, a kin only guess at whit ye'v been throu, but were awe a'hint ye. Whitever ye decide tae dae, tak yer time tae cum tae yersel, but cum back tae us, Alasdair."

This was the most heartfelt speech Alasdair had ever heard. Rena stepped back and wiped the tears that were slowly running down her cheeks.

"A dinna want tae … whit dae ye call it, Brian… emotional blackmare? But Susan is far tae young, no nearly ready tae jine the practice. Doctur Henderson his come oot o' retirement tae help Brian but he's getting' on in years, yea ken. So cum back when yer ready… the village misses yea. Ye'll see some fine changes wi the new surgery since ye left and there's always a place fur ye in oor braw new hoose."

"I think that's enough, mother. Alasdair needs to leave before the whole village wakes up," Brian interrupted Rena. "And Tom needs to drive him to Leightham Station to get the train and be back in time for the church service."

"It's alright, Brian. You drive me in my car, and I need to start…"

"That's enough o' your bliddy cheek. A'll decide when a've said enough, Brian. Am still yer mither." But Rena withdrew from the conversation, as it suddenly came to her that their beautiful new house had been bequeathed to them by some mysterious benefactor who had also given many other benefits to the village. It was …it had to be Alasdair and Janet. But where did they find that kind of money?

"Alasdair, I hiv tae ask ye aboot oor hoose. Did…?" Rena shouted after him.

But Alasdair had already jumped into his car.

Chapter 8

ALASDAIR couldn't believe he had told a complete stranger, a young woman he had just met, about his past, but what a relief to get it off his chest.

"Well, now you know the whole story. I left home and just walked and walked with no real plan or the desire to communicate with anyone. I wanted to put as many miles between me and the recent past as possible, if I had any hope of recovery." He shook his head as if trying to block out his memories. "And, at this point in time, I have no desire to ever return home." *Return home... to what?* he thought.

Míriam came forward and put a comforting hand on Alasdair's arm. Looking down at her he saw her eyes were full of sympathy. This young woman, with long, dark hair and dark eyes, understood how he felt. For a moment she reminded him of someone, who at times had shown the same compassionate understanding.

Looking up at Alasdair, Míriam had wondered why a young man with no luggage except a backpack dumped on the sand, was swimming in the sea at this time of year. "You have lost the love of your life and you are blaming yourself. I know because soy una bruga!"

"A what?!"

"A witch! And you have arrived at the right time to forgive yourself and put the past behind you. This is Semana Santa, Holy week, Easter you would say in your country. In Spain we celebrate for the whole week." Míriam smiled. "What's your name, Señor?"

"Alasdair, but that's all you need to know."

"Mm…that's difficult for the local population to pronounce and I guess you want to remain… anonymous? Si… yes?" Míriam nodded to him. "Do you have a middle name?"

Alasdair hesitated to give her that information. "Que…what is your middle name?" Míriam prompted him again.

"Alexander."

"Ah bueno, from now on, you will be introduced as… Señor Alejandro. Perfecto! Welcome!"

"But that's still a first name; won't people wonder about my surname?"

"All in good time, Alejandro, all in good time. In Spain you can marry and take your wife's surname if you wish." Míriam grinned up at the man, thoroughly enjoying his discomfort. Strange he had no problem with her seeing his naked body, but the suggestion of marriage had him almost quaking in his boots.

"I will get you settled in the village, which is larger than it looks. My brother, Gonzalo, has a 'finca'…a small farm on the outskirts with a… cottage? We only use it for the odd weekend and in the summer. It will be perfecto for you. Tranquilo… peaceful. It is a little farther up the hill with vistas hermosas …beautiful views of the Mediterranean. There is a cool breeze in the evening after a hot summer's day, perfect to sit outside and enjoy San Miguel. Oh! And ice can be delivered along with paraffin for the lamps and wood for indoor and outdoor fires. The outdoor fires are lit in summer because the mosquitoes are pests and the smoke helps to deter them."

"Who or what is San Miguel?"

Míriam burst out laughing. "Cerveza! Beer, the best drink in the world next to your Scottish whisky, but much less potent, so you have to drink quite a few to get the same effect. So will that arrangement do for you, Señor Alejandro?"

"Very nicely. You have been so kind, thank you... gracias, Míriam." Alasdair smiled. "And I will pay you rent, as soon as I contact my bank in Gibraltar. They will exchange my Bank of Scotland notes for pesetas and I will open an account in the Banco de Málaga. I think I saw the bank as I passed through the town."

As the couple made their way slowly from the beach, Alasdair began to wonder if he had the right to feel this content. But life goes on; today becomes tomorrow and tomorrow the next, so no point beating himself up about something he could not change.

"You speak perfect English, Míriam. Where or how did you learn?"

"My papà travelled to many countries and realized a considerable portion of the world's population spoke English: Australia, New Zealand, the Indian sub-continent, East and South Africa and obviously most of America except down in the south east. In New Orleans and Savannah, towns in Georgia and Louisiana, the native tongue is French. It is the same in Canada, mainly English, but French in the south east of that country. They are all colonies past and present of the English and French gobierno... governments and the populations are kept in order by armed forces whose day will end; nothing lasts forever. Spain has a similar history in South America. There they speak Spanish.

"Papà sent me and my brother to the English school in 'He-ibraltar' for English lessons in our summer holidays. Now I teach the children English in the local school. Please respect my honesty Alejandro, but very few British people learn to speak another language whatever country they are living in, other than French which they are taught in schools."

Alasdair felt she was absolutely right, but he decided it was time to change the conversation. "You are right. You would think by 1913 things might have changed, especially with the news from Germany. I don't know anyone who speaks German. Perhaps it is because it is not a Latin-based language. No more politics, Míriam. Why is there so little evidence of fishing along the coast?"

"De acuerdo… agreed; no more talk of war or politics. Spanish people love fish. The main fishing fleet area is in Málaga, but nearly all the villages have fishing boats. We will walk along the beach in the evening and we can eat all the pan-fried sardines you want… no charge. But my favourite fish is dorada caught in the Mediterranean and baked in a salt crust. It might come as a surprise to you, but instead of being a fishing community, San Pedro is a farming one. The main crops are azucar…sugar, maize… wheat…algodon… cotton and pimientos, that's green peppers. We have made great progress in the primary experimentation and mechanization of agricultural equipment and used steam-driven engines as far back as 1862. Well?" Míriam couldn't wait for his answer.

Alasdair shrugged his shoulders. "All I have to say is in Scotland we are also a fish-eating country and have given many engineering contributions to the world over the centuries for such a small country. So I guess eating a lot of fish accounts for an intelligent nation!" Alasdair laughed out loud at his own joke.

"Keep eating fish, Alejandro, because you will have to put your money where your mouth is and you *will* join me in the children's classes to help them with conversional English and they will help you to speak Spanish."

"Spanish and English with a Scottish accent?"

Míriam smiled, before informing Alasdair that he could not have arrived at a better time, as in every village and town there were processions throughout the week to honour the capture, the trials, crucifixion and resurrection of Christ.

Chapter 9

"S ANTA SEMANA, a good time to reflect and pray for healing and reconciliation with the past. You have missed Palm Sunday, the commemoration of Christ's triumphant entry into Jerusalem. The women cover their heads with the falda and, holding long thin candles, fall on their knees outside the church. A man, on a donkey, rides through the village and blesses the palms waving in the air and the branches strewn on the street at his feet. The crowds vie for the palms to make crosses with them, symbols of victory, triumph, peace and eternal life. Our procession is a small one compared to the one in Málaga... that would take your breath away.

"A life-size statue of Christ, with an enormous star-pointed gold halo on his head, astride a donkey, is placed on a massive, deep catafalque or platform, covered with tall candles, crosses and flowers. Metal poles are slung through the base of the catafalque which is borne on the shoulders of at least two hundred men, dressed in white long robes and white, tall, pointed hoods. The penitents carry it through the narrow streets of the old city to the beat of drums, heralded by processions of trumpeters signifying Christ's triumphant entry to Jerusalem. It takes hours, nearly all night, with the bearers swaying and twisting as they turn through the narrow streets.

"I have heard there is an organization in the southern states of America known as the KKK, that wears something similar, but I assure you they have *nothing* to do with the Catholic faith!! I believe it was established mid-1860s to promote white supremacy and terrorize people of colour. They encourage prejudice and hate. How they can call themselves Christians, I will never know." Míriam for the first time looked angry as she spoke. She was thinking not only of the Africans who had been exported there from Africa.

"I agree, Míriam. It is the peak of man's inhumanity to man, but will it ever end? I don't think so. The wonderful procession you just described must have been the high point of Christ's earthly ministration, considering what was to follow." Alasdair made a mental note to write to Tom about it. Tom would have loved this conversation and would have joined in. Alasdair felt his own contribution was pathetic.

"Commemorations are held each day in every village and town and you should not miss the other religious traditions this week. We will travel to Málaga on Good Friday for the procession to remember the crucifixion of Christ. You will never forget the sight of the man who died on the cross, so everyone could be forgiven for their sins. That experience will help you, Alejandro."

Alasdair just nodded his consent, hoping the lecture was over, but there was no stopping Míriam.

"Time for tapas, I think, before I take you to the finca."

"Tapas?"

"Si, tapas.

It originated in Andalusia. The word tapa translates... to cover. A saucer with the tapas is placed on top of a glass of vino and it is mainly served at lunchtime, but it can be served more or less any time of day. In other centuries it was served to the workmen to keep the dust, sand and flies out of their wine or beer. Perhaps you would call them snacks. Delicious Serrano ham, chorizo, olives, cheeses and bread help counteract the adverse effects of the alcohol. History tells us it began from the time of the 13th century. King Alfonso X111, while recovering from illness could only eat small amounts of food at a time. The afternoon siesta is almost over, so let's go to Pedro's bar. He's always open."

Míriam was right. Tapas were served throughout the day in the local bars and, as she said, were delicious and very welcome, as were the glasses of Spanish vino underneath the saucer. Míriam introduced Alejandro to Pedro and Alasdair got the feeling he would probably spend a lot of time with Pedro, so the quicker he learnt to speak the language the better. Much refreshed, it was time to move on.

"Muchas gracias, Pedro…thank you?" Míriam couldn't stop smiling at Alasdair's Scottish accent.

"De nada, Señor Alejandro," Pedro replied. Alasdair nodded to the man, delighted he understood what he had said.

On the walk up the main street to the 'finca', Míriam waxed lyrical on the subject of other festivities in Spain. She explained that although Spain was a religious catholic country, there were celebrations and festivities Alasdair would enjoy, perhaps more than the religious ones.

"Nearly every town and village in Spain enjoys a week of street parties, fiestas, often to honour a saint, but it's not a religious occasion, instead it honours their lives. They are colourful, very noisy affairs and great fun. The streets, houses and patios are decorated with garlands and pots of flowers and all the women and girls are dressed as I am today. Is that why you looked twice at me on the beach? I was giving this feria dress an airing and I will take it off when I get home," Míriam explained.

"No, Míriam. For a fraction of a second I thought you were someone else."

Míriam decided it was better to ignore that comment. "There are processions of loud noisy drum beats and tambourine bands. The horses are decorated with pompom-embellished reins and the men riding the horses wear gold embroidered matador jackets and tight trousers. Women dressed like me, ride side-saddle behind the men. And wait till you see the flamenco dancing! The women are in colourful, long, tiered, frilled, feria dresses, trimmed with fringes and wearing the traditional mantilla, a headdress of black lace, held at the back with a comb… like this one." Míriam pointed to her head.

"The flamenco dancers click their metal-heeled shoes, in time with the castanets. Castanets are two wooden shell-shaped discs, held together with colourful string and fit into the palm of the hand and are clicked in very rapid rhythmic succession, together with the feet… very exciting. During the fiesta the Spanish guitar is played in every bar and eating place that serves as much food as you can eat and of course as much vino or beer as you can drink while you are still standing." Míriam stopped. Alasdair couldn't believe she wasn't out of breath… she wasn't!

"No one really knows how or when flamenco arrived in Spain, but this form of Spanish culture evolved with it, for sure. History scholars think it was brought from the Far East by the Romanies, a very insular race of people, who keep themselves to themselves. Oh, and you might like to attend a bullfight, but the bullring is quite a distance from here in Ronda."

"Pass, on that invitation, Míriam, as I have seen enough human blood to last a lifetime. I have no desire to see it in animals." Alasdair cringed at the very thought of blood-sports in any form.

"It was just a suggestion. Well… if you feel homesick or alone, every evening in the summer months, the villagers come out to sit and be cooled round the fountains and enjoy the evening air. In the centre of the village square, in front of La Iglesia de la Encarnación, is the main fountain. You will be astonished by its size. Join the villagers and listen to the melodious, peaceful, sounds of running water. Fountains are on nearly every street corner here; they are so peaceful. Look at this one in the Fuenta de la Plaza, the Cabeza de la Medusa with its tiny, colourful, mosaic tiles. Mm, perhaps not so peaceful, but…

"You could visit the Convent de la Santísima Trinidad y la Cruz de Malta. They welcome people to sit and meditate. Or take a walk along the coast and look at the Faros' lighthouses and pass the towers that used to observe shipping and approaching enemies and there are the ruins of castles to explore. What about visiting the Roman baths in the countryside on the way to 'He-ibraltar'? Or simply go hiking in the Sierra Blanca mountains behind the village. Better still, take tapas with you and climb La Concha, *The Seashell* which is over to your right. It's shaped like an oyster shell and you can climb it in a day. If these activities don't help you to make your peace with the past, nothing will, Alejandro."

Míriam was on a mission to encourage Alasdair to stay, but Alasdair was already sold. He wasn't going anywhere soon.

On that walk to the finca when Alasdair first arrived, Míriam and he smelt smoke. There was a fire at the rear of the cathedral. Alasdair sent Míriam to alert the fire brigade, and disregarding the danger, he ran into the burning building and rescued many of the villagers who were attending a service there. He attended to the burn victims before getting them to the hospital. That was how someone discovered he was a doctor. Alasdair kept his hand in by volunteering to help the local doctors working in the hospital Real de Spain, a small state and charity-funded care facility that tended to the sick, the poor, the chronic and terminally ill.

They also, with sparse funding, concentrated on providing food, clothing and hospital attention for the poorest families. The local population was grateful to have such services and Alasdair's input was welcomed, even more so once he got a grasp of the Spanish language, which at times caused the staff and the patients to laugh, as he confused 'guantes', gloves, with 'guisantes', green peas! Alasdair had arrived and was one of them.

Chapter 10

WHERE HAD THE TIME GONE? It was 1916. Alasdair looked back to three years ago, just after his arrival, in horror at his disgraceful behaviour towards the woman who in the long run, probably saved his sanity. He had taken Míriam's body to relieve his own selfish misery, in the dark days of winter, when his moods were as dark as the nights. Alasdair shook his head with embarrassment when he thought of the times that he carelessly shoved his tongue into her mouth and almost down her throat, massaging and licking parts of her body, before straddling her and relieving himself of his own sexual need without a thought for hers. He had deliberately withdrawn prematurely before there could be any long-term repercussions, his seed running down between her legs or over her stomach. He cringed at the thought, as he remembered passing out, collapsing on her body, to sleep a short, deep, post-coital, oblivious sleep, before waking up and reaching for a cigarette. Selfish... so selfish, thinking it would stop the crazy thoughts in his head.

But Míriam knew Alasdair was using her. She knew it was part of the healing process and that the anger and taking his revenge for Janet leaving him would pass. She would be waiting for him.

On a peaceful evening with the sounds of the waves, and the gulls crying out above them, almost a year after he had arrived, Míriam and Alasdair walked in silence along the golden sands. The sun was setting, the moon rising, the light scattering the sea with glittering, silver crystals. Alasdair was fighting with the guilt at his own behaviour and his shame of how he had used the most compassionate human he knew. He was spent. It was time for closure.

Míriam seemed to sense the change in Alasdair and turning in front of him stopped him going any further. Reaching up she put her arms around his neck, pulled his head close to her breasts and whispered, "I love you, Alejandro. I have loved you from the very first moment we met, perhaps at this very spot. I cannot imagine life without you now and we will put the past behind us." Alasdair collapsed to his knees, sobbing uncontrolled tears of relief, and held on to Míriam as if he would never let her go.

Míriam and Alasdair were married in La Iglesia de la Encarnación, a year after Alasdair arrived. Padre Roberto informed Alasdair he did not have to convert to the Catholic faith, *but* it would be a full Catholic marriage ceremony, including nuptial Mass. Alasdair had been warmly accepted by Míriam's family and Gonzalo, his best man, and soon to be brother-in-law, guided him to the altar as they entered the church by a side door. Leaving Alasdair, Gonzalo then escorted his mother, Maribel, the mother-of-the-bride, down the aisle to the front pew.

Míriam, carrying a bouquet of orange blossom, broke with tradition and instead of wearing black had secretly gone to Gibraltar, to have a white wedding dress and veil made for her. Ramón proudly walked his daughter down the aisle. Grinning from ear to ear, Ramón thought of a new era for his family and the many nietos to come. A traditional Spanish bodas, celebration, followed and was thoroughly enjoyed by the whole village, drinking, partying and dancing the whole night through. The next day Alasdair had a very sore head!

The couple left on honeymoon and arriving in Gibraltar, booked into the Bristol Hotel. Locating the Presbyterian Church, Alasdair registered their wish to have a blessing in St Andrews Kirk by the Scottish minister, the Rev Mr Campbell, who would be delighted to give the couple a blessing during the Sunday morning service. It would make a change from the usual Sunday morning worshippers mainly comprised of Scottish sailors, based at Gibdock, who had taken advantage of the cheap booze and were nursing their hangovers while they waited for repairs to Royal Naval ships, or the loading and unloading of the cargo of the merchant ships before setting sail.

Alasdair at first felt humble. Did he deserve the joy he felt being with his new wife? But the feelings of guilt were gradually fading and becoming a distant memory. During the day the couple climbed the Rock and admired astonishing views of Africa. Africa was so close you felt you could almost reach out and touch the Pillar of Hercules on the other side of the gateway to the Mediterranean. It was great fun to feed the Barbary macaques, although Alasdair had had to chase after one of them who had stolen Míriam's handbag! They consummated their marriage, making love in their hotel bed and in the sandy coves hidden on all sides by the Rock itself.

One autumn evening, Alasdair was sitting in the rocking chair his mother-in-law, Maribel, one of the kindest women he had ever met, had given them a year ago; a gift to welcome their son Nicolás Alejandro Gonzalo Colón, christened by Padre Roberto, the Padre who had married them. Alasdair sat rocking back and forth with his new infant daughter. But what was different this time was there had been a point of contention between Alasdair and the family regarding the baby's name. Míriam, backed by her mother, Maribel, insisted the baby would be christened Juanita, Spanish for Janet. Alasdair protested it would be too painful a memory for him. Míriam understood why he felt this way. It might be painful to begin with, she argued, but it was important to honour the woman he had loved, and Míriam wanted to remember Janet, the woman who had given her Alasdair and the gift of their children.

Normally on Alasdair's side, Ramón and Gonzalo, who was to be godfather, threw their hands up in the air and walked away from the whole business; they knew who would win. Alasdair had to give in gracefully as his wife and mother-in-law were a force to be reckoned with. In that case, Alasdair insisted his daughter would also have her grandmother's name, Maribel. Maribel laughed. "Alejandro, in the catholic faith, you can give your child as many first names as you wish!"

"In that case Padre Roberto will christen my daughter, 'Juanita Maribel Marjory'. I think Marjory means pearl of the sea and we met by the sea… remember Míriam?"

Alasdair gave Míriam a questioning look, thinking of how they fabricated an excuse to go with baby Nicolás to Gibraltar the previous year. *Another trip to Gibraltar,* he thought remembering how delighted Rev Campbell was to give baby Nicolás a blessing, in the Scottish faith. Míriam was no fool. She was delighted to accompany Alasdair; whatever made him happy made her happy. Anyway, it made sense for her to go. Who would feed baby Juanita for a whole day without her? Her mother, Maribel, would babysit Nicolás without asking any questions. Alasdair also knew that if his children were registered in the church records in Gibraltar, it was possible that at some time in the future, if they wished it, his children could claim dual citizenship.

Chapter 11

"**GOOD GRIEF**, when was this posted?!" Alasdair took the letter from Gonzalo who had collected it from the Correos in Malaga.

"I think it's been there for a while. I usually go once a month, but not recently. Much of the mail is delayed from Britain because of the war. I'll leave you to read your letter in peace."

"Muchas gracias, Gonzalo." Gonzalo grinned as he turned to leave. *Well the accent was improving.*

Alasdair went indoors, handed the baby over to her mother, poured himself a glass of vino, and sat down on the rocking chair. He could see the army post mark, July 1916. It had taken weeks to arrive and it had been sent by Tom Mc Dougall, from the Somme.

My Dear Friend,

At last I have found time to bring you up to date with the situation here, in this hellhole known as the Somme.

[Alasdair winced and shook his head at the word hellhole. Tom using language like this?!]

I was granted leave recently and went home as soon as I could, but now I am back in France. I have little good news to give you from home. Life was going on much as usual in the fishing villages, apart from the fact that many of the boats have been requisitioned as minesweepers and are now at the bottom of the 'drink'. So, there are fewer fishing boats and less fish for sale. Many of the villagers crowd the newsagents for the Fife Free Press to get the latest news of the war.

There is no easy way to give sad news, so I won't dwell on it. Isabel informed me, your aunt Marjory died suddenly from a heart attack. I know your mother was dependent on her, but it will be a comfort to know Marjory arranged for your mother to be admitted to an old people residential home before she died. I am so sorry, Alasdair, but your mother was admitted with dementia and has totally lost her memory and reason. Isabel visits her on a regular basis, but she has no idea who Isabel or anyone else is. Please don't waste your time on an unnecessary visit; your mother wouldn't know who you are either.

Two young lads from Pittendreal both named Robert, have been killed. One, an engineer, was on deck helping to lower the lifeboat after the ship had been torpedoed, when one of the Laskers panicked and let go the rope. He was knocked unconscious and fell into the sea and was drowned. He was 22 years old. His grandmother is heartbroken; she says he was a grand swimmer and stood no chance. The other, a gunner, was shot while manning a machine gun on deck. His brother, John Gardner, was the first man in the village to join up.

He writes to his family from Lebanon, informing them he is well and when he is given free time, has been walking among the cedar trees... prophetic really. The Cedars of Lebanon are mentioned in the Bible several times as symbols of strength and eternity. Hundreds and thousands of young men have certainly gone for all eternity, killed in this war. I wish I was there to walk with John Gardner, if only to experience a little peace and quiet away from the endless sounds of explosions and gunfire. Some of the soldiers have inhaled poisonous mustard gas, a new invention of the devil. I am at a loss as to what to say to them.

I am writing to you because we desperately need medical help and I have all but lost my faith in God. Initially appalled at the amount of alcohol the clergy were drinking, now I don't blame them. Now, I never know who to comfort first: the dying, the injured, the nursing and medical staff or the young men suffering from a new condition called shell-shock. It sickens me to hear these young soldiers being called cowards when they are out of their minds with fear. It must be terrifying for these young, sometimes very young men.

I am told the doctors in the field-ambulance units give anti-tetanus injections for shock and perform urgent lifesaving operations under difficult conditions. Shells explode in the trenches and the worst injuries are to the legs that are blown to shreds. At least they have now acquired a modern invention called a splint: a metal cage which supports broken and damaged bones. Machine gun fire rips open the internal organs and the slightest wound can become infected and gangrenous.

The medical tents behind the lines house the wards and in the rear, operating theatres, operating under difficult circumstances twenty-four hours a day. Staff have been giving blood transfusions before surgery. Apparently, it helps reduce wound infections and alleviates terrible gas-poisoning burns to the skin. But the wards most welcomed by the patients, are the casualty-clearing stations, to get them home as soon as possible. You have medical and surgical experience, Alasdair. Working here would be a walk in the park for you, especially with the experience of treating the burn-victims you described in your letters to me when you first arrived in San Pedro.

The army commanders tell me they are beginning to realize something is very wrong. All's fair in love and war, but not in this war. The Germans seem to have found a way to intercept wireless messages from command centres to the troops in the trenches and on their way to the battlegrounds. The German soldiers are ready for them, hiding in the forests waiting, as if they already know where and when they will be attacked. The accuracy of the Germans bombing of the trenches is unbelievable, not only killing and injuring the troops struggling to take cover, but also the men inside the bomb shelters, as the roofs collapse on top of them!! Slaughter on a grand scale.

Alasdair, do you remember the day before you left Pittendreal? I quoted from the Book of Ecclesiastes, words of comfort for you that meant something for me also. I have written my own version:

> *A time to hate; a time to kill; a time of war.*
> *A time to weep; a time to mourn.*

Will there ever be an end to it? I have saved the worst news till last. The hospital tent Brian Mc Kay was working in, took a direct hit last night and Brian was badly injured, prompting me to write to you. Whether he survives or not is in the lap of the Gods. I have lost my faith. I try to persuade myself that God is on holiday and the devil is in charge. There is only one thing that will restore my belief in religion and that is you joining us... me. I spoke with the medical commander-in- chief and he assures me you don't need to go to the War Office to enlist. Just get here, for God's sake. These are desperate times.

> *Regards, hoping I will see you soon, my dear friend,*
> *Tom*

PS Perhaps you could bring a chess set with you? Brian's set was lost in the bombing and it does take the mind off the nightmare for a short time...

I have just received the news that Brian didn't make it. Is there a medical condition that means numb? That's the way I feel right now, Alasdair – numb.

Chapter 12

"TOM, YOU OLD FOOL! What's this, a summons to appear in Hell? Thank you very much." Alasdair waved Tom's letter at him as the two comrades met and embraced each other. "Here, Tom, dry your eyes with the letter. On second thought, no. I don't want the ink running down your face as well as tears. It can't be as bad as all that."

"Oh, Alasdair, it's worse. You have no idea. It's been going on for weeks and there is no end in sight. It was supposed to be over in days. It might be years yet. I did not want to minimise the conditions here when I wrote that letter… no emotional blackmail. I wanted to make sure you would come because you wanted to and knew what you were facing. But you will never know what a relief it is to see you."

Alasdair had done exactly what Tom had suggested, and had travelled over familiar Spanish territory as he had done a few years earlier, crossed the Pyrenees and then into France. He only had to follow the endless sounds of explosions and gunfire to arrive at his destination on the Somme. The ear-splitting noise took his mind to the heart-rending sounds he had left behind when Míriam had torn Nicolás's little arms from around Alasdair's neck as he shouted, "Papà…papà," and Míriam's reassuring voice, "Come home safe and sound as soon as the war is over."

"Well, good, bad or indifferent, here I am, old man." *God, Tom's aged.* "Do you think I could refuse a request like this from my oldest friend? To be honest I had begun to feel more than a little guilty sitting safe at home in Spain. I heard many Gibraltarians had joined up. I convinced myself I had children to think about. What a pathetic excuse when so many men may never know they are to become fathers, never see their infants or children. So here I am ready to do my duty."

"Right, let's get out of here; nowhere is safe. Play dumb, keep your head down, acknowledge no one. You are not wearing a uniform. Believe it or not that offers you a measure of protection, unless you are captured that is! There are snipers everywhere and saluting tells the enemy that person is an officer! Let's get you settled." Tom paused for a moment, as they walked towards tents marked Red Cross.

"Because of the constant heavy bombardment, to get out of the trenches and face the enemy is almost suicidal. The auxiliary medical staff who are constantly under fire, face the almost impossible task of getting stretchers out of the trenches which are clogged with mud. The number of wounded is overwhelming the medical system. Mercifully, thanks to generous donations to the Red Cross, we have motor ambulances, but in terrible terrain we have to use horses. So, it's a non-stop, stitch, patch-up job for you to do, Alasdair, and the best treatment is to get the wounded home as soon as possible, that's their best chance of survival.

"I am told they have discovered how to stop blood clotting by using heparin, an anticoagulant, whatever that means, and a way to store donated blood for up to four weeks. Tincture of iodine, boric acid and olive oil are used for trench-foot, which is a terrible condition for the soldiers. Tunnels offer the best protection, but even they can collapse and completely block-up the entrance with the soldiers still inside. Now we must part. Captain Wells, Royal Army Medical Corps, will welcome you to the operating tents. Oh, I forgot about the use of sphagnum moss when supplies…"

"Stop, Tom!! That's enough. I can work it out for myself." *That* was too close to home for comfort as Alasdair remembered a young woman who probably saved his hand and arm, if not his life with her use of sphagnum moss.

Tom gave Alasdair a questioning look. Why had he snapped at him? Alasdair realized Tom would have no idea what had triggered that response. Changing the subject Alasdair asked, "Right, Tom, put me out of my misery. Is there a canteen? Do they have good old British tea? I am gasping for a cup."

Tom smiled. "Yes, old man. Let's go and I will get you the finest cup of tea you will ever drink, strong enough to put hair on your chest, boiled for hours and thick with condensed milk, served in tin mugs! Sorry, no china here. And fresh milk? You must be joking."

"Sounds good to me. Tom, you know how I feel about religion, but this is different. Three years ago, had the war begun then, I would have been one of the first to join up glad to enlist and I would not have cared if I lived or died, but I care now. I want to live and return to my family. Rekindle your belief in God, Tom. Your doubts are only temporary and say a few prayers for us both as you did when we went to see Janet's memorial in Pittendreal cemetery... that was very comforting, especially the lines from the Book of Ecclesiastes. Then I will tell you all about my lovely family and my beautiful new daughter's first name."

* * *

"Sophie, when you finish reading the above chapters, your first question will be 'What happened next?' To be honest I am not absolutely sure. Researching documents and war records is difficult at the best of times. If Alasdair did go to the Front, he probably would have been considered a volunteer, as there are no official records of him. Spain certainly was not involved in WW1 and Alasdair may have used his Spanish surname to remain anonymous. Should he survive, he could go straight back to Míriam and not be faced with the additional trauma of being sent to Pittendreal and questioned by bereaved families or pressured to return home for good. Probably in Alasdair's mind there was nothing to return home to Scotland for. I would like to think what I have written is as close to the truth as I can make it. First of all, there was no proof of his death and I wanted a happy ending for the man who would have been my great-uncle had he married Janet.

"My heart went out to him when my 'great-aunt Jane', grandmother, told me his story many years ago and years later, I found two letters, sent back from the Somme. The first, Tom McDougall's letter pleading with Alasdair to join him in France was among my grandmother's belongings. It's my guess Alasdair did join Tom and took the letter with him and it was returned to Isabel with Tom's belongings by the War Office after Tom's death at the battle of Passchendaele. Helen McDougall must have found the letter years later when she cleared out her mother's belongings and gave it to my grandmother along with an old chess set.

"Then among your great-grandmother Rena's belongings, your dad and I found the letter of condolence from Tom to her on the death of her son, Brian, your great-uncle, posted from the Somme. What a waste of young life and for what reason? These letters had quite a paper trail, but the relatives did receive them, along with letters of condolence on behalf of King George V. My doubts began to grow of ever finding evidence he was there and let's face it many were buried in unmarked graves. But there is good news: he did survive. When I returned to Spain, not so long ago, I decided to visit the cemeteries along the coast from Marbella to Gibraltar and my search paid off.

"My journey took me through the most beautiful cemeteries in the Christian world. Row upon row of white marble and stone monuments with Christian symbols, life-sized figures of angels on the tombstones, looked down where the dead were interred and the families' names were engraved on the plinths. There was unusual tier upon tier, rows of very deep, high, multi-layered walls, with the coffins interred inside them one above the other, with oblong alcoves in front filled with flowers and candles. Some of the tombs look like mausoleums, with intricate stained-glass windows that allowed the sun to shine on the coffins inside. How many Colóns could there be? But luck was on my side, just as I had almost given up.

"Before crossing the border and going through border control on a trip to Gibraltar, on impulse I parked the car on the main street in La Linea outside the cemetery there and bought a bunch of flowers, intending to put the flowers on the first gravestone I came across with the name Colón on it. A young man about your age was in the cemetery. He walked towards me and asked why I was putting flowers on *his* family burial site!! Initially I explained I had been taken aback by the stunning white marble effigy of an angel, but then I confessed I had been looking for a particular family with that surname, although it was unlikely the family I was looking for would be here so far from San Pedro.

"You won't believe me, Sophie. He looked straight at me and I knew right away he was related to Alasdair Forman. He told me his family had moved from San Pedro after WW1. He introduced himself as Alejandro Colón; I couldn't believe my ears. He told me all about his family and *he* had been named after his great-grandfather, a Scotsman, Alasdair, who returned home after the war much to the relief of his great-grandmother, Míriam. He remembered being told by his grandfather, Nicolás, Alasdair's son stories of the celebrations in San Pedro after his safe return. The young man went silent for a moment before wistfully telling me he had had a great-aunt, but she died before her third birthday.

"The loss of the three-year-old child Juanita was probably the reason the family decided to move to La Linea because it was too painful for Alejandro's great-grandfather to continue to live in the village where she had been born. Perhaps he thought he might have been able to save his daughter had he not left and gone to war. Alejandro also said that the little girl's name had a special meaning for his great-grandfather.

"His grandfather, Nicolás, also told him of his great-grandfather's need to be near the Presbyterian Church of Scotland in Gibraltar, where his and Míriam's marriage had been blessed and their children had received a blessing. His great-grandfather had been right: his descendants had the right to dual citizenship. Alejandro grinned as he told me that his great-grandparents had five more children after he returned from the war, but he didn't know why the little girl who died was named Juanita, as it was not a family name. I just replied I didn't know either.

"Before we parted the young man told me his great-grandmother, Míriam, died before his great-grandfather. His great-grandfather made the decision to have her body taken back to the *old* cemetery in San Pedro and buried in the same grave as their baby daughter. Alasdair stated at the time, he wanted to be buried with them when he died. His grandfather, Nicolás also told him, Alasdair's funeral was very moving. A Church of Scotland minister was given permission to conduct the funeral service in the catholic cemetery. A Pipe Major, in full ceremonial dress wearing the kilt, came from Gibraltar with him. They met the cortege at the entrance to the cemetery. After the minister's service, the piper played, *'Flooers o' the Forest.* His grandfather said the lament echoed round the cemetery, as the coffin was being lowered into the grave.

"The young man shook my hand and we left agreeing to meet again sometime in the future, and without further ado I made to leave. Suddenly, the young man called me back. Looking shyly at me first, he announced he had decided to let me into a family secret, a secret his grandfather told him. He first explained that there never had been any financial problems in the family, although they never knew the source of the wealth. Not long after Miriam died, so did Alasdair's beloved German shepherd dog. Sophie, the hair began to rise on my forearms!

"Grinning from ear to ear, the young man told me Alasdair had threatened the local priest in San Pedro, that if he didn't allow the dog to be buried in the family grave, he would exhume the bodies and have them reinterred in the protestant cemetery in Gibraltar. Remember, Sophie, in the catholic faith they don't believe animals have souls. The threat did the trick and the dog was buried awaiting her master. Both the church and the gravediggers were *well* compensated for their trouble.

"Shaking like a leaf I ran to the car to recover, thinking of the man and his dog; was it him I thought I saw briefly on the beach in Pittendreal, so many years ago? What I saw might not have been a real person after all. I don't believe in ghosts and spirits, but this was mind-blowing!!

"Quickly finishing my tax-free alcohol, make-up and perfume shopping in Gibraltar, I made my way back to Puerto Banus, but decided to make a detour to San Pedro. I found the old cemetery and the gravesite, easily identified by a magnificent, life-sized, white marble angel that reminded me of the one in Pittendreal on Janet's grave. Alasdair's full Scottish and Spanish names and Miriam's and Juanita's were engraved on the plinth, but no mention of the dog. I guess the priest drew a line at that. I thought it was a very fitting, final resting place for all of them, especially with the Scottish lament.

"A lament is only ever played at funerals throughout the Christian world and the *Flooers o' the Forest* was written to commemorate the deaths of those who were killed in the Battle of Flodden in 1513, an ancient war where so many were slaughtered, a war remembered in Scotland to this day. I think it also confirmed Alasdair's involvement in WW1. He must have witnessed the same number of needless deaths that occur in all wars. I left the cemetery with a deep sense of calm.

"Now over to you, Sophie."

* * *

"Wow, well done mum and you got your wish. Alasdair Forman's story did have a happy ending... five more children!! And goodness only knows how many grandchildren! I think he died a happy man and had made his peace with the death of Janet and his baby daughter, just as Míriam and Janet would have wanted him to. But mum, maybe you are a Scottish bruga... your witch's thumbs? And remember what you thought you saw, a man on the beach in Pittendreal when you were visiting your grandmother as a young woman walking with a German shepherd dog that suddenly disappeared and the two girls when you first moved into Leightham House?!"

"Okay, that's enough about that. Right, file these papers, Sophie, and get on to the next chapters."

I wonder what they are about?! Sophie wondered.

PART FIVE

Chapter 1

Restoration of Leightham House
Second Visit

S OFIYA got the taxi driver to drop her at her parents'
house on the way back from the airport to say hi and
pick up her car. No doubt her dad would have it shining
clean inside and out considering the state she left it in.

"Mum, dad, I'm home! I had such an amazing trip to
Spain. Can't wait to tell you all about it. I might even
consider buying a house there one day. Spain is for
relaxation, swimming, eating wonderful Spanish food.
Doubt you two would like it though. It's a bit on the garlicky
side."

"Welcome back, young lady...oops! Lady Leightham."
Jim made an exaggerated bow, while indicating he wanted to
kiss Sofiya's hand. "Love the suntan."

"That's enough of that, dad. By the way the suntan is
more likely my freckles have all joined up than a suntan."

"Well...how did you get on in Spain? Did you find what
or who you were looking for?" Jim asked.

Before Sofiya could answer, Ina interrupted them. "No,
Spain's not for me. I hate flying and I can't stand the heat.
Ask yer dad... Jim, what was I like in Malta? I wanted to
come home early. Luckily your dad persuaded me to stay or
we would have missed having you and I'm not curtsying to
you."

"Maybe it's me who should be bowing and curtsying,
considering what I have put you through, mum, dad.

"Spain was fascinating and not too hot at this time of
year and boy did I find out exactly what and who I was

looking for, even after more than half a century. But I am home for a bit. How's the work going at the house? Are you pleased with the progress, dad? But first I have to go back to Mount View and unpack before I return to Leightham House and this time it will be me that teases Dixie! Revenge is sweet, dad." Sofiya gave them both a hug.

"Do you think Sam will remember me, dad?"

"Don't be daft. Cats never forget and I think you will get a surprise when you visit Leightham House."

"Right, I am off to spend time with Irene's granddaughter, Harriet. How is she doing?"

"Not too well. She is just out of hospital again. The wee soul seems to be plagued with chest infections. That bairn's no right, Sofiya. Nobody, not even the paediatric consultants seem tae ken what's wrong, Cathie keeps telling everybody!" Ina added as an afterthought.

"That's not good news, but thanks to antibiotics, she should recover. Right! I'm off to give Irene and Cathie support. See you at the weekend. Tea, mum and a round of golf, dad?" Sofiya attempted to defuse the situation, which she knew would erupt as soon as she announced where she was going next, but it was hard to fool her dad.

"Dad, I know you will be dead against it, but my next trip *will* be to Russia. Not immediately because I will have to go with an organised tour. No one is allowed in unaccompanied. I'll apply for a visa but goodness knows how long that will take." Sofiya ran out of the room and got into her car to avoid confrontation with her dad, but she could not avoid hearing him shouting after her,

"Do they allow visitors in Russian Gulags?!! And you better not go wearing miniskirts or hot pants! Take midi…"

Sofiya stuck her head out the car window and yelled back, "What was that, dad? Sorry, I couldn't hear you. Never mind. I am going to a Rugby match on Saturday, the last match this season at Murrayfield with Neil. We might call in on the way back."

Chapter 2

S OFIYA LEFT MOUNT VIEW for the Leightham Estate. Several weeks had passed since her return from Spain. She had been feeding Harriet, giving the baby her antibiotics and taking her turn on the nightshift to look after the infant, who never seemed to sleep for more than an hour at a time. She had been unable to leave Mount View, but at last things had settled down and she was on her way to inspect the progress Dixie was making. She couldn't wait to wind him up!

"Good grief," Sofiya gasped. The place was unrecognizable. Her dad had warned her it looked like a building site, but she wasn't prepared for this. The first thing she saw when she arrived was the rusty, old, metal gate, that was now virtually hanging off its hinges and propped up against the hedge with the sign, 'DANGER! NO ENTRY' on it. The second thing she noted was that her dad, true to form, had ordered Dixie to deal with the back entrance to the house before her return. So no longer were there ruts and potholes. They had been filled with a temporary surface of, what did her dad call it...blaes? *It certainly makes a difference,* Sofiya thought. She got halfway along the drive before having to reverse all the way back to the main road as a lorry piled with debris was bearing down on her.

Mm, this needs temporary passing places. How am I supposed to visit my own house if I have to back up every time to let a lorry pass? The driver doesn't know who I am and he's not going to back up and let me pass first.

What a difference since the last time I was here, she thought. The roof was more or less complete. "Wow! I think Dixie has employed more than a few roofing slaters to get this far never mind the number of carpenters. Why did Dixie say he needed joiners? I remember… they are the men who do the work in a workshop and carpenters construct the building on site. What's that odd looking prefab doing here? Where is Dixie? You are talking to yourself again, old girl."

Leaving her car in a relatively safe spot, Sofiya went to find the man. That was not difficult as she seemed to have arrived in the middle of a row. Shouting could be heard above the sound of sawing and the dogs barking. Dixie's voice above the din was shouting the loudest from behind the unidentified structure.

"Ye daft, baw-headed, bugger!!"

"What are ye gaunna dae, Dixie?! Thraw that at me?! Gaun…gaun, a dare ye… auld man!"

"All gie ye a skelpit erse fur yer cheek, Billy Gibson!!"

Dixie appeared to have some kind of saw in his hand and a piece of wood and was pretending to throw the saw at Billy.

"A guid ye the measurements fur this bit o' wid… an look at the mess ye made o' it and stop termentin' thay dugs! Dae ye think money growes on trees?"

"No, but that bit o' wid did." Billy, laughed at his own joke.

It looked to Sofiya as if Billy and Dixie were enjoying themselves. Billy was ducking and dodging as he encouraged Dixie to throw the saw at him and at the same time, he continued to torment the dugs.

"You youngsters are richt pains in the…Oh my gawd, it's Mrs Leightham! Sorry… yer ladyship, I'll get yer name richt wan o' thay days." Dixie took his now repaired, deerstalker hat off as Sofiya approached. "A didna hear ye arriving."

That's obvious considering the language you were using, Sofiya thought. *Better ignore it.* "Never mind,

Dixie. It looks like work is making good progress. The drive certainly makes access to the house much easier, but we need passing places, as I had to reverse all the way back to the main road to let a lorry out. But I can't believe my eyes. The roof is more or less completed, but what is this?" Sofiya indicated the prefabricated building.

Dixie shook his head. *Do women never stop complaining?* Pulling his deerstalker back on Dixie explained: "That's the workmen's bothy. We canna dae withoot that! That's whaur we get oor tea and oor dinner. I blaw the whistle and awbody kens its time tae down tools and eat. Billy, get the nipper tae pit the tea cans on the fire. Her ladyship will want a cup o' tea, once av taken her round the site tae let her see the progress we've made, afore she laves. And fund a hard-hat fur her ladyship, Billy. Whit wus that ye said!? Ya, impudent young… wait till a get a haud o' you later…They youngsters hiv nae respect they days, yer ladyship.

"You'll be interested tae ken we hid nae bother getting a warrant fae the council tae restore and renovate Leightham Hoose. A thocht the young lad in the office wus plaised tae hear o' the restoration. Some o' the retired locals are auld enough to mind o' the hoose in its hayday, an hiv heard the news and they're plaised as weel."

Kitted out with the hard hat that was threatening to occlude her vision, Sofiya thoroughly enjoyed her tour. She could see piles of wood waiting to be sawed and what looked like an even more odd-looking pile of wood 'happit' up. Dixie explained it was to prevent the wood being soaked if it rained. There seemed to be trestle tables everywhere and it was impossible to walk anywhere without being ankle deep in sawdust. Maybe she should have worn her welly boots! Sofiya remembered the dogs from her last visit and had brought a couple of raw bones for them. The dogs were now happily lying down and chewing at them.

"Aye, like I said at the beginin', oor first job wis tae mak the hoose wind and waterticht. That means labour intensive and sometimes dangerous work. A hid a look at the architect's plans and got a lot o' information. The main roof is a hipped roof. So, ma skilled workers hid tae lay the timbers frae the builder's yard, on a flat surface, measure the building and cut the various lengths. You didna need tae ken aboot widths, spans, gables, runs, but Leightham Hoose his a fairly steep-pitch roof, say aboot 40 degrees? Once the carpenters hid finished, it wus time tae get the slates on.

"A fairly steep-pitched roof is needed fur Scottish slates, but the last Scottish slate quarry ceased production in 1955, but a fund them in demolition yards in the area. It widn'a surprise me if some o' them cam frae the hoose when it was demolished. But am warnin' ye there's a lot o' wastage in adaptin' reused slates. It's been an expensive job. But the end result is whit ye said ye wanted and there's the proof, a sicht tae gladden the hert."

Without looking at her, Dixie continued thoroughly enjoying showing off his superior knowledge. Sofiya was not going to let on that she had no idea what he was talking about, but nodded as if she understood everything.

"Noo, let's get inside. It's no exactly safe, that's why ye need a hat."

"But I don't see any of the workmen wearing hard hats, Dixie."

"Ach, that's up tae them. As ye can see, we hiv cleared a' the vegetation, weeds and tree roots, afore we begun. Look!" Sofiya did as she was told. "The existing flair was in a puir condition, so we broke it up and pit in a layer o' hard-core and a layer o' sand. Next, a damp-proof membrane, then new thick concrete...a'll no bore ye wi the details o' the upper flairs, or the new balustrade and ornamental, wrought iron and wood handrails fur the new staircase. We're lucky there's nothin' wrang wi the original, rectangular, stone stairs themselves."

Had Dixie swallowed a builder's dictionary?

"And this provides us wi safe access tae begin repair a' the wa's. As ye can see we're testin' fur ony auld boss plaster. That means it's lost its strength and adhesion. It his tae come aff, afore the walls are repaired and repointed where necessary. Oh, bit o' guid news! We fund a sample o' the original cornicing and it's been sent tae the factory suppliers tae be copied. A've ordered the best quality electric cables and lead piping and every wall will be lined wi insulation quilting between the partition studs. We're doing the very best tae avoid rising damp, and dry rot. We're well on oor wi tae restorin' this braw hoose tae its formur glory. Here's the design and interior decoration team arriving. A telt the lads you were likely to come the day."

Dixie might as well have been speaking in Chinese for the last half an hour and I haven't studied Chinese! Sofiya thought.

Nate and Harry arrived wearing their hard hats. "Your ladyship, I hope you are well after your visit to Spain? This is Harry Fairgrieve, our interior designer."

"I am very well, thank you, Nate." Sofiya nodded to Harry.

"Just call me Harry and I am delighted to meet you, your ladyship. I believe our families are distantly related. Nate and I have known each other since our college days. We managed to get visas to study old palaces in Russia during our summer holidays, which I believe is a country you have an interest in. We had a special interest in the work of Catherine the Great's Scottish architect, Charles Cameron, and his Neoclassic and Palladian styles. We secretly photographed every square inch of his work.

"I have sourced a reproduction, modernised, Victorian kitchen, Shanks toilets, and brass chains to flush the cistern. And a free-standing bath, that has beautiful, decorative, wrought-iron feet, that you almost have to have a step ladder to get into. Well not quite. And Robert Adam fireplaces for the hall and downstairs rooms. Nate and I both feel a connection to this house's antiquity and it deserves the best we can do to make sure it resembles its historical past. I believe you have many beautiful artefacts and paintings? I will see to it that they are displayed as they would have been in Leightham House years ago.

"Your ladyship, might I suggest, instead of coal fires in the open fireplaces we fit gas fires that resemble wood fires? They are so realistic now, you won't know the difference, except no ash to clean out every day or wood to bring in. I have ordered similar Georgian-style frames and window sashes and reproduction Rennie Mackintosh windows for the upper hallway, overlooking the main hall. Dixie will make sure the deep cornicing is in place and the large ceiling rose is ready to take the weight of your Italian chandelier."

"My Italian chandelier?"

Harry grinned. "Your ladyship, while you were away your dad gave Nate and me the keys to Cards House in Edinburgh. In the basement we found a huge unopened wooden crate. We found tools in the garage and broke into it. We knew you wouldn't mind. Inside, was one of the most beautiful, crystal Italian chandeliers I have ever seen. It has pendants hanging like dew drops from every branch so there will be rainbows reflected all around the ceiling when it is lit. At present it is being converted from candle to electricity. I suggest we choose a neutral colour matte paint for the main walls, so the pure white matte on the cornices, skirting boards and the wall plaster décor, stands out. Oh, Dixie, what about an emergency generator in the grounds? Doubt there will be gas cuts, but you never know with electricity."

"Well said, Harry," Nate agreed with his friend. "To be honest, I don't have that much more to add until I can inspect the whole building and am satisfied with the results for insurance purposes. Let me quickly explain the ground floor as we are standing in the hall with the main door behind us. Over there, on the right, under the staircase, will be the concealed door to the basement kitchen and store rooms. Here is where the double doors to the lounge will be and that leads on to the Victorian conservatory. On the left, the dining room double doors and at the back, a door leading to the study. Harry will make that very comfortable for you to sit when you feel like a bit of privacy."

"Sorry, Nate, *no!* Have you seen the view from upstairs? I have not yet, but I know it will be stunning. I believe you have permission from the structural engineers, to put in weight-bearing beams for the lounge and master bedroom to enable bow windows to replace the old, long narrow ones? So, Mr Fairgrieve, Mr Irvine, please collect my grandmother's old Parker Knoll chairs and my coffee table from Mount View and have them placed in the bow window of my bedroom, so I can relax and look to the Mary Isle and fall in love with the uninterrupted view. But it's unlikely I will be uninterrupted for long, managing the estate!" Both young men smiled. No point in arguing with her about anything. After all she who pays the piper…

"We will deal with it, your ladyship, and make sure the furniture is placed exactly where you want it." Nate glanced in the direction of Dixie. "Dixie is waiting at the front door for you. We are finished, but…" he dropped his voice to a whisper, "Dixie has sworn us to secrecy, but I can't help telling you. We have a surprise for you when you come back, thanks to our student days in Russia." Nate put his finger to his lips and nodded his head.

Sofiya wondered if this was why they had told her, they had studied in Russia, before turning to find Dixie.

Handing her hard hat back to him, Sofiya got into her car. Straight faced and without a trace of humour she announced, "Mr Dixon, I will be away for much longer this time, but where is the nursery to be? I didn't hear any mention of that during this visit from you, Mr Irvine or Mr Fairgrieve."

Dixie's facial expression was priceless as he began to stutter a response.

"Don't worry, Dixie, it's not urgent. I am far more interested in completion of the ground floor: the hall, the lounge, the dining room and conservatory. I want them to be completed by the time I return for my...my...wedding reception which will be a grand affair, with a banquet for hundreds: Scotch broth, steak pie, Scottish trifle with raspberries, custard and sherry; space for playing the bagpipes, accordions and fiddles, Scottish country dancing... you know, the sort of thing we Scots are famous for!"

Sofiya's only regret was she didn't have a camera to photograph Dixie's face as she spoke, as his jaw dropped open. Dixie had offered her a cup of tea when she arrived, but Sofiya was now of the opinion that Dixie could do with a wee dram of Scotch!

* * *

"I have such happy memories of these days Sophie, being involved in the reconstruction of Leightham House. Your dad and I married very soon after he proposed to me, but many of the guests I wanted to invite were unable to travel to Edinburgh. Leightham House, the kitchens and the grounds were not sufficiently completed for us to have our reception there. I wanted a second reception once the house was restored, because so many people, including those involved in the restoration, estate workers, the house staff and the villagers had been unable to attend the first one in Cards House. Believe me that night more than made up for it. And I did dance more than once with Dixie.

I also vividly remember my conversation with my father when I left for Russia."

"Well, I hope you know what you are doing, Sofiya," he announced. "I should think very carefully about what you have decided to do and if you are determined to go to St Petersburg (now called Leningrad), remember you will be in the USSR, behind the Berlin Wall and away from the British Embassy in Moscow. No one can help you and even their help is limited. I know you don't want my advice, but I suggest you get a new passport before you go. Your old one has nearly expired anyway, so apply for a new one now. The number of American visas and entry stamps on the old one? They won't like that in Russia."

"I am well aware of that, dad, but I told you when I returned from Spain that I have traced Alasdair Forman to Spain. Now I must find out how one of my Russian forebears found her way to Scotland and nearly married the man, *and* my new passport has arrived." I answered.

"As you can imagine, Sophie, I made a quick exit and a few weeks later found myself sitting in the first-class departure lounge in Edinburgh airport waiting for my flight to Gatwick. I had to take a flight to Sweden from there and the boat to St Petersburg, as there were no direct flights there at that time.

"After I returned from Russia, Sophie, I then went straight to Kenya without visiting Leightham House in between."

PART SIX

Chapter 1

Russia

"THIS WAS DIFFICULT, Sophie, but I have done my best to put together the facts from the information I gleaned from the research I did in Russia. Keep in mind that these events took place before my grandmother, Alice Gardner, arrived at the Skavronsky Palace to be companion to the princesses. She never spoke about the princesses' grandmother except in one of the chapters where she mentioned that Miss Chambers told her that Prince Alexander's wife had died during a typhoid epidemic. I subsequently found out this was misinformation to hide the truth, but by the time Alice Gardner arrived in Russia the princesses' grandmother was probably dead.

"Both in St Petersburg and in the countryside around it, where I did my research, very few senior Russian citizens were willing to speak to me, or stated they had no memory of their grandparents telling them about the Skavronsky Estate, the Pogroms or the flu epidemic which had occurred in Russia in 1889/90. But this is what I did find out and have written in the same way my grandmother had me write her story. I think it makes more interesting reading if the story is written as fiction."

* * *

Prince Andrei found his father sitting by the fire enjoying a cigar in his study and decided it was time to get answers.

Over the years while he was growing up, he became aware of rumours among the palace staff about his mother. When he asked his governess, Miss Chambers, if they were true, she didn't look him in the eye but said that she had no idea what he was talking about and had quickly changed the subject.

"Papa, I know I am still young but I have fallen in love with Princess Ekaterina and I will marry her, but I need to know about my mother first before I do. Something is not right. Is it not about time to 'come clean' to use an English phrase?"

"She died from typhoid, Andrei."

"No! Papa, it's time you treated me like an adult; please don't insult my intelligence by telling me stories that are not true. You don't control everything. I threatened to have my tutor, Pyotre, fired if he refused to take me to our family's cemetery on the pretext that I wanted to lay flowers on my mother's grave."

Prince Alexander raised his hand to stop his son from asking any more questions, but it was obvious the young man was not going to give up easily.

"No, papa, I insist. I found the grave of my grandmother, Princess Sophia Skavronskya. She was the one who died from typhoid, not my mother. Not one name or date on the grave site of our forebears could be found to corroborate your story about my mother."

Alexander realized he was defeated, "Andrei, you are right and you are old enough now to be told the truth. But first I must ask, no, beg you, to never discuss what I am about to tell you with another living soul. It's all in the past and I don't want the subject ever brought up again… it is too painful for me." Andrei nodded his head and reassured his father he would tell no one.

"Your mother was still alive until a few years ago. We could tell no one what happened because of the danger to your sister, Princess Sophia."

Andrei felt as if he had been punched in the stomach. He collapsed into the nearest chair. "Sister?!" he gasped.

"Your mother developed a condition the doctors describe as puerperal psychosis, although I had the impression they didn't fully understand the condition any more than I did. My beautiful wife, your mother, first showed signs of the condition after you were born.

"But after the birth of your sister, she changed out of all recognition from the woman I married. Her condition spiralled out of control. She refused to get dressed or socialise with anyone. She had shown little sign of interest in you after your birth, but took an active interest in your sister lulling us all into a false sense of security. One day, the nurse caring for her could find neither your mother nor the infant! We will never know how she made the journey to St Petersburg.

"A young clerk, Vadim Yakushin, who was working in Merchants Row in St Petersburg saw a young woman in a nightdress, with an infant in her arms. Confused, he observed her walking towards the end of the embankment just staring ahead and he had the wits to run out of his office. He persuaded the woman to give him the baby and he was able to guide her back to his office. His swift action saved both their lives. He had no idea who the woman was, but heard her say Skavronsky and he got a message to us.

"We employed extra staff to care for your mother. Psychiatrically disturbed people are not responsible for their actions and can be very cunning, but she seemed to calm down. One night, Suleiman, who never seems to sleep, heard the front door open. He discovered it was your mother with the baby by the edge of the lake and about to jump in!

"A guard was posted outside your mother's bedroom twenty-four hours a day. We moved the baby with her nurses to the other side of the palace. Again that seemed to work for a while. One night the whole palace was wakened by shouting from the outside palace staff. I ran outside. Oh my god, Andrei! Your mother had managed to escape from her room, and had made her way undetected along the corridor to the baby's nursery. She had snatched the baby and to everyone's horror there on the palace roof was your mother, with the baby in her arms, about to jump. Somehow Dmitri managed to get behind her and risking his own life, prevented her from jumping.

"Something had to be done at once. Her doctors decided radical, urgent action had to be taken to protect your sister *and* your mother. They informed me it was unlikely your mother would ever recover. I agreed and she was taken immediately to the Novodevichy Closed Order Convent for her own safety. The weekly food is delivered through a hatch in the wall and once a week a priest is permitted entry to hear confession and conduct a Mass, although what the nuns have to confess about is a mystery to me. Even then, twice your mother almost managed to escape from the convent, but was caught in time.

"I had to make the heart-breaking decision to send your little sister away to a secret location where her mother wouldn't find her. The palace staff who knew what had happened were sworn to secrecy and others were told your mother had died from typhoid and it was her dying wish to be buried in the convent grounds. But people whisper and gossip and that's how you heard the stories.

"Your sister lived in one of the family's smaller isolated estates east of the Great Peterhof Palace. Some would say the palace was more like a cottage. Yes, it is small, but very comfortable, with surrounding grounds, forests and a stream that widens and flows into the Neva River and subsequently the Gulf of Finland."

Throughout his father's stunning revelations, Andrei sat speechless. He could hardly take it all in. He didn't even know about this other palace.

"Do you keep in touch Papa? Does she know who she is? Can I go and visit her now the danger is over?"

"Andrei, I did start the process with the help of her companions and her staff, to begin to gradually introduce her to the idea of a holiday away from the palace. I didn't want to alarm my daughter, still a young girl, who knew nothing about us or herself and had never left the estate. And yes, I received monthly reports from Jacob, her palace manager, but then everything had to be put on hold. First of all because of the on-going Pogroms with their savagery against the Jewish people and some of the staff are Jewish. I also thought it was safer to leave her there with her staff who never left the estate and were unlikely to catch Russian flu that was spreading like wildfire and decimating the population at an alarming rate at that time."

"You seem to be talking in the past tense, Papa," Andrei frowned.

"I am, and here is the worst news of all that I received from Dmitri. I had to send him to the palace to find out what had happened as I had not heard from Jacob, which was unusual. On his return Dmitri was almost in tears. The Palace had been torched, burnt to the ground by a marauding group of slaughtering fiends of hell. Almost all of the staff had been killed. But your sister, my little daughter, is missing. No one in the surrounding area, when Dmitri questioned them, admitted to knowing what had happened. I had the feeling they were too afraid to speak to him. Anyway, how could they know? Very few people knew of her existence and I don't want to think about what might have happened. It all happened a long time ago, Andrei, but I will never forgive myself...never."

Chapter 2

HANNAH AND JACOB, warmly wrapped in their fur coats, were sitting outside, drinking cups of hot Russian tea with slices of lemon, a short distance from their young charge, who was staring at a sheaf of papers in her hands. Winter was on its way. Soon they would be able to enjoy troika rides within the estate.

"I am worried, Jacob. Life seems to have changed out of all recognition since the death of Tzar Alexander. Violence has erupted periodically over the last hundred years. We are Christians, but our parents chose Jewish sounding names for us. We are isolated here but that's not a guarantee against marauding anti-Semitic groups. Do you know what Pogrom means, Jacob?"

Jacob shook his head and shrugged his shoulders as if he didn't really care.

"It means to wreak havoc and Pogroms have certainly done that by terrorising decent people. The marauders are bent on the destruction of people and property."

"Hannah, you are overreacting on a subject that diminishes into insignificance considering the local rumours. Savagery or disease… take your pick. I heard from the man who delivers the weekly house supplies, that the scientists are calling it the Russian flu. It is a disease out of control and recent estimates say a million people have died already. It appears to have spread through hundreds and hundreds of miles of the Russian railroads and via shipping from the Volga trade routes. By November it spread to St Petersburg and from there round the world. The disease is unstoppable and no country has been spared.

"We are isolated here, Hannah, but maybe the disease arrives by the very air we breathe. Do you think the young girl knows anything about it?"

"Why do you ask that? She doesn't seem to want to leave the estate and never asks questions about her life."

"You must keep what I am about to tell you a secret, Hannah, or we could lose our jobs… worse still, be banished to Siberia,"

"What are you talking about, Jacob?!"

"One night, a while ago, I heard something unusual. When I looked out of the kitchen window, I saw a lamplight in the faraway bushes swinging back and forth, signalling, and the girl slipping out of the side door. I smiled and almost laughed and just let her go. She must have been meeting someone. It was not as if she was going alone into the forest. So, out of curiosity, I followed her and I recognized the old guy who met her. It was Abraham, the old apothecary from the village with his wife, the old witch. Maybe I was wrong to take such a risk, but she has so little fun and has no one but us, her tutors and servants."

"Let's face it, Jacob, she is denied nothing. Her every whim is catered for."

"Hannah, the one time I thought she might ask questions was when I told her about the box hidden in an old portmanteau at the back of the guard-dogs' kennels and the clothes on the shelf there. The dogs know her and she feeds them on a regular basis. I stressed that should the need arise, she must change out of her regular clothes and dress in the garments she will find on the shelf and take the portmanteau with her, guard its contents with her life and allow no one to open it.

"She looked straight at me and said, 'I understand, Jacob.' Then she ran off into the forest surrounding the palace. I swear she thinks of the bears and wolves as her pets!"

"Rubbish, Jacob!!"

Chapter 3

DRESSED IN A WARM FUR COAT and boots, she sat on a chair by the stream, her favourite place on the estate. Tapping her lips with a pencil, she stared at the homework in front of her that Monsieur Pierre, her tutor, had left her to work on. It was a list of words to be used to compose an essay, before he returned the following week. She was to write about her favourite season, but she loved all the seasons. *How can I choose one of them?*

Monsieur Pierre had been her tutor for close on five years. He was very well paid and had been sworn to secrecy, with the threat of being sent to Siberia if he told anyone about the young girl living on the estate.

Every week, Pierre was thoroughly searched by a young man before being admitted through the main gates to the palace. It was a pleasure to work with her, because she took such an interest in the homework he had left with her and she came up with some incredible answers.

Now what am I supposed to do with this? Staring at the list of words Monsieur Pierre had given her, she wasn't sure which season she liked best. Was it spring, sitting by the stream hearing the birds singing in the trees, as if they were singing only for her? Or listening to the whisper of the spring breezes sending flurries of silver birch leaves like showers of silver sequins overhead. Or the sound of gurgling from the stream, as it broke free with ear-splitting cracks from the winter ice melting in spring, the rush of water celebrating its freedom till it reached the wider stretches of the river and ultimately to... where? She wasn't sure. She had never been allowed to follow its rolling progress any farther than the edge of the estate.

Perhaps Monsieur Pierre's list of words better described the long, long summer days when the sun shone far into the night. Then she was allowed to go boating and swimming in the estate pond and ignored Jacob's voice shouting to her to come back because she was swimming too far out. *Perhaps autumn?* No, she preferred the fast approaching, silent, freezing winter. The edges of the pond were already beginning to freeze. She looked forward to her favourite winter occupations of sledging down slopes thick with snow, and sleigh rides in the forests of the estate. Looking around at a recent light fall of snow, flakes of snow began to swirl around her as she sat. She looked forward to the times she would watch the snow from her bedroom window, as fierce gusts of wind blew it up like clouds into the air before it fell, knee-deep on the ground. It looked like autumn was over for this year, so perhaps writing about winter would be better.

Soon there would be only a few hours of daylight left, but the palace would be warm and the crackle of the log fires acknowledged the arrival of winter. She loved listening to the wolves at night. They were her friends. They howled to each other, oblivious of the freezing temperatures, protected by their thick fur winter coats. Many of these seasonal activities had been somewhat curtailed this last year and she didn't know why, but it had not prevented her night-time visits to Abraham and his wife, Leah. She felt certain Jacob knew of her nightly visits to the old couple, but he had no idea what Leah was teaching her, or he would have put a stop to it.

This thought made her pause momentarily. She wasn't naïve, wasn't unaware of the possible dangers of living in isolation so far from civilisation. Jacob had never explained why she had to know about a box hidden in an old decrepit looking portmanteau in the dog kennels or why he instructed her to change into the clothes that looked like something a peasant would wear and never to allow anyone to open the portmanteau. The only thing he did tell her was that in an emergency, there was a letter in the pocket of the coat that would tell her who to get in touch with. It was all very strange.

Enough! Forget about that. Probably nothing will ever happen… it never does. Now what are the words? I think I will write about winter. Oh dear, these words don't reflect winter. Maybe whispering does, but not trickling, gushing, gurgling, rolling, bubbling and rushing. Nothing rushes or makes a noise in winter. In winter the world around me, around here, is virtually silent.

These thoughts were suddenly shattered. The earth seemed to tremble under her feet, followed by the ear-splitting, sound of explosions. Not understanding what was happening, her first thoughts were there had been an earthquake. She had only read about them but although the ground had trembled it had not split open. That thought quickly disappeared with the sound of wood splintering in the direction of her home. Looking towards the palace she could see a fire blazing, the flames reaching upwards and clouds of black acrid smoke. The palace must have caught fire! Trembling and frozen to the spot, she thought of a poem she had read, 'Dante's Inferno', but there was no gunfire in the poem. She saw the staff being marched in single file out of the palace to the lawn: maids, servants, grooms, dog handlers and cleaning staff, all protesting in surprise.

She heard Jacob yelling at her: "Run, run! Run and hide for God's sake!!" Refusing to run without her beloved friends or leave all the dear people who had looked after her for as long as she could remember, was out of the question. She had the presence of mind to throw the chair out of sight and quickly found a thick clump of bushes close by to hide in. From her hiding place she could see a group of rough, unshaven men gulping down liquid from bottles and laughing as the glass shattered when they threw the bottles on the ground.

Pushing the servants with their rifles towards Jacob and Hannah the men ordered the women to remove their underclothes and the men were ordered to form a row and kneel down. Systematically, the gunmen walked along behind the row of kneeling men and shot them in the back of their heads, laughing at the cries of pain from the men they had failed to kill, before shooting them a second time. Some of the women screamed, "We are not Jewish!" but that fell on deaf ears. The men dragged the women by the hair, viciously hitting them across the face till they fell on the ground writhing in pain or mercifully unconscious. They stripped the defenceless women and threw their clothes up into the air before pulling something out from between the legs of their trousers and throwing themselves on top of the women jerking their bodies up and down and grunting with pleasure.

Frozen with horror at what she was seeing, the young girl wasn't sure what to do. Vaguely in the back of her mind she remembered a worrying conversation she overheard once when she was with the old couple, about a group of marauding, drunken, savages, several years before, ravaging the country looking to expel the Jewish people and there were still uncontrolled groups out there. This must have been what they were talking about.

All feelings and thoughts vanished as one of the ugliest men that the girl had ever seen shot Jacob right in front of her, as he tried to prevent a second man dragging Hannah by the hair. The girl couldn't speak, couldn't shout. She just stared through the grass and bushes at the scene unfolding in front of her. They tore Hannah's clothes off, threw her to the ground and straddled her one behind the other. One of the men forced her legs open and as Hannah screamed for mercy, he opened his wide baggy trousers and pushed something from between his legs between hers.

The other man was kneeling on her chest. Hannah, realizing what was about to happen, stopped pleading, clenched her teeth and closed her mouth tight. Reaching inside his pants he drew out a thick, round, swollen object that resembled a short stick of wood with a knot on the end of it and tried to force it into Hannah's mouth by holding her nose till she could no longer breathe. Hannah was forced to open her mouth gasping for air, and the man pushed the object into her mouth. Like the man behind him he started to raise and lower his knees on her shoulders as if he was riding a horse.

Suddenly, the man on Hannah's chest rocketed back, cracking the skull of the man behind him who fell backwards with blood pouring down his face from his nose and mouth. It looked like his front teeth had been knocked out. The man in front had stopped riding Hannah, and was screaming, but seemed to be unable to free himself from the source of his agony. He couldn't move. Hannah had clenched her teeth down tight on whatever it was he had put in her mouth and was refusing to let it go, however often he hit her across the face. The young girl, not fully understanding what she was seeing, watched as the man, obviously in agony, fumbled in his coat. He drew out a gun and shot Hannah through the temple.

The young girl lay still, silent, terrified they would find her. She continued to watch the two men who were so close to where she lay hidden. One was gagging in pain with every footstep, holding the bleeding object which looked different, with the knot of wood at the end of the stick now missing. The other man appeared to be unable to speak. He looked as if he was grimacing, his broken jaw frozen in one position and he was nursing his bruised swollen face.

It felt like the day would never end, but at last it was almost dark and the only sound was the crackling of the embers from what had once been her beloved home. Emerging from her hiding place, she walked past the palace which was now totally gutted. In a strange state of mind she seemed to be unaffected by the bodies all round her. Her mind had shut down. As if in a trance, she walked towards the sound of the dogs barking and let them out of their cages. She went to the back of the kennels and numb with shock, changed into the peasant clothes, as Jacob had instructed her to do. Taking the portmanteau, she ran and ran through the forest till she could run no more. Unaware she had taken the paths she had taken many times in the past, she collapsed, exhausted and freezing on a doorstep.

Responding to a strange noise at the door and disregarding Leah's warning, "Abe, be careful. We are not expecting anyone and the girl came just yesterday," he went to the door and found what looked like a peasant girl curled up on the doorstep and took her in.

"Mercy, Abe, it's the girl and look at the state she is in! Get a hold of her bag." The girl felt the bag being taken from her and with the first signs of life returning, gasped in a hoarse voice, "No no!"

"It's all right. You are safe now. We won't take your bag, but you must let Leah help you, miss. You are frozen and might lose your fingers or toes from frostbite if you don't. That sheepskin coat isn't as warm as the one you usually wear. You have never told us your name. Please trust us, and tell us your name."

"I don't know," she managed to croak the words.

Abraham realized the girl was telling the truth as she just shook her head. "Please tell us what has happened, so we can go and tell your family to come and collect you. They must be very worried."

It wasn't long before news travelled to the village of the carnage on the secluded estate that no one had ever been allowed to go near. No one said very much for fear of retribution, even the man who delivered the supplies and the gatekeeper kept quiet.

Later, Abe told Leah, "This is more than worrying, Leah. It was probably to do with the Pogroms. We must get her away from here. When you were bathing the girl, I went through the pockets of her coat and I found a letter. Now calm down... I am glad I did. I opened it and to my surprise read only two words, 'Lermontov' and 'boat'."

"But what on earth does that mean?"

"This morning, I went into the village and found the local Russian Orthodox priest, Father Michele, who wasn't pleased to see me, but agreed to answer my questions. It seems he's a real history buff. With much pondering and stroking his beard, he announced that Lermontov is the name of a dead, famous Russian poet. Father Michele suggested that the poet's name might be linked to a small country beyond the Baltic States over the North Sea, a country named Scotland and Lermontov's forebears had probably emigrated from there to Russia, many centuries ago. What about that?"

"The priest also added, although it is impossible to be certain, that Lermontov may have been descended from Scottish nobility. I asked him what he would do with such scant information. He said he did not want to know why I was asking him, but he would take a boat to that country to find out more and that's exactly what we will do."

"I am not leaving my home! I am too old to care what happens to me, Pogroms or not!"

"Not us Leah, the young girl. One way or another I will find a way to get her to a port in Finland, then on a ship, or fishing boat sailing to that country and get her away from any further danger. The priest also agreed to write a note of passage to 'whom it may concern' using the name Lermontov so when she arrives someone might be able to help her."

Chapter 4

"**SOPHIE,** I arrived nearly a hundred years later and many documents such as those related to shipping for instance, had been destroyed. Therefore, it was impossible to prove how a young girl journeyed to Scotland, as she might have sailed from either St Petersburg or Helsinki in Finland. But luck was on my side. Old documents and registers of shipping arriving and leaving were still available at the shipping office in Leith and many were signed by a Captain Melville. A word caught my eye…Lermontov.

"How the young girl found her way to auld Tam's cottage remains a mystery. The stories my grandmother told me about Janet did not give an explanation, only suggestions of how she came to Pittendreal. But her description of the young woman's aristocratic features, demeanour and waking up at night terrified, confirmed my suspicions. And the clothes she was wearing also suggested to my grandmother that she might have fled from the Port of Leith as they didn't recognise the surname and been picked up by gypsies, or the Romanian people who intermittently visited Scotland. Somehow she got left behind the night auld Tam found her and took her in. I believe Alasdair Forman guessed her origins before that awful accident. The contents of the portmanteau, the sealed scrolls which were sent to the library, convinced me she was Princess Sophia Skavronskya, my great-aunt.

"I managed to organize a trip to the area where the young girl was last sighted in Russia. Half of the stone walls of the estate had been removed, the rest crumbled to a pile of stones. The walls of the palace, however, were still standing, a bare, stark, burnt-out shell of its past, full of weeds, trees and tall grass. I was not surprised to see all the metal gates and railings were missing. They would have been removed and sent to the Russian iron foundries to be melted down for guns and ammunition to be used in the various wars.

"As I made to leave and get into a decrepit old Lada taxi, a young man approached me. Looking furtively around, he indicated I should move out of earshot of the taxi driver. He had heard that someone was asking questions about the old palace, had information and wanted to do a deal with me. In exchange for information, I was to give him clothing for his sister, risking both of us being arrested as I had been warned I might be asked for clothing and under no circumstances was I to give anyone anything, including toilet roll! I found out toilet roll was in very short supply when going to the toilets in the palaces and museums. A woman sitting outside gave me two pieces of toilet paper!

"However, I agreed to the deal and he told me his great-grandfather had been the gatekeeper to the palace and had been present on the night of the attack. His great-grandfather had described how a marauding group of savages had torched the palace and, being terrified he might be killed, had hidden and witnessed the most awful atrocities being committed on the staff before they were murdered. The young man further added it was rumoured that the beautiful young girl who lived there had somehow escaped with the help of two local villagers, but that was all he knew. We arranged to meet later and I gladly gave him armfuls of my dresses, trousers, blouses and wished him well. Maybe he did have a sister or just sold the stuff to make money. I didn't hang around long enough to find out. But I left Russia with no doubt in my mind that Janet or rather, Princess Sophia Skavronskya, was my great-aunt.

"By the way, Sophie, when I returned to Russia after the millennium, I noticed incredible changes from my first visit. McDonald's was there and the shops were full of Western goods. There was even plenty toilet roll! And now here is what I found out in my search for my parents in Kenya."

PART SEVEN

Chapter 1

Kenya

"S OPHIE, although I held little hope of a positive ending, I had to try to find out why my birth parents sent me back to Scotland and what had happened to them. This is what I discovered. It seems like a long time ago now. Please read on."

* * *

On the East African Airways flight to Kenya, Sofiya had time to think back and remember her visits to her grandmother. But it wasn't until after the reading of the will, that Sofiya discovered who her birth parents were. Never did her grandmother even hint that her parents were her grandmother's own children, or why she had her adopted. But Sofiya vividly remembered the meeting when her grandmother read the stories she had written about WW2 and again emphasized they were fiction.

Sofiya read the letters her mother, Ana Davidson, sent to her grandmother from Ceylon. They were painful to read as Ana constantly begged for a reply and it seemed, at this point, my grandmother made the decision to move back to Pittendreal from Edinburgh. She had posed as a distant relative of Sofiya's adopted family and told them she had recently returned from Canada and her wealth was from bidding in New York auction houses for the possessions of displaced Russian refugees. Most of this was untrue. She was the daughter of Aggie and Wullie Gardner. The Russian refugees fleeing the Bolshevik revolution barely had the clothes they stood up in.

Her grandmother seemed to have thrived on intrigue and duplicity. So where had the old lady's body gone? How had she arranged that, on her death, there would be no trace of her body? If you have no financial restrictions, you can arrange anything and she probably was confident her granddaughter would try to find out where she was buried and subsequently find her parents. *Maybe I am more like my grandmother than I thought. Kenya... it's obvious.* There was only one way to find out...go there.

Cathie had discovered the body in the lounge and over and over again stated quite categorically she never went back to the lounge. She had been told that Sofiya's aunt Nan, would take care of everything and to pack a bag and leave and she did just that. All enquiries at the doctor's surgery drew a blank. It appeared all records of Alice Gardner's death had disappeared. Her GP had left the practice and was unable to be contacted to confirm she had died or that he had signed the death certificate. Sofiya had employed lawyers and private investigators to search every council office, every cemetery and crematorium from Pittendreal to Dundee and Edinburgh and they had all drawn a blank.

Sofiya had to respect the fact the woman *had* done everything in her power to stop her son and daughter meeting. Alice Gardner knew exactly where her son James was and that he had been adopted by Fred Paxton, the owner of tea and coffee estates in Ceylon and Kenya. She also knew full well the kind of socialising that would go on in war time. The tea estate owners and the British people living and working in Ceylon would enjoy socialising with the armed forces. The thought passed through Sofiya's mind that she had been so lucky, both physically and mentally not to have suffered as others had done when their parents were so closely related, but sadly not every child was spared.

Sofiya also knew from reading Ana's letters, her parents had moved from Ceylon to Kenya, just before Ceylon gained independence in 1948. Kenya had gained its independence in 1963 and was still a young country. So Sofiya hoped to find out where the Paxton Tea and Coffee estates were. There might be Kenyans who could help her find her parents. She could not stop thinking about the birth parents she had never known. On the long journey to Kenya, she wasn't sure if she was glad she found out about them or sad. She felt guilty because she should have had more feelings for her parents. But how could she? She had only found out about them recently. Sofiya felt her saving grace was the fact her adoptive parents were the most wonderful people in the world and no one could take the place of her dad, Jim.

Everything pointed to the conclusion that her grandmother had orchestrated Sofiya's adoption and her own burial! But why and where?

*   *   *

The flight attendant announced over the intercom: "Return to your seats, please. Fasten your seat belts, put your trays in the upright position, remove all earphones. We will be landing in Nairobi in the next thirty minutes." As the plane began its descent to Embakasi Airport, it was difficult for her not to wonder what she would find out, considering the recent terrible battles for Kenya's independence. Tribe had fought against tribe, and fought the British army and police who had nothing to be proud of in their treatment of the Kenyan people. Was it endemic in man's DNA, man's inhumanity to man, attacking their own countrymen, invading and attacking other countries?

What Sofiya had discovered on her recent visit to Russia had shocked her and made her sad for such a beautiful country. It had some of the kindest people she had met, who, although hesitant at first because of the culture they lived in, had become her friends. Perhaps someday a leader would encourage the German people to pull down the Berlin Wall and hopefully someday a Russian President would be elected, who would end the USSR and the Cold War and open up Russia. Russian people could then freely travel abroad and learn more about democracy, freedom of speech, unbiased elections, freedom for lawyers and free, fair, justice for all.

But the way things are going with the Cold War and the development of nuclear weapons, perhaps the apocalypse is closer than we think, so what happens in Russia won't matter if we are all blown to smithereens. Stop thinking about that, Sofiya. You are becoming morbid. Concentrate on the reason you are here which is to find out what happened to your grandmother and how they felt about having to part with you.

Chapter 2

"**WE HAVE TO SEND HER HOME** now, James! It's not just the mosquitos or the other serious gastric infections babies develop, regardless of the number of times you boil the water. It's the worrying uprisings in Kenya. They want their independence, James."

"Well, I have handed over my father's Ceylon estates and I am not handing my Kenyan estate to a country that is not yet independent. I will make that decision if or when independence comes! And in any case, send our baby where? To your mother's? Are you crazy? I know Ahinsa doesn't want to come with us and that doesn't help, but there are ayahs in Kenya. They love children. I have to go and find out what is happening at my dad's tea estates. Maybe you should go home to Scotland with the baby, make up with your mother. She won't turn you and her own grandchild away. I can arrange a passage for you with Joe and Sadie. They have already packed and are ready to go."

"No, I am not leaving you, James. Maybe we should all go home, make a new life for ourselves in Scotland. It's only a matter of time till the Mau Mau win and we will have to leave anyway."

"Well, until that day comes, I am not giving up any more of my father's lifelong work and that's my final word. I can persuade Ahinsa to come with us so we don't need an ayah if that makes you any happier!

"I remember my dad taking me with him when I was very young. He spent several years at his Kenyan tea estates. I had an ayah... Fatimah. Yes, now I remember I used to call her Tuma! She was wonderful. I loved her and she carried me everywhere in her arms. She laughed when I copied the shamba boys weaving back and forth cutting the grass with their pangas."

James smiled as he reminisced about the past. "I also remember Ayuba and Chege, the houseboys my father trusted to look after the bungalow with his estate manager when he wasn't there. They were well taken care of, well paid. I can't see them turning against their employer's son."

"How far outside Nairobi is the tea estate, James?"

"Not far, thirty miles or so. The largest estate is in Nakuru."

"I am still not convinced. The reports that are arriving here, although few and far between, are frightening. Nationalist Jomo Kenyatta of the Kenyan African Union has been pressing the British government in vain for political rights, land reforms, and valuable holdings to be redistributed to African owners for years. Somehow, I can't believe you will agree to that."

James realized he wasn't on a winner and changed the subject.

"Do you remember our wedding, Ana? And do you remember how late you were in arriving? I had almost begun to panic. I thought you had changed your mind!"

"Of course I remember. How could I forget? Anyway, I thought it was traditional, the bride's prerogative to keep the groom waiting? I received a rather terse letter from my mother that morning! I had written to tell her that we were getting married and I thought I would never hear from her again. She had been so angry at my joining the Navy, but believe it or not she wished us well and our children no harm. It was very strange. She said she had come to terms with my marrying you, but gave no details as to why. She wrote she had too many sad memories living in Cards House and would be moving away from Edinburgh.

Enclosed in the letter was the address and name of her personal lawyer, stating, if at any time in the future I wished to get in touch with her, I was to write to him at his law firm... a Mr Norman Cunningham. It doesn't make sense, James."

"Life doesn't make much sense these days Ana, but one thing is for certain, we should not have any more children for the foreseeable future until our future is settled."

Ana had lost her argument against the move to Kenya. She never thought she would have to leave her beloved Ceylon or the tea estate and resettle in a strange country, but she would deal with James later. In the meantime, Ana's thought went back to that wonderful day, her wedding day.

*   *   *

Ahinsa artistically coiled Ana's glorious auburn hair round a crown of blue water lilies that grew in abundance everywhere in Ceylon. Ana's bouquet of matching blue and white flowers had been specially chosen as they were the colours of the Saltire, Scotland's national flag. Tall and slim in the beautiful silk dress she was wearing the first time she met James, Ana couldn't believe how well it had been repaired. All traces of salt water had been skilfully removed and the soft insecure silk buttons that had split open during the New Year Ball in Government House had been replaced with tiny, solid, silver, secure ones, inside the back opening so there was no chance of them bursting open again as they had done that night.

"Come on, Ana. Hurry up! I know it's traditional for the bride to be late, but this is too much. James will leave the church. He might think you have changed your mind about marrying him," Alison complained very un-Alison like. "The transport has arrived for JD and me. We have to get going."

Ana folded the letter she had just received that morning and carefully put it in her going away case. Joe and Sadie who were taking her to the church were due to arrive after the girls and the nurses, who had been invited to the wedding, had left.

"You know, Alison, it's alright to feel nervous before you get married," JD quipped in her usual positive, bright fashion, as the two bridesmaids stood at the door of the Dockyard Church in Colombo. "I know I will be when my time comes."

"What do you mean, when your time comes, JD?" Alison asked, the large, Ceylon sapphire engagement ring Stuart had put on her finger glittering in the sunlight. JD nervous? Not likely.

Before JD could answer, the Church of Scotland minister, Mr Balfour, walked up the aisle to the church door dressed in full, clerical vestments for a wedding, to the sound of the bagpipes that drowned out JD's answer.

The *Graynog* had berthed the previous day and the crew had managed to shift all the ship's cargo onto the docks. The ship also brought more troops and nurses. The wedding invitations had gone out to the ship's crew to join the festivities. The nurses on board, hearing about the wedding, needed little persuasion to join the sailors after the long tedious sea-voyage and delayed their departure to the various hospitals. On board Chippy Thompson and Scottie Mc Kenzie practised playing the bagpipes and the sound sent the local Ceylon dock workers flying in all directions! Well, wasn't that what the bagpipes were supposed to do in times of war... terrify the enemy?

JD and Alison felt emotional when they heard the skirl of the pipes as they waited outside the church door. By the sound of it, it was as if the whole Scottish Dragoon

Guards were playing. But where was Ana? The heat was beginning to get to all of them. The minister, poor soul, was dabbing his forehead. The two pipers had decided to wear wide-sleeved shirts with their kilts because of the heat. Alison and JD in their long, sleeveless, silk bridesmaid dresses were dabbing at their foreheads, hoping it would prevent the sweat pouring down their cheeks. JD was worried her mascara would run.

By this time James was seriously concerned. His best man, Robert Keay, in his white tropical lieutenant commander uniform, was finding it hard to reassure James. Everyone had arrived except the bride, so the pipers stopped playing. Inside the church a soft low muttering sound started to rise in volume. Matron Morton's and Commander McLean's commanding voices rose above the others, until a weel kent voice assaulted the congregation.

"Coo-eee!" Sadie Rodger shouted, "Hurry up, Joe! Keep up wi me; they're awe waitin in the kirk." Sadie was out of puff, her face not much different from its usual red colour. But the heat wasn't helping, neither was the puce coloured silk jacket she was wearing with a long-skirted dress. She and Joe had brought Ana to the church.

"It's that Heshan; he's nearly burnt the gears oot. We hid tae stop at the garage fur water, the engine wus overheating. A keep telling Joe, we need tae get a new car, but Joe kens best. He's convinced Ceylon will get its independence afore long, so there's nae need fur a new car. Ach, he's an auld Scottish skinflint, jist savin' his bawbees."

"That's enough, Sadie. Sorry girls, and to you Ana. It was the brakes, no the gears. Well, well, jist look at the three o' yea…whit braw lassies." Joe looked up to the heavens and in a silent prayer gave the good lord Harry grateful thanks that JD's bridesmaid's dress covered her bosom, as the memory of the Admiral's Ball flooded back, when JD's dress barely covered her breasts and he didn't know where to look, he had been so embarrassed at her over-exposed cleavage. That had been quite a 'heady' moment even for Joe. This time he wiped the sweat from his forehead because of the heat, not embarrassment.

"Right, Joe, it's time," Sadie ordered the poor man. "I'm awa doon the aisle. Joe, tac Ana's airm. Her left airm, ye eejit! Yer gonna gie her richt wan tae James. An' you lassies, get ahent Ana." Sadie shook her head looking at the girls, before turning to Ana. "My, my... yer beautiful, Ana, awfie braw. Oh, my goodness! Is that the gown ye wore at the ball? It's perfect. A wis worried ye micht get married in yer uniform." Sadie reached into her voluminous bag and produced a man's huge handkerchief, dabbed at her eyes and took off down the aisle at speed.

"Whoo, that's a relief," Joe announced now Sadie was out of earshot, "Well, are ye ready, lassie? You're sure? No wantin tae change yer mind, Ana?"

Ana looked straight at the smiling man. "Never, Joe. James is the love of my life... I can't imagine life without him."

"I canna wait tae see whit James's face looks like when he sees ye. Tak ma airm, hen. Let's gan find oot."

Chapter 3

ANA WONDERED where the time had gone since she and James had had that conversation and had packed all their furnishings and household goods in Ceylon and sent them ahead to Kenya. They arrived at Kilindini Harbour in Mombasa. James had refused to change his mind, even when recent reports of native uprisings had given him pause for thought. Ana had put every possible obstruction, every argument she could think of against the move, but James was adamant, determined. He said that the police and the army would take care of them and not all Kenyans were for independence.

Ana and James disembarked from the boat with Ahinsa who had the baby in her arms and their personal possessions packed in many suitcases and wooden trunks were round their feet. On the quayside, they waited for Chege their Kikuyu driver, to collect them. Ana didn't like the fact that his tribe, the Kikuyu, championed the struggle for independence. James was fussing, un-James like, over a wooden crate that looked like it had been left unattended on the wharf for some time. Yelling at the top of his voice and scaring the Kenyan dock workers half to death, he demanded to know why the crate was still there.

"Sorry, Bwana, I'll deal with it. Jambo memsahib, jambo. Habari gani? Mtoto… mzuri sana."

"What is he saying, James? And why are you shouting?" *No wonder the British are so disliked by Kenyans,* Ana thought. *I don't blame them. James is being so arrogant.*

"It's none of your business that I am shouting and from my limited Swahili, he is greeting me as the Big Boss and you the Lady Boss and a word Mtoto means a baby, a child, and mzuri sana, very good, fine, Kenyans love children. Let's face it, between disease and starvation, it's a wonder any of them reach adulthood. You will soon learn Swahili, Ana. And before we go any further... I am the Bwana-kubwa here, the top man. You better get used to it. The British government office in Nairobi advises taking all your jewellery off. We can put it in the safe at the bungalow and if you decide to drive anywhere, or go to Nairobi to do shopping, leave nothing on the seats of the car, lock everything in the boot after you park!" Ana had never seen James so anxious or arrogant.

"James, not only have you scared the Kenyan dock workers half to death because a stupid crate is still here, you have scared me as well." Ana felt the hairs on her arm rise up. She had begun to feel afraid and they had only just disembarked. Ahinsa looked ready to reboard the ship for Ceylon. A great start. So, this was what the future looked like? "What is in your blasted crate?"

"My Kenyan Arabica, long bean coffee, grown in the high, rich, volcanic soil of the Blue Mountains of Kenya, the finest coffee in the world, you idiot! The quicker we get to the estate and get them unpacked and planted into the ground, the quicker they are packed into foil-lined wooden boxes and sent off to companies that deal with the auction and export coffee to other countries. I believe my father's coffee grinding machines are still there just waiting to be restarted. And there's a good source of Kenyan workers glad of the work, even if they have to pick the crop high up in the mountains where the air has less oxygen. The locals are not affected by the altitude, but your cakes might be. They need extra raising agents to make them rise!"

"Never mind that… I don't plan to bake cakes! What companies, James?"

"Thompsons in Scotland is one of them. The profit from the Kenyan Blue Mountain variety will be enormous. I hear there is a growing market for coffee. Maybe, just maybe, I will consider returning to a land I think I was born in, but I have no memory of living there. Only once I have made a million, only then I might be persuaded to return. Do you think I will suit a kilt, Ana?" James seemed to have returned to his usual self. "Now where can Chege have got to? He used to be a houseboy, now Chege is a driver. I wonder if he will recognize me. I doubt I will recognize him!"

* * *

Ana had been more than a little surprised how easily she had slipped into her new life. The bungalow staff never stopped smiling and nothing was ever a problem. It was the same with the shamba boys. Ahinsa, to her disgust, had had to accept Fatimah's help with the baby as James insisted on employing her. Ana did not mind the isolation or the fact she did not have to raise a finger to cook, or do the washing and ironing, and better still, to do housework, which she hated. Everywhere she went on her walks with the baby in her pram, all the Kenyan estate workers and local Kenyans, shouted, "Jambo, mcmsahib," as she passed by, whether they knew her or not. It was not unlike life in Ceylon, but with one big difference: the lack of a sense of security!

The one change Ana had to adapt to was, if she was on her own driving the car to Nairobi, which she liked to do, she had to make certain she left in daylight and returned in daylight. Kenya is close to the equator so with one hour difference between summer and winter, there are only twelve hours of daylight and there was no street lighting anywhere.

But most of all, Ana loved shopping in Nairobi having found a wonderful row of open-fronted shops in one of the back streets, selling everything from home-grown fruit and vegetables, wonderful smelling spices and hand-held Indian delicacies to eat: bhajias, samosas, mandazi, koftas and cassava chips… irresistible and delicious. So was falooda, a drink. The main flavour was rose syrup and although having a thick texture, it was drinkable like a milk shake. There was also a wonderful selection of dress fabrics, with dressmakers ready to sew whatever design she chose without using a pattern.

She also loved having coffee in The Thorn Tree café, right in the middle of the main street while reading the British newspapers that arrived a day late. Although she had only been a few times, some of the English ladies having their lunch started to greet her and asked her to join them for lunch on her next visit. They said to make sure she went to the wonderful lakes at Naivasha and Kisumu with their incredible flocks of pink flamingos which were pink from eating the algae and to take a holiday on the coast with its fabulous, white, sandy beaches in Kilifi and further up the coast at Malindi. Ana began to wonder if they were working for a holiday company! She had the feeling that as far as these women were concerned, Kenya belonged to them. It was their home and they would never return to Britain, independence or no independence and they were trying to recruit her to feel the same.

However, Ana wasn't that enthusiastic about joining them, listening to their artificial, frightfully posh accents and treating the waiters as if they didn't exist, except to complain to them. The waiters in their spotless white jackets and red fez hats, bowing profusely, backed away, murmuring "mimi-samahani". Ana soon discovered that meant sorry and she began to realize how financially important it was for them and their families that there were no complaints against them as they might lose their jobs. She also noticed the disgusted looks on the English ladies' faces when she gave generous tips to the waiters. "Asante-sana, memsahib, asante-sana, thank you." The waiters clasped their hands together as if in prayer and called after her, "Guahere, guahere. Goodbye, memsahib."

Ana and Ahinsa had got used to the distant sound of drums coming from the forests outside the estate almost every night. At times they sounded much closer than they actually were, but after a hard day's work, James fell sound asleep in one of the living room chairs, totally unaffected. Chege informed Ana that the local villagers brewed their own liquor, warige, a sort of Kenyan moonshine, from sugar cane, but also from anything that they could get their hands on to ferment... bananas and maize, brewing it for days, before drinking it once it was cold. Chege said that the potent alcohol could be lethal and one glass could render the drinker senseless or even dead. He grinned, adding, "Maybe you drink bottle of your Scotch, to get the same effect, memsahib?"

Chapter 4

ON THE NIGHT OF TERROR that brought matters to a head, James camped out on the veranda with a rifle on his lap. Ana and Ahinsa tried to get some sleep by sleeping under the bed. The baby, thankfully, heard nothing and slept on. The metal frames protecting the windows were already in place and the heavy metal door frames were locked and chained. Sounding closer and closer, the beating of the native drums grew louder and louder. When the drumming temporarily stopped, the silence was broken by long gargling, high pitched sounds from the women's throats, interspersed with shouts of "Harambee...harambee...harambee!!" Chege explained it meant "All pull together." *That wouldn't be a bad motto for many countries, but not tonight,* Ana thought. She also knew it was time to get the baby home to Scotland. Ahinsa had threatened to leave even if she had to walk to Mombasa, to get a berth back to Ceylon.

"That's it, James, I have decided and I won't take no for an answer." James tried unsuccessfully to interrupt Ana, till he finally raised both his hands and his voice.

"Ana, please!! I agree with you! I almost shot Chege by accident last night. The poor man had come back from his hut, to check on us. I know he's a Kikuyu, but he has been a faithful servant to my father and me since he was a young boy. I knew things were heating up, but thought the government would quell any riots. But I am not going to leave. My first crop is about to be harvested and I will not leave it to wilt and die. I have invested too much in this estate and before you think I am putting money before my family's lives...Well, that's just not true."

"I am talking about our daughter's safety, James! I am no coward. I was willing to make a dangerous journey from Portsmouth to Ceylon in 1942 but that pales into insignificance. You think I can't carry a gun? Try me. To my surprise I have fallen in love with this country and its wonderful people. I want us, you and me, to stay. I refuse to give up the daily drop-in clinics I have started with the Dutch nuns from the local convent. We help the sick and injured Kenyans, who have neither the money nor the transport to access any form of medical care. Soon I will organize ambulance transport to the hospitals in Nairobi. We have many cases of TB that need long-term care. I am not leaving you, but I cannot…I will not have my daughter's life put at risk."

"If you would just let me get a word in edgeways, Ana. I telegrammed Mr Norman Cunningham, the lawyer in your grandmother's letter, informing him I want to arrange a flight from Nairobi to London Airport for Ahinsa and Sofiya and I gave him several dates. Yesterday, I received a telegram back informing me that the baby will be met at London Airport and taken care of." James frowned a little. "Not sure what 'taken care' of means. He also assured me that someone will make sure Ahinsa gets a passage back to Ceylon. Happy now? We will miss our baby dreadfully but it's her safety we must think about. How about a second honeymoon on the beach in Malindi? It might help as a distraction from the way we are feeling."

Ana threw herself into James's arms as if she would never let him go. With tears flowing down her cheeks, Ana swallowed hard and told James, "That's little consolation for parting with our daughter, our baby, but we must ensure her safety."

Chapter 5

SOFIYA arrived at Embakasi Airport after a very pleasant seven-hour flight from London and prepared to disembark. Descending the aircraft steps she thought, *I believe my parents knew they would not survive and they would never be reunited with me. And in a way I also feel a deep sense of gratitude to my grandmother for not telling my parents I had been adopted.*

Walking to the entrance of the airport building to clear security and customs, Sofiya heard a shout from the viewing terrace above the entrance doorway. "Your Ladyship! Lady Sofiya!"

Sofiya looked up and knew right away it was Moonira, the librarian she had recently contacted to help her with her research. Moonira or Moonie as she insisted on being called, waved at her with both arms and was grinning from ear to ear. Moonie shouted, "I am going to wait for you in the arrival hall! Meet me there!"

By now the other passengers were pushing their way past her, encouraging her to move. Security was easy. "Jambo, memsahib. Habari...welcome," the custom officer added in English as he took her passport. He scarcely glanced at the passport or bothered to look to see if she had a visa. "Mzuri sana, memsahib... all good." Noticing her address, he smiled and said, "You are Scottish?" Nodding his head as if in approval, he signalled she should go to claim her luggage. Rows of suitcases were waiting and some of the passengers were being asked to open their luggage. No one seemed interested in hers and looking round for a trolley, she was virtually assaulted by Moonie throwing her arms round her. "Leave that, Lady Sofiya."

"Just Sofiya will do... please." Sofiya smiled at Moonie.

"OK. Juma our driver will deal with your luggage and I insist that you come home to stay with me and my family. I have told them all about you and they can't wait to meet you, especially since we have close family relatives living in Scotland."

"But are you sure you have room for me?"

"Sofiya, my uncle Anoo and my family own a large farm, estate would describe it better, five miles outside Nairobi. Now get in the car and I will tell you all about it and them."

Juma was obviously an experienced driver as he weaved his way in and out of the chaotic traffic on the road to the farm. Sofiya was spellbound by the views from the car windows. High up in the hills the temperature was a pleasant 25 degrees, with a cool breeze blowing. Arriving at the farm, Sofiya realized it was without doubt more like an estate, but this one had high, security metal railings round it as far as the eye could see, with double security gates, which mysteriously swung open as they arrived.

Two Kenyans both carrying rifles and two very angry looking German shepherd dogs, straining at their metal chain leads, barking their heads off, were standing guard.

"Security guards are on duty twenty-four hours a day," Moonie told her. "You have to be careful, Sofiya. We are lucky to be in a position to employ guards, not everyone is. When independence was declared, the British, who had been here for more than half a century, left. They just vanished without making any provisions for their loyal workers.

"You cannot imagine the number of decent, older men arriving at the doors in spotless, white houseboy coats, begging for work and presenting impeccable references from their previous memsahibs. The houseboys were left penniless and the new government is struggling with finance as it is. So, if some Kenyans steal anything that isn't nailed down you can't blame them. Here we are. Oh, my goodness, what a line up."

"Well, I hope they don't curtsey, Moonie!"

Moonie just laughed. "OK, handshakes only. This is my darling mum, Shamim. Wait till you taste her food; it's delicious. I hope you are not on a diet, although you might need to go on one when you get back home. And this is my lovely dad, Taher. He's a brilliant teacher; if you want to learn to speak Swahili, he's your man. My two sisters, Yasmin and Suraya. You have arrived just in time as we are all about to emigrate to Canada. And this lovely lady is our grandmother, or as we say, Mootiema. The name is not really a name from a proper language, Indian or Kenyan, but we love it and her. She is the dearest, kindest, most patient person in the world. Oh, by the way, she may not speak English, but she knows and understands every word. Be careful what you say in front of her. I am sure nowadays she would have gone to university… she is so intelligent. It's a shame really. She's the person to follow into the kitchen if you want to learn how to cook.

"Oh, before you leave us, don't let me forget to give you the names and addresses of my lovely cousins in Scotland. Zain is studying medicine at Glasgow University and his sister, Saira, law. So, if you ever need a lawyer, she is the one to contact. My dad says she is worse than a terrier dog. Once she gets her teeth in, she never lets go. She will never let you down. I don't think they will ever return to Kenya as they both have Scottish partners. Don't let Mootiema hear that; it's strictly against our culture," Moonie laughed.

"Come on, let's get you settled. I will take you to one of our guest bedrooms. It has an en-suite bathroom… you will be very comfortable. If you need anything the bed-pull is at the bedside and one of the house-boys will come. Feruzi is waiting. Give him your suitcase keys and he will empty your suitcases, hang everything up and sort out stuff to go in drawers and put your toiletries in the bathroom. He has already made you a cup of tea. Go sit by the window and take in the view. When you are ready, he will bring you to the garden. I will wait for you there. Did you take your medicine to prevent malaria?"

"Yes, my doctor prescribed chloroquine for me. As I am only here for a short time, I opted for a daily dose, not a weekly one."

"Good. Relax… see you in about half an hour. I want to take you round the grounds and the farm and we cannot go on ignoring why you are here. The quicker we get it over with, the quicker you will be able to come to terms with what I found out when I did my research for you… some sad, but also some comforting information. And then I want to take you on a tour of this amazing country before you return home, so you will want to return someday under different circumstances."

* * *

"These buildings over there are the cowsheds."

Sofiya, refreshed by a thirst-quenching cup of Kenya tea with lemon, walked through the most beautiful well-attended gardens. She was surprised to see how many plants were the same as at home. There was a vast expanse of roses, carnations, lilies and gypsophilla in abundance, and one she didn't recognize. Moonie informed her it was the unofficial national flower of Kenya, gloriosa superba, the flame lily, or poor man's orchid.

"My goodness, Moonie, how many cows does your uncle have?" Sofiya gasped as they approached the cowsheds. "And why aren't they in fields?"

"I wish I hadn't told you what they were. I should have avoided bringing you to see them."

"Well, you have to tell me now."

"They are not cows. They are male calves being fattened up for their meat, veal. They are very well fed, but housed in restricted, separated narrow stalls, so they are unable to move which makes the meat very tender."

"I understand, Moonie. I just wish I hadn't seen them. Anyway, I don't think I have ever tasted veal, but I have to confess I love a beef steak." There was a second reason she wished Moonie hadn't brought her to the cowsheds. It reminded Sofiya of the happy days she had spent in Texas, thoroughly enjoying thick barbecued Texan steaks with Johnny. Sofiya stopped walking and turned to face Moonie. "It's time, Moonie. Tell me what you found out or I won't be able to sleep tonight and I need to get it over with."

"Sofiya, both your parents are dead." Moonie paused to let that sink in. "There was one terrible night, not long after you were sent home to Scotland when the Kikuyu, known as the Mau Mau, rose up in protest against the imprisonment and treatment meted out by the British police and army against thousands of Kikuyu. I refuse to give you any more details. It is distressing enough to learn of their deaths without me elaborating on what happened. I was told they didn't suffer. In fact, the person who gave me the information said they probably died together while they slept in their bed. So tomorrow we will leave for Nakuru by car. Juma will drive us and there is someone there waiting, desperate to meet you."

* * *

The next day, Moonie indicated to Sofiya that she should go up to the old bungalow by herself and reminded her nearly all the tea and coffee estates were now owned by Kenyan planters. She also told her, not to get a surprise or be upset as probably the gardens round the bungalow would have all been dug up and banana trees and crops like maize planted. "They have to eat, Sofiya, so they cultivate where they can. There's no ground wasted on flowers."

Sofiya walked up the short hill on her own, to the place from where she had been sent back to Scotland and where her parents had died. She suddenly thought, *Lord, I should have brought flowers.* But there was no need. An elderly, virtually toothless old African gentleman wearing what looked like a very old, hand-knitted, woolly bunnet, appeared from out of the cornfield with an armful of native flowers. He called out to Sofiya, "Jambo, Jambo, memsahib. You were mtoto last time I saw you. Habari? I'm Chege... habari?" Chege handed Sofiya the flowers and beckoned her to follow him.

Further up the hill, on a flat piece of ground near the bungalow, Chege stopped at a rough mound of earth. "We bury mama na baba here. No mzuri, no good business... Samahari, sorry, sorry, memsahib. Now, B'wana Kuba, big boss come with box. Said had to put in grave!"

Sofiya stood for a moment by her parents' grave, comforted by how well the local people all these years ago had honoured them and given them a decent funeral and burial place, but best of all was that Sofiya felt sure her grandmother had been reunited with her children in the same place. The recently disturbed mound of earth was evidence of that. When she returned to Nairobi she would ask Moonie to help her organize a grave stone, to mark her parents' and grandmother's grave site. Placing the flowers

Chege had given her on the mound of grass-covered earth, she turned and walked back down the hill.

Moonie left Sofiya to her thoughts as Juma drove them home. Just before they reached Nairobi, Sofiya turned to Moonie. "Back home we mourned for a woman who my family and I thought was my great-aunt Jane. It was only a short time ago we discovered who she really was. I felt sad I had not known this before she died. Now I have said goodbye to my grandmother. Thank you, Moonie."

"But... your parents, Sofiya?"

"If there is a God I hope he forgives me, Moonie, but I felt nothing, had no feelings at all for my birth-parents. How can you mourn for people you never knew existed till a few months ago? We were all victims of the time. My only regret is that I wasn't brought up in this wonderful country."

Chapter 6

ON THE FLIGHT BACK from Nairobi, Sofiya couldn't help wondering, who was the B'wana kubwa, the boss Chege spoke of and who had obtained a death certificate, when no one had informed the local council of her death? And where had her grandmother been cremated, when all the investigations, in local crematoria Sofiya had made, came up negative? She doubted she would ever find out. But her birth parents and her grandmother were together for eternity, and her grandmother's wishes had been fulfilled. These thoughts made her journey home calm and very peaceful.

When Sofiya arrived back at Mount View having gone to her parents' house first, she was met as usual by Cathie at the front door. "We're awe that gled yer back, safe and sound, Miss Sofiya."

"How's baby Harriet?"

"Much better… they antibiotics did the trick. But afore ye unpack yer stuff, gan awa in tae the sitting room. Here's an important looking letter that arrived when ye were awa. Sit doon and read it." Cathie handed a large brown envelope to Sofiya. "We didna ken if it wus important or no, but there wis nae wey we could get it tae ye. Then awa up an see the bairn."

"Thank you, Cathie. A cup of tea would be appreciated." Sofiya recognized the company stamp on the envelope.

"A'll awa an pit the kettle on." Cathie nodded, as she saw Sofiya open the envelope.

Dear Lady Leightham,

I work for the lost person research company you employed to try to find the whereabouts of a relative of yours and as you know my company, after intensive research, failed to trace your relative. I apologize for taking the liberty of continuing the search without your permission.

Our company is normally employed to trace people who are still alive and with advertising, talking to relatives and neighbours, and even a paper trail, they can be traced. In this case, 'we hit the wall' at every turn. But I was not convinced we had tried hard enough and refusing to be defeated I continued the search in my own time and it paid off.

It seemed to me that, if I decided I did not want my relatives to be upset by having to plan my funeral, whether burial or cremation, I would find a way to have my body taken somewhere else, without their knowledge. And that is exactly what this person did.

I finally tracked down a funeral director in Glasgow who was willing to tell me of a rather unusual case. It appears he had been approached by a lawyer from Edinburgh, a Mr Norman Cunningham. The funeral director said he was very impressed by the man's genuine affection for his client and the lawyer had presented a letter confirming the arrangements to be made when they died.

In the middle of the night a few months later, the funeral director received a phone call from the lawyer who directed him as arranged to urgently send an unmarked hearse and two undertakers to the address he had been given. The lawyer had received a phone call. No one spoke. Hearing very faint breathing before the line went dead, he went right away to the house and looking in the lounge window realized the person was slouching in a chair and not breathing. He ran back home to collect a set of house keys the client had given him and phone the funeral director. To be honest, he wasn't sure what he would have done otherwise if it had been during the day, but it had gone to plan and he could fulfil their wishes. The person was elderly, there were no suspicious circumstances and Mr Cunningham would meet them at the address in Fife.

The only minor problem that night was they had taken longer to arrive than expected. Mr Cunningham returned to the house and waited in the porch for the undertakers to show them where to go for the body, but to his horror, the housekeeper had come downstairs and found the person had passed away! Thankfully the woman was so distressed he saw her flee with her bag from the house.

The funeral director, as instructed, took the body to Glasgow. Apparently, Mr Cunningham presented his credentials to the crematorium and to the director's astonishment the lawyer demanded an immediate cremation and that the ashes be given to him right away as his client had instructed that the ashes be taken by him to Kenya, for burial.

Perhaps you already know of this person's final resting place, but I thought you should know the details I discovered and the circumstances of what I must confess, is a very unusual, almost unbelievable history of what happened. I hope it gives you peace of mind that all this person's wishes had been carried out.

I remain,
Yours truly...

Sofiya could hardly believe what she had just read. *So that's who Chege described as the Bwana Kubwa!*

Sofiya reached out to put the letter on the coffee table and realized the table was missing and so were the two Parker Knoll chairs!

PART EIGHT

Chapter 1

Leightham House Restored

"SO, YOU GOT OUT THEN?! Not charged as a British spy?" Jim had spent many sleepless nights waiting for news of his daughter and he snapped at her from sheer relief that she had returned safely from Russia and Kenya.

"Give it a rest, Dad. I knew the risk before I left, but I met some decent people in both countries. And in Russia not all of them have been brainwashed with communism, but they have no option but to obey, whether they agree with the regime or not. The prospect of life in a Russian jail and worse is terrifying. But Dad, it almost brought tears to my eyes, and you know I don't cry easily, when I met my great-aunt, Princess Kseniya. She is now over 70 and when she looked up from her chair in the ballet school's retirement home and saw me, she stared at me and in perfect English whispered, 'Miss Alice, Miss Alice, you have come back for me!' Marina calmed her down and asked her if she knew where her sister Lera was. She gave some furtive glances round her and looked blank as if she was afraid to speak in case someone overheard.

"Marina confided in me later that Lera had probably been captured and killed by the Bolsheviks or the newly formed Red Army and they would have destroyed all the evidence. It was an unexpected joy to meet the old lady, but she said very little about her past or her life as a young princess. I got the feeling she was afraid to acknowledge she was Russian Royalty, or who she really was, but for survival most people of her age group were too frightened to admit to anything regarding their past.

"I bet my grandmother regretted not taking the girls with her when she fled in 1917 because of the Bolshevik uprising. My visit to both countries was an experience I would not have missed for the world. So please, no more on the subject of Russia or Kenya, Dad. I am back and unlikely to ever return to either country and please don't press me on the subject of my parents… it's too painful. The good thing was the comforting news that my grandmother had had her ashes taken to Kenya and had them interred in my parents' and her children's graves.

"Where's Mum?"

"Well, as we had no idea what time you would be back and grace us with your presence, your mum went to visit her aunt Lil, you know the one who lives with the ex-nun who was put out the nunnery in Rome because she was too worldly? Apparently, she was looking at the hats in the shops. I think it was more likely she was looking too much at the other postu…."

"Dad!! That's her business and we have all known for years about my great-aunt Lil. So what if she uses Brylcreem in her hair and wears brogue shoes? She is one of the kindest, most generous people I know. I think it's sad she has been born in a time when women are expected to marry, have children and stay in the kitchen rolling out pastry! It's about time attitudes change. The poor woman suffered three ghastly months of marriage to please her family, before she divorced George Chalmers."

"I don't dislike your great-aunt's friend. I suppose she didn't have much choice. She was one of thirteen children and her family decided she was to become a nun and sent her to Rome. When she was asked to leave the convent, she then decided to train as a nurse and that's where Lil met her, when Lil was working as a sister tutor in Nottingham and brought her back to Scotland with her.

Poor as a church mouse when she pulled up her chair and supped at Lil's table, as your old granny would say. Lil's no short o' a bob or two and the woman's a lot younger than Lil. Now Lil's building a fine bungalow for them to live in; they're calling it *The Dykes,* as they both come from towns with the syllable 'dyke' in it."

"Dad, Lil's found love and support in her relationship with Ciara Nugent. After what I have experienced in the field of love, with a man, it might have put me off for life. But I have found someone, but I doubt there's much chance of him arranging for us to jump out of a plane, parachuting down and proposing on one knee once we hit the ground to impress me. But I have been there. I am not bitter, but that kind of romantic love is for the young. Neil knows all about me and my past. His love and support are all I need, and it wouldn't surprise me if he got his mother to buy the engagement ring for him, *if* he decides he does wants to marry me. His medical mind and brains are on another planet, except at Rugby matches.

"Right, give Mum a hug for me. I'm off. I will go and see what's happening at my house, but I can't wait to move in, Dad."

Grinning from ear to ear at the thought his daughter might need resuscitation both when she saw the house and what was going to happen next, he told Sofiya to go to the main entrance, not the back one. For a fleeting moment, Sofiya wondered what her dad was grinning about.

* * *

Sofiya did as she was told and as she turned into the main drive her jaw dropped! Gone was the one remaining stone animal and the crumbled pillars. In their place and restored to their original splendour were two refurbished

229

pillars with tall, majestic, black wrought-iron gates. Two stunning gilded deer atop the gates locked antlers when the gates were closed. But these gates had now mysteriously swung open! Jim had placed the automatic fob in Sofiya's car so the gates would seem to open by themselves, just for her.

The long main drive, previously impassable, now resembled the drive of its heyday. Sofiya smiled, remembering the story of Alice, arriving for the first time as a young girl to work at the big house and walking up the main drive and being ticked off by the estate worker, Stanley Whitehill, and sent to the servants' entrance at the back. Thick overgrown grass on the verges had been cleared and replanted with new grass seed. A huge field where one of the original cornfields had been, large enough to house a football or cricket pitch, had also been cleared and planted with grass seed. The road had been covered with fresh tarmacadam. The old Scots pine trees on either side, looking incredibly majestic, had been pruned. Sofiya put the car in gear and continued on her way.

Gobsmacked, was the word that came into Sofiya's mind to describe how she felt. Parking her car at the side of the now unrecognizable renovated house, she ignored several other cars parked there and made her way to the front entrance. Standing at the bottom of the semi-circular, stone steps to the front door, stood Dixie, Nathaniel and Harry. Sofiya was surprised. How did they know she was coming? The three men stepped forward in unison and bowed. Dixie presented Sofiya with a large bouquet of yellow roses, and Nate and Harry gave Sofiya a large, heavy Georgian door key sitting on a silk cushion, before inviting her to walk up the steps to the solid wood front door.

"Welcome home, your ladyship," Dixie murmured, adding "Got it right for once."

Almost overwhelmed, Sofiya managed to nod her head, but all she could say was, "Thank you, guys."

"You won't thank us when you get the bill, your ladyship."

"You got it right for once, Dixie, and you know full well the bill will surprise no one." Sofiya smiled at the man.

In his whole career, Dixie had never enjoyed working on a project as much as this one. He considered it a privilege, had put his heart and soul into it, realizing it was highly unlikely he would ever get a project like this again. But he felt certain her ladyship would turn to him for future repairs and maintenance.

The ancient, heavy Georgian door with its years of weather damage and green mould, had stood the test of time and now cleaned, the outer edges of the original six long panels had been outlined with impressive brass nobs. On either side of the door were portals of freshly repaired and scrubbed stone. Above the lintel, a semi-circle of carved stone with the number 1755, freshly chiselled where the original number had been, completed the awe-inspiring entrance.

Sofiya unlocked the door and proceeded through the newly-tiled vestibule. Opening the glass inner-door, she entered the reception hall.

Clutching at her throat, her eyes stinging with emotional tears, Sofiya couldn't take it in, but one phrase kept going through her mind. *I am home. Home with three hundred years of Leightham family history.* "I think my heart will burst with happiness, lads; I am almost speechless. It is the end of an old era and the beginning of a new one. Thank you."

Again, a fog of happiness engulfed Sofiya as the three men explained in turn what projects were still left to be finished, but certainly this grand reception hall wasn't one of them. A deceptively real-looking wood log gas fire burned in the Adam fireplace. The sun shone through the tall windows lighting every painting, every artefact. A magnificent gold inlaid French Boulle Cabinet, the only piece of furniture, stood against one wall.

"The windows are reproduction Charles Rennie Macintosh, double glazed and framed in oak," Nathaniel explained. "Astral bars have been inserted to maintain their authentic, traditional appearance. All the ceilings and walls are now sound."

Harry Fairgrieve spoke up next. "All the authentic Georgian plaster moulding, swag and drop design cornice have been copied and inserted between ceiling and wall. A narrower variation put up as a picture rail below the cornice and Georgian moulding to architrave, round doors and windows, walls and matching moulding to the skirting board."

Not to be outdone, that seemed to spurn Dixie into announcing his part in all of it. How the walls had been tested and plasterboard sheeting mounted to all internal wall surfaces and re-plastered where necessary. Dixie flicked a brass electric light switch and the magnificent crystal chandelier, hanging from the decorative plaster rose in the centre of the hall ceiling, burst into a thousand magical lights, beautifully illuminating a painting.

"My painting...my painting! Dixie, you are a genius! I can hardly recognize it. It's so...so..."

"Clean? Aye, the lads did a grand job wi bread and a coat of very light varnish."

"Bread?!"

"Aye, the best cleaner fur auld oil paintings."

Dixie could be a pain in the b-t-m at times, wanting all the praise for himself.

"Aye, your ladyship, Irene and Cathie wanted everythin tae be perfect for your return. Awe your own belongings, furnishings from Mount View and lorries full of stuff stored in Cards House fur years wus brung oor frae Edinburgh, ready for you to move in. That life-size painting of the Russian girl or princess on that incredible black stallion was the first object dealt with and a new coat of gold leaf was applied tae its ornate frame to restore it to its former glory."

Sofiya suddenly remembered Nate and Harry had intimated to her before she left last time that there might be a surprise on her return.

"Wait! Stay still, your ladyship. Look down at the floor. This is your surprise, a gift from us, *from Russia with love* but with one change, the central design."

Dixie searched in his pockets for a handkerchief, but Harry found his unused one and looking away, slightly embarrassed, handed it to Sofiya whose eyes shone with tears. What a reward for all the unbelievable hard work of the skilled joiners who had studied the requirements to be able to cope with the insanely difficult work required.

"Oh, my, god, it's the parquet floor from the Skavronsky Palace! How did you find all the different coloured woods?"

Dixie was ready to burst. "Do ye remember the last time ye were here? Ye nearly spilt the secret. Remember the pile o wid happit under the tarpaulin ye wanted tae look at? It wis this. We hid tae keep the different woods waitin tae come intae the hoose, till the hoose wis waterticht. The parquet blocks are less prone tae moving and warping and hiv tae be acclimatized and the flair under it… dry as a board tae prevent it warpin. It's been sanded and a coat o' fine varnish on it tae prevent it fadin' in the sunlight and marked wi onythin bein' spilt on it."

"Sorry, Dixie, give me a break," or it will be your blood spilt on the floor, Harry thought. "Your ladyship, we photographed every square inch of the Skavronsky Palace and this is the design, but with one exception. Look down at your feet. For generations, your family were fishing folks in the East Neuk, and your dad and aunt inWW2 had connections to the sea. We know some of your own history, of studying and travelling abroad. Yes, it's a compass. Your dad lent us his to copy. You are standing on the south point, looking north and on your right the east and the west to the left. Where will you travel to next, your ladyship?"

"Nowhere, Harry. I am home for good! I could not love your design more. I... Oh, what on earth is that noise?" Sofiya enquired.

Suddenly the dining room doors burst open. Champagne corks exploded into the air! Sofiya's whole family and dear friends pushed their way in, led by her dad with an open bottle of champagne in one hand and another ready to open in the other, followed by Susan and Neil Martin.

"I don't believe it! You are a romantic after all!" Sofiya gasped, as Neil came forward with his mother pushing him, muttering, "I wouldn't say that."

Neil went down on one knee and opened a box containing a glittering diamond engagement ring,

"Will you marry me, Sofiya? Don't worry, I have asked your dad's permission."

"I am not worried whether you have his permission or not," Sofiya grinned with a fleeting glance at Jim, surely the best dad in the world, "Yes...yes, I will marry you, Neil!"

A deafening roar erupted from everyone present and more champagne corks exploded as Neil and Sofiya embraced and kissed each other. Jim was almost in tears with sheer relief. There was a God after all and he couldn't wait to escort her down the aisle and the sooner the better!

Dixie interrupted the romantic scene nervously, "Like a said, yer Ladyship, the champagne will no spile the flair, ye see we pit..."

"Yes, I know, Dixie. You varnished the floor, but no dogs on it yet! Now I know why there were so many cars at the side of the house when I arrived. It was you lot... Granny, aunt Nan, aunt Jessie, Margo, Phil, you came all the way from England? Mum, you didn't go to visit aunt Lil. You were here all the time. I must be losing it in my old age."

Out of the corner of her eye, she could see Paula jumping up and down shouting, "I'm going to be a flower girl, I'm going to be a flower girl," while her brother, Tony, looked disgusted at the thought of having to wear a kilt.

At the end of a wonderful evening, Cathie came forward to hug Sofiya. "We are on our way home with the baby. It makes no difference to her whether it's day or night. We all love her and thank you for arranging a night nurse. Irene and I have put everything you need here in your beloved new home. Will Neil stay with you?" Cathie asked innocently.

"Cathie, I love you! Go home, take care of our girl. See you soon."

The next morning very early, Sofiya stretched and yawned, waking up after her first night in the most beautiful bedroom she had ever slept in, when she became aware of voices, yet no one was in the house but her! Slipping into her dressing gown, Sofiya went out to the upper hall, but there was no one there. It was Saturday and no one worked there on a Saturday. Running back into the bedroom she opened the curtains and looked out of the window.

She couldn't believe it. There on the lawn, were two young girls with their arms around each other making their way towards the cornfields. She couldn't see their faces, but one was slim with vivid red hair and wore a simple housemaid's dress. The other a shorter, chubbier girl, was wearing a very large flower-embellished hat, and seemed to be giggling, laughing and colliding into the other more sober girl in fun. Sofiya blinked again, opened her eyes, but the girls had disappeared! She must have been dreaming or had drunk too much champagne last night!? Or, Sofiya felt with a strange warmth, was it the Leightham House staff from days gone by, come to reassure the Leightham forebears, the house was in good hands? Sofiya never saw or heard them again.

* * *

"That was spooky, mum."

"Strangely enough, I didn't feel the least bit frightened and, like I said, I never saw, or heard any ghosts in the house or gardens again."

"But mum, they were not the only 'ghosts' you ever saw, were they? What about the man with the German shepherd dog you wrote about on Pittendreal beach when you were a young woman." Sophie reminded her. "And in Russia, Hamish the dog, and the prince with his two little princesses in the gardens of the Skavronsky Palace?!"

Sofiya smiled a poignant smile. Sophie thought her mother was looking back, but it was not the memory of the man on the beach Sofiya was remembering… it was her marriage to Neil.

"Sophie, here are the last of my memories for you to read about my younger days and nothing to do with ghosts. They are very personal. They are regarding my marriage to your father and not up for discussion." Sofiya handed her daughter a few pages of hardcopy and indicated to her she should leave now and read them in private.

Chapter 2

S OPHIE SAT BESIDE her mother wondering what would come next, what was so private? She heard her mother muttering about reading this chapter when she was totally alone and to remember it was both painful and sad for her to write and for the part she played in it.

"As a family we fared better than most..." Sofiya shook her head. "How lucky young people are now to be able to live with their partner before committing to each other for the rest of their lives, to get to know each other, socially, physically and sexually, without relatives or neighbours disapproving and insisting on marriage before they are positive about making a long-term commitment.

"Celebrate my life, Sophie. When the time comes, don't mourn my death. Remember the quotes I like. 'It is better to laugh, than to cry'. 'Think of the good times and draw a line under the bad'.

"I know, when you read this, it will bring back many happy memories of your young life but also there were times, however hard I tried to conceal our arguments and differences from you, you overheard and were aware of our unhappiness. You certainly were aware of that before the last disastrous trip your father and I took together.

"Your dad and I married too soon after he proposed to me. It was my fault. I didn't insist we wait a little longer, to get to know each other and I am not proud of my motive for marrying him. I was on the rebound from Johnny Geiger, knocked for six by being jilted by him.

"It left me devastated, robbed me of my confidence and made me deeply depressed. After being with Johnny for several years and giving my all to him... ready to leave my family and move to another country to be with him, he just walked away! My family and close friends thought I would never recover, but with their support I did. Sometimes I think men are more in control of their emotions than women. But I have struggled with my conscience. I loved your father, a medical soul mate, but I was never 'in-love' with him, whatever that means."

Sophie watched her mother put the document on the coffee table. It was hard to get what her mother had just said out of her mind and it was obvious her mother was also thinking about the contents of the document.

* * *

Neil and Sofiya left their wedding reception in Cards House very late on Saturday night. Arriving back at Leightham House, Sofiya went down to the kitchen and found the cold supper Cathie had left for the newlyweds on the kitchen table. Sofiya put the kettle on as Neil took the luggage up to their bedroom to unpack. Sofiya smiled to herself wondering what Neil would think of that beautiful master bedroom. She had instructed Cathie to leave the bedside lights on and the curtains wide open. It would be so romantic. Taking two mugs of tea and the plate of sandwiches upstairs, she found Neil emptying one of his suitcases all over the bed and the floor. A pile of books and papers were already on the bedside table.

Sofiya wasn't too sure what to do next. Neil was now stacking medical books and journals against the bedroom wall and totally ignoring her. She walked over to the window, sat down and drank her cup of tea. If she and Johnny had been separated for any length of time, Johnny could hardly keep his hands off her. Neil knew full well she was no virgin bride, in fact there was nothing he didn't know about her past.

Sofiya didn't know anything about Neil's past relationships with women before he met her. He was a bit older than she was and he must have had at least one long-term relationship. His mother wasn't going to give her that information any more than Neil was. It seemed to Sofiya that Susan had done everything in her power to get Neil to propose and marry her as soon as possible. His mother had gone full-pelt into organizing the wedding, before anyone could change their mind, by making sure the Banns were called the very next week in Leightham Parish Church. Susan had also phoned a fine-dining company in Edinburgh to provide the wedding dinner at Cards House, much to Ina's irritation. That was her job, as mother-of-the-bride, but who argues with doctors? And who argues with their mother-in-law-to-be? Maybe Susan wanted to be a grandmother before she got any older.

Sofiya would love to have a family, but at this rate it wasn't going to happen anytime soon. She thought that wanting children might have been another reason for her decision to marry so quickly. Apart from the fact they were both doctors and shared a liking for Rugby, what other interest did they share? Only time would tell. The old proverbial saying, "marry in haste..." also went through her mind.

At last Neil looked up. "Done! I've put my toiletries in the bathroom. Just give me a minute."

"No problem, Neil. I was beginning to think you had forgotten all about me."

Neil ignored that comment. "Just going for a shower Sofiya... what a luxury."

Sofiya dropped her voice. "Thank you, Neil." She tried not to sound too sarcastic.

By now it was almost the middle of the night. Neil, having taken his time, came out of the bathroom grinning from ear to ear. "Your turn, Mrs Martin," he announced.

Sofiya showered as fast as she could and quickly changed into a beautiful French peignoir and nightdress. Suddenly Sofiya was overcome with a sensation she rarely felt... shy. She realized this was the first time she had been totally alone with him. Walking to the bed and keeping her eyes down, she wondered what to do next. Should she take her dressing gown off, then slip the thin straps of her nightdress down and let it fall to the floor? Scottish men were not exactly known for their romantic gestures so it was unlikely Neil would do this. A bunch of flowers was as much as she received in the last few weeks and she was certain Susan had bought them for Neil to give her.

The sound of pages being turned roused her from her dilemma and made her look up. She couldn't believe her eyes. Neil was still in his dressing gown stretched out on the bed with his reading glasses on and seemed to be totally unaware of her. The man was absorbed in reading a handful of hand-written medical notes. Sofiya slipped out of her dressing gown and lay next to Neil. She stared nervously at the ceiling.

My God is this what my life is going to be like from now on? Am I to play second fiddle to his work... even in bed?!

Neil, dropped the paperwork onto the floor, took his glasses off, stood up and stripped bare before lying down on the top of the bed. Sofiya turned to face him. Her jaw dropped open, as she looked at his already erect penis. Without a word, he calmly removed Sofiya's nightdress, pulled her astride his hips and whether she was ready or not, entered her by pushing her buttocks up and down, until he reached his own climax, then moved her back to her side of the bed. *Well at least I didn't get a mouthful of his chest hair as I did with Johnny.* Johnny was an accomplished lover. Neil was not.

To make matters worse, Neil turned to face Sofiya and announced, "We are not going to France for our honeymoon on Monday as I had planned. There is a medical conference in Amsterdam next week on the theories of porphyria. We will go there instead. I know you are keen to keep your medical information up to date and we will be joined by Imdad, Abe and their wives. We can all have dinner on one of the canal boats in the evenings."

Sofiya took a deep breath, got up as Neil fell asleep, put on her dressing gown and went downstairs for a glass of water. She couldn't take it in. Not only did Neil suffer from premature ejaculation... he was a control freak as well. *Better get used to it... you married him!*

* * *

Time passes at an alarming rate. "Oh, not again mum! ... Italy then Utrecht. Where next are you and dad going?!" Sophie wailed. "It's almost Christmas. Dad promised me he would help put up the decorations this year and light the bonfire for Hogmanay. He said I am old enough to stay up now! It's not fair. Who are you going to palm me off on this time, granny Ina or grandma Susan?"

"I know, darling, and I am sorry, but your dad has agreed to give a lecture to the medical students in Stockholm on his latest research into human DNA fingerprinting. I know you are not interested, but I am and very proud of him and the research team. He says they can work on just a teaspoon of human blood and in another ten years, all they will need will be a single drop of blood, just one cell to get the same results and he is working on that now.

"So, who is it going to be? We will only be away three days and will be back in good time for Christmas."

"Granny Ina. I always have a good time with her and granddad. She taught me to knit when I was only four, and how to chop vegetables to make soup, and we need to make our bramble jeelie. She said last week she had defrosted the brambles we picked in September, boiled them and strained them through the jeelie bag. All we have to do is add the sugar and simmer it till the bramble jeelie thickens. We can also make granny's home-made ginger wine for Hogmanay at the same time and granddad's black bun. Yuk, I hate black bun. I always get the currant seeds in my teeth!" Sophie had cheered up. "And I love going down to the cove with granny and granddad, even in the winter and it looks like snow this weekend. I can go sledging!"

"Down the beach, Sophie, in winter?!"

"Yes. Granny and me make…"

"I, Sophie. Granny and I."

"Granny Fairgrieve always has a poke ready for me when I visit her on Sundays with iced gingerbread, her home-made Scottish tablet, and Smith's crisps. Granny and I will make a poke of goodies to take with us to the beach. We will make scones before we go as well and we'll both get covered in flour," Sophie giggled. "I like them better than pancakes on the beach. Pancakes crumble before we get there. Granddad puts the windbreak up, then the folding chairs, granny says for us to coorie doon on, then granddad lights the primus stove to heat the milk and water and makes us hot cocoa. It's delicious. Mm."

I hope he doesn't lace his with Scotch whisky! Sofiya thought.

"OK you win. I will get them to come over on Friday."

When Neil arrived back home from Edinburgh, he threw his coat and bulging briefcase on the kitchen table, gave Sofiya a perfunctory kiss on the cheek before hugging Sophie and scrunching up her hair, much to her annoyance.

"Don't, dad. I am getting too old for that." Sophie went towards the stairs to the hall.

"Sorry, young lady," he called after her.

"Sofiya, I have just had an invitation to give a lecture in South Africa, but I will have to fly out on the 22nd and I have booked your ticket to go with me. Sophie can stay with my mother for Christmas. It's too important for us… for me to miss."

"This is the last straw, Neil. On our wedding night, when you told me you had rearranged our honeymoon and we would be sharing it with other people, I thought you were a control freak! You are a married bachelor *and* a control freak!! No! When we get back from Stockholm, you are on your own. I am not spending Christmas in South Africa and don't bring Imdad and Abe or their wives into it. They are lovely people, but Christmas isn't really their celebration."

"There will be plenty of other Christmases and Hogmanays to celebrate. This is a once in a lifetime invitation. Please yourself… don't come! I am going for a shower."

"Thinking of yourself as usual. What about thinking of your daughter for once?! Damn you!"

Sophie heard her parents shouting and arguing. Usually her parents' disagreements were very one sided, as if her father was wearing earplugs, but not today.

* * *

Sofiya arrived back from Stockholm in a taxi, in the middle of a snow storm. "Hi, everybody! Susan, I wasn't expecting to see you. Neil wouldn't stop talking to his professorial colleagues, I'd had enough. I wanted to get home before it got dark." Sofiya busied herself brushing the snowflakes from her hair and tried not looking at anyone in particular.

"The Stains Road is getting worse with the subsidence from the coal mines. It's like a switchback railroad and even more treacherous with the ice and snow. I would have tried to phone Neil at the airport to warn him, but he's probably left." Sofiya took her coat off before becoming aware of an ominous silence. Looking up she could see Cathie and Irene and her daughter's white face.

Sophie ran towards her mother and burst into tears. A cold hand gripped Sofiya's chest. Fearing the worst, she asked, "What's wrong? Why is everyone here?" Sofiya held her sobbing daughter close, stroking her hair, trying to comfort her.

"You had better sit down, Sofiya... Neil's dead," Jim told her. "He was killed on his way back home. Sergeant Wilson phoned us with the news. Apparently, there was a car full of young men...joyriders. The driver, only eighteen, had just passed his driving test and was driving at full speed over the top of one of the worst subsidence mounds. He lost control and skidded right into Neil's car coming in the opposite direction. Neil's car was hit full on, the car spun and rolled over several times, flattening the roof and ended up in a ditch after hitting a tree." Jim took a breath. "He didn't stand a chance, Sofiya. All the young lads died as well. God help their families and us." Jim walked over to the drinks cabinet and poured himself and Sofiya a large glass of Scotch.

* * *

"I want you to remember, when you read this Sophie, it happened a long time ago and although it took time, I have forgiven myself for the part I played. The hard part was forgetting. And in those years children rarely attended funerals. Thankfully, a number of years later I met Charles and he helped me come to terms with your father's death. Well, I've talked enough gloom and doom. I'm fine now." Sofiya smiled. "Your dad would heve been so proud of you and his grandchildren, but I bet he would have had a soft spot for Sophia. She aims high and like him, very single minded and never lets anything get in her way. Off you go now and give my lovely grandchildren a big hug from me."

PART NINE

Chapter 1

SOPHIE dropped her daughter off at the Leightham Mall to meet with Selina and Alex, Sophia's school friends, to go shopping. Iain had taken the other three children to the cinema to watch the latest Walt Disney movie, which gave Sophie the whole of Sunday afternoon to spend with her mother. Continuing on her way to Leightham House, Sophie smiled. There were times she wished she could 'freeze-dry' each of her children at a certain stage of their young lives, so she could enjoy them for just a bit longer, as they seemed to grow up so quickly. Sophie remembered playing with her pram and dolls until she was nine or ten years old, but Savanna had more or less discarded her toys by the age of eight, much to her grandmother's disbelief.

Apart from taking Savanna swimming, Sofiya saw little of her granddaughter these days, which was unlike her daughter's and her own childhood. They had spent a lot of their free time with their grandmothers doing jigsaw puzzles, baking, knitting and learning other practical skills. Nowadays her grandchildren did nothing but play electronic games on their Apple iPads, which apart from homework, seemed to absorb their every waking minute while at home. 'Dit-dit machines', Sofiya called them in disgust. She felt at times neglected by her grandchildren who rarely heard her arrive at their house when she visited.

There were no longer shouts of "Grandma!" to greet her or the hugs and kisses that used to follow. Sophia had to be dragged out of her bedroom to say hello to her grandmother, that is if she wasn't absorbed with social media and texting her friends. It was the same when she left. Sophie had to shout, "Grandma's leaving!" That always worked. Bedroom doors were flung open and the pounding of feet on the stairs heralded the children coming to say goodbye, rapidly followed by them running back up the stairs to their bedrooms to continue playing their on-line games with their friends. Sofiya began to think that when she was asked to babysit, she was only there to make sure her grandchildren didn't set fire to the house!

Sofiya knew how important it was that her grandchildren were mod-tech literate, but at times she wondered how safe they were spending so much time alone, isolated in their bedrooms. There were reports of children becoming depressed and worse, especially if the parents were not aware of whom their children were communicating with. And weren't they missing out on other activities in their young lives, activities she had had with her grandmother? Her daughter told her she remembered reading in one of the chapters of her mother's previous work, that one of her forebears had wisely said that life was short at its longest. How very true. With the blink of an eye all her grandchildren were out of nursery school and in primary school or in Sophia's case about to leave high school. Where had the time gone?

The year had passed with lightning speed and it was December again. Driving along the rhododendron-lined rear entrance of her childhood home, Sophie noticed a light sprinkling of frost on the ground and on the leaves of the evergreen trees and plants. These were changed days from her childhood when the branches of the trees on the estate sagged with the weight of fallen snow. The oak and beech tree leaves, recently an autumnal red and orange colour, were now stark, bare, brown skeletons devoid of their leaves, as were the handkerchief tree and the golden magnolia, the leaves of which Ronald and the estate staff diligently cleared as they fell, sweeping them into large wire mesh containers to be used as mulch the following year. Douglas fir and Scots pine trees were growing in readiness 'for the Christmas-tree markets.

One very large holly tree with bright red berries was ready to be cut down for the great hall of Leightham House. Her mother insisted on having one each year, irrespective of its prickly needles. Sofiya had argued in the past that because of the tree's bright red berries, only fairy lights needed to be added as it didn't require further decoration, but this would be the last year a tree would be cut down. In future Sofiya decided she would have a much smaller holly tree, dug up and rooted in a plant pot in the hall, which would be replanted back in the estate grounds after Christmas. Sophie knew copious bunches of mistletoe collected from the woods round the estate would be hung on the hall doors, much to the delight of the children, Iain, the house and estate staff during the Christmas-day celebrations.

In April, Sophie had been desperate to begin reading her mother's work, but it had been impossible to get time to concentrate during the weeks that followed and it seemed like every weekend there had been some function requiring her attention, such as the boys' birthday parties and taking them to their friends' birthday parties in return, as well as sleepovers and play-dates, a modern invention designed to let parents off the hook for the night.

The seven weeks of the entire school summer holidays were always spent at her mother's villa in Marbella, sunbathing on the beach, swimming and jumping over the swirling surf of the Mediterranean and building sandcastles. Sofiya's favourite occupation with the children was taking them beachcombing for seashells and crazy misshapen pieces of driftwood that resembled skeletons, animals or ancient human faces. Friends who were also on holiday joined them for numerous pool parties and barbeques.

Relaxing on a sunbed with a cocktail in her hand, Sophie generally read the silly romantic novels she had picked up at the airport's newsagents, as they didn't require much in the way of concentration while basking in the Spanish sunshine. It had been impossible to concentrate on reading her mother's more serious work because of enjoyable family trips to water parks, eating out and excursions to Gibraltar, to take advantage of the duty-free perfumes and cosmetics while the younger children enjoyed excursions up 'The Rock' to watch the antics of troupes of Barbary Apes that roamed free there.

Sophie had returned to Spain in October for a week, with five of her friends, and was grateful for her mother's villa which meant they didn't need to book into a hotel or worry about making a noise. On her return home, her mother seemed a little subdued, but when Sophie asked her why, Sofiya offered no explanation. Halloween and Guy Fawkes celebrations followed her return, which is why it had taken Sophie so long to finish reading the hardcopy her mother had given her.

At last she had finished. With Christmas looming, her time would be taken up with preparing for the festivities and arranging Sophia's and Savanna's birthday parties which were both in December. Sophie wondered at times if her mother thought she had lost interest in reading what she had challenged her mother to write in the first place. But she had not. Quite the opposite. Sophie, when she had the time to sit down and read, was loath to put the chapters back in the desk drawer and at times, resented the need to pay attention to her family's constant interruptions.

Sophie had been absorbed by the descriptive details in her mother's story, to the point where she felt she was actually there, as if she knew the people, and the countries they lived in. Her mother had graduated MBChB, but

Sophie thought she would have been better to have studied for an English degree and become a professional writer. When she finished reading chapter after chapter of such in-depth, personal memories, as well as those her mother had indicated were fiction, she thought that they were definitely worth publishing at some time in the future. Sophie was saddened by this thought as her mother had made her promise not to publish anything until after her death, just as Sofiya's grandmother had done and to date Sofiya had honoured that promise.

Her mother had visited her grandmother, to hear directly from the old lady then write her story from her birth to her death. Sophie, realized her mother must have inherited the same vivid imagination as her grandmother. Sofiya had written her own life-story up to the present day and Sophie hoped that they could now look forward to the future together. Her mother had promised Sophie would either be told the last chapters or be given them to read. Perhaps today might help her mother come to terms with certain unhappy events in her past. Sophie would try to help her mother to forgive those who had hurt her, to gain peace of mind and closure, even although she knew her mother would forgive, but doubted she would ever forget.

Sophie parked her car at the rear entrance of Leightham House. Picking up the jotter and slinging the fake Louis Vuitton bag she had bought at the Marbella market over her shoulder, she made her way to the back door. She smiled thinking of her mother's disgust at her buying 'knock-off bags' when she could have the real thing, but money-wise Iain thoroughly approved. In any case, they all loved the local Centro Plaza Saturday markets while on holiday. The boys haggled for football T-shirts and the girls loved the sundresses, fake jewellery and in particular the fake designer bags and purses. It was a great place for the children to spend their pocket money!

On the rare occasions when they were alone together, Sofiya had answered the occasional innocuous question for Sophie, but nothing more. Her mother had stipulated that she would not answer serious questions until Sophie had read all she had given her to read. "I will decide then whether to tell you the ending face to face, or write it down for you to read." Sophie had arranged to meet with her mother today in their favourite room, her mother's bedroom. Its bay window was wide enough to accommodate a coffee table and the two high-backed comfortable chairs from Mount View, and the room offered a glorious view of the river.

The day was cold and wintry. Sophie was glad of her zipped up puffer coat and UGG boots. She remembered when she was at university, stuffing her feet into her leather boots with several pairs of socks on to try to keep her feet warm and pulling the pompommed, woollen hat that Bunty had knitted for her over her ears and almost down over her eyes to keep warm. She had had to wind her extra-long woollen scarf several times round her neck and grasp at her coat to stop it flapping in the wind to keep out the cold.

What Sophie had read over the months filled her with pride. Her mother had been deceived by the woman she thought was her great-aunt, never knowing she was her grandmother. Sophie suddenly felt angry at the woman, who knew the truth about her own children and spoke of them frequently by their first names in the stories she told their daughter. To be told of her true birth-parents by a lawyer days after she was to have been married was a double blow for anyone. Her mother had painfully described her journey as a young woman, full of love and hope, looking forward to a new life in America with the man she loved. Instead, she was discarded by a shallow, pathetic man who had deserted her.

How did her mother rise above such overwhelming adversity? Sophie couldn't wait to hear or read the conclusion to her mother's story today and in particular the answer to what troubled her. Why did her grandfather throw her mother out of the house? Sophie also wanted to read the letter that had arrived from America in April and what had happened in October when she and her friends were in Spain? And what was in the mysterious package she and Gillian had found in the attic so many years ago, the contents her mother would not let Sophie read last April? What was its significance?

The back door was always left open. Bunty and Vivienne MacKay went to Edinburgh or St Andrew's for afternoon tea on Sundays. Letting herself into the kitchen, Sophie switched the kettle on and turned to the tea tray on the kitchen table, which was set up with a silver tea service and fine Crown Derby cups and saucers. Bunty insisted on no 'cheenie' mugs on a Sunday, only the best china and a plate of Perkin biscuits! Her mother must have developed a taste for the ginger-flavoured biscuits during her visits to her grandmother. Sophie shook her head thinking nothing much changes. *Here I am repeating history.* When her mother had visited her grandmother Cathie had left the tea ready for them. Now Bunty left the tea tray ready for her and her mother, but with Kenya teabags! Teabags! The 'great-aunt Jane' would have been horrified!

Sophie filled the teapot with hot water from the kettle, slung her bag over her shoulder and tucking the jotter under her arm picked up the tea tray. Making her way to the hall, she paused as always to look at the life-size painting of the girl on a black stallion, who she now knew was a Russian princess. Gingerly, Sophie climbed the stairs to her mother's bedroom, hoping that after today, she would not regret her demand that her mother should explain the reasons for her melancholic state every April.

Chapter 2

SOPHIE reached her mother's bedroom with her heart thumping. Would her mother tell her the whole story? How would she feel when she left?... happy, sad or wishing she had never started the whole miserable business in the first place? Sofiya had written extensively and Sophie appreciated being taken into her mother's confidence and being told the story of her life in such detail. Sophie wondered, *will I regret asking the questions or hearing her answers and where to begin? Perhaps I should start by asking why granddad threw her out before asking why Irene's granddaughter was never reunited with her mother in Australia and why was the baby given the name Harriet?*

Sophie knew from history that that name is usually associated with Harriet Tubman, an African-American heroine, who was involved with the movement to free the slaves, arranging safe passage along the 'underground railway' from the South to the North. She had been a political activist against slavery, an abolitionist and recognized for her bravery. It wouldn't surprise Sophie if some racist person in power disagreed with the proposal to have Harriet's picture on the $20 dollar bill as it was a reminder of the American Civil War that freed the slaves.

Walking over to the coffee table, Sophie laid the tea tray on it, took her notebook from under her arm and put it down on the table beside the tray, at the same time noticing a small pile of hardcopy. She also recognized the handwritten letter from last April and the package from the loft. *So mum has decided to write the last chapters!*

Sofiya continued to look out of the window, as if she had not heard her daughter enter the room. It never failed to please Sophie to see how beautiful her mother still was. Sofiya belied her age. No one guessed she was ten years older than she looked. *Just look at her,* Sophie thought, shaking her head, *standing there in her skinny jeans and cashmere sweater, tall and slim with her vibrant auburn, thick, straight, shoulder-length hair.* Sophie could not remember it in any other style. She wondered if in the past her mother at a younger age had been '... *a dedicated follower of fashion*' especially the more dramatic ones.

Her mum must have been glad to trade her panty girdle, suspenders and nylons for tights, and have welcomed the introduction of underwired push-up bras. Her grandfather had said that stiletto heels were only fit for planting leeks and the stiff, starched, net petticoats were so wide, her grandmother Ina said, she couldn't pass her daughter in the door! Had her mother worn Cuban and wedge-heel shoes, knee-high leather boots with hot-pants, plastic go-go boots with mini-skirts, ankle boots with midi-skirts or agonizing wooden Scholl sandals? If granny couldn't pass her mother in the doorway with her sticking-out petticoats, she would have had an even greater problem with the 1980's shoulder pads!

She wondered what her grandfather would have said about the huge, wide, shoulder pads in every coat and blouse, the jackets with tight waists and deep frilly peplums from waist to hip, the exaggerated long, curly, back-combed hair, popularized in the American TV series *Dallas*. Fashion seemed to change so rapidly. It was hard to keep up. There was also an obsession with royal-blue coloured garments in the late 1980s. After WW2 women seemed to prefer trousers to skirts. There had been straight-leg trousers, palazzo pants, flared bottom trousers, jogging bottoms, jump suits, track and trouser suits, leggings, jeans and now jeggings. What next?!

Sophie reflected that as far back as she could remember, her mother stayed with the classic Vidal Sassoon straight haircuts. She could not imagine her mother with the back-combed, high bouffant hairstyles of the late 1950s. Did her mother ever copy the bee-hive, glued in place with lacquer, the Afro look, or Mary Quant pixy haircuts of the 1960s and 70s or Twiggy with her long spider-like eyelashes? Looking back Sophie realized the introduction of the hand-held hairdryer, heated Carmen rollers, self-gripping Velcro rollers and straighteners, meant women no longer had to sit for hours under a hooded hairdryer. It seemed to Sophie her mother always looked the same: confident, classic, and *not* dictated to by fashion. In fact, her mother's style was a tribute to the legendary Jackie Kennedy's simple, unfussy, classic style, including her pill-box hat!

Sofiya turned away from the window.

"Pour the tea, Sophie, and put these Perkin biscuits in my bag. I will feed them to the ducks. I don't like them and they remind me too much of the past. I must have given Bunty the idea I liked Perkin biscuits and every time I have a guest to tea she produces them. I don't want to hurt her feelings, but…" Sophie smiled remembering her mother's grandmother's obsession for them and the flak Cathie and her mother took for trying to change them for something else… Kit Kats did not go down well.

Sofiya picked up her teacup and drank some of the tea before looking straight at her daughter. "You won't need your notebook. I have written everything down. My memory isn't quite as sharp as it used to be, so I have written the concluding chapters, so that I did not forget any details. It is all true, just as it happened. However, I did write it in the same format as I previously did, and as if you are reading a novel, but this is the last, this is the end. It is the truth, not fiction. Leave the letter and the package until I return. Please don't judge me until you have read everything and after today there will be no more discussion, no more questions. We must agree once and for all this is the last chapter… The End."

Standing up, Sofiya picked up the printed pages from the coffee table and handed them to her daughter, then made to leave the room.

"Where are you going, mum?"

"I won't be long. I am going for a short walk. I want to give you time by yourself to read without me looking over at you. When I return, you will read the letter that arrived in April."

"But mum, I wanted to ask you about Irene's granddaughter."

"There's no need… it's all in there."

Sophie hesitated for a moment before asking, "Why did granddad put you out?"

Sofiya shook her head and smiled. As she left the room she heard Sophie repeat her question in a much louder voice.

"Why did granddad put you out? Was it because you were rude to grandma?!"

Sofiya went downstairs. She comforted herself, thinking whatever her daughter thought of her after today… confession is good for the soul whatever the consequences. Sofiya felt a weight had been lifted from her shoulders. She had for too long lived in the past. Now she felt free, free from her innermost secrets and her past with Johnny Geiger.

But most of all she was grateful to her grandmother, for leaving her all the documented evidence from those who were involved and to her husband, Neil, for his research into DNA finger-printing in the 1980s which had left her all the indisputable proof she had needed to deal with Mr Geiger! It had also confirmed Sofiya's need to plan for the future of Leightham House.

Chapter 3

S OPHIE REALIZED her mother had no intention of answering her questions till she returned. She looked down at the sheets of paper her mother had handed her. To her astonishment, she saw that the first page was a letter to her! Why?

My dearest daughter,

Before you begin to read the last chapters of my life story to date, I want to explain how things were for women prior to1968. I know you are aware of changes that took place around the time you were born in the 70s, that dramatically changed life for women, but that era is now long forgotten. Neither you nor your generation have any experience of how things were for women before an act of parliament decriminalized 'termination of pregnancy'. I hate the 'A' word... it conjures up pictures of desperate women going to the back-street abortionists, who performed a service which was the only way to help women who had no other option.

It is also important to remember that, not so long ago, the wedding vows stated the bride must love, honour and obey *her husband. In other words, if he forced his wife to have intercourse with him, he could not be charged with rape, irrespective of how many pregnancies the woman had previously and regardless of her health, or her reluctance to bring yet more children into her family. She was forced to endure pregnancy and childbirth as a result of her husband's demands. That too had to be challenged in the courts.*

In the 1960s, doctors were able to prescribe the contraceptive pill for married or soon to be married women, but it took until the 1970s before doctors and family planning clinics were permitted to prescribe the contraceptive pill for all women. Until then if the couple had premarital sex and the woman became pregnant, the man was under no obligation to acknowledge parentage. He could walk away scot-free.

It brings back memories of my days in the gynaecology wards when I was a medical student. A woman in Edinburgh who provided the 'A' service to procure a termination, mercifully would direct the woman to go right away to hospital should anything go wrong. Perhaps it was an act of kindness or to save her own skin and a jail sentence if she were found out. Either way it was a lifesaver for many women. And believe me, no unmarried woman who has ever had to make such a decision will ever forget the relief, followed by the guilt and would never forget the need to keep the termination secret until her dying day.

However, there were unfortunate women who either because they did not know how to find the back-street abortionists, or could not afford their services, resorted to terminating their pregnancy themselves. How many women over the centuries not only lost their baby, but their own lives from haemorrhage or sepsis? I remember vividly one woman, the terror on her face and her only question, "Was it away yet?" No... sometimes it wasn't, but the gynaecologist could not treat the woman until she began to show signs of losing the pregnancy and then only if she was infection free! The last time I saw that patient, she was being wheeled from the ward to the artificial kidney unit, her kidneys going into failure from sepsis.

Prior to 1970s, an unmarried woman had no choice but to proceed with an unwanted pregnancy. She would be admitted to the 'home for unmarried mothers' not the

261

'maternity hospital', to hide her shame and nearly always the baby was put up for adoption. It was very unlikely she would ever be able to acknowledge she had had a baby, or ever see her son or her daughter again after she was discharged. It is unthinkable in today's modern world for a mother to be parted from her child, to see an innocent infant as illegitimate or a bastard, another ugly word... unimaginable! Her pregnancy was seen as a sin, or proof of her inability to control her sexual desires. She was condemned as a fallen woman, branded as loose or worse. A husband expected his wife to be a virgin on their wedding night, although it was perfectly acceptable for men to have had previous sexual experiences. Women were denied the right to have the same desires and needs as men because of the risk of pregnancy.

Mercifully the law changed and the termination of pregnancy was permitted in 1968. A woman has the right to her own body, and not to be dictated to by the clergy, or politicians, men or other women. A woman has the right to choose what she wants to do. It is her body, her decision, no one else's. Sadly, with every step forward there can be a step back. I remember an old doctor saying 'the pill liberated the men' and with the frightening increase in sexually transmitted disease, he may well have been right.

Why am I telling you this or reminding you of a time you have no experience of? Women of my age would prefer to forget the past, but I cannot. Until you have read all I have written, I beg you not to judge me too harshly. I wanted you to read this letter before the last chapters, to remind you of the times I lived through.

The final chapters will answer your questions that I refused to answer since last April. The most burning one is, "Why did my father throw me out of the house?" It seems so long ago now, although I wrote in a previous chapter that I couldn't believe my father was capable of throwing me out and telling me to do what I had to do to sort myself out and not to return until I did. That's not strictly true as you will find out when you read my next chapters.

I did go to the States, but I will never forget the feeling of the hell I was about to face in those weeks and months ahead when I returned, as if life was no longer worth living. I write this as if it happened yesterday, because for me every April brings it all back, every sad, heart breaking memory of rejection and the heart-rending decision I had to make because of the times I lived in and who I was. So, keep this in mind as you read the last chapters. I beg you please don't judge me too harshly. I did what I thought was right.

Sophie, you are my family, you Iain and my grandchildren are my life and I love you all so much. What would I do without you?

Mum.

'Oh, Mum! How can you even think I would form any kind of judgement on your past? We are all human and humans make mistakes. I believe in your honesty and decency. Whatever happened to you, I have doubts that you were the only person to blame in whatever it was.'

Sophie put the letter down on the coffee table and continued reading the pages her mother had handed her before she left, wondering what was the need to write her such an explanatory letter?

263

Chapter 4

SOFIYA JUMPED out of bed, washed and dressed before throwing her nightclothes, toiletries and make-up into her totebag, then ran downstairs to avoid the possibility of her parents returning earlier than expected and her mother refusing to let her leave. She picked up her passport and held it between her teeth. With the suitcase her dad had taken downstairs for her in one hand, she opened the front door and looked round her home one last time. Reaching down, she picked up the cat basket with Samson now silent and curled inside as if resigned to his fate. *Samson you don't know how much I wish I could change places with you, instead of facing my own self-inflicted unresolved nightmare.*

Leaning over the back seat of the car Sofiya lifted the box, carelessly thrown there by her dad, that contained her wedding dress and stored it in the boot. Sam, no longer loudly protesting as he usually did on the way to the vets was now safe on the back seat in his basket. Sofiya got into the driving seat and drove away. The long dangerous Stains Road had been damaged by subsidence due to the coal mines underground and this made it like a switchback railway as she drove to Mount View. With a wry smile on her face, Sofiya shook her head. *What a performance, Dad! You should have been on the stage! What an actor! You gave a performance worthy of an Oscar. Mum was completely fooled, completely taken in. But I'm glad I am not in your shoes. You'd better hope, Dad, she has a good supply of Valium to calm her nerves when you get back.*

* * *

Oh, my God!! Sophie could not believe what she had just read. She was in a state of utter disbelief, flabbergasted. *What on earth?!* Her granddad, the kindest man on earth and her mother had worked this out between them! Sophie looked down at the page and reread it in case she had misinterpreted something, but no, there it was in black and white. Sofiya had been thrown out of the house by her father in such a harsh manner to fool her mother! But why? Why was there the need to orchestrate such a performance between them to trick the family? Sophie took a few moments to digest what she had read before continuing to read.

* * *

Sofiya realized that by now her parents would have returned home and no doubt her mother would have made a number of phone calls, in a voice loud enough to ensure her father heard her wherever he was in the house. Phone calls to her grandmother, cousin Margo, aunts Nan and Jessie, telling them Jim had thrown *her* daughter out for no good reason and the poor lassie wasn't that well and she wouldn't be speaking to him until Sofiya returned home. Sofiya could almost hear their gasps of disbelief and horror at the news. She knew they would want to know when she would return and to be honest Sofiya had no idea herself when that would be. *You are right, Mum, I am not well but more in my head than my body.*

Thinking of her family and driving along the same road brought back memories of her childhood and the times she and her family had travelled to visit great-aunt

Jane. The journey took the same turns and bends on the road until the river and the Mary Isle came into view. Sofiya knew nothing much ever changes in that part of the county. She remembered the hawthorn and beech hedges on either side of the road and the pavement on one side that week-end walkers could use.

The fields were now mostly bare. The winter vegetable season of potatoes, carrots, turnips and cabbage was almost over. The rich arable land was resting, waiting to be ploughed for spring planting of barley that would be sent to the Haig distillers to be fermented into Scotland's famous Scotch whisky. The barley was also essential for making traditional Scotch broth. Wheat would be planted then harvested and sent to local millers to be ground into flour before being sent to bakeries and shops. And what would Scotland do without oats for morning porridge?

In the spring and summer as in a pastoral scene, the cows would graze on rich pastures calm and placid awaiting milking, milk the whole community enjoyed in their porridge and tea. Rich summer soft fruits would be sent to restaurants and hotels all over the country. Harvest thanksgiving church services would give thanks for a crop safely gathered. What a rich heritage she had just inherited with Leightham House! Was she up to the challenge of maintaining all of it? Sofiya was thankful she did not have to think about it yet because she had a far more pressing problem to deal with.

The journey had seemed long and tedious for her as a child, despite the family singing Scottish songs and reciting Scots poetry to amuse her and Margo. But she never forgot the moment as a child and young woman, the exact bend in the road when she would see Leightham House, the house with no roof that had led her to her present predicament. But today the house seemed to have a golden glow. Was it the promise of better things to come? No, the golden glow was not from the house itself,

266

but from the masses of golden daffodils swaying in the breeze in its gardens. This house that had bewitched her from early childhood with her obsession to find out more about its history and by a quirk of unbelievable fate, Leightham House now belonged to her.

Sofiya vividly remembered the part in her grandmother's story about her friend 'Alice Gardner', pregnant and fleeing to avoid the stigma of having a child out of wedlock because she had no proof of her marriage to Lord Robert Leightham and no one would have believed her without proof. But out of that marriage, her parents' unfortunate marriage resulted and her inheritance in her grandmother's will, she was now Lady Leightham facing a similar predicament. Was she a reincarnation of her great-aunt and where had her head been for the last six months?

* * *

Coming to the end of the main drive to Mount View, the drive that Johnny Geiger had skidded out of barely six months ago, Sofiya could see Cathie pacing up and down the front doorstep, as usual waiting for her to arrive. Sam had also realized they had arrived, had perked up, was now clawing at the sides of his carry-basket and screeching at the top of his voice to be let out, as only Siamese cats can.

"Come awa in, ma lass, and let that beast oot o' his cage. He kens fine whaur the backdoor is and dinna worry he'll fund his ain wae aboot... he's nae daft."

"Thank you, Cathie."

Following Cathie's instructions, Sofiya released the cat and picked up her totebag. Cathie lifted the suitcase out of the boot and put it at her feet and turning quickly, she darted a glance from side to side to make sure the coast was clear. Cathie instructed Sofiya to get back in the car and to drive round to the back of the house. She handed Sofiya the garage keys and told her to park her car in the last garage which was never used and to make sure, she pulled the door right down and locked the padlock behind her.

"That garage is niver yaised, so naebody wull ken its yer car that's in there. I've ordered a taxi fur ye fae Edinburgh this efternin' and it'll tak ye tae the airport tae catch yer flight tae London, in guid time tae get the flight tae America the nicht. A' only wish a can cum wi ye"

"Cathie, what would I do without you and Irene? But I need to deal with this myself."

"Ach, yer like ma ain bairn and ye'll nae be the first or the last lassie tae suffer from the same predicament. Let's hope his 'majesty' wull dae the richt thing by ye… although a hae ma doots. Noo wae a wee bit o' luck nae one wull hiv seen ye arrive. A've got the taxi fae Edinburgh because the local taxi drivers wid recognize ye *and* a've got a heavy headscarf and thick, black framed, but normal glesses fur ye tae wear when ye lave. Noo, awa' wi the car. Irene's got the kettle on fur a cup o' tea and a bite tae eat. Jist look at ye. Ye're as whites as a sheet and ye're still as skinny as a matchstick. Naebody would guess whit's wrang wi ye! And ye wull need tae get yer bluids done. Ye canna gan on like this much longer."

"I know, Cathie, but it's not for much longer."

"Richt, awa wi the car. Keep yer heid doon and get back inside the hoose as quick as ye can. So far we've been lucky."

A few hours later the taxi arrived and Sofiya left with Cathie's and Irene's reassurances ringing in her ears that all would be well and they were there to support her whether she stayed in America or returned home. They had asked Sofiya just to phone and let them know if she was returning so they could plan what to do next.

Chapter 5

BOARDING THE PAN AM FLIGHT from London to New York, Sofiya thought, so this is what it's like to travel when money is no object. The first-class lounge had been luxury personified: individual, comfortable, secluded seating, low lights, coffee tables, hostesses and stewards circulating with trays of as much food, soft and alcoholic drink as one could want. The lounge seemed awash with champagne. Sofiya thought it would be a wonder if the passengers were sober enough to board the flight when it was called. And for passengers arriving from long-haul flights with time to spare before boarding an on-going flight, there were individual showers, expensive soap, shampoo, moisturiser, toothbrushes and toothpaste available on request. Thankfully the lounge had very few passengers. Better still, everyone was keeping themself to themself and Sofiya wanted it to stay that way. She had no desire to talk with or befriend anyone. Finally, the call came softly over the tannoy and first-class passengers were the first to board.

The flight attendants offered glasses of orange juice and champagne as the passengers entered the first-class seating compartment. Stewards helped the passengers to their private seats and stowed away hand luggage in the overhanging bins. The airline had placed latest television screens in front of each passenger and there was a selection of movies and new modern earphones that blocked out the noise of the engines. The earphones brought back memories of cheap plastic ones on flights in her student days in economy class. Before settling down to sleep with fresh blankets and pillows brought by the hostess, Sofiya had watched the latest James Bond movie, while dinner had been served on fine china and with silver cutlery. Sofiya tuned into her favourite classical music channel to help her relax and hopefully sleep. She listened to Carl Nielsen's 'Sinfonia Espansiva' and that brought back the memory of when she first met Johnny Geiger.

What was the ill-fated, unbelievable chance of Sofiya meeting an American Airline pilot on his way home to Texas on an internal flight from New York? Johnny should have, like all off-duty airline staff, been travelling first class, but no seats were available there, and that was how he ended up in economy, sitting next to Sofiya. God, he was so handsome, strikingly good looking in his pilot's uniform. She had been hypnotized by Johnny Geiger's soft, southern, Texas drawl. Where had it all gone wrong? Little did she know at that time how closely related they were. Maybe that's why they were so attracted to one another?

It was hard not to look back at her engagement to him and the life-changing disaster that followed the freak August storm that had wrecked the gardens of Mount View the day before their wedding. Worse still, the reading of her grandmother's will was etched in her mind forever. Sofiya would never forget the horror of Johnny Geiger abandoning her. Or Cathie throwing that piece of stone she had brought from the ruin of Leightham House at his face, or the trickle of blood running down his cheek or Johnny, driving like a lunatic onto the main road in Pittendreal as if he couldn't wait to get away. It seemed like a lifetime had passed since then. Sofiya had heard nothing from Johnny and she began to wonder what kind of reception she would receive, especially with the news she was about to give him. With that disturbing thought in mind Sofiya tried to get some sleep.

The rest of the flight was uneventful and as one of the privileged first-class passengers, she left the aeroplane first, was whisked through customs and security to a private car waiting for her, with her luggage already loaded to take her to her hotel. Sofiya gave a wry smile and thought once more that she could get used to the life of the idle rich and famous.

Sofiya arrived at the luxurious Waldorf Astoria overlooking Central Park and began to unpack her suitcase. Normally, Sofiya would have gone for a walk, but the temperature was below freezing and she realized she had only brought her old duffle coat from her student days with her. Instead, she decided to try and catch up some lost sleep. Even with the luxury of first-class accommodation on the flight, she had been unable to sleep. Sofiya had been in touch with her friend in Texas, Mary Smith, and asked for her help in contacting Johnny, as all her efforts had been ignored. Mary had put her fiancé, a psychiatrist, Bob, on the job and through various contacts, managed to get hold of Johnny Geiger and said he would hold him accountable at his next airline pilot psychiatric assessment if he didn't meet with Sofiya. As luck would have it, Johnny was flying into New York that same afternoon.

Lying on the bed she felt the baby move for the first time. Perhaps only now she was allowing herself to accept the fact that she was pregnant. Suddenly the telephone rang by the side of the bed. Sofiya was startled for a few seconds but lifted the receiver. The hotel manager informed her she had a visitor. Sofiya asked him to delay sending her guest up to her room, and said she would phone back when she was ready. Sofiya rushed to the bathroom and had a quick shower wearing a bath cap, as she had no time to dry her hair. Applying a little extra make-up on the black circles under her eyes and a little extra rouge, she hoped to disguise how tired and pale she looked. With her hands trembling she called the concierge at the main desk and asked him to send her visitor up.

* * *

"Oh, Mum. Mum!" Sophie gasped. This was the first time Sophie had an insight into what had happened to her mother. But Sophie was slightly confused. This chapter related to February. Sophie realized there was more to come, but she just could not imagine or comprehend how her mother coped with this secret for so long or the misery she had gone through. Sophie wished her mother would come back right now, so she could hold her tight and reassure her all was well. Didn't the bible tell us 'Judge not lest ye be judged' and 'Let he who is without sin cast the first stone'? Sophie wiped a tear that ran down her cheek and now understood why her mother had written the letter for her to read first.

Chapter 6

JOHNNY GEIGER entered the room and casually chucked his pilot's cap on the bed almost with contempt.

"Well ma'am, yah've gotten me here. What do yah want? Ah thought ah made it perfectly clear when ah left Mount View, ah niver wanted to see or hear from yah'all again."

Listening to Johnny's Texan drawl made Sofiya shudder.

"Well!" he snapped, "Yah ill or somethin'? Gawd dammit, yah've dragged me here...yah look well enough to me so git a move on. Ah've gotten a flight to catch back to Texas tonight and ah can't waste mah time." Irritation was written all over Johnny's face.

Sofiya momentarily wondered if she had had a narrow escape with Johnny deserting her last August. But Sofiya was not going to be intimidated by him. Narrowing her eyes, she looked straight at Johnny, now lounging nonchalantly in the chair and in a cold voice began to answer him.

"I am glad you are sitting down, although I didn't invite you to." Johnny shuffled slightly, but cocked his arrogant head to the side as if ready to argue with Sofiya. "As you can see if you bothered to look closer, I am well physically, but a mess emotionally and mentally."

"Surprise me! Our mutual, psychotic, great-grandmother Elizabeth Leightham wer the same. Maybah yah'all take after her." Johnny shrugged his shoulders.

Sofiya realized this was going nowhere. She decided there was no point in delaying the reason she had wanted to meet with him any longer. Removing the wide coat she was wearing, Sofiya revealed her expanding waistline.

"This has nothing to do with psychosis or mental illness... I am pregnant!!" Sofiya almost shouted at him. "I need help."

That temporarily shook the man and his cheeks began to turn red under his bronze Texan tan. "Aw my Gawd, ah don't believe yah. It must be six months since we parted. How in the hell did this happen? Yah were on the pill, so it can't be mine." Johnny searched in his mind for words to belittle Sofiya and because he couldn't think of any, ended up sneering at her wealth. "Yah'all got plenty of dough. Git rid of it!" But Sofiya could see Johnny was genuinely uneasy, shuffling around on the chair.

"I *was* on the pill damn it!! I don't know what happened. Well yes, I do know how it happened... that's obvious!! I have gone over and over in my mind our last days together in Texas before I left for our wedding in Scotland. Maybe I packed the pills in my suitcase or maybe I didn't unpack them till a few days later. Maybe it was the time difference... or jetlag? Maybe I needed to see my GP for a repeat prescription because I had finished the last packet in Texas. I don't remember, but so what? Within days we were to be married and it wouldn't have mattered, but I assure you I did *not deliberately forget* to take the pill. Why would I? You obviously have remained unaffected by what happened to us, but I have not. I have virtually been in a state of denial since that dreadful day at Mount View, psychologically blanking out the memories. Do you think I wouldn't have considered termination, if it had been possible? I didn't realize I was pregnant until a couple of weeks ago. It's too late now, Johnny.

"My dad recently guessed what happened to me. He arranged the flights and hotel. He even pretended to pick a quarrel with me, announced he was throwing me out of the house, so none of my family would know about the baby or where I am. My father would prefer us not to marry, but he thinks you should be given the chance to put things right."

Johnny ignored Sofiya, because he knew full well what her dad's opinion of him was, before and certainly after he abandoned his daughter virtually at the altar. "So...whit do yah want me to do about it?" Johnny's tone softened somewhat and that made Sofiya begin to hope there was a possible amicable solution.

"We could get married Johnny and give our baby a name."

"*Whaht!!*" Johnny exploded, "Yah cannot be serious. Wait! A have the solution. A have a friend in the pharmacy in town. Ah will go and git some abortion pills. It's never too late."

Sofiya cringed at the word abortion. "How dare you!" she hissed at him. "Do that and I will report your friend to the American Department of Health and Human Services and have your friend's licence revoked. Don't push me, Johnny. I assure you they will take the word of a doctor's complaint very seriously. It's so simple. Just marry me. We can fly to Las Vegas this evening. I brought my blood test results with me and we can get our marriage licence in hours. Help me avoid the disgrace, the humiliation, of bringing an illegitimate child into the world. We can divorce after the baby is born. Then I swear to you, I will return to Scotland and tell my family it didn't work out and you will never hear from me again and as you have just reminded me, I need no maintenance or financial help from you."

"Gimme a break. Ah'm engaged to a Texan girl from mah college days and mah mother and family are delighted. She knows nothin' about us and ah wants it to stay that way, understand? Ah've gotta git out o' here!"

"Well...heavens to Betsy, sir. How yah'all surprise me. Well ah do declare." Sofiya realized she had nothing to lose aping Johnny. "Your mother Betsy Geiger is delighted? That doesn't surprise me. She never liked me anyway because I could see right through her neurosis."

Johnny just shrugged his shoulders and didn't look straight at Sofiya, because guilt was written all over his face. He knew the baby was his and Sofiya was telling the truth, but he was still going to marry another woman. Johnny got up and went as if to retrieve his cap ready to leave. Sofiya moved and stood right in front of Johnny, stopping him. She was not going to leave it there, even though she realized she had lost.

"You accused me of being like our great-grandmother Elizabeth Leightham. It's more likely you have inherited your genes from our grandfather Robert Leightham. But he married my grandmother, a common servant girl, pregnant with his child, without telling anyone, in a secret wedding service. Worse still, he survived the Titanic disaster but did not return to Scotland to save her from humiliation and recriminations. He abandoned her and she thought she had no way of proving she was married to him. Ha! But the joke's on you. He entered a bigamous marriage with *your* grandmother Rachel Harrison… your mother is illegitimate, as our baby will be!! You are as cold, calculating and inhuman as he was, deserting me, as he deserted my grandmother. I am *not* like Elizabeth Leightham but you…you are the reincarnation of her son Robert Leightham!"

Johnny moved in close to Sofiya, staring down at her face with contempt written all over his. "If yah eva dare try to contact me agin or tell anyone the baby is mine…ah will git mah college friends to say they had sex with yah…not me. Do yah understand? Ah've hid enough of this."

That was the last straw for Sofiya. Johnny had virtually called her a prostitute. How low could he sink? Sofiya saw red, lost control and clenching her fist she punched him in the face. The crack echoed round the room. They both stood frozen in shock for a few moments, as a slow trickle of blood began to run down from Johnny's nose. Sofiya had to control herself from laughing hysterically, because for the first time she could see on Johnny's cheek the mark of a healed scar from the stone Cathie had thrown at him. *Cathie will love hearing about this when I tell her!*

Johnny began frantically searching in his pockets for a handkerchief. "Damn it! Ah must have left mah handkerchief in mah overcoat and ah can't git blood on mah shirt. Ah don't have anither with me for mah flight back."

"Here, take this and put it in the wash basket. You are in America, remember the rules. Don't try to flush it down the toilet, I don't want a bill for a blocked drain," Sofiya ordered as she handed Johnny a clean hotel napkin.

Johnny went into the ensuite bathroom and once the bleeding stopped, returned, buttoned up his pilot's jacket, reached for his cap and looking in the mirror to admire himself, arranged it on his head to his satisfaction as he prepared to leave.

"Thurs nuthin' more tuh sigh." Johnny raised his eyebrows, giving Sofiya a nonchalant look of boredom. Sofiya saw he had simply lost all interest in her or the situation. He left without a backward glance.

Sofiya realized she had lost Johnny forever. She would never see him again. She lifted the phone and asked for the overseas operator to put a transatlantic call through to Scotland. She could hear the sigh of relief in Cathie's voice. There was no point in staying any longer.

Sofiya finished packing her suitcase and went into the bathroom to collect the few pieces of clothing she had put in the clothes basket including the blood-stained napkin. The last thing she wanted was to leave it behind for the hotel staff to find. Picking up her make-up bag, toothbrush and hairbrush, she couldn't believe her eyes. On closer inspection, she realized her hairbrush had strands of black curly hair in its bristles!! "The arrogant, fat-headed, full of himself, ill-mannered, rotter! He used my hair brush. How dare he! What impudence! Who does he think he is?" She was raging and realized what a narrow escape she had had. Her first instinct was to bin the brush, but she didn't want the hotel staff to find that either so dumped it in her suitcase with the rest of her toiletries. She just couldn't wait to get home and fall into the loving arms that were waiting for her.

* * *

Sophie was saddened by the confirmation of her mother's pregnancy, then remembered the letter she had just read regarding what life was like for women at that time. *So Mum did meet Johnny Geiger on that return visit to America! My mother was pregnant to Johnny Geiger and he abandoned her when she was so vulnerable. How low could the man sink? But what happened to the baby? Was my mother forced to have the baby adopted? Do I have a brother or sister I know nothing about? You said what you have written would answer all my questions. But to be honest, I feel I have more questions now than I did when I started reading today.*

Chapter 7

"I HATE THIS BABY," Sofiya hissed, arching her spine as another excruciating labour pain engulfed her whole body. Sofiya's throat was dry and she was hoarse from crying out. She was exhausted and began to think that the pain would never end. She thought of the gas and air the mothers inhaled during labour, the merciful injections of pethidine she had given them for pain in the delivery room and what she would give to have access to either of them now.

"Ma lass, jist keep on wi yer breathin'…three deep breaths wi the next contraction jist like we practised, then tap the mattress wi yer fingers and sing yer song 'She'll be cumin' round the mountain when she comes'… yer duin fine."

"Aye, yer duin fine," Irene echoed Cathie's words.

"If you repeat what Cathie says one more time, Irene, I swear…Ah-h," Sofiya stopped mid-sentence as another contraction seemed to start in the middle of her spine and ended in her ankles and ears, before she once again fell into a short, exhausted sleep.

Irene, remembering her own labour pains, realised Sofiya was making no progress and mouthed to her sister, *We need to talk.* Once outside the bedroom door, Irene stated in no uncertain terms, "This his been gaun on far too long. Somethin's no richt Cathie."

"But whit can we dae? Naebody kens she's here."

Irene stood thinking for a minute. "There's only wan thing tae be done. We need help or we're gaunna hae twa deed bodies on oor hauns and a jail sentence!"

"Whit!!?"

"Listen, a've been thinkin'. A ken what tae dae...Dr Martin."

"Dr Martin? I thocht she'd retired?"

"A ken that, but she's been keepin' her haund in and dayin' the odd shift in her auld practice. She'll ken what tae dae."

"At this time o' nicht? Oh, my Goad almichty, there's her ladyship cryin' oot again. A need tae gan back aside her."

"Aye, awa ye go in. Am gawn fur the doctur Cathie, we canna lave this ony longer."

The weeks had passed relatively quickly since Sofiya had returned from America and moved into Mount View. The sisters had devoted their time to caring for her and so far, so good. Sofiya had been able to walk round the gardens after dark, just as her great-aunt Jane had done when she was in hiding with the Phimister sisters. Irene had spent her time making delicious soups and milk puddings, which Sofiya hated. Cathie had forced her to drink tumblers of milk, telling Sofiya it was "Guid fur ye and the bairn's bones". It was all beginning to get on Sofiya's nerves and if anyone had told her morning sickness could last all day and much longer than three months, she would not have believed them.

* * *

One dull rainy afternoon, Irene drove them along the narrow back roads to Tayport and over the Tay Road Bridge to Dundee to do some shopping and she and Cathie ended up looking at things for babies: gauze and towelling nappies, vests, cot blankets, prams and cots and Cathie discovered a new all-in-one garment called a Babygrow was made in a new factory in Kirkcaldy. She privately wondered what happened to flannel barricoats and the long nightgowns worn in the first months of a baby's life not so long ago. And to Cathie's astonishment there were packets of something called Pampers... disposable nappies of all things! What next? Getting out for a while had cheered Sofiya up, but realizing that there was no point in buying baby clothes and equipment saddened her and made her present situation all too real.

Cathie and Irene happily occupied themselves knitting for the baby even knowing full well this baby would never wear the garments, but they could be donated to charity or sold at the church fetes in the summer. And with the guile of the innocent, Irene informed the shop assistants in Cormack's wool shop on Leightham High Street, the baby wool she was buying was for her daughter in London who was expecting, just in case the fact that she was buying wool for a baby got around Pittendreal. But soon there would be enough bootees, matinee jackets with matching bonnets for triplets, and if her ladyship didn't go into labour, there would be enough for quadruplets and the local gossips would wonder what was going on.

Cathie and Sofiya practised the latest *Lamaze* controlled breathing and relaxation techniques to help Sofiya when she went into labour. But Sundays were saved for jigsaw puzzles and board games, Scrabble and Monopoly. As there were only three of them, they couldn't play bridge, Sofiya's favourite card game. In the evening Cathie insisted on watching *Songs of Praise, Sunday Night at the Palladium* and no one missed the nine o'clock news and the weather forecast, but Cathie prophesized on a regular basis, it would be a good summer because the crows were building their nests high in the trees; if the cows were all lying down in the fields it was a sign of rain.

Sofiya usually took herself off to bed after the nine o'clock news, but this Sunday she just could not get comfortable. She felt restless and paced up and down the living room. Cathie and Irene nodded knowingly to each other. Maybe it was beginning at last. After dark, Sofiya left the house and walked round Mount View gardens in the hope of stimulating labour. Sofiya was worried and well aware of the fact this baby was long overdue.

At breakfast on Tuesday, Sofiya insisted they go over their plan for once the baby had arrived. Irene hastened to assure Sofiya the plan was watertight and ready to go... it couldn't fail. As soon as the baby was born, Irene who had already secreted the old baby travel cot and blankets used for her daughter from her old house in Pittendreal, would wait till after dark, put the baby in the car and drive to the Church of Scotland's Mother and Baby Home in Edinburgh to leave the baby there for adoption. And no one would be any the wiser. She would tell the matron she found the infant abandoned on her doorstep and, as she had no way of feeding the infant at that time of night, had decided to bring the baby right away. Irene would give her old address in case they needed to contact her, but other than that she would give no further information.

Chapter 8

CATHIE was wringing her hands in despair. The last hour seemed interminable. It seemed like a lifetime had passed since Irene left to fetch Dr Martin. *Maybe the doctor didn't want to get involved. Maybe Dr Martin had decided to phone the community midwives to attend Sofiya or had just phoned for an ambulance to take Sofiya to the maternity hospital near St Andrew's or worse, had called the police to arrest them!* Cathie's vivid imagination was working overtime… *Lord, help us,* Cathie prayed.

There was still no sign of either of them and Sofiya seemed to have sunk into a coma between contractions. Every time Cathie tried to hold Sofiya's hand, stroke her brow or bathe her forehead with a cool wet cloth, Sofiya brushed Cathie's hand away, croaking hoarsely, "Don't touch me! Don't touch me!" as another contraction engulfed her body.

"Oh, thank Gawd, that's somebody at the front door at last!" Cathie ran out of the bedroom and looked over the stair banister. To her relief Irene and Dr Martin had arrived. "Am that gled tae see ye doctur…up here… up here!!" she shouted.

"Hello, Cathie," a calm reassuring voice called up the stairs. "Sorry, but I had to make a phone call to the maternity hospital, then drive there to collect some equipment I might need. Then Irene and I went to the surgery to collect the drugs that I don't keep in the house." Susan turned back to Irene. "Do you have a fish kettle for steaming salmon in the kitchen?" Bewildered, Irene nodded yes. "Good, take the forceps I brought from the hospital and boil them in case I need them. Here, Cathie, help me with the entonox cylinder and let's get to the bedroom."

Susan walked over to the bed and, even with all her experience in obstetrics, was more than a little disturbed at the sight in front of her. It was obvious that this young woman should have been in the maternity hospital days ago. On the journey to Pittendreal, Irene had filled her in with all the details as to why Sofiya was with them in Mount View and although she didn't agree entirely with Sofiya taking such a risk, she was a fellow doctor and Sofiya must have had her reasons as to why she was unmarried and pregnant. Susan was well aware that if this got out it would create a local scandal!

"Cathie, roll Sofiya onto her side and I'll give her an injection for the pain. It will take about twenty minutes to take effect, so put the gas and air cylinder next to the bed first." Sofiya opened her eyes, saw the mask and knowing what it was, wrenched it out of Cathie's hands and sucked in the pain-relieving gas like a drug addict.

Less than half an hour later, Susan, Cathie and Irene stood round the bed staring at the tiny infant in front of them.

"That wus quick, Doctur Martin. Whit was wrang?" Irene asked.

"The baby was the wrong way round, Irene. The back of the baby's head pressing against the mother's spine is very painful and labour takes much longer. Sofiya was fully dilated so a quick injection of oxytocin, a few manipulations, and here we are. I'm glad I didn't need the forceps or that would have meant stitches."

"It's a girl," Cathie whispered. "What's wrang wi her, doctur? She's hardly movin and why is her heid a funny shape?" Cathie sucked in her breath in horror, "Ah, look at her feet!" Cathie burst out.

Irene, wide eyed with shock, stared at Susan. "Doctur Martin, this wee bairn has black curly hair, her Ladyship is a red head, and she looks like she's frowning."

"Irene, the colour of the baby's hair is the least of her problems. On the way here you told me of your plans for the baby's future. Well, that's well and truly out of the window now. We need to think of a plan B." Susan drew her brows down, "Irene, did you say you had put it about the town that your daughter in London was pregnant?" Irene nodded. "But she isn't?" Irene nodded again. "That might be a way out, an answer to the predicament." The three women stood silent, each with her own thoughts. Susan's initial reaction to the deformities had been to cover her up and let nature take its course. That might have been kinder in the long run and save a lot of heartache, but with Cathie and Irene looking on that was unthinkable… they wouldn't understand.

"Right! First things first." Susan who was used to taking control, went into action. "This wee lamb needs urgent hospitalization. Get her ready, Irene. I'll phone the paediatric cardiac consultant in the Sick Kids' Hospital and take her there right now. I will make up a simple, but partially true story her mother is unwell and can't be with her. They are very discrete and won't ask any questions because the primary reason for her admission is obvious… to save her life." Privately, Susan wondered how the hell this happened. "This baby is fighting for her life. If she survives and it's a big *if*, it's unlikely she will ever be adopted or even fostered, but we can worry about that at a later date. Let's see what we can do for her right now."

"Dinna ye worry, doctur. Ye deal wi the bairn and your richt, we wull decide whit's tae be done when the time comes. Maybe wi a young doctur livin' wi us, the Social micht agree tae let us become her foster parents?" Cathie said hopefully.

"Doctur! Cathie! A've got it! A'll tell awbody ma dochter's hid her bairn, a wee lassie in London the day. Naebody need tae ken the bairn is in the hospital in Edinburgh. Then when its time fur the bairn tae be discharged, a'll pretend tae gan tae London, collect the bairn

285

frae Edinburgh and bring her back hame wi me… am her 'granny' efter awe. We dinna need tae involve the Social. And because the bairns no weel, if onybody asks, a'll tell them ma dochter canny baith work and tak care o' her wee lassie at the same time and she's been offered a guid job in Australia… which is true… and she is aboot tae gan awa there. Whit dae ye think? And the bairn will be wi her real mither."

"That makes a lot of sense Irene; let's hope your daughter agrees to cover for Sofiya."

"Aye, she wull, doctur. She wus freens wi her ladyship at the scuil and when a explain the situation she'll agree and she'll never brek her confidence. Onieway, she'll no be back in Scotland fur a lang time."

Sofiya wouldn't be able to see her baby for many weeks yet and this could be a blessing in disguise, Susan thought. And it gave her time to discuss the situation with her from a clinical point of view and not an emotional one.

"Irene, bring the car round and let's get on our way as quickly as possible. I don't have access to oxygen and this baby will almost certainly need oxygen and I don't have paediatric intravenous equipment to keep her hydrated either. Cathie, relax, don't worry. The injection I gave Sofiya won't wear off for a number of hours yet. Just let her sleep. I'll call back when we return and break the news to her myself."

Racing through Susan's mind was the thought that her son, Neil, a scientist, would be interested in this child's history. With Irene out of the room and Cathie busy taking the entonox cylinder downstairs, Susan quickly got a syringe and needle out of her bag and withdrew a sample of the baby's blood from the umbilical cord. She decided she would store this in her freezer, irrespective of what happened to the infant. The results would be interesting, once DNA human fingerprinting had been perfected and her son and his colleagues in haematology were close to perfecting the process.

Chapter 9

PLAN B was certainly the best option for the baby who was now safe in the Sick Kids' Hospital and it should have been for Sofiya. Susan did her best to encourage Sofiya to face reality and discussed, step by step, all of her baby's medical health and physical needs, and possible future problems once the baby was discharged from hospital. Sofiya already knew what the future held for the baby from a medical point of view, but felt no emotion. She would never be able to acknowledge the infant as her daughter. Susan had done her best to keep her consultations with Sofiya professional, but most of the time she realized Sofiya was not listening. Never once did Sofiya ask Susan about her baby or exhibit any motherly anxiety. It was as though she had never had the child and she cut most medical discussions short by staring out of the window. Cathie reported her concerns to Susan about Sofiya's withdrawal and was deeply concerned as to what Sofiya might do to herself.

At times Sofiya began to wonder if the 'grey rain' that dripped endlessly inside her head would ever stop. She had treated new mothers for post-natal depression in the past, but she never realized until now how cruel the condition could be. Sofiya knew the depression could vary in depth and duration, but for most new mothers, with a little one to care for it passed relatively quickly. In other cases, thankfully few and far between, some post-natal mothers showed no interest in their baby, crying out they didn't want the child. Sofiya had known that they required urgent hospitalization and psychiatric help. When she was in labour, she remembered telling Cathie that she hated the baby and because she had never seen the infant, who might not survive, began to wonder if it had all really happened. Sofiya built a deep protective wall to shield herself from any emotional involvement with the infant and from the heart-ache, the pain and guilt, the last months had inflicted on her.

"This his tae stop!" Irene, remembering what her own minor post-natal depression felt like, decided it was time to act. "This is no richt. It's been gaun on far tae lang. There's only one thing tae dae, Cathie."

"I couldna agree mair wi ye, Irene. I wis gawna tell Doctur Martin that Sofiya needs tae be moved tae the hospital. But what are ye suggestin'? "

"Am awa tae phone Jim, her faither, Cathie. He kens awe aboot this, richt frae the start. She'll listen tae him and its aboot time she got back tae her ain life, irrespective o' whit happens wi the bairn. She needs a project tae tak her mind aff awe this." Irene frowned. "What wis it she wanted tae dae? Oh aye, rebuild Leightham Hoose. Well she needs tae mak a start afore the hail thing collapses intae the grund." Irene wisely nodded her head, tapping her teeth at the same time and while still thinking about the situation went downstairs to make the phone call.

Jim arrived less than an hour later, at the same time as Doctor Martin and, without mincing his words, challenged his daughter. "So you don't want to see your own baby, eh? Look at me!! And you've never held her in your arms? And never taken an interest in her at all? Well... doctor Martin, whether you agree or not... get that infant here as soon as possible, preferably this afternoon. My daughter is not poor. She can pay all the expenses for transportation, private nurses, house visits from doctors, so get her here *now*!" Jim stood directly in front of Sofiya and put his arms out to hold her. "How do you think I would have responded to a child of my own or my adopted daughter should she have been born with any special need? You are my beloved girl and your wee lassie will mean the same to you, whatever the future holds for you both and you are made of stronger stuff than this. I'm ashamed of you." That worked. Sofiya stood up and blinded from the tears of sheer relief, she collapsed into her dad's arms.

"Jim… You don't mind me calling you Jim?" Susan asked. "No? Well, that's what I came to tell you all. The baby is ready to be discharged and I have volunteered to take care of her on a daily basis, until you feel strong enough to look after her yourself, Sofiya. The hospital will transport her by ambulance and supply oxygen tanks and plastic nasal tubing, everything she needs in case of an emergency." Susan looked at the people in front of her. "Listen to me. No one with any kind of illness can come near the baby and Jim… *no smoking*!! You will blow us all to smithereens with an oxygen cylinder in the house and, Jim, take my word for it, under these circumstances you can't do better than our National Health Service."

Digging into her pocket, Susan turned to Irene. "Here is the train ticket to Edinburgh and I have booked you into The Carlton Hotel for two nights. The ambulance will bring you back with the baby and with a bit of luck no one will notice."

Susan was glad to see smiles of relief all around her. "Cathie, go get your coat on. Jim can stay with his daughter. You and I are going to Dundee to buy all the equipment, bedding and baby clothing Sofiya will need for her daughter… and I hear there's been a fair bit of knitting going on…?" Susan laughed.

Three days later Irene appeared back with Sofiya's baby daughter and Susan has been right… no one noticed their arrival by ambulance. Sofiya held out her arms, took her baby from Irene and with tears running down her cheeks, looked down at the tiny infant in her arms, overwhelmed with guilt and remorse. She vowed whatever happened, whatever path their lives took, as long as she was alive, her daughter would want for nothing.

Strangely enough, no one asked any questions, neither the gardeners nor the villagers. A brand-new Silver Cross high pram appeared in Pittendreal. After Cathie and Irene finished squabbling as to who was going to push the pram, they proudly took the baby out for walks and later on pushed her in her wheelchair. The sisters could hardly walk a hundred yards along Pittendreal High Street or the Mid-Shore without half the shopkeepers and the local population, initially concealing their surprise at the physical appearance of the infant, gathering round the pram with a silver coin in their hands doing their best to get the "bairn" to hold it in her hand to ward off the devil. Villagers and the village children took the little infant with her black curly hair to their hearts and the village matrons reassured the sisters that they could babysit anytime, and offered a multitude of advice on how to keep the bairn warm and what was, in their opinion, the best baby milk powder.

* * *

"Who names this child?" the Rev John McDougall asked, a few weeks later looking round the members of the baby's family and friends gathered round the Victorian font which his grandfather, the Rev Tom McDougall had found in the basement of Pittendreal Parish Church many years ago and had had it restored and placed in its rightful place at the side of the altar.

"I am her godmother," Sofiya answered the minister.

"Ah, Lady Leightham, and what name are we giving this little one?"

"Harriet."

290

The Reverend reached out to take the infant from Sofiya. The baby was beautifully robed in her forebears' Victorian christening robe, petticoat and the bonnet, Maggie Bowman had made for her granddaughter, Aggie Gardner's baby Alice Jane.

Sofiya knew her birth-father, James, had been christened by the Rev Tom McDougall in Pittendreal, in the same robe as she had been christened in, in Ceylon before her parents moved to Kenya. She also knew the robe had been sent back in a box to her great-aunt Jane with her mother's silk wedding dress and personal documents, prior to her adoption by Jim and Ina. Cathie made a mental note that after today these would be returned to the same box and carefully stored in the loft thinking the robe might never see the light of day again.

The Rev John McDougall gently smiled, thinking perhaps he was the only person in the church, besides Sofiya, who realized the significance of the choice of the name Harriet. Sofiya's dad, standing across from his beloved daughter, smiled and gently nodded his head in support and respect for her bravery. Removing the baby's christening bonnet, the Reverend leaned over the font and with holy water from the River Jordan, performed the naming ceremony and welcomed the infant into the congregation of the Church of Scotland, in the name of the Father, the Son and the Holy Ghost.

As they left the church, the congregation of Pittendreal church jostled each other to take the baby's photograph, nearly knocking the camera out of the hands of the official photographer from Ireland's, the photographers in Leightham. The church had been relatively full for baby Harriet's christening, but it was packed to standing room only a few years later, for the funeral of the little girl with black curly hair, Harriet, whom the village had taken to their hearts.

Chapter 10

SOPHIE sat utterly astounded by what she had just read. Taking a few deep breaths, she lay back in the chair and reflected on all she had read to date. Just like the stories which her mother had been told by her 'great-aunt Jane' so many years ago, this was not fantasy or fiction, this was the truth. She was in awe at the strength of her mother's character, to have endured the appalling revelation of who her real parents were, then to be abandoned by Johnny Geiger, rejected by him, the father of her baby. Sophie now understood why the Victorian christening robe in the attic had never seen the light of day since her sister, Harriet, had been christened in it: it would have brought back painful, unbearable memories for her mother.

Sophie also admired her mother for travelling to other countries to look for her real parents and trying to discover what happened to her grandmother who, along with her parents, may still have been alive in the 1970s. Her mother had then travelled to Russia, prior to perestroika and glasnost, searching for the possible link between herself and a Russian princess who had mysteriously arrived in Scotland at the end of the 1800s, Alasdair Forman's unfortunate fiancée known as Janet McDougall. Sophie shook her head knowing that she could never have undertaken such heart-rending, emotional journeys.

Today's chapters confirmed what Sophie had suspected for the last six months. Her mother had given birth to a disabled infant and had only been able to care for her baby from a distance because of the times she lived in...so cruel. And in order to be involved in her child's life she had become her godmother, not admitting to being her mother!

The situation must have been unbearable. Sophie could not imagine the pain. The only positive outcome was that at least her mother knew where her baby was. Other women in the same position suffered the cruelty of being forced to have their illegitimate infant adopted, never knowing who adopted their baby or what happened to it and going on useless quests to try to find their child in later years. Thank God we have moved on from being judged when we have a child out of wedlock. Judge not lest ye be judged… obviously that didn't count in past years and centuries.

How did her mother cope without ante-natal care, with prolonged labour and serious post-natal depression without professional psychiatric support? And staring her in the face, the truth about her infant's physical condition and African forebears. How did she overcome feelings of guilt and blame when the one person who should have shared them had abandoned her… opted out?

She would never know how a mother could come to terms with making the agonising decision to give her child up for adoption, only to discover her baby's physical problems would mean long-term institutional care instead. Could she have lived with her mother's memories, her conflicting feelings of love and guilt? Mercifully, Sophie had never been in a position to have to decide whether to part with her daughter, Sophia. Her mother had always assured her she would support and respect any decision she made regarding her own body and now Sophie knew why.

Sophie realized she was never told Harriet was her sister, in case she might have accidentally revealed the secret; the disgrace and humiliation would have been unbearable for all of them. It is no wonder she had loved the little girl she had played with at Mount View, thinking she was Irene's granddaughter. They were sisters and she could not have loved her more knowing the truth. Sophie held her hand to her throat remembering that although she was very young herself the painful memory of Harriet's funeral at such a young age. Now it all made sense. It was crystal clear why her mother dreaded April when memories came flooding back to haunt her. The sins of the father are visited on the child and in Harriet's case, the unwitting sins of her real parents, half-brother and sister, had been visited not on her mother, but on her innocent child.

Sophie smiled, thinking of how the local community had taken her little sister to their heart. They could show the world how to treat human beings of all races, religions and creeds. As a memorial to her sister, her mother had used her inheritance to convert Mount View, once it was no longer in use, to accommodate people with a special need, so they could live independent lives, renaming it Harriet House. But Sophie knew who had really pulled her mother through her darkest moments, supported her through dark days... her grandfather Jim, her grandmother Susan, Cathie and Irene.

I am going to insist I help and support mum solve whatever situation has arisen by the arrival of that letter! Her mother had taken Johnny Geiger's letter with her, but the package was still on the coffee table. Maybe the contents held the solution?

With that thought in mind, Sophie leaned forward to put the sheaf of papers she was still holding down, when she suddenly realised there were still a few more pages stuck together with a paper clip at the back of the last chapter. The sound of the dog barking alerted Sophie to her mother returning from her walk. Faintly she heard the sound of water running in the kitchen: *mum must be making tea for us before she comes upstairs...what a cool customer.* Looking down at the pages, she realised it was another letter! Not sure if her mother had deliberately left the letter for her to read, Sophie decided to go ahead and read it to save time. Again it was written in the style her mother used when she wrote about the past.

Chapter 11

L IZZIE TARVET was sitting by the kitchen fire knitting her hundredth pair of socks. She remembered her granny's words: "You shid aye hae a sock on the needles, the deil macs work fur idol hauns". Lizzie had plenty of 'idol time' on her hands. A knock at her front door startled her. *Wha on earth can that be, richt at tea-time?* Lizzie put down her knitting needles and made her way to the door. There stood the postie with a big brown envelope which he handed to Lizzie.

"Sorry, Miss Tarvet. This arrived late the day, oor late fur the second delivery, but it looked important so a brung it fur ye on ma wi hame."

Lizzie frowned, shrugged her shoulders and took the envelope. She had no idea who it could be from. Going back inside she sat down, tore open the envelope which contained a letter and two other sealed envelopes.

Leightham Estate,
Aberdeenshire,
December 1912.

"Mercy on us! Its frae his Lordship in Eberdeen! Noo, whit can he be wantin'? Wi awe they fine estate folk oot o' work thanks tae his daughter-in law and his grandson… he's a bit late tae offer them work on his Eberdeen Estate or apologize noo." Lizzie continued to read his lordship's letter.

Dear Miss Tarvet,
The enclosed envelopes arrived here just after we heard about the ship, the Titanic, *going down. They had been re-*

directed here by the post office, as obviously Leightham House no longer exists. Initially I wasn't sure what to do with them as they are not addressed to me, but I can confirm this is my grandson's handwriting. I placed them in my filing cabinet, meaning to deal with them later. I was in a state of shock and sank into a depression thinking I would never see my grandson again and I am ashamed to admit I forgot about them until last week, when I asked Mr Jameson, my butler, if he knew the person to whom they were addressed.

As you can see, they are addressed to a Miss Alice Gardner, care of Leightham House and Mr Jameson informs me she was a housemaid, a member of your staff and he thought you would know where she is and would forward them to her. I have respected my grandson's privacy and not opened the letters but I have no idea why he would be writing to this woman.

Further to this, I must beg you to treat with complete confidentiality the information I am about to give you. When my grandson, Lord Robert Leightham, set off to resolve the financial debts his mother left behind in Scotland, London and Monte Carlo, before leaving France in desperation, he sent a telegram to a distant wealthy American relative of his mother in America to ask for financial assistance. (I believe Elizabeth's forbears emigrated to the States from Scotland many years before. Apparently they were originally plantation and slave owners, but were 'couthie' enough to sell up and move north before the Civil War.) My grandson boarded the ill-fated Titanic, as instructed to do so by that relative, with the promise of financial help.

I believed Robbie had drowned and he was the last of the Leightham family line. Incredibly I received a telegram from America from Robbie to tell me he had survived the sinking. To tell the truth I was utterly astonished and cried from sheer relief! He had been taken to a hospital in Canada with spinal injuries and was now living in New York.

As you will remember, earlier this year, I instructed Mr Jameson to inform you my grandson had survived.

Then a letter arrived from my grandson. In his letter he gave me the heart-breaking news, he was not be returning to Scotland. He had no option but to stay in America. His mother's uncle, Andrew Harrison had made the proviso: to receive financial aid Robbie had to marry his granddaughter, Rachel! The Americans are fanatical about British Royalty and titles, and for his daughter to become Lady Leightham was too tempting an opportunity to miss and it appears she agreed with her grandfather and they are now married.

I have no idea who Alice Gardner is or what her connection is to my grandson. I feel certain you will know her whereabouts and ask that you forward the letters to her. I might have a vacancy for her to work for me on my estate if she is willing to travel north and is still unemployed.

I remain, yours truly,

Lord John Leightham.

Lizzie nearly choked on the last sentence. *What a bliddy cheek. Oh, ye will offer her some employment will ye? A weel, your lordship, it's too late and I hiv nae idea whaur she or her family are but luckily for ye I ken somebidy wha micht.* Lizzie reached for her shawl and wrapping it tightly around her head and shoulders against a biting north wind, with the envelopes in her hand, made her way to the Phimister household.

* * *

"Goodness, Lizzie Tarvet! I couldn't think who would be at the door. What are you doing out on such a terrible night. And it looks like it's going to snow. What can I do for you?"

"A weel, Miss Phimister, the postie drapped they envelopes aff at ma hoose late this efternuin. There wus a letter for me as weel frae Lord John Leightham, apologisin' fur no senden' them sooner. A' thocht that ye micht ken whaur Alice Gairdner micht be as naither she nor her family his been seen fur months? And a've no seen nor heard o' hur since that awfy day when we cleared oot the big hoose."

"What makes you think I would know, Miss Tarvet?"

"Ach, ye ken whit local gossips like, Miss Phimister. A' dinna want tae speir aboot the faimlie ony further… it's nane o' ma business. But they look important and the postmarks on baith o' them show the letters were posted in April, from Liverpool! And we awe ken whit happened in April…" Lizzie ducked her head with respect.

"You did the right thing Lizzie. Leave them with me. Thank you. Now get away home with you before it starts to snow." She could hear her sister, Rosie, shouting from the living room, "Who is at the door?"

"It's alright, Rosie! Nothing to worry about."

Fimmy had already decided what was to be done with the letters. Carefully opening the seals, and reading the contents, she resealed them with glue from the kitchen dresser. *There's only one thing to be done with these documents which will be of great importance to Alice. What an unfortunate lapse of memory the old duffer had. He might have saved Alice from a great deal of misery had he forwarded the letters when he should have. Helen McDougall knows Alice's whereabouts, I'm certain of that, because she more or less told me when I caught up with her in Lightman's tea rooms in the summer, buying children's toys for Alice's young charges in Russia. Helen will post them on to Alice, wherever she is.*

* * *

I bet the letters are in the package and mum will let me read them when she comes upstairs, Sophie thought. *At last, she's here,* as Sophie heard her mother coming up the stair.

298

PART TEN

Chapter 1

S OPHIE PLACED THE SHEETS of paper on the coffee table and rose up to embrace her mother as she entered the bedroom, but Sofiya indicated she should sit down. Crossing to the window Sofiya laid down the tea tray. Sophie couldn't believe her ears... her mother was humming, and looking as if the weight of the world had been lifted from her shoulders. It passed through Sophie's mind, that if they had been catholic, her mother was acting as though she had just been to confession and said however many Hail Marys the priest had given her, to absolve her of her sins.

"Mother?!" Sophie gasped.

"Sophie, relax. After so many years of supressing the truth, this has been one of the happiest days of my life. I am free, free from the heart-rending, shameful burden I have had to hide since my youth." Sofiya looked pensive for a moment before continuing.

"But I was one of the privileged few in a position to decide what to do with my illegitimate baby, the innocent victim of the times in which she was conceived. Many young women had their babies taken from them without their consent, and their babies were adopted here at home or exported like goods to another country without an invoice, a receipt, or legal documents. And in recent years, when they tried to trace their children, the mothers discovered many of the adoption records were missing, disposed of, or burnt, and remember there was no obligation for the adoptive parents to inform the children they had been adopted. But I knew. I knew where my little girl, your sister, was, and is. Every April, from now on, we will celebrate Harriet's birthday. No more mourning and I don't give a hoot what people say anymore."

Sophie quickly butted in. "To coin a phrase, mum, I doubt anyone would give two brass razoos. They couldn't care less what happened to you all these years ago; the times, thank goodness, have changed since those days."

"You don't take sugar, do you?" Sophie shook her head in awe of her mother, in her strength and thinking, *You are an amazing woman*, as she watched her mother calmly pour the tea, totally unfazed by the emotional journey they had been through this afternoon.

"You know I don't."

"Yes... yes. I bought some Kit-Kats from our local Pakistani corner shop in the village. They are always open on Sundays. Ah, I see you have read the letter from Lord John, my three-times great-grandfather. Interesting...? Yes?"

"Why don't you give me the letters to read, the ones he sent to Miss Tarvet?"

"All in good time, Sophie. But there is always a fly in the ointment. First read the obnoxious letter from Johnny Geiger, the one I received last April." Sofiya handed the letter to her daughter. "You might need a whisky, not a cup of tea, once you have read it."

Sophie took the letter her mother handed her. It began...

My dearest Sofiya,

"He's got a nerve, Mum."

"Just read the letter, Sophie. No comments till you have finished, please."

My dearest Sofiya,
I have taken the liberty of addressing you as my dearest. I would not blame you if you tore this letter up and refused to continue reading but hear me out. Not a day has passed without you in my mind and in my heart since that awful day

I walked away from you in Pittendreal and then abandoned you in America, when you were at your most vulnerable. My excuse... I was weak and too cowardly to stand up to my mother. I know, I know... a pathetic excuse. Attitudes mercifully have changed since those days and I offer you my sincere apology. I was wrong. I bowed to the times we lived in and to my family's prejudice.

The week before our wedding, you will remember, I spent a few days with my parents in Austria. My mother had discovered the relationship between your parents and the fact we shared a grandfather and great-grandmother on both sides! My mother did not become hysterical as you, who knew her, would have expected. Instead, she quietly and calmly informed me of the genetic risks, not only from your parents but also from our forebears; secrets that had been kept from me till that week.

Gradually mother reverted to the woman you remember, agitated to the point of hysteria, but not before she reminded me that our mutual great-grandmother, Elizabeth Leightham, had been addicted to gambling and drugs and had committed suicide. My grandmother, Rachel Harrison, had spent her later years in a mental institution. My mother went on to say that we could not marry, not only because of your parents, who you and I both know, were the unwitting victims of incestuous love that led to their marriage, but also because of the drug addiction and mental illness that plagued other generations on both sides.

I feel certain if you researched your Russian, royal, in-bred forebears, you would find evidence of mental and physical disability among them, I have no doubt.

My mother begged me not to marry you, emotionally blackmailing me, saying she would harm herself if I did. To my shame I acquiesced. My dad had to return to America with my mother. There was no way she could have attended our wedding, even if I had insisted on going ahead with it. But, we were also victims, the unwitting prisoners of our feelings for each other. I apportion no blame. But over the years I have asked myself, why didn't your great-aunt Jane tell you as soon as she knew of our relationship... and put a stop to it? She would have saved us so much pain if she had not left it until we were about to marry. To have the truth revealed at the reading of her will was disgraceful!

"He's blaming your grandmother, mum!!" Sophie burst out.

"Just ignore that, Sophie. He knows the reasons and I didn't know my parents had adopted me and adoption was rarely revealed to the child. Read the rest..."

Sophie turned to the next page...

I seemed to have inherited Robert Leightham's characteristics. He was a weak-kneed, spineless man, terrified of his mother. His abandoning of your pregnant grandmother, Alice Gardner, not informing her he had survived the sinking of the Titanic. Worse still, cheating my grandmother, marrying her despite knowing that he was already married, although there is no proof of that. Our grandparents' marriage was arranged by Andrew Harrison, a cousin of our mutual great-grandmother, Elizabeth Leightham. He made a deal with Robert. If Robert married his granddaughter, Rachel, he would clear Elizabeth's debts, and also give Robert sufficient funds to save the Leightham Estate and house. But, as we both know, it was too late to save the house.

To my everlasting shame, I abandoned you in New York, calling you despicable names, accusing you of behaviour I knew to be untrue. I was so certain you would give our child up for adoption and avoid the shame of bearing a bastard child. In all honesty I cut myself off, wanted to put the past behind me and forget you existed.

Revenge is sweet, but I know it is not in your nature to either look for or relish revenge. But if you want revenge...

here it is. I married a woman knowing full well I did not love her, which she quickly realized. My wife was a career woman. She worked for the government in Washington and was rarely at home. She had no desire to have children, so I am the last of the Geigers. I know you have a daughter who is married with four children. I envy you. Today I am a childless lonely widower.

It is such a pathetic plea, but I ask for your forgiveness. I have loved you from the moment we met and not a day has passed that I did not think of you and I bitterly regret my actions. Every day when I look in the mirror and see the scar from the stone Cathie threw at me on that fateful day in Pittendreal, the stone from Leightham House, it reminds me of what I did. My wife has been dead for several years now and I know you have been a widow for a considerable length of time. Do you think you could find it in your heart to let me make it up to you in our retirement years and marry me now?

With no legal documents of your father's birth proving his parentage, I am therefore the rightful Lord John Leightham. I am Lord Robert's heir and should inherit both the title and his estate. We will be Lord and Lady Leightham. I like the sound of that. And take my word for it, the Leightham dynasty is secure in your hands and, because I have no heirs, I have no desire to change that. I look forward to being a step-grandfather to your grandchildren and having a long happy retirement with your... our lovely family!

I know you will never forget, but I believe forgiveness is the first step towards closure. You may have looked on me as your unrequited love over the years, but now with all my heart I want to change that.

With all my love,
Johnny

Chapter 2

SOPHIE WAS READY for that whisky!

"The impudent b...d! Draw a line under the past! That does it!! I told you last April, we would work it out together. Well, we have dealt with the past, but this is the present. Your 'unrequited love'!! That's a joke. Geiger... the cause of all the misery you suffered over the years. Who does he think he is?" Sophie nearly choked on the words. "He will be some sort of grandfather to my children, over my dead body! The...the arrogance of the man is beyond belief...the...the cheek! And he wants his rightful place as Lord Leightham?!" Sophie stood up and making a fist with both hands placed them on her hips.

"Let battle commence, mum. I'm ready to take him on. Now, where do we begin?"

"Hang on, old girl, or I'll go and get you one of my blood pressure tablets," Sofiya laughed. "No need to do anything, darling. It's all been settled, dealt with."

"I don't understand, mum. We should plan how to deal with Johnny Geiger, now, once and for all!"

Sofiya laughed again. "Sit down, Sophie, or I *will* go and get you a whisky. I hate to take the wind out of your sails, but there's nothing to be done. I have already dealt with the man once and for all. I assure you, we will never hear from him again."

"How on earth did you accomplish that? Mental telepathy?"

"No! Do you remember during the school holidays when you and your girlfriends returned from Marbella, in October?" Sophie nodded. "You said you thought I was a little mm ...flat?"

"I remember. I was worried you might be developing flu, because you had not yet had your annual flu vaccine."

"No, it wasn't that. It was the confrontation I had just had with Geiger, who turned up unannounced and having to clean up the mess he left behind."

"Geiger was here?! He timed his visit well. We were all away and the children were with Iain's mum and dad. 'Clean up the mess'...Did he break something?"

"No, listen. As soon as he left, I wrote the whole visit down for you so I wouldn't forget any of it, as I want you to know everything that happened. Revenge *is* sweet. And just in case I suddenly snuff it and Geiger still tries to claim the title and the estate, you will have all the necessary documents to defeat him even in a court of law."

Sofiya lifted up the brown package, broke its seal, withdrew her notes and at the same time a considerable number of documents, certificates and letters fell out of it onto the coffee table.

"God bless Miss Reid, Elizabeth Leightham's maid who brought all her mistress's possessions back from Monte Carlo; Mr Jameson, Lord Robert's butler; and Mr Montgomery, the estate manager, for their prompt action the night before the roof was removed in 1912; Billie Gibson's grandfather, William Gibson's letter confirming what happened that night. And also Lord John, for sending my grandfather letters to Miss Tarvet, who took them to Miss Phimister, who forwarded them to Alice Gardner my grandmother via Helen McDougall... an amazing paper trail. And most of all, a letter your dad and I found in the Aberdeen house. God bless the woman I thought was my great-aunt, Jane; she knew I would need the evidence someday, the letters sealed in a package and the most essential certificates hidden in the secret base of the Ormolu clock. She never met Johnny Geiger, but she could read him like a book, because she had personal experience of the erratic behaviour of Elizabeth Leightham. She knew I would need the verification of our forebears to fight Johnny Geiger."

Sophie was stunned.

"Blood is thicker than water. Without a doubt, none of that information would have been any use on its own without DNA fingerprinting carried out by your dad and his colleague. Read for yourself the results of the scientific work he did and you will know we have the indisputable proof and evidence to feel confident we will never hear from that man again, in or out of court. And don't worry, I don't plan to snuff it any time soon." Sofiya laughed.

"Here, get on with it, read. I'm going to enjoy my cup of tea. Hurry up, it is almost my 'Happy Hour' and you need to get on your way. Iain and the children will be waiting for you at home. Hamburgers tonight… no cheese for you, right?" Sofiya laughed.

Chapter 3

I T WAS THE LAST SUNDAY of the October school holidays and Iain had taken the children to their other grandparents for the day. Sophie was in Spain with her friends. Sunday, the Lord's Day, a day Sofiya looked forward to. From the end of October to March the Leightham Estate Café and Restaurant were closed on Sundays and Mondays, except for December, in preparation for Christmas. Bunty and Vivienne had already left for Edinburgh as usual and Sofiya heard them 'nattering' all the way to the end of the drive to wait for the bus, as if they had never set eyes on each other all week.

The men were no different. Jimmy's and Ronald's argumentative voices erupted from the kitchen, on the merits of Saturday's football match, whether the goalkeeper had saved the match or lost it. On Sundays the men looked forward to a pint and a game of darts in the Leightham Arms, or if there was a Sunday football match on the pub's TV, shouted themselves hoarse again. Today the 'discussion' turned to the merit of draught beer versus canned. Ronald had bought cans of flavoured beers from the new Fallen Brewing Company and stashed them at the back of the kitchen fridge.

"Ye canna pit the pub's draught beer in the fridge, Jimmy. Ach, yer ower auld fashioned—set in yer weys." Ronald had tried several flavours of Fallen Brewery beer, liking the Inertia flavour best, but he conceded the other varieties were equally good. Ronald also liked the eye-catching, different, artwork on the cans, but didn't recognize the artist. It had caught his attention that the company used all renewable sources and minimized waste wherever possible.

"That company's protecting the planet, wi its recycling, Jimmy!"

That hit the spot with Jimmy. Recycling was his personal crusade to save the planet for the generations to follow. The latest reports on climate change, global warming, forest fires out of control, flooding, drought and the polar ice caps melting at an alarming rate, had worried Jimmy. He announced he would change to Fallen beer and get the Leightham Arms to stock it.

Sofiya heard the outer kitchen door slam shut as the two men left for the pub. Sofiya liked a beer herself at times and made a mental note to pinch a can of Ronald's beer; after all it was in her fridge, in her kitchen... she didn't need to ask permission to help herself, did she? "Peace, perfect peace at last," Sofiya muttered as she settled down to enjoy a cup of coffee in her favourite place, her bedroom bay window looking out over the Forth, and began to open the Sunday papers. The only sound in the house was music coming from Classic F*M* on the radio. Suddenly, Sofiya became aware of a car coming up the main drive.

That's odd, she thought. "I don't believe it! So much for peace and quiet! Now who on earth can that be? I am not expecting anyone," she spoke out loud to herself.

Looking out the window, she saw a car driving at speed up the right-hand side of the main drive. It looked like a rental car. Maybe the driver had got lost and was looking for directions? The man parked the car and slammed the door behind him. Sofiya put down her coffee cup and newspaper and made her way downstairs. Remembering she was alone in the house, she went to the back of the hall, opened the kitchen door and called for Laila. The dog slowly mounted the kitchen stairs, yawning and stretching as if to say *"I've been for a walk... what do you want now?"*

The front doorbell rang and with the dog at her heels, Sofiya went forward to answer it.

"Can I help you?"

The man holding a large bouquet of red roses in one hand and an obvious small square jeweller's box in the other, apparently was admiring the view. He turned to face Sofiya full on. It was Johnny Geiger! She wasn't surprised. She had been half expecting him.

Johnny made an exaggerated bow to Sofiya, offering her the flowers at the same time.

"*Lord* Johnny Leightham at your service, ma-am." Johnny, grinning from ear to ear continued, "Wow, jist as beautiful as ever."

Sofiya disgusted, wondered, *Why doesn't he just say, "Here's Johnny!"?*

Ignoring the flowers, Sofiya quietly demanded to know, "What do you want?" And added: "And don't B-S me, Lord... Johnny?"

"Well...what kine o' welcome is that? Kin ahh come in?" The southern drawl had returned.

Sofiya indicated he was to follow her. The dog, walking behind Johnny, was wagging her tail and nuzzled her nose into Johnny's hand hoping for a biscuit while drinking in his scent at the same time. Once in the study, Sofiya indicated he should sit down and put the flowers on the coffee table. Johnny jerked his hand away from the dog and slipped the jeweller's box back into his pocket.

"At least I am offering you the courtesy of a seat. When we last met, you helped yourself to one and you will need to sit down to save collapsing, once I have given you my answer to your letter and the information regarding your claim to the title and the estate. Don't take your coat off, Johnny. This won't take long."

Johnny tentatively felt for the arms of the chair before sitting. This wasn't going the way he had confidently anticipated.

Sofiya went over to the desk, took out a large brown package and after placing it on the coffee table, sat down. "Let's make it perfectly clear," she stated icily. "You made a big mistake refusing to marry me. If you had, you might have had a legal claim to the title through me. As it stands you have none. We are only related through Elizabeth Leightham. Lord Robert's mother was a cousin of the Harrisons. She was a Leightham by marriage, not birth."

"That's garbage! You cain't prove nothin'."

"Here, to save time I have all the information ready for you: DNA documents, birth, marriage certificates and letters from my forebears, people who thankfully had the Leightham Estate's best interest at heart."

Johnny began to think he might lose the battle before it even began. He started to get up out of the chair. Raising his voice, he announced, "Ahh'm not listening to any more of this. Ahh'll see *you* in court." Laila had been lying quietly at Sofiya's feet facing Johnny. The dog's tail stopped wagging and she began to push herself up onto her front paws.

"Git that dawg out o' here or ahh'll call the police."

"And tell them what? Sit down!!" Sofiya commanded sharply. Both the dog and Johnny promptly sat down. "I will tell the dog when to release you. I knew this day would come and you would turn up and I refuse to go round in circles trying to convince you. I have all the evidence right here. My friend and right-hand woman, Wilma Paterson, has researched and verified everything. The handwriting has been analysed by a graphologist to certify the writer of each letter. Wilma researched entries in town council offices and church records in Scotland and newspaper cuttings back to the mid-19th century in America. Here, take them with you... see you in court."

Sofiya shrugging her shoulders, pointed to the package, pretending she couldn't care less, but her heart was pounding.

"Ma-am, ahh sure kin find out whit's fact and whit's fiction in this woman's claims, at the touch of a keyboard."

"Do you remember my dad, Johnny? He said 'brag' was the middle name of all Americans. I disagreed with him because all my American friends and work colleagues were genuine, decent people but you... you take the biscuit!"

That silenced Johnny. "Jist git on with it!"

"Before I start, let's get something clear. What is *not* up for discussion is why I was adopted. I know why and I have the proof of who my birth parents were and my true birth certificate, but that's none of your business." Sofiya let that sink in before she continued. "Also, the woman we both thought was my great-aunt Jane was in fact my grandmother Alice Jane Gardner. Again, not up for discussion.

"And how dare you hint in your letter, bring into question the sanity of my Russian forebears. I know what you are referring to was the Tzar's family, and inbreeding. To clear the air and because you hinted about it in your letter, the only history of insanity in my Russian family was my grandfather's first wife who developed puerperal psychosis, an unexplained, psychiatric condition that *only* occurs after childbirth in otherwise normal women. They can be a danger to themselves and the infant. After the princess was found on the Palace roof about to jump with the new-born infant, she was admitted to a convent for her own safety. The story of the princess dying in childbirth was untrue, put out by the family to protect the child. There was no cholera epidemic, but the little princess did go missing.

"I also found out, when I visited Russia, that dates given were incorrect. The little princess who disappeared would have been younger than her brother, Prince Andrei. Therefore, she would have been Alice Gardner's step-daughter by marriage to Prince Alexander. I found out how she made her way to Pittendreal and was known locally as Janet McDougall throughout the late 19th century and into the 20th. Before the terrible accident that killed her, she had treated Alice Gardner for a serious condition, after the birth of my father, James, but neither of them knew how closely related they were.

"Rena McKay, my late husband's grandmother saved the blood-stained clothes of Janet, and my husband, in the mid-1980's did Janet's DNA fingerprinting, which gave indisputable proof princess Sophia was my Russian grandfather Prince Alexander's daughter. I am telling you this because I am profoundly grateful to my Russian forebears. Thanks to them I inherited an enormous fortune. I owe a great debt of gratitude to them. Never raise their names again! I have my own DNA fingerprinting, which is primarily Scottish and also proves my Russian blood and an unimportant trace of Nordic genes which probably accounts for my red hair, but most of all proves who my parents and grandparents were on both sides of my family."

That silenced Johnny.

Sofiya was tempted to say, *Are we sitting comfortably? Then I'll begin,* which was the introduction to a BBC children's radio programme, Listen with Mother, she had listened to as a child, but she wanted no interruptions and to get this meeting over with as soon as possible. From the coffee table, Sofiya lifted the package containing the information she needed to destroy Johnny's claims to the estate and opened it.

"Here! All the information I have. No need to give this one much attention because you already know the gist of it. Robert Leightham informs his grandfather that he is alive after the sinking of the *Titanic*, but will not be returning to Scotland and will be marrying Rachel Harrison. Lord John forwarded that information to the housekeeper, Miss Tarvet, and as you can see the second and third letters are addressed to Alice Gardner. Her name and the dates they were posted are the most relevant pieces of information."

Johnny took the letters. Robbie had written:

April 1912.

My darling Alice, how much I miss you and I can't wait to return home, but I have no option but to travel to America. My mother's uncle has made a financial offer, to save the estate, that I just cannot refuse. It will haunt me for the rest of my life; leaving you having our baby. I am fully aware how close you are to the date our baby is due. I might not get back in time to register the baby as my own. I don't care whether it is a boy or girl. I will be the happiest man on the planet.

I am going to have this letter witnessed and signed by my valet Edward Richardson, in case you have to register the baby by yourself and the council clerk doubts your word. Take it with you to prove I am the father. My love, I can't wait to get home to announce our marriage, have our baby christened and be a family. I have to hurry because I am about to board the Titanic, *bound for America; that is why the post mark says Liverpool.*

All my love, Robbie.

"Does that look like it has been made up? We both know Alice's baby was my father, James, adopted by Fred Paxton. The false birth certificate named Fred as the father... mother unknown. Please... ridiculous! Mother unknown, give me a break?! In London the man obtained a false birth certificate and there's no record of the birth being registered in any of the London council offices, but I have my father's true birth certificate, registered by Alice with the following proof from his father and obviously my mother Ana's birth certificate re-registered in Edinburgh." Johnny began to speak. Sofiya held her hand up. "No! Read the next one."

Alice dearest, Richardson has just brought to my attention our marriage certificate which he found in one of my jacket pockets! I was in such a rush to get to Monte Carlo, I must have stuffed it into my pocket. After our wedding and with the stress of the situation and having to leave Leightham House in such a hurry, I forgot all about it. Richardson was packing my clothes in the hotel in Monte Carlo and he found it after I had left Monaco to go to France (I will explain later). I wrote my letter to you regarding our baby, on the train from London to Liverpool. As soon as Richardson witnessed my letter, I rushed to post it, or I would have posted them together. Here is our marriage certificate and this covering note from me and counter-signed again by him verifying our wedding, the name of the church and the minister who married us. Go right away to the registrar and register our marriage!!

With all my love, Robbie.

Johnny could hardly contain himself. "That done prove nothin'. Jist a love-sick young man writing to a pregnant girl in his village. That's easily disproved… won stand up in a court of law. Lord, it's nearly a hundred years ago! All that evidence will have disappeared and ahh' don believe it anyway."

"That's ugly even for you Johnny, and don't raise your voice, the dog doesn't like it. When you get back to America, have the handwriting verified. There must be samples of my grandfather Robert's writing in your

316

possession and look at the date, December 1912. The letters were sent to Miss Tarvet from Aberdeen, months after Alice left for Russia. Was I just a village girl you got into trouble and left to face the music alone? But you walked out on me by choice. I was unmarried, and having our child. Cruel circumstances forced *my* grandfather to leave his pregnant wife. You chose to abandon me." Sofiya shook her head in disgust. "You are unconvinced? I have a third letter written to Lord John by my grandfather, Lord Robert, from America… but that can wait."

"*Our* grandfather. Where is this mysterious letter?" Johnny interrupted.

Sofiya thought of a phrase from an old American movie, *Just cut to the chase. Let's get this over with.*

"Scotland has Parish registers dating back to the 15th century and the General Registry for Scotland, certifying that my grandparents were married in a small church on the outskirts of Leightham in February 1912 and registered in 1918 by my grandmother on her return from Russia when she received the letters and certificates from her friend, Helen McDougall. Over the years, as other birth and marriage certificates came into her possession: my own birth certificate, my parents' marriage certificate from Sri Lanka, which was then Ceylon; they were all re-registered in Scotland by her and hidden in a secret compartment in the Ormolu clock. My grandmother knew I would need them some day."

"So what? *Written* evidence that means nothin'."

"Take a deep breath, Johnny. Listen to me. I have the absolute proof of who you are and it is not who you think you are. Our only mutual forebear was our great-grandmother, Elizabeth Leightham."

"You're joking! You expect me to believe this…this!" Johnny raised his voice with contempt.

"Stop raising your voice, Johnny. You are making the dog anxious. I am grateful to Elizabeth's maid Miss Reid, who on the night of Elizabeth's suicide, packed all her mistress's belongings in Monte Carlo and brought them back to Leightham House."

"Ahh' don give a damn what she packed. The blasted roof was removed. How the hell do you expect me to believe you found any of her belongings in a pile of ancient rubble? That proves nothin'."

"Here is the letter that proves what I have just told you."

"Hu' another bit o' paper. You have no proof, just paper evidence. You cain't prove nothin'." Johnny sneered.

Sofiya just shook her head.

"To save time I will read it to you as it is in local dialect and you wouldn't understand most of it. It was brought to me by a young man, Billie Gibson. His grandfather William had worked on the estate in his youth and he writes..." Sofiya read the letter out loud.

Dear Billie,
A wee note that might be of interest to you.

"Et cetera, et cetera." Sofiya missed out some of the superfluous sentences.

I know Her Ladyship will be very interested: The night before the roof was removed from Leightham House, I heard hammering at the door and several other doors in our street. Mr Jameson, the old butler, told me to get dressed and get up to the front entrance of the big house right away. Mr Montgomery, the estate manager, was next door at the Fairgrieve's house instructing the two housemaids, Ella and Babbie to do the same.

When we arrived, there were other estate workers there and a row of vans and covered wagons outside. We were all sworn to absolute secrecy, and instructed to get into the house and use crates marked 'Aberdeen' and pack everything we could lay our hands on. We stacked the crates in the waiting transporters outside before the official removal vans arrived next morning. Well, we did as we were told and took as many of the fine furnishings, silver, china and paintings we could cram in.

Once I got home, I heard the sound of the vans and wagons driving through the village in the direction of Dundee, not Edinburgh where the auction houses were. I thought no more about it till about a week later when I met Ella and Babbie in the street. They had been taken to the family's private rooms and told to pack everything of Lord Robert's and Her Ladyship's personal belongings, and to leave nothing behind. Ella Fairgrieve said that the suitcases Miss Reid had brought back from Monte Carlo were there and had never been opened.

But what upset Ella was when she emptied the bedside drawers in Her Ladyship's bedroom, a box full of needles and syringes burst open, some still filled with blood! Ella grabbed at them in case they smashed on the floor and stabbed her hand with one of the needles. The poor woman had a bandage on her hand from a septic infection from the stab wound and she had to pay the doctor to drain it for her and lie about how she got it! Well, well... she's recovered now but has an ugly scar on her hand.

Let me know how you get on.

All the best, granddad Wullie.

Sofiya let that information sink in before continuing. "When my late husband and I went up to my Aberdeen Estate, we emptied the loft and the outside building and found everything that had been spirited away from Leightham House that night. We found the suitcases Miss Reid brought back from Monte Carlo and they still remained locked. My husband saved the blood from Elizabeth's syringes and Lord Robert's razor and hairbrushes till DNA fingerprinting could confirm their genetic patterns.

"I think we should take a break. I am going to make a fresh cup of coffee and if you value your skin, I advise you to sit still till I get back. This breed of dog is very obedient and I assure you she will not let you move unless I tell her to. Don't worry, Johnny. Everything is a game to her." Laila had begun to follow Sofiya who turned and put her hand up and commanded the dog to "Stay!!" Laila obeyed Sofiya. Disappointed, the dog turned and with her head drooping, slumped back down at the side of Sofiya's chair, but Laila then looked directly at Johnny and positively grinned in anticipation.

Chapter 4

S OFIYA RETURNED with the coffee to find Johnny sitting as if paralysed in the chair. Neither he nor the dog had moved. Putting the tray down, Sofiya served Johnny with a mug of coffee and gave Laila a dog biscuit from her pocket. "Good girl," Sofiya praised the dog.

"I have proven beyond doubt with more than sufficient written evidence, to confirm you have no legal claim to the estate. But there is one letter from Robert Leightham living in America, the one I withheld from you when we began and an American newspaper article." Johnny almost choked on his coffee.

"It is from my grandfather, Robert, to Lord John, dated 1914. Here, read it for yourself." Sofiya handed him the letter. Johnny put his mug down on the coffee table and reluctantly took the letter from her.

My dear grandfather,

I cannot explain how difficult it is for me to write this letter. I feel I am being punished for something, unknown to you, that I did in Scotland before I left. I have had to come to terms with the fact that the injuries I sustained when the Titanic *sank have left me impotent. To put it bluntly, I can never father a child. Rachel knew this when we married, but insisted on going ahead with the wedding, claiming it was only the title she wanted. She had no interest in Scotland whatsoever.*

Unknown to me, she organized a large dinner party for the Harrisons and friends and in the middle of it, announced she is delighted we are going to have a baby! I have agreed to say nothing so the Harrison family will

accept the child as ours and its inheritance will not be affected, but I assure you the child is not *mine. Nothing matters anymore, but I will never forgive myself for leaving Scotland on a useless quest, instead of enjoying a future that would have given me a family and you such joy.*
Robert.

"So what, Sofiya? It's all in the past. Let's look to the future." Johnny began to wrestle in his pocket for the ring.

"No, Johnny, don't! I will never marry you or even consider living with you. I still have the beautiful engagement ring you gave me all these years ago when you proposed, when we landed after jumping out of the twin-engine aeroplane and parachuting to the ground! It was so romantic. Don't spoil the good memories. Draw a line under the bad...I have. See... I had the diamond made into a necklace." Sofiya indicated the necklace round her neck.

"But are y'all not lonely?"

"Lonely, Johnny, me? I know I have been a widow for a long time, but I have never been alone. I have a wonderful family, friends and a special friend, Charles Macintosh. Charles is a widower. We enjoy each other's company and have many mutual interests. We respect each other and have a great platonic 'no-ties' relationship. I would go as far as to say we love each other but we are not in love. That's for the young." Sofiya smiled at the sceptical expression on Johnny's face. "Keep the ring, Johnny. You are still a good looking man and still have a head of curly hair although now grey. Go on one of those websites. Lots of people are looking for relationships," Sofiya said patronisingly. Johnny positively scowled.

You are sailing close to the wind, Sofiya. Change the subject.

"Now please, can we get on?"

Sofiya took the last piece of written American evidence from the package. "Wilma flew to America and did an extensive amount of research in Georgia for me. The *Augusta Chronicle,* first published in 1785, had the names of the slave owners, and the National Historic Museum of Georgia had the names of cotton plantations and lists of slaves. There are also Captains' Logbooks, documenting the names of the cargo ships and including a list of slaves bought by a Mr P Harrison, circa 1850s. One name jumps out, a slave named Matilda, bought by a Mr Harrison."

"He probably bought many slaves. What's so important about this one? They were given numbers in transit and only first names by their owners."

"Wait, Johnny, you will see why and it is very important. Wilma found a column in the *Atlanta Herald* circa 1859. Here, read this…" Sofiya calmly drank her coffee, but watched for Johnny's reaction, over the mug.

*A*tlanta *H*erald *June 1859*

*W*e were sad to hear a well-known member of our Wesley Chapel, Methodist community, Mr Peter Harrison has sold his plantation and is moving north to join his family in New York. The Scotsman easily identified by his bright red hair and very white skin informs us he gets his coloring from his Scottish and Viking ancestors and states his white skin suffers under the Georgian sun; his reason for leaving. He is sorry to go and hopes he will find his favorite Bourbon Whiskey in New York or he will return! Mr Harrison never *married, but takes with him his two adopted, curly-headed, suntanned children and an African slave he freed, Matilda Harrison, to look after the children, as she has cared for them since their birth. We wish him and the children well.   Editor*

"Looks like he just got out in time, Johnny. You know the Civil War began in 1861 to end the scourge of slavery. You should feel proud of him. But taking only one slave with him... why? Matilda was the mother of his children. Come on, you are beginning to have doubts yourself." Sofiya felt a moment's sympathy for the man, but not for long.

"What's the point of all this trash, Sofiya? Yah cain't prove they were his children and so what? Letters, birth certificates, newspaper cuttings, all from the Dark Ages? What's it got ta do wi me, a possible ancestor freed a slave? What's next... photographs of the dead? Ahh, don accept non of it. Now tell that dowg to let me go...or...or ahh *will* call the police!"

"Be patient, Johnny, almost there. You are right... I have no birth certificates relating to your forebears, but I have your blood and the blood of a young relative of yours, and a photograph."

"Are you kidin' me? Damn right you have nothin on me or my family. Y'all have my blood and somebody else's? Not possible. The only time ahh lost any blood near you, was when Cathie threw the goddamn brick at me in the car park of Mount View and if ahh' remember right y'all was at the back o' her. And that picture that fell off the wall that day... shattered next to me but none of the glass hit me. You have nothin' to prove your claim." Johnny rubbed the side of his cheek remembering that day.

324

"That painting haunted me for years. I sold it and good riddance and are you suffering from selective amnesia, Johnny? Let me remind you of a night etched in my memory for ever… the hotel in New York? I rarely lose my temper but between your denial and insults I landed you a punch Mohammed Ali would have been proud of, remember? I gave you one of the hotel napkins to stop the blood trickling down your face… might have dripped on your precious pilot's shirt." Sofiya couldn't resist being a little sarcastic. "I did not want the hotel staff to think there had been a fist fight in the room and I saved the napkin and my hairbrush that you brushed your hair with in the hotel bathroom, before you put your pilot's cap back on. I put them in a polybag, brought them back to Scotland and stored them. Looking back, I don't know why I did this, but I am thankful I did."

Johnny sat silent. He could not refute what Sofiya had just told him and he did remember that night only too well.

For some unknown reason, Sofiya suddenly remembered a nurse's hospital badge she had seen, awarded at the end of their first year staff nursing, at one of the hospitals she had worked in: a pelican feeding its young with drops of blood from its breast, a symbol representing charity and a level of self-sacrifice to others. It was so kind and heart-warming. She didn't know why she thought of that at this precise moment, perhaps it was to remind her to get on with the scientific haematology results and put Johnny out of his misery.

"Forget the written evidence. You have assured me you believe in science. I doubt you will be able to dispute or dismiss what I am about to give you. My late husband, Professor Martin, worked in the field of genetic research and forensic profiling; his work was highly respected. My own genetic markers conclusively show the inherent diseases I miraculously escaped, such as heart disease and others sadly associated with the close relationship of my birth parents."

Johnny still sat silent. Sofiya wasn't even sure if he was listening.

"Beginning in the 1980s, initial research DNA fingerprinting required a teaspoon of human blood. Now it is down to one cell. Every cell in the human body confirms a human being's individual genetic, ethnic, dominant, natural or cultural history and today can pinpoint a person's birthplace to within a five mile radius. Here are your results, Johnny.

"The results I am giving you are indisputable and right up-to-date. Scottish, German … but did you know you also have Italian genes?"

Johnny's jaw dropped.

"Wilma found no evidence to support Italians owning plantations, which is not really important, except you have a quarter of your grandfather's Italian genes, a quarter of your grandmother Rachel's, but *none* of Robert Leightham's. It's my guess Rachel Harrison had an affair with an Italian and your mother Betsy was the result. Robert Leightham's letter confirms it."

Johnny continued to stare at Sofiya.

"Johnny, you have African blood in your DNA." Sofiya delivered her most potent verbal attack.

"What the…?!" That brought Johnny to life. "Go to hell!!"

"There is no doubt. Peter Harrison's children were his and Matilda's."

"What are you talkin about… a slave's children? Y'all have no proof."

"Sit still Johnny. I have to get something from the desk drawer." Sofiya got up and returned with a photograph and two small envelopes, sat down and held both next to her breast.

"I have mourned every April since I had our baby. The times have mercifully changed. Illegitimacy is no longer a stigma: no longer the woman's and the child's shame. Nowadays the woman is not made to feel she had committed an unforgivable sin, nor is she shunned like a fallen woman, but my grandmother did. These two letters that I kept are heart-breaking, poignant, accounts from a sixteen-year-old girl writing of her gratitude to the two women who took her in and the note she left in her son James…my father's cot, begging forgiveness for abandoning him and confirming she and Robert Leightham were married and of their love for their son. But I will not allow you to read, or give you the opportunity of making the disparaging and flippant remarks you did with my grandfather's letters. You must take my word for it, that they were written by my grandmother and I have other letters written by her and they are all in her handwriting.

"Once it would have distressed me to meet with you in this manner and I might have denied the past and said our child had been adopted. Although I will *never* forget what you did to me, I learned over the years that forgiveness is the beginning of closure. Forgiveness is a better cure for anger, hatred, recrimination, than the bitter desire for revenge." Sofiya realized at that moment she was free. "Revenge is not sweet, Johnny. It can leave a bitter taste in your mouth. I am truly sorry if what you say in your letter is true, that I am your unrequited love…but *you* are not mine."

Ignoring what Sofiya just said as if he couldn't care less Johnny asked, "You tryin to tell me you didn't have it adopted? Where is it?" Johnny looked around for evidence.

"She, *she*, Johnny, our daughter. I named her Harriet for obvious reasons. Here is her photograph."

"So, you know where she is?"

"In a manner of speaking. Although I could never acknowledge she was my daughter, mercifully the love of my dad, Cathie and Irene saved my sanity; they supported me because I had none from you. Yes, I know where she is. My grandmother suffered because of the cruel circumstances and prejudice of the times she lived in and for a long time she had no idea where her son had gone. My father was legitimate, not illegitimate as our daughter was."

Sofiya leaned forward and tried to hand Johnny the photograph of her holding Harriet, an infant dressed in the family christening robe. He refused to take it. Johnny just looked at the photograph. His face drained of colour as he fell back in the chair and clutched at his throat.

"Do you want a glass of water?" Sofiya asked, as she put the framed picture down on the coffee table beside the documents. She knew Johnny to be arrogant, self-opinionated and over confident, but he was no racist and might even agree that the southern white supremacists should have their DNA examined before joining their racist factions. But what was going through his mind?

Recovering, Johnny began to bluster. "No! But…but this… infant has …"

"African colouring?"

"She couldn't be mine. Even if there were African-Americans in my family's past, that's four, five generations ago," Johnny hissed at Sofiya, who was aware of the dog becoming agitated.

Sofiya reached forward and held the dog's collar. "Calm down, Johnny. She is your daughter. It's in your genes, not mine. Harriet is what is called a 'throwback'. It is rare but it happens. My mother-in-law had the presence of mind to take a specimen of her cord blood the night she was born and my husband proved her ancestral genetic heritage. Believe me, the last thing I would sully is our daughter's name with denial of her roots."

"Well, if you didn't have her adopted, where is she? Did she get married? Is she here?" Johnny looked around him as if looking for proof.

Sofiya, swallowing hard, told him. "Our daughter would have spent her life in residential care. Her physical genetic disorders you can place entirely at my door, but not her African-American blood. But you should be on your hands and knees in gratitude to Cathie and her sister, Irene, as I was. They refused to allow Harriet to be taken into care and thank God for Irene's daughter, who was about to emigrate to Australia. She gave Harriet her surname and fabricated a story about being unable to take a child with special needs with her. My dad, Jim, knew everything and saved me from a life in a mental institution with his support and I also had the support of my mother-in-law to be, Dr Susan Martin. They all insisted I became my own child's godmother so I could take an active part in her life." Sofiya breathed in at last. She could look back and not feel ashamed.

"I could never admit publicly she was mine...but I was her mother and she was my daughter. Can you imagine the scandal, late 1960s... Her Ladyship with an illegitimate child? I didn't need to worry about her. The Pittendreal community took our Harriet to their hearts. My daughter, Sophie, loved her like a sister, never knowing, until recently, she was her half-sister. The teachers and children in the nursery school played with her, wheeled her about in her wheelchair and loved hearing her laugh. I guess special needs and racial prejudice don't exist in children. Maybe it is we adults who teach them that."

"Where is she now?"

"Dead, Johnny. She had serious heart defects at a time when there was no transplant surgery and she also had other incurable inherent physical anomalies. Still a child, she died young. So, take your flowers and go to Pittendreal cemetery. You will pass Mount View on your way, now renamed Harriet House. I named it in her memory. I had the house converted to accommodation for young people to live independently. Lay the flowers on your daughter's grave. It's easy to find. A small white marble angel, with 'Harriet' carved on the plinth, marks her final resting place. Take the documents with you as well, Johnny, but I advise you to leave and never return. I never want to hear from or see you again."

For a fraction of a second, you could have heard a pin drop. Johnny sat as if digesting the fact that he had lost, but he was seething inside. Sofiya's calm voice was like a red flag to a bull. Johnny jumped up and virtually spat in Sofiya's face. "You think you have won, don't you? You haven't heard the last of this or me!!" he shouted at her.

Sofiya lunged forward and just managed to grab Laila's collar with both hands. The dog's hair was standing up on the back of its neck and it was straining to get at Johnny. Johnny, like a spoilt child throwing a tantrum, snatched the photograph and threw it to the floor, smashing the glass to pieces. Grabbing a fistful of documents, he shredded them, threw them up into the air. They fell like confetti at a wedding. Sofiya just shook her head thinking, *Pathetic Johnny. A bit too late. You had your chance to marry me, share the title to the estate and spend time with our little daughter and you blew it.* "Get out, Johnny!! I don't know how much longer I can hold her," Sofiya shouted, as the dog was now twisting and turning to be free. Laila's instinct to protect her beloved mistress was fuelled by both love and the feeling this person might harm Sofiya.

Trying to keep the dog behind her, Sofiya managed to get Johnny out of the study. He took off getting through the hall and halfway out of the front door before Laila finally twisted free of her collar. She shot after Johnny and narrowly missing him as she pounced at the back of the half-closed door. She slammed it shut with her body weight and front paws before clawing and tearing the paint off; then, bowing down, tail in the air, she went nineteen to the dozen drinking in the smell of the man at the closed door.

"Laila!!" Sofiya shouted. "Stop!!"

Laila turned. The look on her face said it all: *That was great fun. Drat, I could have got him by the sleeve! I'll get him next time.*

Sofiya couldn't help laughing at the dog, as the war-cry of William Wallace rang through her head, *Freedom! What a wonderful feeling. Freedom from the chains of the past. Hallelujah.* Clasping her hands together, Sofiya gave up a silent prayer of thanks to whoever was listening.

"Come on dawg. Let's get down to the kitchen. It's almost happy hour and that meeting has given me a thirst. I think I *will* try one of Paul Fallen flavoured beers and you will get an extra dog biscuit…good girl." The only word Laila recognized was the word 'biscuit'. Laila shot down the stair in front of her mistress to claim her reward.

Chapter 5

S OPHIE LOOKED at her mother. "If I hadn't been holding this paper, I would have been hanging on the edge of my seat!" Sophie was aghast at what she had just read. "No wonder you looked the way you did when I got back from Spain. Oh my God, mum. Thank goodness you had the presence of mind to get the dog from the kitchen. I don't want to think of what he might have done to you. On the other hand, you might have packed him another wallop in the face, and this time... no need to keep a sample of his blood!"

That broke any tension between mother and daughter and they burst out laughing.

"And now I know why you said you had to clean up the mess he left behind! Well done, mum. But I think forgiving him hurt more than the thought you didn't love him. I don't think he was expecting that in a million years. He must have been raging inside and feeling a right fool. Sorry, mum, I apologize for being so graphic... no, I am not going to apologise, but... but to smash a photograph of an innocent little baby regardless of who's baby she was, disgraceful... Johnny Geiger is an ass-hole mum!"

"Sophie!"

"You shouldn't have been so kind, so nice to him. From what you have told me about the man, his arrogance, he was running true to his family history."

"What do you mean... family history?"

"Well, think about it. His grandmother, Rachael, marries your grandfather only for the title. And don't tell me Geiger didn't know when, he married his wife, she had no intention of having a family. I bet she held a senior position in the American Government and he would benefit from the privileges it offered. And after all these years he bothers to get in touch with you, why? Running true to form, taking after his forebears, he frankly admits it in his letter that he wants to share *his* title and *his* estate with you. Boy, he must have got a shock when he realized that with all the evidence you had proved he had no chance. But I am worried, mum. I can't stop thinking about the threats he made as he left you... Oh my goodness." Sophie suddenly remembered the documents. "Great-aunt Jane's letters and certificates you found in her Ormolu clock, Dad and the professors' DNA results. Mum, he shredded them! You might need them."

"Give me a break, as they say. Do you think for one minute I would have given him the originals? They were all copies. He thought he was destroying the evidence. I have the originals under lock and key and, let's face it, I have heard nothing more from him since. Now let's change the subject... Christmas."

"I hope it's not an ominous silence. Maybe we should think about more security."

"Well, I have the ultimate deterrent."

"The dog!!" both women chanted together.

"It's a good job Laila is in the kitchen or she would be barking her lungs out with excitement at us shouting. German Shepherds are an incredibly loyal breed of dog and people probably don't realise most of their behaviour is a game to them. But you are right. Laila didn't like Johnny, I admit that. She sensed he didn't like her, but she didn't put a paw wrong until she joined in the chase as he ran out the front door. Don't worry, he won't get within a hundred feet of the house. You should have seen her drinking in his smell... aftershave and all, and dogs never forget a scent. Laila will let me know if he's around and heaven help him, she will tear off his jacket and shred it for fun. Let's hope she doesn't grab him by the B-T-M as he runs away. Now I am being graphic. But to be on the safe side, I will let her sleep in the hall with the kitchen door open. She'll think all her birthdays have come at once. She's jealous of Samosa being allowed to sleep on my bed. Now get off home. Let's meet next week to finalise all the last-minute Christmas details. Oh, by the way, I like my grandson's suggestion."

"Mum, don't let anyone know you sleep with a Samosa. They will think you are in bed with an Indian chilli pastry." Sophie smiled at the thought. "What did Arran suggest, mum?"

"You know we have decided to donate the money we normally spend on Christmas gifts to charity? Well, he suggested to me we pick a name out of a hat and each of us buy a gift of less than five pounds for that person. I think he called it Secret Santa? He thought it was a bit sad not to receive anything at all and I agreed. I will let all the staff know and organize the draw. Make sure you tell Iain's parents."

"I think they are going to Iain's brother's this year, mum. Karen and Alan are expecting them and they enjoy being with their other granddaughter, Lara. Oh, before I forget, will Charles be with his family till after the New Year?"

"Yes, but he will be back in time for the performance of Handel's *Messiah* on the second of January at the Usher Hall in Edinburgh. We already have the tickets. Oh! I phoned Mr Ellis, the manager of The Dome, my favourite restaurant on George Street; he assures me they will be open for afternoon tea as usual on the second, but closed on the third to take the Christmas decorations down. So afternoon champagne tea for Charles and me before the performance. It might be The Dome's historical connection to the site of the old Physicians' Hall, built in 1775 that is the reason I like going there. I can hardly remember my days in the medical field, it seems so long ago now."

"Are you getting 'maudlin', sentimental in your old age mum?"

"Enough of your cheek. Now, away with you. See you next week." Sophie and her mother hugged each other tight and waved goodbye.

Sophie picked up her bag and went downstairs to collect her coat. She still felt troubled but it wasn't about Johnny Geiger. It was about something else and she had no idea how she and Iain would tell her mum. On her way home in the car, she thought… *I need a drink!*

Chapter 6

"HER LADYSHIP says, this his tae be the best Christmas ever," Bunty announced, as she and Vivienne rechecked the Christmas shopping lists for Aikman the grocer and Carrick the butcher. "I admire her ladyship insisting that Leightham Hoose supports the local tradesfolk, when that mony shops his gan oot o' business wi Supermarkets openin' in thay shoppin' centres. Awbidys encouraged tae spend their bawbees in wan place.But am gled the Co-op is still gawn strong. Reminds me o' the auld days and the excitement when the Divi wus due.

"But niver mind that. It seems tae me her ladyship's hail attitude tae life his changed recently and it's no jist Christmas. Since October she's been like a new wuman. Dae ye remember that Sunday when we got back frae Edinburgh?" Vivienne nodded. "A' think something happened that day when we were awe oot. When a' cam back, a' went richt tae the kitchen tae mak share she hid eaten the crisp bread and cottage cheese I had left fur hur supper. Yae ken whit she's like. She's back on her 'Breakfast like a king, lunch like a prince' and nae supper. Ha! Her healthy eating programme...! And there's no a pick on her oniewey. A weel, there she wus in the kitchen, wi a great big grin on her face, dancing roond the table, Laila barkin' her lungs oot. Barkin' mad the pair o' them. A' thocht, she's ether drunk or on drugs!"

Vivienne laughed. "Maybe she hid a veesitor that pit hur in a guid mood. It couldna' hae been Mr Charles. He wus awa wi his grandchildren fur the school holidays."

"Aye, ye micht be richt but she's aye that particular aboot gettin' peace and quiet on a Sunday efternuin. Her ladyship says it's the only day o' the week that she gets tae hersel." Bunty thought for a moment whether she should say more or not, but decided to go ahead and, lowering her voice, continued.

"Puir sowl. That wis an awfy secret her ladyship hid fur awe they years, Vivienne. Naebody could care less noo, whether a bairn's got a faither or no. A' mind o' talkin' last April wi Sophie aboot her mither's state o' mind and telt her it wus aboot time she got it oot o' her ladyship what in heaven's name wus wrang wi her. We'd awe hid enough o' tip-toein' round the hoose and keepin' oot o' her mither's road every April. Enough wus enough! Am gled a' did and it wus Sophie that came back and telt me awe aboot what had happened tae her mither awe they years ago, and aboot Harriet. The only regret Sophie said she hid, wus she was sorry she didna ken the wee lassie wus her sister. So, whatever happened in October, if it hid somethin' tae dae wi that, then a'm awfy gled fur her ladyship," Bunty whispered and nodded her head.

"That wus an unusual name tae gee the bairn," Vivienne whispered back, thinking... *Why am I whispering? Now I'm going barking mad! There's no one in the house to hear us.*

"Harriet Tubman was an African American slave wha escaped. An abolitionist, she helped tae hide the slaves when *they* escaped, took them intae safe hooses, known as the Underground Railroad. A' looked it up on Google," Bunty announced proud of her research. "A' mind o' the bairn, what a fine wee duggie-mel, as my granny would hae said. And Cathie and Irene... What would her ladyship hae done withoot them? Cathie aye pit a bonnie pink bow in the bairn's black curly hair. Puir wee sowl, she wisnae very weel maist o' her short life. The hail village thocht the bairn wus Irene's granddochter. The

337

guid book says, 'Judge not lest yae be judged', and they twa decent Christian wumen kent everythin' aboot the bairn and never judged her ladyship."

Vivienne was surprised Bunty knew about Google as Bunty always claimed that she was modern technology illiterate.

"Bunty, the less said aboot it the better. It's awe in the past, better forgotten and she wisnae the only lassie that suffered. At least she kent whaur her bairn wus. Hoo mony lassies didna ken whit happened tae their bairns?"

"Aye, yer richt, Vivienne. The lassies dae ken hoo lucky they are noo adays. Thank the guid Lord fur they awfy grand *peels* the Docturs hiv been prescribin' fur mair than forty years noo, that stop them hain' bairns until they want them. And wha cares if they are mairret or no? A' used tae think the mairriage certificate meant buyin' a pair o' Marigold rubber gloves, a licence tae wash the dishes!" Bunty burst out laughing at her own joke. "But we'll pit awe that aside. A' think the hail year wull be better noo her ladyship's secret is oot. It's like the wecht o' the world's gan aff her shoother's. Nae mair gloom and doom."

"Bunty, let's concentrate on the grocery list, please."

"Aye, yer richt. Sophia tells me she's a... a vegeta-turean noo."

"Vegetarian, Bunty." Vivienne raised her eyes to the heavens. Then turning her attention back to Bunty noticed she was tapping her lips with her fingers, as if she was deep in thought and hadn't heard a word she'd said. So, what was new?

"A've always wanted to cook some o' they vegetable dishes. I saw a recipe in *The Peoples Friend* fur beef Wellington, but made wi vegetables: roasted red peppers, beetroot, kale and mushrooms, layered up wi goat's cheese and the pastry glazed wi Marmite. Sophia can help hersel tae awe the other vegs we're hiven': the roasted and mashed totties and parsnips, sprouts, carrots and a'll mac a fine vegetarian gravy, wi plenty bay leaves, carrots, celery, herbs and a wee splash o' white wine tae gie it flavour jist fur her. Aye." Bunty nodded enthusiastically, well pleased with herself.

"That'll be awfy grand fur the lassie, Bunty. A' think a'll hae a wee taste o' it masel. Noo, thay lists should hiv been finished yisterday. Hoo mony did yea say were comin…?"

The ladies turned their attention to the task in hand, making sure they had ordered everything they needed for the big day and were grateful that Jimmy and Ronald would deal with the wine order, so they didn't need to bother with that.

Chapter 7

THE BUILD UP TO CHRISTMAS may well have
been more exciting than the day itself, with parties
and a trip to the Christmas market in Princes Street,
Edinburgh; the local Christmas Fairs, carol services at the
school and the Church to attend; shopping for food and
baking the Christmas cake well in advance of the big day,
in good time to be marinated with brandy before
decorating it with marzipan and royal Icing, but there was
to be no Christmas pudding. In Bunty's own words, "Am
no makin' a Christmas pudding, but a traditional Scottish
clootie dumplin, wi silver sixpences in it fur the bairns tae
fund and Savanna will help me stir the mixture fur guid
luck."

Sofiya loved the excitement and anticipation on her
grandchildren's faces as they did their Christmas shopping
and she watched them wrapping their gifts to put under the
Christmas tree and writing their Christmas cards to be
posted with Christmas stamps. But best of all, the family
loved helping Ronald and Jimmy put the decorations
outside Leightham House in gardens and the driveway. To
help them stop shivering with cold when they had
finished, the day was made even better with Vivienne's
hot chocolate with whipped cream, marshmallows and hot
mince pies waiting for them in the estate's coffee shop.
Preparation for the event seemed to require weeks of
organization and this year had been no different from any
other.

At last, Sofiya, the family and the rest of the guests fell
back in their chairs absolutely stuffed with one of the
finest Christmas dinners Bunty and Vivienne had ever

cooked. Spoons rattled off dessert plates as the last of the traditional Scottish trifle and clootie dumplin with custard had been consumed. Rubbing their stomachs and pursing their lips, the look on their faces said it all and they could only express how they felt, by blowing through their lips… "Whoo!" Then the compliments were thrown around the table: "Delicious", "I couldna' eat anither bite", accompanied by "That wus awfy guid". Bunty announced there were still mince pies and the chocolate truffles that she and Savanna had baked that needed to be eaten.

"Later, Bunty. I think we will all burst if we eat any more. But Iain, Ronald, Jimmy, ladies… liqueur, brandy, or coffee? Or should we do Secret Santa first?" Sofiya asked. "Secret Santa!" echoed round the room.

"Arran and me are going first!" Alexander shouted, as he jumped up almost knocking his chair onto the floor. The boys made a dash out of the dining room to the hall, where a large pile of gifts lay at the side of the Holly tree with only the recipient's name on them.

"I…Arran and I," Iain corrected his son's grammar,

"No! I want to be first. Alexander always gets to go first," Savanna complained, running after her brother.

Iain got up from the table. "I'll go sort that pair out."

"Ache, lave thay bairns' alane, Iain…it's Christmas," Bunty advised. "They're awe growen up oor fast. They'll no be bairns much longer," added Vivienne and both nodded their heads knowingly.

"Don't worry, Dad. Let me go." Wise words from Sophia, who was a good few years older than her brothers and sister and she had the knack of resolving Savanna and Alexander's squabbles.

The calm after the storm found the adults sitting around the tree, with the children cross-legged on the floor waiting to receive their gifts. The boys planned to give their gifts together and had negotiated the arrangement with Sophia in advance and for the sake of peace and quiet she had agreed. Alexander had previously exchanged the name he had picked out of the hat with Savanna, who willingly cooperated, as she preferred to buy her present for a woman rather than a man.

Iain was suddenly suspicious. He had given the boys money to go to the shopping mall alone to do their Christmas shopping and had no idea what the boys had bought and was now thinking that might not have been the best idea and that the pair were up to something. Giggling and bumping into each other, Arran and Alexander handed the gifts to Ronald and Jimmy, instructing them to open the parcels together. The two men, initially surprised, did as they were told and opened their gifts to find plastic toys, which when squeezed, made very loud, rude noises and gestures!!

"Boys! Just you wait till I get you home..." Iain spluttered.

"Naw, naw, lave the lawdies' alane, Iain. It's guid tae hae a laugh. It minds us o' oor school days, ay Ronald?" Jimmy and Ronald squeaked the offending toys again and again, laughing together with the boys and other male guests and thoroughly enjoying the boys' cheeky pranks.

Billie Gibson thought it was a right laugh. Billie had retired several years earlier and had gone to live in Glasgow with his family, but he always came back to Leightham House with his wife for Christmas dinner, at the invitation of his previous employer. His gift instructed him to adopt an elephant and his wife, was given a book on *How to be a Good Wife,* which raised a lot of eyebrows and laughter as it was well known that Jenny was the boss in the Gibson family.

Secret Santa gave Iain a carpenter's level and he saw his daughter grinning and nodding her head in his direction. *Maybe the shelves still in their packet would finally be put up in her bedroom. There was no excuse now.*

All the ladies were delighted with their boxes of chocolates, bubble bath and hand cream. The guests, estate staff and the family had mutually agreed to forgo the usual gifts and had collected a considerable amount of money for the Hospice and Children's charities instead. Everyone agreed to do the same every year and Arran's '£5 only' Secret Santa idea had gone down well apart from their rude squeaky toys!

When the guessing game of who gave what to whom came to an end, everyone suddenly realised, her ladyship had received nothing, that is except Jimmy and Ronald who seemed to be preoccupied with examining the ceiling for cracks. Someone spotted a large parcel still hidden at the back of the tree. Iain went over and pulled the box out and saw the name *Sofiya* on the label.

"This is for you, mother-in law, dearest!" Iain winked at Sofiya, "But it's not from me!"

Sofiya tore off the Christmas paper to reveal a large cardboard box. When she opened it, it contained multiple layers of scrunched up brown paper. By this time the children were impatient to see what the mysterious gift was and started to help pull out the paper, until finally, individually bubble wrapped mysterious circular objects were revealed. Sofiya knew at once what they were, and this was confirmed by a handwritten note…

Drink yer ain Fallen beers and lave oors alaine!

Sofiya burst out laughing. No one present had a clue as to who had given her a dozen cans of beer, but she knew who the culprits were right away, £5 eh? Sofiya gave a surreptitious nod and smile to both Ronald and Jimmy, who had decided there was nothing wrong with the ceiling and now had a look of innocence on each of their faces.

"Right! Everybody, back into the dining room," Sofiya announced, "Divide into two teams. I have gone mad this year…no expense spared!" she joked. "I bought two second-hand, Gibson's limited edition, Christmas jigsaws from eBay! What a steal! I don't think they have even been opened. So let the games begin. The first team to finish their jigsaw will get a chocolate Santa each! Oh no, boys! No dit-dit machines on Christmas day," Sofiya called out, as she saw the pair of them about to slip away unnoticed to the family room, to play games on their new iPads. "Jigsaws first please and then word games. Why do you think there are notepads and pencils on the sideboard and the playing cards? Old Maid and Snap, after that!"

"I'm not playing Old Maid!" Alexander objected. "Neither am I," Arran added.

"Well, I've got an idea. What about 7s? You know, that card game you taught me?"

"Yeah, brilliant idea, grandma… definitely. We always win, you always lose."

Alexander grudgingly gave in, remembering his grandmother did usually lose and shrugging his shoulders made his way to join the others, although perhaps it was the thought of chocolate Santas that might have had something to do with it.

* * *

The guests had gone home with their gifts and the mince pies that no one could eat. Savanna instructed them to eat them on Boxing Day as they had been made by her and Bunty, using their own special pastry recipe. Christmas Day had come and gone at lightning speed as it always did. Sofiya found herself tired but happy saying goodbye to her family as they left for home. Iain and the boys made their way to the car with the boys shouting back to their grandmother a chorus of, "We had a fabulous day", "See you at Hogmanay. Alexander and I will do the Dashing White Sergeant with you grandma…love you".

"No I won't!! I hate dancing!"

Arran nudged his brother in the ribs. "Alex ...she doesn't need to know that yet." Arran pushed Alexander into the car, in case he announced he wasn't going to wear a kilt either! "Shut up, Alex, or Grandma will hear you. She'll have forgotten by New Year...you know what old folk are like..."

"I heard that!!" Sofiya shook her head, laughed and waved to the boys, then turned her attention to the girls.

"Merry Christmas grandma, it's been a wonderful day, one of the best and please, tell Bunty for me, in case I don't see her before Hogmanay, I loved her vegetarian Wellington and the gravy. I could almost drink it. M-m, it was delicious." Sophia hugged her grandmother and blowing her a kiss, walked towards the car.

Savanna, who always hung back, was almost the last to leave. Throwing her arms round her grandmother's waist, she looked up at the woman with whom she had a special bond. Sofiya was reminded how closely Savanna resembled her grandmother Alice Jane Gardner, the only red-haired and blue-eyed child of her four grandchildren. And why did her daughter name her Savanna? Was it in memory of the child's great-grandmother Tatiana, known as Ana? Might well have been the reason.

"Merry Christmas, grandma. See you next week!" Savanna untangled herself from Sofiya and, with her bubble bath and a bag with a few left-over mince pies in her hands, she ran to the car.

Only Sophie hovered on the doorstep, ignoring Iain's shouts to hurry up, because "It is too cold to hang about!"

"Savanna is right, mum. This has been one of the best Christmases ever. What a difference a day makes or in our case, what a difference the last three months have made. New beginnings for all of us? Oh, don't forget you promised you would babysit. Well, you know what I mean. Sophia is old enough to babysit, but come and eat with us on Hogmanay."

"What do you mean, babysit? I know Sophia is perfectly capable of babysitting, but I don't mind keeping her company. Most of the village will be out celebrating in the Leightham Arms till about eleven. Ronald will come and take the dog out, then light the bonfire ready for midnight, so I might leave a little earlier. Where are you going, anyway?"

"I forgot to tell you. Gillian and Simon are home from Malaysia. Iain and I want to go out for a drink with them to catch up on all their news. We will be back before eleven but, if you leave earlier... no problem." Sophie seemed to hesitate. She didn't want to spoil such a wonderful day, but there was no alternative, the subject had to be broached. She couldn't avoid it any longer. It just couldn't be put off and Iain was threatening to tell Sofiya himself which would be a disaster.

"What is it, Sophie?! I don't like the look on your face."

Sophie blurted out: "I'm sorry, mum, but there is something Iain and I have to... to discuss with you. It's not urgent, certainly *not* life threatening, so don't worry on that account, but we decided to wait till next week, so we could all look forward to a New Year. We felt that would be the best time to deal with any future changes."

With that statement ringing in Sofiya's ears, Sophie hugged her mum, turned and ran to the car before her mother could ask any questions.

Chapter 8

HAVING HAD LITTLE communication with Sophie since Christmas, Sofiya arrived at her daughter's house to 'babysit' on Hogmanay. Sophie had prepared a light supper, on the grounds that everyone's waistline was beginning to expand at a rapid rate. Unfortunately, the otherwise happy evening was marred by a feeling of tension among the adults. Iain had decided earlier in the day that matters couldn't wait any longer and whether his wife liked it or not, he had to speak up. Looking distinctly uncomfortable he chased the younger children out of the dining room. Sophie knew exactly what Iain was going to say and began to shuffle around in her seat.

"Maybe it's too soon, Iain," Sophie whispered, looking at him over the table.

Sofiya frowned and remembered the way she had parted from her daughter on Christmas Day and began to wonder, maybe this was what it was all about?

"No! Sophie, you and I have agreed, it's more than time. I am sorry, Sofiya, but Sophie has decided without any pressure from me... she does *not* want to inherit the title, or the estate. My partner Brian and I have built up several dental practices over the years and once our children have left home, we will sell up and enjoy an early retirement."

"What?!" Sofiya exploded.

Sophie, shamefaced, sat staring at her dinner plate.

Sofiya felt as if the feet had been knocked from under her. She was astounded. If someone had punched her in the stomach, she could not have been more shocked. She certainly was not prepared for this.

"Sophie just wants to be plain Mrs Haig. She has no desire to become Lady Leightham. We have big travel plans and will be away from Scotland for months on end. Sophie wants to do the Trans-Siberian railway to get a feel for Russia and I want to do the Trans-Canadian railway and include a cruise to Alaska. We might even buy a holiday home abroad or a boat and sail whenever the notion takes us. No one can run Leightham House and the estate long distance. We don't want the work... or the worry. Sorry, Sofiya... it's just not going to happen."

Sofiya had controlled herself long enough and in a voice tense with anger, she hissed through her teeth, "Are *you* speaking on my daughter's behalf, Iain? Yes, obviously!" As Sophie was still staring at her plate.

Sofiya threw her napkin on the table and angrily turned on both of them. "So, what have you two collaborators connived to do with me in the meantime, have me admitted to an old folks' home now I am in my dotage!? Am I allowed to go home one more time to sack the house, café and restaurant staff? Tell them they are now unemployed and no longer needed, to go home and join the dole queue? You are too cowardly to do it yourselves? Oh, and before I forget with my old-age, short-term, memory loss... does that include the ground staff? And will I have to withdraw funding from Cards House and evict the young people living in Harriet House?"

Sofiya stood up, her voice rising, "How about, I casually pop into the Council Chambers next week and tell them I will not be attending any more of their meetings, or supporting local charities; call a meeting with the local town council and nonchalantly shrugging my shoulders inform them... sorry, the tennis courts, cricket pitch and the grounds are closed! No more Guy Fawkes bonfires or firework displays. Oops! Oh dear, sorry folks… Christmas dinners and Hogmanay celebrations are cancelled from now on, along with the spring and summer music festivals and concerts that bring in money for local businesses.

"Worse still, am I to leave my beloved Leightham House and before I go, have high, chained, metal gates erected at both entrances and encircle the house with barbed wire and leave it to become derelict again, the way I inherited it?! But this time have the privilege of watching the roof cave in from a distance from sheer neglect!! Does that suit you *both*?!!" Sofiya was now shouting at the top of her voice and red in the face with temper.

"Mum, *please,* sit down. Watch your blood pressure."

Sofiya, infuriated, sat down. "I couldn't care less about my bloody… blood pressure, Sophie! At this moment I don't give a damn about me, but… you… you're the cause of all this! Sitting there like a dummy! Don't you care about your childhood home… the history of your forebears, your family descendants, or the estate that I have spent my life working for? I *don't* own the estate. I am its caretaker for future generations and *you* are the next generation, you and your children. How can I rest in peace when my time comes?"

Sophie, incensed, started to rise up in protest, threw her napkin down on the table, pushed her chair back and would have left the room, but for her daughter's intervention.

Sophia had sat quietly listening to the outpouring of emotions and horrified, decided she couldn't keep quiet any longer. "That's enough!" Her voice rang out: "Grandma, Mum, Dad, *please…* calm down… You are behaving like children. There is no need for this." This was about to turn into a full-scale family war, with the likelihood of no one speaking to each other for the foreseeable future.

Chapter 9

SOPHIA HAD GROWN into a beautiful, intelligent young woman, who knew her own mind. Mature beyond her years, anyone who knew her knew you could not argue with her and win. She had already decided what she wanted to do with her life and realized it was time, time for her to make her announcement. Unfortunately, it would have to be now, sooner than she had hoped but it couldn't wait any longer. In her heart she knew what she wanted more than anything.

In a resolute voice that brooked no interruptions, she continued, "Please, it's Hogmanay, New Year, new beginnings. I am an adult and sorry, Mum and Dad, I *will* give my opinion regarding Leightham House whether you like it or not." Turning to face Sofiya, she spoke directly to her. "Grandma, give me time to complete my degree in aeronautical engineering and to gain some experience in that field. Once I have gone as far as I want to go in my professional life, *I will* take some of the burden of the Leightham estate from your shoulders."

Iain's, Sophie's and Sofiya's jaw literally dropped, as they stared dumbfounded at Sophia. Iain, in disbelief, managed to ask his daughter, "Sophia, are you having me on?"

Sophia stood up, ignoring her father. "I want to inherit Leightham House and the estate, but, Grandma, that's not going to happen for a long time yet. In the meantime, I need you to work with me and teach me everything you know."

Jumping to his feet, Iain protested, "That was quite a speech, Sophia, but *you* are *not* going to…"

Cool as a cucumber, Sophia interrupted: "I am not finished yet, Dad. Please sit down, and in any case how are you going to stop me?" The assembled company sat stunned, but there was no use arguing with her, as Iain had just learnt.

"Mum, Grandma, I have done something without your permission and I am glad I did. While you were both out, I went through your desks and drawers. Grandma, I have read everything you wrote about the times you visited the woman you thought was your great-aunt, and the papers you gave Mum to read this year. Having read everything you went through, Grandma, from the bottom of my heart, I have admiration and respect for you. Don't worry, I have replaced all the documents where I found them and I have made a copy from Wilma's memory stick to my own for safe keeping.

"Look at my female lineage. How can I fail to succeed you? Would I have survived finding out that *you* weren't my great-aunt Jane but my grandmother? Just think of the hell she went through; a victim of the times she lived in, just as you were a victim of the times you lived in. What went through her mind when she discovered that your parents, her son, James and daughter, Ana, had married after meeting in Ceylon during WW2? And the horror, when she thought that it was all going to happen again, between you and Johnny Geiger. Your grandmother's sudden death made sure you would know the truth at the reading of her will, because she couldn't tell you herself. The truth was corroborated because she had the presence of mind to hide every scrap of written evidence, letters, photographs and registration documents in her antique clock for you to find.

"Maybe she had a premonition that one day your right to your inheritance might be challenged. And recently it was! It was fortunate that you saved the blood-splattered napkin that Johnny Geiger wiped his nose on; the blood that ultimately proved without a doubt, he had no legal claim to the estate! That astonished me! And the coagulated blood in needles, syringes and razors from your forebears that were stored on the Aberdeen estate… many would have thrown them in the bin as rubbish.

"But my grandfather Neil decided to save these precious drops of blood, which in the lab showed that Geiger was not related to any of the Leighthams. And my great-grandmother Susan had the presence of mind to save a sample of Harriet's cord blood which confirmed Harriet was Geiger's daughter. He is a cold-hearted, pathetic man, smashing her baby photograph in a temper because he couldn't deny she was his.

"And what about my great-great-grandmother, Rena McKay saving Janet's blood-stained clothes? My grandfather, Neil and his colleagues extracted the DNA from these clothes, proving Janet's Russian origins and she was your grandmother Alice's step-daughter. Your legitimate claim to Prince Alexander's Edinburgh property, Cards House and the valuable contents he brought from Russia before the Revolution was disputed by the Russian Embassy at the time of your grandmother's death. Fortunately, your claim was upheld.

"My heart goes out to your grandmother, Alice Jane Gardner. You were her only grandchild and she couldn't acknowledge you. She had you adopted to prevent you finding out who she and your birth parents were. Did you suffer, as she must have done, from the heart-breaking decisions she had had to make? Not from what I read. Ina and Jim were decent, honourable, people who loved you as their own, especially your dad, Jim. He never judged you. He supported you through what must have been a nightmare."

Sofiya shook her head… No, she hadn't suffered.

"You will never forget what happened, grandma, but closure begins with forgiveness." Sophia seemed to be on a roll and hardly pausing for breath, carried on.

"We Scottish women have survived many situations and tragedies. Look at our stoic East Neuk, hard-working fisher lassies, my forebears. Without complaint they carried heavy creels of fish on their backs, gutted and packed the fish in boxes of salt, their hands blistered and gnarled with rheumatism. It must have been agony. And the hours they must have spent in their lofts, mending heavy fishing nets, so the men could go out and fish to earn the money to feed their families. No nets, no fishing—no fish to sell, no food on the table.

"As well as bearing children and caring for their families, these women also followed the fishing fleet from here to Peterhead. They stood on the harbour walls in all weathers, with only a shawl to protect them, desperately scanning the horizon after terrible storms, anxiously watching and waiting to see if the fishing boats would return safely or if their menfolk had been lost at sea. We are directly descended from them."

Sophia showed the first sign of emotion and paused for a moment as her dad silently offered her a glass of water.

*   *   *

"There are times we forget the heroines, whether born in Scotland or not, who shaped the face of Scotland over the centuries.

"St Margaret of Scotland, a Scottish Patron Saint, although she is thought to have been born in Hungary; she was the Queen Consort of Malcolm III of Scotland and was canonized by the Pope in 1250 for her services to the poor.

"Isabella MacDuff was a significant figure in the fight to retain and defend Scotland's Independence in the 13th century. It was her family's hereditary right to crown Scotland's kings and she crowned Robert the Bruce. She was captured, endured unimaginable cruelty, but survived being hung in a cage on the walls of Berwick Castle for four years by the English king, Edward I. He had hope that Robert the Bruce would try to rescue her. He didn't fall into that trap and I guess she would not have wanted him to!

"Mary, Queen of Scots became Queen at six days of age and reigned in the 16th century. She had a legitimate claim to the English throne, but because of her Catholic faith, would have faced opposition by some of the nobles in England. Mary, however, and later her son, James, allowed people to practise their own religion. Mary and James did not burn so-called heretics at the stake as Mary Tudor did, nor did they hang, draw and quarter people for practising their faith as Elizabeth 1st did. Mary was beheaded on the orders of Elizabeth. Mary's son, James VI of Scotland, a Protestant, succeeded Elizabeth and became James 1st of England. Mary, a devout Roman Catholic was interred in the Anglican Westminster Abbey a few feet from the woman who had her beheaded! I don't think she rests in peace!"

Sophia quickly moved on to avoid any discussion on the subject of religion.

"Lady Agnes Campbell, a 16th century heroine, daughter of the Earl of Argyll, played a leading role in the Irish resistance to English rule. Scotland and Ireland were close allies and, a formidable leader, she directed her own Scottish troops against the English forces occupying Ireland.

"Flora McDonald is said to have disguised Bonnie Prince Charlie as a serving maid, thus aiding his escape to France after the defeat at the Battle of Culloden. She was imprisoned in the Tower of London for her actions but was pardoned in 1747... few people know that. I didn't know till I did some research on her life.

"Mary Slessor, born in the late 18th century, was a Dundee mill girl, who became a missionary. She worked tirelessly to improve the lives of the poor in Scotland and Nigeria. I hope I am not boring you?"

"No, please go on, Sophia. But I am beginning to realize what I am up against... Scottish women." Iain raised his eyebrows. Sophie and Sofiya, smiled nodding their heads in agreement with Iain.

Chapter 10

S OPHIA GRATEFULLY took a sip of the water before continuing. "Grandma, would you have graduated from Edinburgh University with your medical degree without the bravery of the Edinburgh Seven? They were pioneering women led by Sophia Jex-Blake in the struggle for women to be admitted to Edinburgh University in 1869 to study medicine. In order to succeed they endured multiple challenges, in the form of segregation, higher academic fees and a multiplicity of abuse, not only from fellow students, but also from powerful academics, in spite of obtaining excellence in their clinical subjects. The culmination of their struggle in 1870, was the Surgeons' Hall Riot, when an angry mob of over 200 greeted them and pelted them with mud, rubbish, howled insults, and refused them admission to sit an anatomy exam, till a sympathetic student came to their rescue and opened the university gates to let them in.

"Not all the male medical students were against them, but others strongly objected... not a surprise when 5 of the top 7 medical students in the final exams were women! They would also have been the first women to graduate at the university, yet in the end lost their battle. Influential members of the medical faculty persuaded the university to refuse their graduation. They appealed to the Edinburgh High Court of Sessions, but it supported the university's right to refuse the women their degrees and their campaign failed in 1873. The Court of Sessions also ruled by a majority, that the women should never have been admitted to the university in the first place! In 1876 they were awarded their MD from Bern, Switzerland and Paris

France. Today the joke would be on those men who obstructed the women from graduating, as there are a higher percentage of women in Scottish universities than men.

"Dr Elsie Inglis, grandma? A physician, surgeon, teacher, suffragist and founder of the Scottish Women's Hospitals, she began her student career in 1887 at the Edinburgh School of Medicine for Women and left after a disagreement with them and founded her own women's medical college. She was a WW1 heroine. In 1914 she thought the Scottish Red Cross would help her raise funds for a hospital to be staffed by women for the war effort, but the head of the Red Cross denied her request, stating the Red Cross was in the hands of the War Office and it would have nothing to do with a hospital staffed by women.

"She approached the Royal Army Medical Corp with her offer of a ready-made hundred-bed hospital unit, to be deployed anywhere on the Western Front, which again was refused. Undeterred, she approached the War Office with the offer. She was refused again and was famously told by the War Office, 'My good lady, go home and sit still'... she didn't! She offered her services to other European allied forces and was warmly welcomed and spent most of her war years in Serbia. There, after her death, a memorial fountain was erected in her honour. I expect you remember the Elsie Inglis Memorial Maternity Hospital, grandma? She was appalled by the standards of care for the poor women of Edinburgh and had it built, but it's closed now, and so is the old Royal Infirmary of Edinburgh."

"Yes I know. It's sad in a way, but these old buildings are too expensive to maintain. I wonder what happened to Florence Nightingale's lamp from the hospital in Scutari that was on the wall in the hall of the nurses' home? I remember a Christmas concert on the stage there. The nurses staged a tableau of the manger with a baby's crib and the nurses sang carols for the patients. One of the nurses had a beautiful soprano voice. She sang something from the *Messiah,* but I can't remember what…" Sofiya seemed to be talking to herself. No one said anything because they didn't know what she was talking about.

"Mum, grandma, I want to tell you something that will make you smile. Listen! Dr James Barry, a highly intelligent Irishman, aided by his family and influential family friends, began studying medicine and qualified as a doctor from Edinburgh University in 1809, although there was some debate about his age. He went on to have a distinguished career as a military doctor. Dr Barry was a skilled surgeon, as well as a pioneer of changes in sanitation, water systems and the treatment of the mentally ill. He performed the first known successful Caesarean section… a miracle in those days! During the Crimean War, he got into considerable conflict with Florence Nightingale, but no one faulted his incredible surgical ability.

"Now wait for it! On his deathbed he demanded to be buried in the bed-sheet he died in and there was to be no autopsy. But to establish cause of death, an autopsy was performed. They discovered he was in fact a woman! Her family had disguised her as a man so she could gain admission to the University in the first place. Described as small in stature, with delicate features, a bad-tempered, squeaky voiced eccentric, she had fooled the British Nation at home and abroad." Sophia enjoyed hearing her family gasp in surprise, then with laughter. The miasma of discontent among them was well and truly dispersed.

"To come right up to date on the subject of strong Scottish women… Grandma, you and your grandmother discussed the need for more women in political power, and you said to give it time. Wise words, grandma, because for the first time we have a strong, female minister in the Scottish Government—who knows how far she will go? Another brave Scottish lady, who believes in her country.

"We may not be directly descended from any of these brave women, but we all have their resilient, genetic fingering in our DNA as do generations of Scottish women who emigrated to other countries over the centuries. I hope, just as those women's families supported them, I have you, grandma, mum and of course you, Dad, to support me. If I have the 'Leightham Three' on my side, how can I fail? So in the fullness of time... I *will* be the next Lady Sophia Leightham!"

The 'Leightham Three' sat quietly digesting all Sophia had said, till Iain felt it was time to address his daughter's determined declaration regarding her future.

"You win. You know we will support you, Sophia, but will we have to dress you up as a man?" Iain pulled his daughter's leg. "But seriously, I have only one question to ask. Supposing you meet someone and want to marry. What will you do if he doesn't feel the same way you do? I have known for a good number of years now, your mother never wanted to inherit what seemed to her a giant burden. Your future partner might feel the same."

"Dad, my grandfather, who sadly I never met, told grandma he couldn't care less about her inheritance, titles, or anything else." Sophia could see her grandmother nodding in agreement. "Believe me, I have no intention of getting involved with or marrying anyone who doesn't feel the same way I do about the estate. Tell me... when you first met and fell in love with mum, are you trying to tell me you cared about anything except how you felt about each other? But my partner will have to support me one hundred percent, before I continue with any further relationship. And in any case who says I will get married? I agree with Bunty... the marriage certificate is a licence to wash dishes! Perhaps we will just live together, or 'live in sin' as they used to say… right, grandma?!"

Sophia's captivated audience had sat more or less spellbound, quietly listening to all she had said. Now they stood up and applauded. The noise erupting from the dining room brought Sophia's brothers and sister running in to find out what all the commotion was about.

"Well said, Sophia. But is the marriage certificate a licence to wash dishes, for the husband or the wife?" Iain continued joking with her. Sophia burst out laughing as he indicated she was to sit down and everyone else was to remain standing. Lifting his glass, he announced, "I want you all to raise your glass and toast… Miss Sophia Haig… the future Lady Leightham!! We wish her all the very best *and* we will all give her all the support she needs."

"What a relief! Maybe I will live long enough to get my birthday card from the queen, now that the long-term stress of running the estate has been lifted from my shoulders. And when my time comes… I can rest in peace."

Sofiya turned to her granddaughter and reassured her she wasn't planning to die that night or any time soon. Sophia happily echoed her grandmother's sentiment adding that her long life would give her time to fulfil her dream of becoming an astronaut and exploring what lay 'beyond the beyond'.

CONCLUSION

THE HOGMANAY celebrations were well under way in the Leightham Arms. Sofiya arranged with the proprietors, Stacey and Gareth Rees, that it would be a free bar and the locals were taking full advantage of her ladyship's generosity. Two lads from Pittendreal, who played at the Dundee Fiddlers Rally every year had been brought in, along with an accordionist to play Scottish country dance music and were presently blasting out 'The Gay Gordons'. Bunty and Vivienne were dancing together, as their menfolk had been busy knocking back one 'pint and a hauf' after the other for the last two hours and weren't in a fit state to dance.

"Oh my gawd, Jimmy! Wid ye look at the time?!" Ronald shouted over the din. "A' promised her ladyship a' wid let the dug oot an hoor ago and get the bonfire lit. Gan oor tae the bar and tell Stacey am awa tae the big hoose."

"A' think a'll come we ye, Ronald. It'll no dae me ony herm tae get a breath o' fresh air. Ma heid's lowpin'"

"Aye that's no a bad idea, Jimmy. Noo awa an tell Stacey we're baith gawn and mind ye dinna fa' awe yer length oor Walter, that Newfoundland dug o theirs, the muckle great beast droolin' awe oor the flair! A' daenae ken hoo they're alloo'd tae bring that dug in tae the pub wi the new Health an' Safety laws?"

"Ach, niver mind the dug, Ronald. It's a big lump o' guid nature."

"Plaise yersel. Am awa tae get oor coats frae the cloakroom, an a'll meet ye at the exit. Hurry up an tak yer time!" Ronald laughed at his own joke. Maybe he had had one too many as well.

Ronald collected the coats and made his way back through the crowded bar to the exit, to be almost knocked back into the pub by two disgruntled men, who from the smell of them, had obviously gone outside for a smoke and were now cursing and swearing about being nearly knocked over by a car mounting the pavement on the wrong side of the road. "Bluidie, effing, drunken eejit," they cursed in Ronald's face.

Ignoring them Ronald got a hold of Jimmy and the two of them made their way on foot to the back entrance to Leightham House. But for no reason, Ronald began to feel uneasy as they approached the house. Something wasn't right. Ronald wanted to hurry, but Jimmy, slightly inebriated, couldn't be hurried, so Ronald decided to go on ahead and told Jimmy he would meet him once he got the dog and they could walk it together and light the bonfire in the bottom field.

* * *

Sofiya was on her way home, having left her family standing on the doorstep. Their goodbyes were ringing in her ears, with Sophia declaring that she would be driving the family now she had passed her driving test, as she didn't like drinking anyway. "Sounds good to me," Iain had agreed. "See you for the celebrations, grandma," Savanna shouted above the others. "Have you got enough of those big, American marshmallows to toast? And tell Ronald to find long sticks to hold them to the bonfire. My hand got too hot last year," she complained.

"Be careful driving along that road, mum. It's late and there's ice and snow forecast! Right! Everybody inside," Sophie ordered. "It's too cold to hang about without your

362

coats on. We will be there in good time before midnight, mum," she added.

Sofiya happily reminisced on the outcome of the evening. What more could she want! Her granddaughter, Sophia, was the best person to inherit all she had worked for. It had also occurred to Sofiya, that as she had followed in *her* grandmother's footsteps, her granddaughter would be following in hers.

Reaching the bend in the road, the road she had travelled with the women in her family from early childhood and then driven herself in her youth, Sofiya was happy knowing that there on the hill Leightham House would come into view. She knew the sad history of the house with her grandmother telling her about its occupants from the late 19th century to the middle of the 20$^{th.}$ It was a history that at times was shocking and unbelievable. But from the time she had inherited Leightham House as a young woman, to the present, 21st century, she thought of the happiness it gave her and others and when the time came, it would be placed in the steady hands of her granddaughter and be safe for generations to come. These thoughts gladdened her heart.

Sofiya drove on, anticipating the view of her beloved home that would now be lit by the outdoor spotlights and probably the bonfire. *Goodness, that's some fire Ronald has lit. It looks brighter than the usual Hogmanay rosy glow. That's odd that it is so close to the house.* Sofiya frowned as she reached the bend in the road.

Distracted, Sofiya had taken her eyes off the road for a few seconds, but turning back, she was suddenly confronted by a car coming straight at her, at full speed, in the middle of the road! Swerving to avoid the car, she ended up in the ditch and cursed out loud. "Damn you!! I thought they had banned all drink driving. Where are the police when you need them?" She also had a vague notion as the car flashed past her, that it had been hired. "Good! I can tell the police to look for a drunk in a hired car!"

Sofiya managed to untangle herself, thanking the good Lord for the airbag and her seatbelt or she might have gone through the windscreen. Opening the driver's door, she slithered down the side of the car, angrily accepting she had no other option but to walk the rest of the way. Thankfully the main drive of the house was close by. Cursing again, she realized she had left her mobile at her daughter's house, where she had forgotten to charge it, so it would be useless now anyway! "We get so damned dependent on modern technology," she muttered. "But in this case…"

Halfway up the drive, Sofiya saw Ronald running towards her.

"Thank God you're back!" he shouted at Sofiya, "A've been trying to get ye on yer mobile, yer ladyship but there wis nae answer. So a' phoned yer dochter, but she telt me ye hid already left," Ronald panted, out of breath. "That's why a ran doon the drive tae catch ye and tell ye tae hurry!" Ronald bent over to catch his breath before standing upright.

"For heaven's sake, Ronald, what are you on about and where's Laila? You are beginning to worry me," Sofiya nipped at Ronald, still a little shaken from crashing into the ditch and she walked briskly ahead leaving the man standing.

Ronald ran to catch up. "That's whit am trying tae tell ye, yer Ladyship. Jimmy an a' left the pub thegither. A didna ken whit but somethin' wis worrying me. Jimmy wis taken oor much time, so a went on aheid. When a' got tae the back door, the dug wis gawn mental, barkin' her lungs oot and clawing at the door. When a' opened it the cat shot oot between ma legs first, then afore a' could get a haud o' her, Laila belted oot!"

364

"Will you get a move on, Ronald? What the hell is going on?!"

"Am tryin' tae tell ye," Ronald panted. "Laila, shot roond tae the front o' the hoose, wi me efter her, but even though she wis stoppin' tae smell every tree and blade o' gress and liften' her nose in the air tae tak in deep breaths as if she could smell somethin', a couldna get a haud o' her. She was on a mission. When a' caught up wi the dug, she wis thrown hersel against the front door growlin' and clawin' at it, wantin' in." Ronald paused for a moment to catch his breath again and to save the man's lungs, Sofiya slowed down.

"It wus then a' saw awe the hoose lichts were oot, and a rosy glow was comin' frae inside the building. At first a thoucht it wis jist a power cut, then a' realized the emergency generator must hae been disconnected or the emergency lichts wid hae come on and the fire alarm wid be gan aff. It wis then a kent the water sprinkler system must hae been interfered wi as weel. It seemed tae me somebidy must hae taken a pickaxe tae them, tae dae that amount o' damage! A ran back tae find Jimmy and telt him tae get back tae the Leightham Arms and tell Stacey what hid happened, jist in case she didna hear her phone wi awe that racket gawn on in the pub and for her tae get awbody here tae try tae save whit we could.

"A' phoned the fire brigade richt awa, but they're at twa other fires, but they'll come as soon as they kin and it sounds like they're nearly here. Then a' phoned the police and telt them aboot the fire and about the car driven by a drunk that nearly knocked they twa lads doon oot side the pub, jist in case it wis the same maniac wha did this." The sound of the fire engines could be heard coming closer. "We've awe done oor best yer ladyship and managed tae get as many o' the furnishins', paintins' and yer belongins' oot o' the hoose as we could, afore the fire took a haud but…"

The gut-wrenching realization of what had happened to her beloved home suddenly dawned on Sofiya. It seemed that Ronald's voice was echoing softly as if from a tunnel and Sofiya felt that she was moving in slow motion with surreal movements, as if watching herself on a film screen. She felt she was experiencing an out-of-body sensation, floating, looking down, observing herself from above and for a brief moment her forebears, Elizabeth Leightham, Robert Leightham and her grandmother Alice Jane Gardner were at her side, watching her, waiting to see what she would do. *Would she turn and flee from the house as they had done?*

Reaching the front of the house Sofiya stood as if hypnotized a few feet from the front door, staring, motionless, at the sight before her. Behind Sofiya stood the men and women who had risked their lives to try to save what they could. The women were huddled in groups horrified, the men struck dumb, silent with the helpless frustration of defeat. They stood paralyzed at the sight of Leightham House on fire. Sofiya heard the cracking of the timbers and saw showers of scarlet sparks shooting up into the night sky, as the timbers fell from the rafters onto the first floor of the house, as if the fireworks for the Hogmanay celebrations had been set off.

Sofiya could see the flames inside performing some exotic dance, mocking her helplessness. It looked like a scene from the inner circle of Dante's inferno. Clutching her hands to her mouth to prevent hysteria, Sofiya heard deafening explosions of glass windows shattering from the searing heat and saw shards of glass spraying the ground around her.

Vaguely, as if away in the distance, she heard Ronald telling her the police had phoned. There had been a bad accident with a hired car hitting a bollard in the High Street. The driver had ignored the 'No Entry' sign and hadn't been wearing a seatbelt and had gone right through the windscreen. The badly injured man was on his way to hospital but unlikely to survive.

Sofiya didn't need to be told about the car, or who had started the fire, or who interfered with the alarm, the water supply and the electricity, or who was driving the hired car that had forced her car off the road moments ago. It was the same car, from the same rental company, that she saw coming up the drive in October. Who else could it be but that man, full of venom, hatred, vowing revenge, shouting in her face with temper when he left her, "If I can't have the house and the estate, neither will you and you haven't heard the last from me!"... Johnny Geiger. Even the dog had recognized his scent.

The two-toned howling of the fire engines' alarm bells and the ear-splitting shrieks of the police cars' sirens coming up the drive, suddenly jolted Sofiya back to reality, rudely waking her from her catatonic-like state. She turned to face the villagers and screamed at them, "No!! No, the paintings are all reproductions!! The originals are safe, locked up in the basement of Cards' House!! No! Where is the only original, the life-size painting of the girl on the black stallion? It can never be replaced!" Sofiya shouted above the noise. Then realizing how selfish she was being and that people had risked their lives to save her belongings, added, "But thank you for trying to save my belongings." The hopeless despair in her voice was heard by all.

"Your ladyship, a'm that sorry, but we couldn't get it aff the back wall in time... the heat... the smoke... I told awbody to tak whit could be lifted, withoot endangering their lives. Ye widna hae wanted that, wid ye?" Ronald put an arm around Sofiya's shoulder to comfort her. He explained that it would have taken less than thirty minutes from the start of the fire to reach this state.

Like a harbinger of the Apocalypse, the two main front doors burst open and were inviting her to come in. Possessed, deranged, Sofiya broke free from Ronald and to the horror of everyone, ran up the steps and into the burning house, shouting back over her shoulder, "Ronald, Jimmy, help me get the painting out!" The two men heard Sofiya's frantic pleading, but Bunty and Vivienne also heard her and clung to their husbands in sheer panic, restraining them, terrified they would try to follow Sofiya.

Ignoring the danger and the smell of acrid smoke swirling round her that made her cough and her eyes sting, Sofiya ran, stepping over the shattered Italian, crystal chandelier; oblivious to the burning cinders falling all around her, she made her way to the back of the hall where the oil painting hung. She didn't hear the wooden beams crashing behind her as she looked up to the portrait of the young Russian princess on the magnificent black stallion. She saw the oil paint melt from the heat and trickle down the face of the young girl. The dripping paint made it look as though the girl was crying, a picture of the despair in Sofiya's heart. A thick grey cloud of smoke began to engulf the painting and, dropping to her knees, Sofiya rocked back and forward as if she was in pain until she was overcome by smoke inhalation and fell unconscious on the floor beneath the portrait.

Arriving at the front door, a dozen firemen in full fire-fighting gear yelled at everyone to "Get back" before running into Leightham House with their hoses set on full-force. The hoses expanded with the high volume of water spewing into the building.

"Her ladyship's in there!!" Ronald yelled, managing to get the attention of the last fireman.

"Ach, dinna worry, man. We'll hae her Ladyship oot in nae time and get the fire under control. A' wis sent tae check the back o' the hoose first an am gled tae tell ye, the rear o' the main hoose, the restaurant and the outbuildings are no affected. His onybody phoned for an ambulance yet? No? Weel dae it richt noo! Tell them tae mak share their oxygen cylinders are full. Her ladyship will nae doubt need it when we get her oot o' there," the man shouted as he disappeared into the burning building, sadly reflecting they were not always successful in rescuing people.

REFLECTIONS

"*I* REMEMBERED *from very early childhood the excitement of being driven along the coast road with my family. Now I was driving along the same road to visit the person who would be waiting for me with Kenya coffee but not Perkin ginger biscuits. I will never forget this beautiful day in late summer, the sun high in the sky and fields of golden corn ripening in the fields."*

Was history repeating itself? Why was she remembering these words? Continuing on her journey, she knew every landmark, twist and turn on the way and when she reached the bend in the road, she had travelled so often in the past, there it was up on the hill, the ruins of Leightham House. Again, why these words that were coming into her head? These thoughts made her wonder should Leightham House be rebuilt? Or should it remain a testament, a memorial to those who had lived, loved and died there? Suddenly as if struck by a bolt of lightning, she remembered where she had read all about the house's past... the memory stick she had carefully saved with over a hundred years of one family's history saved on it. Maybe it's time... time to publish the story and the history of The House with No Roof.

THE END

Glossary

Aye	Yes
Sma	small
Awfy	awful
Skelpit	smacked
A	I
Yersel	yourself
Awa	away
Sair	pain
Bairn	child
Beilen	septic wound
Bobby	East coast for the Police
Bonspiel	a curling match
Braw	beautiful
Craiter	creature beast or devil
Cannae	cannot
Cauld	cold
Dinna'	do not
Dae	do
Dye	East coast for Grandfather
Fou	full
Gaun	go
Haar	mist from the sea
Hapit	cover
Haun	hand
Himsel'	the boss
Haud yer wheesht	be quiet!
Masel	myself
Naw	West coast for no
Ken	know
Lowp	throb
Maun	you must
Mauna	must not

Neeps	turnips
Ower	over
Oor	hour
Poke	a paper bag

Printed in Great Britain
by Amazon

22990198R00215